I0580862

The Third Generation Series

Book 8

Elisabeth and Tanya: Blood Calls to Blood

&

Book 9

Erin: The Call

By

Margaret Gregory

i

Copyright © 2020 by Margaret Gregory
All rights reserved.
ISBN: 978-1-925332-69-8 (print)

No part of this publication may be reproduced, distributed, or transmitted in any form or by any means, including photocopying, recording, or other electronic or mechanical methods, without the prior written permission of the author, except non-commercial uses permitted by copyright law.

Cover designed by msgdragon
Cover image: © Can Stock Photo Inc. /

Also by Margaret Gregory
TYMOREAN TRUST SERIES:
Book 1 - Power Rising
Book 2 - Great Ones
Book 3 - The Return to Earth
Book 4 – Earth Mission
Book 5 – Alien Contact
Book 6 - Invasion
ATAPI SORCERESS SERIES:
Prequel – Korvu: The Beginning
Book 1- The Wild One
Book 2 – Atapi Sorceress
THE THIRD GENERATION SERIES:
Book 1 - Wanda: From Bad to Worse
Book 2 - Wanda: Choosing Crime
Wanda – Early Days (anthology) Book 1 and 2
Book 3 – Wanda: Risking Life to Live
Book 4 – Erin: The Forcing of Wisdom
Book 5 – Wanda: A New Life Part 1 – Hidden Secrets
Book 6 – Wanda: A New Life Part 2 – First Mission
Book 7 – Wanda: Full Circle

For permission requests, address the request to the author c/o
Permissions,
C/o TAT Indie Publishing
PO Box 2728
Rowville, Victoria, 3178
www.tatindiepublishing.com.au

The Third Generation Series

Book 8

Elisabeth and Tanya: Blood Calls to Blood

By

Margaret Gregory

Table of Contents

Chapter 1

Senator Charles Willard and his daughter Elisabeth emerged from the limousine and looked around them. They had driven from Los Angeles, where it had been overcast and threatening rain, to the foothills of the San Bernardino Mountains where the sun shone from a typically bright cloudless Californian summer day.

"I know this place," Elisabeth said quietly to her father.

Willard glanced at his slender, blonde haired daughter and then at the low prefabricated buildings they had stopped next to. He knew she had never been to this out of the way location before. They had needed to pass through a secure checkpoint at the gate – they had been expected but he had still been required to produce his identification and credentials. Elisabeth, as his administrative assistant, had needed to produce identification as well.

"It's a training facility, quite secret," was the Senator's equally quiet reply. "A rather surprising place for a meeting." He seemed to ignore his daughter's earlier comment.

"Not if Wanda and David have been living here," Elisabeth murmured.

"Maybe they were, and maybe not," he said as if the people mentioned meant nothing to him. They did, but very few people were privy to that fact. "I do know that the Martin couple have not been seen for several months and if what I have been told is true, neither has one of the top OSI operatives. However, that information was highly classified. I wonder why they want you here."

Charles Willard was trying not to betray his inner worries to his daughter. His relationship to Wanda Martin was a highly classified secret. Wanda Martin was his eldest child, but she had cut herself off from him for many years, and then had gone into the witness protection program. "Have you heard from Wanda?"

Elisabeth shook her head slightly. "Look, there's Mr Cooper."

Senator Willard recognised the white haired man who was walking out to meet them. He had been with his eldest daughter the last time he had seen her. "So that's it..."

"Senator, Miss Willard, thank you for coming. You may not remember me... Jim Phillips," the white haired man shook Elisabeth's hand and then the Senator's.

Neither commented about the different name. Phillips nodded as if satisfied that these two people would be discreet.

"I will take you to the meeting – this way."

Phillips led them into the nearest building, past an unobtrusive security control room, and on to a room that contained a large circular table with about twenty people already seated about it. Three chairs remained vacant, and he led his guests there, and then seated himself.

The other attendees glanced briefly at the newcomers before returning their attention to the chairman, who was seated with the window behind him and a direct line of sight to the door. It seemed he had been waiting for the last arrivals.

"Ladies, Gentlemen, most of you already know me. For those that don't, I am Magnus Goldman, Director of the OSI. Welcome, all of you. You have all been invited here for a specific reason, and I wish to emphasise that what you hear in here today is not to be discussed outside of this room. Many of you are here to report on investigations made at my request. Each team is only aware of part of the whole situation and it is necessary to maintain that state of affairs."

Goldman glanced around before continuing. "Before I begin, I want each of you to read the sheet of paper on the table before you, and sign it. If any of you do not feel that you can – come and see me."

Elisabeth reached for the paper and began to read.

"National Security Act?" she queried her father, who was also reading.

Jim Phillips answered. "A formality. No one who was invited here is considered as being a security risk."

"From this, I gather that my eldest daughter has come to the attention of the OSI," Charles Willard murmured to Phillips.

"Not in a negative way," Phillips assured him quietly. "Are you aware she has some intriguing talents?"

"In addition to disreputable ones? Yes, I have an idea," Willard agreed.

"Magnus Goldman agrees with my evaluation of her," Phillips added.

"I'll accept that for now," the Senator agreed, seeing that the signed papers were being folded in half and passed to the head of the table. He reached for Elisabeth's paper, folded it with his own and handed both to Jim Phillips to pass on.

The first team leader was invited to give her report. The woman stood up and nodded to the chairman.

"Team Alpha was assigned the task of tracing the whereabouts of person one," the woman began. She went on to outline the steps and techniques taken to try to locate the person she referred to only by number. She concluded by admitting that no trace had been found.

A man replaced her. He was the speaker for Team Bravo and his report followed a similar pattern with a similar lack of success. Two more speakers also reported on attempts to find certain people.

Elisabeth sat quietly, listening carefully to what was being said. But what was not being said was enlightening. She noticed too, that some people in the room, Jim Phillips included, were listening intently to all the speakers. She guessed that they did know to whom each team was referring.

All she was sure about from the first report was that the first missing person had once been in the armed forces, and had later become some kind of celebrity. In an instant of revelation, Elisabeth put a name to the facts. Colonel Aldrin, she realised, remembering that Wanda had mentioned his name the last time they had met.

Now that she had the key to the matter, Elisabeth considered the identity of the second subject, someone who had a few years ago, gone into the witness protection program. The speaker, it seemed, felt he should have been able to trace the person, as he had access to the classified files. They had even done a thorough search for unidentified victims of accident or crime that matched the person's description.

Goldman had betrayed no hint of his thoughts. He just nodded when each report was finished, thanked the speaker and dismissed them before inviting the next one to speak.

The third speaker had a comprehensive report on his subject – but had no details of his life prior to three years ago. When a mention was made of cosmetic surgery, and undercover work in a corruption investigation, Elisabeth was certain that he was talking about David Martin and the speaker before had been as well. She knew more about David than the two groups had discovered.

Therefore, she was not surprised that the fourth speaker also had a negative report. It was to be expected, since if his subject had been Wanda Dean – all but a handful of people believed her to be dead. And many of that handful were in the room. Her appraising glance suggested that Goldman, and possibly the older man sitting beside him, both knew Wanda Martin's background.

It seemed that the thrust of the investigation had been to check if anyone had been making enquiries about her, perhaps disbelieving the reports of her death. That group had even tested the proof of her death and concluded that there was no likelihood that the subject was alive.

Again, Elisabeth knew more than the team of investigators. They had not even discovered that Wanda Dean was now Wanda Martin and had been Gwen Willard. Wanda had done a masterful job of hiding her true name, and Jim Phillips had arranged the 'proof' of her death.

All of a sudden, Elisabeth knew the reason for the meeting and its secrecy. The idea was totally wild, and she had all but forgotten or discounted what Wanda had once said to her. Wanda, David and this Colonel Aldrin, had gone off somewhere together. All were missing – not somewhere on Earth out of America – but somewhere off it. And that would be the reason for the secrecy – no one sane would normally give credence to the 'taken by aliens' theory. But even that was more believable than the 'walked to another planet' idea now in her mind. Yet she had experienced it – on a smaller scale. Wanda had walked her out of a house where she had been taken by a psychotic criminal, to a safe outside place – in three steps. The second being to a dark twisting place. She had fainted on arrival, and discounted her memory when she woke – but it had to have been real. And perhaps, she had once done it herself.

Elisabeth slumped back into her chair and saw her father give her a concerned glance. She shook her head, and her father returned his attention to the speaker.

Having the key pieces of information in her mind, she fully understood what she was hearing. Everything possible was being done to determine if the three people Wanda, David and the Colonel, were anywhere on Earth – alive or dead.

After the first four speakers had reported and departed, there were reports from the FBI, CIA, DEA and a few other groups Elisabeth hadn't heard of. Each reported and departed.

The feeling of those still in the room should have been that the people being looked for where dead. However, instead of grief, there was a sense of excitement tinged with apprehension.

The number of people in the room had dropped to seven when Goldman called a recess and refreshments were brought in.

Jim Phillips moved away and returned with a grey haired man, who looked frail but whose eyes were still a piercing blue. When Elisabeth looked up, it seemed the man could not stop staring at her.

"Do I know you?" Elisabeth felt compelled to ask, for it almost seemed as if the man thought he knew her. "You look so much like someone I once knew," the elderly man apologised. "So much..."

Jim placed a gentle hand on the man's arm. "Stefan, a moment. I would like you to meet Senator Charles Willard and his daughter Elisabeth. This is Stefan Krinsky."

Charles shook the man's hand and controlled his curiosity. Elisabeth had recognised the name and was controlling her excitement.

"I wanted the three of you to meet," Jim explained. "Senator, you haven't had any contact with Wanda Martin for a while, but Stefan's daughter Tanya, and Wanda Martin could pass for twins."

"And your daughter, Senator, is the image of my dead wife, Ivana Tatarovich Krinsky."

Willard was stunned. "My first wife was Katya Androv, but before her first marriage she was Katya Tatarovich."

Elisabeth took her father's hand and squeezed gently in excitement. Her father looked at her and asked, "This isn't exactly a surprise to you is it?"

"No," was her admission.

A voice behind them interrupted further talk.

"I think it is time to reconvene the meeting. We will be moving to a smaller room," Goldman said quietly.

He led them through a door to the left of the one they had entered by. In the smaller room the chairs were in a more informal arrangement.

Goldman introduced all the remaining people by name. On his right was Stan Russell, the Secretary of State and on his left was Rowan Wallace a scientist of some renown. Elisabeth learnt that Stefan Krinsky was a Russian scientist, now residing in America. Jim Phillips was introduced as a Special Projects Director. Elisabeth was introduced as the daughter of her Senator father.

The Secretary of State nodded faintly in Jim Phillips's direction and showed surprise at Senator Willard's presence. The two had met but did not know each other well.

"Let us proceed," Goldman prompted. "I am now able to be less mysterious about this meeting. All of us, with the exception of Secretary Russell have met, or know Stev Aldrin, or Wanda and David Martin. Some of us know that the three of them have been undertaking a classified mission for the past six months. What is not generally known is that no contact has been received from them since they left here on..."

Charles Willard frowned, and then became aware that the Secretary of

State was watching him. When he met Russel's gaze, the Secretary of State glanced away and considered Professor Krinsky.

Goldman was addressing Krinsky. "Professor, were you aware that your daughter and Mrs Martin were undertaking a program of experiments into various psychic abilities?"

"Yes, Mr Goldman. My daughter confided in me. And I, myself, am convinced that the two of them could indeed speak mind to mind."

"What else did she tell you?" Goldman prompted.

"Well, this is something I find hard to believe, but she insists it was not some after effect of the anaesthetic. She's just had her appendix out or she would be here too. She told me that one night, she walked in her sleep – but walked through a wall, through a twisting blackness to the outside of the fence here – in three steps."

Elisabeth noticed the Secretary leaning forward. His attention fixed on the former Russian.

"Did she say why she walked? What else was in her mind?" Goldman asked.

"She must have been dreaming. She said she had heard a voice in her mind – calling her – calling for help that she could give."

"Where is this all leading, Goldman," the Secretary demanded.

"Please be patient, Sir. What I believe to be the truth is not an easy concept to accept. I want to present you with the information that I received and see if you draw the same conclusions."

"Very well, continue."

Goldman did. "Mr Secretary, on the same night that Tanya Krinsky was found outside the east security fence, Wanda Martin disappeared from near the cottage she shared here with her husband. We have security film that shows her walking out of the cottage and simply vanishing. That film was tested thoroughly for tampering. We are convinced it is authentic. She was found the following day, about twenty miles east of here – up in the mountains. Her memories of the events are identical to those of Miss Krinsky. The two women were not in contact with each other before being debriefed."

Elisabeth caught Goldman's eye and was given permission to speak. She met the gaze of the Secretary as she began. "On that same night, I also 'sleepwalked'. My brother found me some distance away – towards the east – still in my pyjamas, and I left my home without using keys to unlock the door. I have never, before that, walked in my sleep and on that night I too remember being called."

"And does that Martin woman talk to you mind to mind too?" the Secretary demanded, sounding disagreeable.

"Mr Secretary," Charles Willard interrupted quietly. "I believe you are aware of some of Wanda Martin's previous history?"

"Yes, indeed." The Secretary made no secret of his distaste for what he knew.

"I share your sentiments, Sir. However, you may not be aware that prior to her first conviction as Wanda Dean, she had officially changed her name from Gwenda Willard. Wanda Martin is my eldest daughter and a full sibling to Elisabeth. And I am convinced that my two eldest daughters have always had a mutual sense of how each other is faring – without letters, without phone calls or any other direct means."

The Secretary seemed about to call Willard deluded.

"I am also convinced, that even as a very small child, Gwen shared something with her mother, my first wife. She told me, that she had shared her mother's pain. And I do not mean that platitude 'I share your pain', meaning I know you are suffering terribly and feel pity for you – but physically shared it. She blamed herself for wishing her mother's death. I think, however, that she helped Katya last much longer than any doctor expected."

"You surprise me Senator," the Secretary said in an even, but slightly derogatory voice. "Are you saying that you think she willed your wife's death?"

"No, Mr Secretary, I am not." The Senator's tone was icy. He had not missed the other man's innuendo. "At the time of her mother's death, my daughter was four years old. I never realised the bond existed, but I did know that when my daughters were with her – she felt much better."

Elisabeth stared at the Secretary and added, "And no, I did not share my mother's pain, but yes, I shared Wanda's pain, misery, as well as other parts of her life. I knew she went to prison. I knew what she went through in there. I know things she has never even admitted to me. Things that would make you cringe. Yes, I knew she was a criminal, and I know why she left home, changed her name and never intended to come back. She wouldn't have either, except for me."

The look of scepticism remained on the Secretary's face.

"And can you, Miss Willard, do all the other amazing things your sister is supposed to be able to do?"

Elisabeth held onto her temper. "Until that sleepwalking incident, I could share emotions, occasional images and a sense of how my sister was. After that incident, I began to be able to hear her voice in my head. She could reach my mind and read my thoughts. The reverse is not the case. I have not heard from her for months, but I don't think she is dead. And you had better believe that where ever she is, she is not just lying down to die. And if the reason I am here is to help find her, and David and Colonel Aldrin – count me in 100%. I owe her my life. She came home when I was critically ill, risking her life to do it. I won't do any less for her."

"Well said, Miss Willard," Rowan Wallace said quickly before the Secretary could comment further. Elisabeth added then, "Trouble is, I don't think anything I can do, will be enough."

The Secretary gave Senator Willard a 'we'll talk about this later' look before turning his attention back to Goldman.

"Miss Willard, you say that you have sensed nothing at all from Wanda Martin?" Goldman asked.

"I have tried to think at her, and all I felt was a sense of darkness," Elisabeth admitted.

"You told Vera you were having nightmares," Charles Willard reminded his daughter.

Elisabeth shrugged that off. "They were just that. I don't think visions of dark, formless, inhuman monsters are significant here."

"Can we get to the point here, Goldman?" the Secretary insisted.

"If you would care to watch the screen, Mr Secretary," Goldman suggested. He touched a switch and a screen lowered from the roof, and the room darkened.

"What you will be seeing are security videos from around the base. Please pay particular attention to the time and date in the bottom corner."

After a series of twelve tapes, the Secretary spoke out. "That's impossible. There must be errors in the time mechanism."

Goldman began another tape, one showing Wanda from a distance, walking from a building, towards the cottage. She seemed to disappear and two seconds later appearing thirty metres further on. There was no change of camera, or background picture.

This time, the Secretary was silent for a full minute. "Tell me your theory, Goldman."

Goldman spoke with deliberation. "I think that wherever Stev Aldrin and the Martin's have gone, Wanda Martin was the one who enabled it. If we are to find them, or get them back – we need to know more about Wanda Martin and her abilities."

Rowan Wallace spoke up then. "I have a record of a conversation involving Wanda shortly after she was returned from the mountains."

When that had been played, Wallace continued, "I also have reports from Colonel Aldrin, from when Wanda was learning about some new abilities that she had developed after the mountain incident. I am about to play a recording from my lab, taken when Wanda was under hypnosis."

When the recording finished, the silence in the room was absolute. Everyone could hear the clock ticking on the wall.

"God dammit, Goldman," the Secretary forgot his position and his own importance. "What have you started here?"

Goldman added every detail he had not yet mentioned about Wanda's abilities and what she had revealed about the alien in her mind. The Secretary seemed to stare at Elisabeth as he spoke.

"Is there anything you want to add, Miss Willard," the Secretary held his sarcasm in check.

Elisabeth met the man's eyes and dared him to disbelieve her. "I was with Wanda, right before she disappeared, I think. She told me that she was being called away, possibly to another world. She needed to know that I would be here for her, when she needed to return. I asked her how she would be going, and she said that she had the voice in her head, but something she had found in a house near there had made the contact much clearer – that it was a key to crossing planes. I think, it was a link between the two worlds – that it was an alien artefact. She didn't actually say how she was going, but..."

"Yes?" the Secretary demanded.

"She had just walked me out of a house, from a room at the back to a clearing out the front, in three steps."

Elisabeth could read in the man's stiffness, that the Secretary had closed his mind to the evidence.

"So what did you hope to gain from this meeting, Goldman? Apart from suggesting that three people from here are now on another planet. If that is true, and I really can't believe it, how will this help get them back? Do you even know where this planet is?"

"Knowledge is power, Mr Secretary," Goldman reminded his superior of a statement he often used. "The more we can learn the better chance we have of acting."

The Secretary stood up and straightened.

Rowan Wallace read the antagonism in the man's stance. He commented,

"Much of what we accept as science today, would have been unbelievable a few decades back. And I agree, what you have just heard sounds fantastic. I have been observing Wanda Martin's odd talents. As far as her telekinetic ability is concerned, I am sure that for her to walk between places, she needs a very good image of it in her mind and an equally good knowledge of the relative direction of where she expects to go."

"Meaning what, exactly?"

"Picturing a sunny beach in the middle of Alaska in winter, won't work," Wallace replied. "She was able to go to a place she knew well, or a person she knows well."

"This is all very interesting, I am sure, but it seems like a wild goose chase to me. I can't see that it should take priority over more urgent matters." The Secretary picked up a briefcase and looked to be ready to leave. "I will advise the President that Colonel Aldrin is still missing and enquiries to date have given no indication that he is in unfriendly hands and investigations are continuing into his whereabouts. As for the rest of the conjecture, I doubt I will need to mention that – unless of course you can bring me some irrefutable proof. Senator – a word with you."

Elisabeth watched her father obey the summons. When the door had closed behind the two men, the tension in the room eased. She muttered her personal opinion of Stanley Russell under her breath and wondered if the deep breath Goldman seemed to take was his way of controlling his own opinion of his superior.

Jim Phillips, who had been sitting with Professor Krinsky stood up and stretched. He had been very quiet throughout the smaller meeting.

"Now that the official reports have been received," Jim spoke to Goldman, "What can we do?"

"I am open to ideas," Goldman invited. "I still believe Mrs Martin is the key to this and I want to know more. I believe I overheard Professor Krinsky and Senator Willard learning they were related through their wives?"

Krinsky was happy to repeat the conversation. Elisabeth now had proof of Wanda's theory that she had to be related to Tanya. Then she recalled a horrid séance she had been to and wondered if she should bring it up.

Jim Phillips saved her the trouble. She hadn't realised that he knew about it. David or Wanda must have mentioned it to him.

"I had an item of information given to me," Jim said, glancing at Elisabeth. "That Wanda's mother had two sisters, one being Ivana Krinsky. The other was called Katrina."

Goldman was immediately interested. "Where did this information come from?"

Elisabeth grinned wryly. "Me. I got talked into going to a séance. I didn't believe in the things, but a presence appeared and claimed to be my mother. Wanda was in my head at the time and it knew she was there and recognised it. Between us, we were convinced it was what it claimed. She, that presence, claimed that Tanya, Wanda and I were cousins. She gave us the names of her sisters and said that they were born in Eastern Europe in a town called, I think, Vrbas."

Jim went on then. "I have been searching for information on the women. Stefan had no idea that his wife had any relatives. Elisabeth, do you have any more information about your mother?"

Elisabeth shook her head. "Ask Dad, he might know more, but he has never spoken about her past to me. I didn't even know she had been married before she married Dad. I only know that she was twenty-four when she died."

"I have no idea where to find the third sister, if she is still alive," Jim admitted. "The other person I am trying to get a lead on is the one Wanda mentioned as being the leader of one of the alien races. A woman who was supposedly born here – somewhere around Crystal Brook. That and the mention of those others who came here. Perhaps one of them was left behind."

"I remember," Wallace said. "Wanda said the woman's father was Matthew Cassidy. All I learnt was that he was dead."

"I can arrange to talk to the family," Jim suggested.

Goldman wrote something on a piece of paper and pressed a button. A young man entered, went to listen to Goldman's instructions, nodded and departed.

"I will have the name run through the computers," Goldman said.

Senator Willard returned and went to sit near Elisabeth.

"Dad, do you know anything about my mother, before you met her? Did she mention her family?"

Charles Willard permitted himself time to think. "I seem to recall her saying that she had no family. I know that she chose to leave Europe after her first husband was killed. I think she was afraid of something, but she never spoke of it."

Jim turned to Professor Krinsky. "Stefan, do you know of the town Vrbas?"

"No. I only live in Russia. I meet my wife there. She was daughter of soldier. Pieter Tatarovich – he died."

"Do you know her date of birth?" Goldman asked, making more notes.

"1957, but not the day," Stefan said.

"Senator, do you know when your wife arrived and how she came here?" Goldman asked.

"She came by ship. I think it was the 'Salonika'. I met her in 1976 and she must have been only 18 or 19. We married the following year."

"Anything else you can remember? I heard you mention her maiden name," Goldman prompted.

"Tatarovich was her birth name. She married a man called Antov."

A silence fell on the group, with everyone trying to think of what to do next.

Rowan Wallace broke it. "Miss Willard, what can you tell me about an artefact that Wanda found?"

"It was some kind of bracelet. Wanda was wearing it – intricate wirework and polished stones," Elisabeth related.

"David didn't mention that to me," Jim said. "But that house you were at – it was owned by a Henry Cassidy. That wasn't at Crystal Brook, it was nearer Wetherby. I will definitely go and see him."

"Has anyone any other ideas?" Goldman asked.

After a moment of silence, Elisabeth spoke up. "Wanda spoke to Henry Cassidy. He showed her a picture of his family. He had a half-sister who has been missing for over forty years. He claimed she was a wild one – always in trouble."

Jim nodded agreement. "Police records for this area might help. Also we might be able to find some police officers, active or retired that might recall odd things that were not put into reports. I'll do that too."

"Could I go with you, Mr Phillips?" Elisabeth asked.

"A hunch?" Jim asked quietly.

Elisabeth shrugged. "I just want to feel like I am helping."

"I don't think there is much more to gain from this meeting," Goldman announced. "I have an assistant starting to check into the Cassidy family. I can organize a search through immigration records for information on Katya Tatarovich Antov. I will also speak to our embassies in Russia and the Slavic states. They can organise searches of local records. We may turn up a lead on that third sister. I will consolidate all findings and keep those of you who are interested, up to date. If anyone thinks of any other avenue to explore, please call me. I will leave word for you to get through to me. Of course, I need not remind you not to discuss these matters with others."

Goldman left with Wallace, ending the meeting. Elisabeth asked her father a question. "What did Mr Russell want? Did he think he was scenting a cover up?"

Willard gave a wry smile. "Something like that. He just wanted to be sure that Wanda didn't get her delinquent nature from me. Seems he was the one to approve her change of status. He wanted to know why he didn't know she was my daughter. So I enlightened him to my ignorance of most of her activities and reminded him that we were sworn to secrecy on the subject. I told him that should word leak out that she was alive he would open a worse can of worms than he had just heard and cause a vendetta on someone who did not deserve to be killed. I don't blame him for disliking what she was, and he had to admit that she achieved a major public service by testifying against those criminals and that she had kept her bargain since."

"Yeah," Elisabeth said, mildly amused. "I am allowed to help Mr Phillips aren't I?"

"Of course. You are old enough to do as you please," Willard agreed. "But I have duties at home."

Jim approached with Stefan Krinsky. "I have arranged a driver for you Senator, and accommodation for your daughter. There are spare units on the base here and a store for necessities. Goldman has to return to Washington and Stefan will be going with him."

"Will I get to meet your daughter, Professor," Elisabeth asked. "I would like to."

"I think she will like to meet you too," Krinsky said looking at his niece and marvelling at having relatives in his new country.

Jim interceded with, "I think that you will meet her. I know Goldman has the idea of bringing here anyone that Wanda might have a link to. He won't object to you staying here."

Elisabeth nodded thoughtfully. "If that third sister is alive, I wonder if she had children."

Chapter 2

Jim read the report on the Cassidy family and made notes in point form. It was thorough. The house where Elisabeth had briefly been a prisoner was the old farmhouse where Matthew Cassidy and his wife Betsy and their six children had lived. It was currently unoccupied – being somewhat rundown.

Henry Cassidy, Matthew's oldest child, lived close by. His original farm was much smaller now. He was born in 1933 and would be seventy-five now. He had twin brothers, Nicholas and Michael, who would be seventy-three. Michael lived in London and Nicholas in Los Angeles. The oldest girl, Eva, also living in Los Angeles was seventy-one. The next sister, Lucy (now deceased) would have been sixty-nine now. She was born in 1939, just before the war. Then there was the youngest girl – the odd one, Jai – born in 1942. She left home at sixteen and last seen less than a year later.

The elder children of that generation had, between them, ten children. Jim passed them over for now. Only Eva's eldest son had a criminal record – the rest seemed to be model citizens.

The dossier on Matthew Cassidy proved to be quite fascinating. As a young man, it seemed, he was a wild one himself. He had never actually been in official trouble, but often warned to mend his ways. As soon as war broke out in Europe, he had gone to England and enlisted in the RAF. He had proved to be a natural and hadn't seemed to care that he had left a wife and five young children – one still a baby – at home.

He flew missions all over Europe, was shot down over Eastern Europe, and eventually reappeared with recovered wounds, months after being shot down. He was sent home at the end of 1941. The report then indicated that he seemed to have matured, for he settled down to work the farm.

A report, unearthed from various sources, indicated that a heavily pregnant woman, Jai Ansuni, had turned up soon after Matthew returned. The odd thing was, the child was born at the farmhouse, and his wife had willingly adopted the child after the mother had died.

Jim found the separate dossier on Jai Cassidy. Her birth certificate proved that she was a half-sister to the rest. It gave Matthew Cassidy as her father, but her mother as Jai Ansuni – an odd name that. It also mentioned the trouble she had often been in. By the time she was sixteen, she had a long record of misdemeanours, had left home, and was wanted for an assault on a local personage of importance.

That had been followed up. The charge was later dropped as she had helped police close down a whorehouse and white slave racket run by the personage. That report, containing official statements as well as police reports had a number of oddities that were hinted at but not stated.

One name stood out – Mosellan. The man had been involved with the whorehouse raid. He had employed Jai Cassidy and one report had it that he had tamed her. Later it was mentioned that Jai Cassidy was granted probation in his aegis. There was also mention of his wife, Ellie, and son, Jonny, being kidnapped and rescued by Jai Cassidy. It was not long after that that Jai was last seen. All presumed that this Mosellan had returned to his own country (unknown or never mentioned) and Jai had gone with him. One of the oddities was that the man, Mosellan, had lived in a small hamlet in the nearby hills. It was hard to get to with no real roads into it. There was a police report of a visit there to talk to Jai Cassidy, and a later one when the police had tried to find the hamlet, and couldn't.

With all these details in mind, Jim Phillips took Elisabeth to talk to Henry Cassidy.

"Why are you interested in my father?" Henry Cassidy asked as he unlocked the door of the farmhouse. "And why did you want me here? We are in the process of clearing the place out."

Jim followed Henry inside, and Elisabeth followed. She began to look around.

"Wow," exclaimed. "This would be a wonderful room if it could be restored. Do you know who designed it?"

"I'm sure I don't know," Henry admitted, diverted from his earlier faint suspicions. "All I remember is that my Da had it done when he returned home from the war. If you must know, and heavens knows, Da can't care now if I tell you, I think he did it for Ma out of guilt."

Henry dragged off the covers from a few chairs and invited his guests to sit.

"You intrigue me, Mr Cassidy," Elisabeth smiled at him. "It's really nothing to do with my real reason for being here, but would you indulge me and I'll get to the point. But guilt?"

Henry grinned at an old memory. "Well, as Ma put it, Da had the unmitigated gall to run off, leaving her with five kids, one only a few months old, to join a foreign army – just to get in one hell of a dogfight."

Elisabeth laughed in delight. "I would have been waiting at home with a frying pan," she claimed.

"She would have been. Except when she knew he was coming home and alive, after us not knowing what had happened to him, well, she just wanted him home. And then, not long after, some foreign woman followed him here and claimed he was the father of her child."

"Oh dear! What happened then?" Elisabeth sounded surprised.

Jim hadn't sat as the others had; he was leaning against the door frame, studying the room. He was enjoying Elisabeth's success in getting the old man to talk.

"The woman was pretty sick, apparently. Dad had her stay with us, and us kids were told to keep away from her. I was something like ten at the time but I remember Ma and Da had a real loud fight. Next day they seemed back to normal. I remember hearing the baby when it was born. Mum birthed all of us in this house too. They called the baby Jai, J-a-i, after the woman who died shortly after."

Jim made a mental note to check local doctor reports.

It seemed Elisabeth read his mind. Though it might simply be she had a very logical mind too.

"Did a doctor look at her?"

"He had another emergency. He was too late," Henry remembered.

"Did he do an autopsy?" Elisabeth asked.

"Here? Back then?" Henry shook his head. "She had told Da that she had no family – that was why she had come to him. So, she died, Dad had her buried in the old town cemetery and we looked after the baby."

"Your mother must have been a saint." Elisabeth marvelled.

"Ma loved children," Henry said simply. "Would have liked to have had a dozen. Da found out, after he'd got back that he couldn't have any more. The injury he'd took before being sent home had done something to him. I don't think Ma wanted to lose the last of Da's children even if she was a little hellion."

"I would think your father was too," Jim commented dryly from the door.

Henry snorted. "I believe so, but the war changed him. He certainly wouldn't take much from us boys. I felt his hand on my backside many a time. Never laid a hand on the girls though. I often thought Jai should've been a boy."

Jim decided they had heard enough about the youngest Cassidy child for the moment – he'd get back to her.

"Mr Cassidy – what we came here about was to do research for a book about the history of the area. We believe that the Cassidy's have lived around here for a long time?"

"Certainly have," Henry agreed proudly. "Almost as long as the Lammonds – longer now – the last of them is dead."

It was Jim's turn to skilfully get Henry to talk about the last of the Lammonds but not right away. He wanted to learn about the earlier ones. He wanted to be sure that the last of them, really had been one of them.

"Do you mind if I take notes," Elisabeth asked with a smile Henry couldn't resist. He was tickled by her interest.

Henry began by saying the original Lammonds had been wealthy, and had come to the area to start a vineyard. Most of their wealth had come from other businesses in the city. Over time, the vineyard had closed down and the property had been transformed into a resort for other wealthy people.

The town had grown up and become famous for its pure water and its mineral springs.

The Lammond family had always been a pillar of the town - regular church goers, doers of good works.

Olivier Lammond had spent most of the war years in the city – overseeing his businesses. His son had joined the marines but was killed overseas. Olivier, when he returned home was a different man – reclusive.

"There was some sort of scandal about him, wasn't there," Elisabeth asked casually. She seemed to be considering her notes.

Henry snorted. "Some sort! The biggest damn thing ever to happen hereabouts. Old Olivier started up a whore house in an old barn just off his property. They reckoned he took girls who had no family and made them work there and had them right convinced that it was no use escaping."

"How did they find him out?" Jim asked, interested.

"Not sure ah know the whole story," Henry admitted. "But I reckon he made a mistake about one of the women he took – tried to take."

"How so?" Elisabeth asked, leaning forward.

"Well, the gossip said he had taken a girl from the village and tried to take her in a way she didn't want."

"What – rape her," Elisabeth asked directly.

"Well – yes. But the girl managed to run off. She told the police, but they didn't believe her because, Lammond was – well he was a Lammond."

Jim nodded, understanding. Powerful family, long history of good in the district...

"Figured out later, he tried something similar with that hellion of a sister of mine. She never let it get that far – she kneed him in the groin and scampered off. She never said a word about it. Probably didn't dare, considering her record in the district. Police figured out it was her – told the folks she was wanted for assault."

"And you believed it?" Elisabeth asked, wanting confirmation.

"Too right!" Henry agreed with emphasis. "This was after she had run off from the farm one time. Da sent me to bring her back. She did exactly that to me. She had no intention of coming back. She told me she'd do it again if I tried to make her. Said she watched us boys fighting. I told her she could go to hell, and told the old man I couldn't find her. I reckon Lammond underestimated her."

"So how did he get found out," Elisabeth repeated Jim's question.

"Some foreigner got the police all riled up because his sister in law was missing. He must've been someone important. Everyone was saying how lots of women had gone missing around the place."

"Do you remember that man's name?" Jim made his question sound casual.

Henry went quiet, noticeably thinking – by the way his brows furrowed.

"Mossell, Moselle, Mosielan...something like that. By all accounts, not the sort of gent to be on the wrong side of. Had to laugh though. Somehow he must have given my sister a job – got the police off her back by promising she would behave. I wouldn't have believed it possible, but I reckon he civilised her. He even got her to wear a dress!"

Henry had a reminiscent chuckle. "I didn't hear the details of the raid – were lots of rumours of course, but somehow Jai was involved – after that the police were saying how good she was."

"So what happened to her?" Elisabeth asked, really wanting to know.

"No one knows," Henry admitted. "Da thought she had decided to go off with the Mosellan gent. She was supposed to have become a maid or companion to his wife. That's what she said when she came here for a bit. We found her with a foreign woman and a boy, by the road when we were coming back from church. She said they had been kidnapped, and escaped."

"What did you think?" Jim asked.

"I'd have said she done something to annoy the Mosellan gent, but when the police came they believed her. That's when I heard they had dropped the assault thing. Didn't see her after that. The kid at the garage asked after her, sometime later, but we didn't know where she had gone."

"Is that kid still living around here?" Jim asked.

"Yeah. Retired now. His kids run the garage in Wetherby. John Masterton is his name."

Jim asked a few more innocuous questions about the history of the district. Elisabeth asked if the ladies room still worked and used that supposed need as an excuse to look around while Jim kept Henry talking.

Elisabeth, when she had been a prisoner here, had only really seen the front room and a glimpse of a kind of dining room, in the dark. Wanda had described where she had found the bracelet and how it had seemed to call to her. Nothing like that feeling had affected her. Admittedly, the last time she was here she had other things on her mind and was also a little 'tied up'.

All the upstairs rooms were empty. If anything else like the bracelet had been here – it had probably been removed. She went back to the front room and gave Jim a slight shrug. Shortly afterwards, they left the house.

"Did you learn anything new?" Elisabeth asked, once they were driving away.

"He confirmed most of what was in the reports I got. I think it is worth talking to this Masterton and I want to find out more about that foreigner, Mosellan. Are you up to interviewing the mechanic?"

"Try and stop me!" Elisabeth threatened. "And can I read those reports too?"

"Yes, I'll arrange it when we get back." Jim was grinning at Elisabeth's enthusiasm. She seemed to be taking a personal interest in this sideline investigation.

Perhaps it was simply wanting to help find Wanda, but he had warned her that this might lead to nothing. It was a long shot, but only worth looking at because Wanda had found something of interest in that old house of the Cassidy's.

"Ok, we'll go see if we can find Masterton. I don't suppose you felt anything back in that house?" Jim asked idly.

"No. Not this time nor last time." Elisabeth had to admit. "Whatever Wanda found had to have targeted her."

"Oh, why do you say that?" Jim was more interested in her answer than he wanted this sister of Wanda to realise.

"Something about her must have caused it to react. And there was probably only one thing like it there. Wanda has always had 'something'. She could sense things, I never could. Now, I can hear her, but no one else."

Jim merely nodded. He felt sure that Elisabeth Willard did have 'something' too – but at a level she wasn't aware of. He recalled her hunch, before he had brought Wanda back to San Francisco for the Franklin's trial. She had warned they would try to kill Wanda.

As for the questioning of Henry Cassidy – that was masterful. He doubted that it was all due to being an attractive Senator's daughter.

"By all means," insisted the son of John Masterton. "He's free. He's been retired for ten years and still can't stop hanging around here. Reckons he likes the smell of the place. I'd say he likes chatting to the customers, but some of them find him a nuisance. The history of this area you say? I'm not sure about that – you will probably get all the gossip. Garage is good for that."

It was easy to get John Masterton to talk. It only took a few casual questions and the assumption that he had a vast knowledge of the district. Jim decided to suggest they moved to the diner opposite when it became apparent they would find it hard to stop him talking.

Jim began by asking about families that had been around longest in the district, and who had founded it.

When the old man mentioned the Cassidy's, Elisabeth broke in. "Yes. We've met Henry C. He suggested you could help us."

John chuckled. "Bit of a wowser that one. Honest though, I'll give him that. All that bunch were the same. The girls were trained to be ladies, and the boys – men. Except for the youngest - she was never a lady and could fight like a boy."

"Bit of a town mystery, that one," Elisabeth suggested.

"Nah! Just a tomboy with lot of guts. That family was too straight laced for her. She was the best of the lot, I reckon."

"You knew her?" Elisabeth asked.

"Yeah. I met her one day, hiding out amongst the wrecks out the back of the garage. Had half the police in the state after her. Heard she had kicked old Lammond in the balls and he – being so high and mighty with relatives in the police – insisted on charging her with assault."

"So you obviously didn't turn her in," Elisabeth challenged as Jim was struck by another thought.

Lammond's only son had died in the war. Nowhere else was mention of other Lammonds. The line had died out. Something else to check.

"Nah!" Masterton went on blithely. "When I heard what that little slip of a thing had done, I'd've helped her any which way. She was a kid, barely sixteen - shorter than you, Miss. Old Lammond was solid, and quite tall. And he'd had a go at my sister. That made her my friend for life."

"So what happened?" Elisabeth asked, leaning forward.

"Oh, when it got dark, I drove her up the road. I dropped her out of town where the hills start. She reckoned she could manage on her own – didn't want me in trouble too."

"Henry said she went off forty years ago. Did you ever hear from her again?" Jim asked.

"Not in the last forty years. But back then I did. A few days later, someone had done a hit run on her. I took her to the hospital – I reckon she had broken bones and stuff. Left her there. I don't think the police found her because the town stayed buzzing for a week before they gave up. Then about a month or two later, she turns up again. I got told the police wanted to see me. I got taken to a guest house out of town. She was there with a police inspector and another guy. They asked me to help set up a raid on Lammond's whore house. I was game for that. We, Jai and I - she was pretending to be a boy – found the place. Hadn't been there long when they knew the police were around. I think that other guy had a way to track Jai. I was thrown out of the place, and Jai was told to get out. She found me down the hill a bit. Things worked out though. Lammond was arrested and then he killed himself. The police arrested a few others."

"A night of infamy," Elisabeth commented. "Were you a hero or an outcast for helping?"

"I kept my mouth shut," John told them. "The whole event was weird. I mean, I wasn't drunk. I'd had a couple when we were trying for this pass thing we needed to go to the whore house, just to seem legit, but it was weird."

"How so?" Elisabeth encouraged.

"Promise you won't tell anyone I said this?"

Elisabeth glanced at Jim, and then promised.

"Well, the place we were sent to could only have been Harris's barn. But that had been a burnt out ruin for years. Yet it was done up like a Sultan's harem inside. And, mind you, I had only been by there a short time before when I was looking for my sister. So, it was no burnt ruin, and there were a couple of times - going there and coming back when I felt weird, as if the whole world twisted. I had gone a fair way down the track, until the guards on that place stopped following me – then snuck back he find Jai. When I got back, the barn was a burnt out ruin."

"That is odd," Elisabeth agreed, sounding perplexed, but actually hiding her excitement. "You must have had a more potent brew than you thought."

"Was that woman they were looking for – found there?" Jim asked. "I heard about someone's wife..."

"Yeah. That other guy – the one with the Inspector – his wife's sister was missing. Yeah, they found her."

"What was he like?" Elisabeth asked abruptly.

John Masterton turned and studied her. "Tall, dark blond hair. Tight curls all over his head. He had an odd bone structure..." He continued to stare at Elisabeth. "A lot like yours, Miss. Are you related to him?"

"Not ...that I know of," Elisabeth said, flustered. "I know my father, and grandfather..."

"Coincidence," Masterton shrugged. "Anyway, he had this way of looking at you as if he could see right into you. The sort of presence where you don't dare do anything wrong because he would know and you would be for it. Jai seemed to have a lot of wary respect for him!"

Jim turned the talk to later gossip for a time, before deciding it was time to be heading back.

"What are you thinking?" Jim asked Elisabeth as they were heading back to Rockwater.

"That we have found evidence of aliens and that Jai Cassidy was in the thick of it."

"I have to agree," Jim said evenly. "What convinced you?"

"That part where John mentioned the weirdness, particularly when he said he felt the world had twisted."

"Why was that?" Jim asked still evenly.

"Because, I have felt that too. When Wanda walked me from the house where Joseph had me. I fainted, after, and I put my recollection of it down to reaction to everything."

Jim nodded. Marjorie Howard, the negotiator, had mentioned something similar, and Jim had proposed the same reason.

"And how the place was a building one moment and a ruin the next," Elisabeth added.

"Hmm," Jim murmured thoughtfully. "Wanda mentioned two groups. I wonder if Jai Cassidy and that man Mosellan were both the same group."

Elisabeth pondered. "Lammond had to be another. What he was doing was barbaric and I'd guess he was Atapi. If Mosellan was keen to get him, I'd say he was the other group. But what was Jai?"

"Wanda said she was half human, half Atapi," Jim revealed. "That's why they hope Wanda will find her. They want to bring the Atapi back to be warriors against the invaders. But it seems she was no friend to Lammond."

"It makes no sense," Elisabeth muttered. "Do they think Wanda is some kind of magician?"

"No, but they must feel she can do it, has the talent for it. Perhaps like you and Wanda can know where the other is – and talk to each other."

"But we are sisters," Elisabeth countered. "That woman vanished forty years ago and we are not even related!"

"And John thought you looked like the man..." Jim said gently.

"How can that be? I know my father's family, and mother was born in Europe. Her father was Russian."

"Goldman is checking over there," Jim said. "But it could be from your mother's grandparents."

"Hmm," Elisabeth hummed. "You know – I have a really strong urge to find out. Do you think that policeman might still be alive? He might be able to tell us more about that man, Mosellan."

"I'll find out," Jim promised. "And I will get Goldman looking for medical records on Jai Cassidy and if Mosellan was a foreigner, there ought to be immigration records of his arriving and departing. If he was some sort of diplomat, we might have to check classified records."

Jim located the former Superintendent Holt at a nursing home about an hour's drive from Rockwater. The nurse there warned them that the old man's mind wandered, but that he did have lucid moments about the past. He would be glad of visitors.

Stephen Holt was but a shadow of his younger self but for the moment was in the present.

"What brings you here to see me, Mr Phillips, Miss Willard?" he asked in a quavery voice.

"Jai Cassidy," Elisabeth said at once, dropping into a chair opposite the wheel chair in which the old man sat.

"Jai Cassidy," Holt repeated. "Has she turned up again?"

"No," Elisabeth admitted. "But her name did. My sister was sent to find her and she is missing now."

"And your sister is?" Holt prompted delicately.

"A special investigator for the government." Jim answered promptly.

"Ah," Holt understood. "A spy." He nodded, probably thinking back. "What do you know of Jai Cassidy?"

Jim summarised what he had learnt from Henry Cassidy and John Masterton.

"There is probably not much more that I can add," Holt admitted. "Except without Miss Cassidy's help, and that employer of hers, I doubt I would have closed down that prostitution racket. They always seemed to know when we were sniffing around, and simply hid – somehow. That young snip of a girl saw things a lot more clearly than some of my men. She told her employer that she believed some of the police were related to that Lammond creature. So when that Mosellan guy, her employer, came to me about his missing relative again – I was more wary about things."

"That relative had been missing for a while," Elisabeth nudged the man's memory.

"Yes, some months," Holt agreed. "So had a lot of other women who had been in the area. He came back to me with an odd tale about his wife, dreaming about her sister. He admitted that he didn't really know if it were possible, but Miss Cassidy had recognised a place his wife had described and a man she'd seen in a dream."

Elisabeth became aware that the old policeman was studying her in much the same way as Masterton had.

"I'm like that with my sister," Elisabeth told Holt, trying to distract him.

"I've seen you somewhere before," Holt told Elisabeth. Some of the brightness was leaving his eyes.

"You might have seen me in the papers. I am Senator Willard's daughter."

"Oh, yes. That could be – but before that..." Holt's voice faded away.

The hovering nurse began to move forward, but Jim waved her back. He let the old man think on his memories.

"Yes! Mosellan, Miss Cassidy's employer – you are like him." The brightness was back in his eyes.

"What do you know about him," Jim asked, but the old man appeared not to have heard the question.

Elisabeth repeated it.

"He was some foreign VIP – or that is what my superiors told me. I had to give him all the help he needed. He wasn't Russian – but from somewhere in Eastern Europe. His wife and her sister were from Yugoslavia or Czechoslovakia – somewhere there – with little English."

"He helped with Lammond," Elisabeth suggested.

"Very much. That creature saw him and was afraid of him."

"Why do you call him – that creature?" Elisabeth asked.

"He was nothing like any of that family," Holt said. "Later I did some checking. There was a period of a few years between the war and when he returned here that I couldn't account for. If the Lammond we arrested was the same man that left the district before the war – something happened to him to completely change him. That is why no one believed at first that he could be involved in anything so ugly and perverted."

"Was he ever in the armed forces?" Elisabeth asked.

"No, but his son was. The son died in Europe somewhere. I can't recall those details. It was idle curiosity so I didn't probe too far."

Elisabeth glanced at Jim, who nodded for her to keep going.

"Maybe Mosellan knew him from Europe," Elisabeth mused aloud.

"Once we had the missing woman back," Holt said, reverting to the previous topic, "that was the last I saw of Mosellan, or Miss Cassidy."

"Did you ever check on either of them?" Elisabeth asked.

"Some years later," Holt admitted. "Matt Cassidy asked me if I could contact the man, to see how his daughter was going."

"And..." Elisabeth prompted.

"Nothing. Couldn't find anything. I had checked the routine things, believing that Mosellan and his family must have returned to Europe. Perhaps with him being a VIP it was all hush-hush. All I could say was, in my opinion, Mr Mosellan was a man of upstanding character who would treat his daughter right, and if he wasn't, Miss Cassidy would know how to handle him."

"All this doesn't seem to help me find my sister," Elisabeth slumped back into the chair. "She, like they, seems to have disappeared off the face of the Earth."

Elisabeth knew her comment had a double meaning. Most people would take it as the colloquial version of disappeared completely.

Holt went rigid. "Just like that village Mosellan lived in when he was here."

"What?" Elisabeth blurted.

The story that followed did sound like the wanderings of an old mind, but the man's eyes were bright.

Mosellan had taken him to the village on one occasion to talk to Jai Cassidy. He had been able to judge how the girl had changed, even to the point of wearing a dress. That had convinced him that Mosellan knew how to handle people. And how to handle Jai Cassidy in a more positive way than putting her into a juvenile detention centre would have.

Holt's narrative wandered back to the Lammond case, but Jim gently deflected him. "The village..."

"We had to walk up to it – there wasn't a road into it. It was all very rustic, no electricity or anything. And Mosellan walked me back down to the road where I had left my car."

"Do you know the location?" Jim asked gently.

Holt gave a precise location of where the trail they followed left the road.

"I didn't know the area well, but two of my men were locals and they had to go up there with Miss Cassidy, but they reached a point where she expected to see the place, but there was nothing there. They reported that Mosellan found them, reassured them, and promised to come and see the police when he finished recalling the men he had out searching for his wife and son. Miss Cassidy joined him, and my men returned."

"Did you try finding the village again?" Jim asked.

"Yup – couldn't. I followed Crystal Spring fire track all the way up. I even got some of the first aerial maps of the area. Not a trace. When they mapped the hills, there was no mention of a village around there. No signs that one had ever been there. By now, though, there have been fires through there."

The hovering nurse returned. "I think that is enough for today."

Jim nodded, seeing the brightness fade from the old eyes. He gestured to Elisabeth and thanked the old man for all his help. Elisabeth went and hugged him. She whispered a thank you to him and saw his pleased smile.

"I don't think we are going to find much more around here," Jim commented as they were driving away.

"A village that was there, and then not there," Elisabeth verbalised what was confusing her.

Jim agreed. It sounded weird but... "That place he described, its location – could have been where we found Wanda."

Jim found a number of reports waiting when he returned. The other investigators found some information, but little that actually helped.

A small hospital on the other side of Wetherby from Crystal Brook, found mention of an accident victim, around the time mentioned by John Masterton, but the name was wrong. The only odd thing was that initial x-rays of the woman victim had shown fractures, but ones taken an hour later did not.

The team checking immigration records found no mention of the man Mosellan – arriving or departing. There was no record of Jai Cassidy applying for a passport to leave the country. Checks in sensitive diplomatic channels came back negative too. If a record had ever existed, those looking had clearance to find it.

However they did have success finding the arrival of Wanda and Elisabeth's mother. They had the dates, ship name, departure point and arrival point, her passport details and a photo. The likeness to Wanda was uncanny, and that to Elisabeth was obvious in the bone structure.

Further investigations were to be made into Katya Willard (nee Androv, nee Tatarovich) at the point of origin of the ship.

The next report Jim read was from the team that had been searching local newspaper archives and they had found something that Jim had hoped for. A photo, albeit a poor one – of Mosellan. It was dated a month or so before the infamous Lammond story, when Mosellan's sister in law had first gone missing. There was also a poor quality photo of the missing woman.

Jim studied both photos – and then went through the files he was keeping on the enquiries. He found a copy of the picture Wanda had drawn under hypnosis.

Uncanny, that's what it was. Not identical, but like enough that the face Wanda had drawn had distinct likenesses to Mosellan and the other woman.

Then Jim studied the poor photo of Mosellan – recalling how two men had seen a likeness between him and Elisabeth. Her hair didn't curl, but if you ignored that – the likeness was there. It was in the bone structure, and the slight slant in the eyes and the shape of the cheek bones. Elisabeth's hair colour, lighter than Wanda's, increased the effect.

Jim sat back and considered what he had in his hands.

Elisabeth, Wanda, Tanya – all had to be related to this man, Mosellan. It had to be through the maternal link. In Wanda's and Elisabeth's case, it could not be through the Senator. His family had been checked back a hundred and twenty years – totally American.

Ok, Jim thought to himself, Mosellan was of the Kumatan group Wanda had mentioned. They had come to control the Atapi group. Lammond, had to have been one of that ilk. Jai Cassidy, Wanda had told him, was half Atapi, half human. She had to have been trusted by Mosellan. Was it because she was half human? Or because, Mosellan had civilised her? But if the Kumatan had followed the Atapi here, surely they could find the Atapi on their own world?

Jim let his mind clear of everything and as he had experienced often before, an idea came to him. The village, that was there and not there. Wanda's mention of crossing between places, no, planes. Perhaps those two words did not have the same meaning here. Perhaps there was a plane where humans existed and one where the village existed, in the same relative place on the world, but only someone like Mosellan could bring people from one to the other. Perhaps Jai Cassidy could do it too.

He mulled over the idea, and even if he did not understand how it was possible, it fit. Wanda it seemed could go from place to place. Could she also cross from plane to plane? They must think she was able to – but why her? Why did they think she – an alien from Earth – could find the missing Jai Cassidy on a world alien to Wanda, when they who lived there could not?

"Earth blood?"

Jim was startled when Elisabeth spoke. "Sorry. I couldn't sleep, and your door was open and you were muttering."

"No need to apologise," Jim said, getting up and inviting Elisabeth to sit with a gesture and going to make sure his door was now shut. "I read those reports I gave you too. And others. I was just thinking that if blood can call to blood, sort of like you and Wanda, and if there are only two people on whatever that world is called..."

"Jim, who is this?" Elisabeth had seen the photo of Mosellan and the colour had gone from her face.

"Sit down before you fall down," Jim urged. "That's the man that Masterton and Holt met with Jai Cassidy."

"Are you sure that Wanda and I are actually daughters of Charles Willard and not this man?"

"I think you can be sure. He disappeared about the time your mother would have been born," Jim told her, emphasising the time difference. Then he moved some papers to show her the copy of the passport of her mother. Elisabeth relaxed as she took in the information on the document and studied the photo.

"It does give that town as her birthplace, and in 1957," Elisabeth said aloud. "It's the same year as Prof Krinsky's wife, Ivana. Could the likeness is ethnic to that area? Wasn't there a third one?"

"Triplets?" Jim said without conscious thought. "There were three girls."

Jim went to the phone and dialled. He asked for Goldman and was put straight through.

"The people checking in Europe. Could you have them be alert for a mention of triplets born in 1957 around that village?"

Elisabeth heard what sounded like an exclamation from Goldman before the voice went soft again. Jim listened for quite a while.

"What?" Elisabeth asked when Jim had replaced the receiver.

Jim didn't speak at once.

Finally. "Tatarovich, the Russian soldier that was father to Ivana. Official sources say that prior to joining the army, he had spent time in Eastern Europe, in 1956-1957. When he joined up he did not say that he was married."

"But?" Elisabeth prompted, sensing there was more.

Jim smiled faintly. "But family sources, close to the Tatarovich family, have admitted that soon after he joined up a couple brought a child to the Tatarovich house and claimed it was his. They had a ring that was a Tatarovich family heirloom and a photo of him and the mother. The Tatarovich family were convinced and not wanting scandal, adopted the child. It helped that the mother was dead. It meant that when their son joined up it was true he was not married."

"He was probably drunk at some time and raped the girl," Elisabeth muttered.

"He could have been in love," Jim suggested, and saw Elisabeth blush.

"Yeah, Yeah. Perhaps," Elisabeth's better nature admitted. "Can we get a hold of that photo?"

"If it is possible, it will be done," Jim told her.

"Ok, but there was one, possibly two other babies born to that girl," Elisabeth reminded Jim.

"I would guess that Tatarovich was long gone by the time the babies were born. The mother might only have had the ring and the photo to identify him, other than his name."

"Supposing the girl had triplets, and died, why did they take only one of the babies to the father?" Elisabeth persisted.

"It depends on how much time passed before that decision was made," Jim proposed. "If the mother died, they would have needed someone to care for the babies. From what I know of the area – the people were pretty poor. Perhaps if there were three babies, they were farmed out to three families and only one wanted to make the effort to take the baby to her father."

"Probably for money," Elisabeth said snidely.

Jim shook his head slightly. Elisabeth usually found a way to see the good side of people. That was twice now she had come in that she'd said something disparaging.

"So it looks like this Tatarovich was my maternal grandfather," Elisabeth summarised. "But there is still my uncanny likeness to the Mosellan guy."

"Yes. He was believed to have come from Eastern Europe, but we have not been able to find travel records for him. We know he was here in 1958. It doesn't mean he wasn't there in 1957. I would estimate though that he would be old enough to be the father of Tatarovich's wife. And I would say that the wife would be about the same age as Jai Cassidy."

"Then he might be my great grandfather," Elisabeth suggested.

Jim shrugged. "We will see if anything else turns up. I feel sure we are still missing something."

"What do you mean?"

"If you are descended from some alien Kumatan," Jim began.

"Thanks," Elisabeth muttered.

Jim smiled faintly, wondering what was affecting her. "And Jai Cassidy was descended from some alien Atapi... Ok, you, Wanda and Tanya have mixed blood. Jai Cassidy has mixed blood. I just think there has to be something more."

"Yeah. My ancestors were aliens!"

Jim laughed softly. "Do you feel like an alien?"

"Of course not. The whole notion is ridiculous."

"Was that the reason why you came visiting?"

Elisabeth shook her head. "Bad dreams, that's all. Probably from all the odd reports I was reading."

"Were your dreams about Wanda?" Jim asked.

"No. I am used to what I sense from her." In the past some of those things had been like nightmares. "I dreamt I was going crazy. A bit like what Wanda described when she suddenly heard everyone's mental voices – only in the dream I was sharing everyone's emotions. I thought I was going crazy."

Jim simply nodded and filed her comments in the back of his mind. It may be nothing, but it might be Elisabeth was reacting to something relevant. He couldn't say yet.

"Get some warm milk and go to bed," Jim suggested.

"That's what Dad would say," Elisabeth agreed, getting up to leave. "You'll tell me anything else you find out?"

Jim nodded and watched her leave. Perhaps he had better take his own advice, and sleep.

Jim Phillips had upped and gone – sometime in the middle of the night. Elisabeth had only found that out when she had asked the question of the base CO, General Addison.

"Called away, Miss Willard," Addison told her impersonally.

"Do you know when he will be back?"

Addison simply said, "I am not privy to his business. I do have permission for you to stay on here if you wish. Dr Wallace suggested that you could."

"I'll go and see if he needs help with anything," Elisabeth said aloud.

"That won't be possible. Dr Wallace left for Washington this morning."

"Sir, is there anything useful I can be doing? Internet research or something?" Elisabeth asked – not used to being idle and not really wanting to go back to Oxnard to help her father.

Addison outlined the recreational facilities on the base and suggested others in the nearby town. It wasn't what she wanted to do.

"Is there a computer I can use?" Elisabeth asked. "I was helping Jim Phillips check out a few things. I could keep on with that."

"The computers here are government ones. You would need to get a clearance to use them. I am sorry, Miss Willard."

"How would I get a clearance?" Elisabeth insisted.

"It's not up to me, Miss."

"Ask your superiors? Ask Magnus Goldman. Ask...I will ask my father, Senator Willard."

Addison smiled politely and made no comment.

Elisabeth managed to leave his presence without acting like she was in a huff – but she felt like it. She went back to her cottage and called her father. Jim had not told her to keep anything from her father – just not to discuss it widely. Anyway, it was his daughter they were looking for too. He had a right to know.

Still, she was not sure how secure the phone line was so she kept things general and asked about clearances.

"I can't pull rank, Elisabeth," he said regretfully. "I don't know if I have enough pull anyway."

"What if you called Goldman?" Elisabeth suggested. "Or do you think I could?"

"Ok, Liz. I'll call him. I'm more likely to get through to him," Charles

Willard agreed. "What do you want to do?"

"Just some family history searches," she said carefully.

"I'll ask," Willard said, having understood her reference.

Elisabeth rang off and began to pace the room; she was feeling like she needed something to occupy her mind. Failing that a gentle workout in the gym might relieve her of the excess, fidgety energy.

"What is the matter with me?" Elisabeth asked herself, finally. "I'm not usually like this – I'm getting like Wanda used to..."

"Wanda?" she thought strongly. This had worked before Wanda had gone off. "Wanda?" She imagined yelling it, concentrating on her sister with all of her heart and soul.

Something – a flicker – then that darkness with its sense of unseen things like her nightmares. Elisabeth shivered. With a curse, she grabbed her workout clothes and gym shoes and walked purposefully toward the gym.

Two hours later, she looked up from the counter on the treadmill and her heart nearly stopped. Her feet did and she nearly fell on the machine.

"Elisabeth?" Tanya Krinsky asked in a voice both once familiar and totally at odds with what she saw.

"I'm Tanya Krinsky. Dr Wallace said you were here. I am really pleased to meet you."

Elisabeth found her voice. "I wanted to meet you too, and I am sorry I stared, but..."

"I know. I am very like Wanda," Tanya agreed. "I am sorry I startled you."

"It's not that. I had been told about you. It's just that – I wouldn't have been shocked if Wanda had suddenly appeared in front of me... I really wished you were her."

Tanya moved and embraced her just met cousin. "I too wish she were here," she admitted as she felt the younger girl shaking slightly. "Just like I wish my mother was still alive. My father said that our mothers were sisters."

Elisabeth pushed herself away from her cousin. Her face was wet with tears. "Sorry," she murmured. "You look like Wanda, but sound like my mother did. I didn't realise how well I remembered her voice. I was only three when she died."

"You feel like the sister I wish I had," Tanya said softly. "Like you would understand me like my mother did. Like Wanda understood me but she was... driven."

"I know, but we were always there for each other," Elisabeth admitted. "I guess cousins are the next best thing." She reached out for Tanya, and realised that some of the tension she had been feeling had drained away.

"Yes," Tanya said gently. "Father is a wonderful man, I know that, but..."

"It isn't the same," Elisabeth finished. "Dad's great, but he has been married twice since my mother died. I have six younger siblings, but Wanda and I are soul mates. And you feel the same. Having you here, gives me hope. I didn't think I could help get Wanda back by myself."

Tanya gripped Elisabeth's hands. "Together we are stronger."

It turned out, Tanya had been assigned to share quarters with Elisabeth. Now that they had met, both were more than happy with the arrangement. Back at the cottage, Elisabeth found a message from General Addison, requesting that she bring Tanya with her, to talk to him when convenient.

She called his aide, and was told they could come right away.

The General dismissed his aide when he had shown the two women in to see him. He invited his guests to sit. "Magnus Goldman has granted both of you limited clearance – to use the base computers. He has assigned you a password and user name. When you logon – you will only be able to access non-classified sites. I expect you will be circumspect about your use. You ought to be aware that all computer use is monitored and inappropriate use will be acted on."

"What I expected," Elisabeth agreed. "Thank you, General."

"Oh, it wasn't me," Addison smiled. "It must have been those strings you pulled with the Senator. I am also to tell you that you may discuss your family matters with Miss Krinsky."

"Any reservations?" Elisabeth asked.

Addison smiled again. He reached to one side of his desk and picked up a piece of paper. "Miss Krinsky needs to sign this. It is to say that what you tell her, Miss Willard, will not be discussed off this base or with people who did not attend the meeting with Goldman last Wednesday."

Elisabeth nodded and explained, "We discussed some things a few days ago when your father was here. I can tell you about them, but you can only discuss them with the people who were there." She listed the people.

Tanya read the document, signed it and gave it to Addison. He in turn handed each of them a sealed envelope with their login names and passwords. He gestured dismissal to them.

Elisabeth spent the next two hours filling Tanya in on the meeting and various related matters including the visits she had made with Jim Phillips.

"So what do you want to do," Tanya asked Elisabeth. "I am not to exert myself until my stitches come out."

"Jim wants to find some connection between Jai Cassidy and us – if one exists. But I want to trace that third sister, Katrina. Did your mother ever mention her?"

Tanya shook her head. "Never. I would have remembered. And where would you look?"

"On the internet. Lots of old records have been posted there now. Can you speak or read anything besides Russian and American?"

"My mother spoke some Slavic dialect. She taught me to read it."

"Good. I will try and see if they have any old birth records from Eastern Europe up on the web," Elisabeth decided.

Tanya had only a very basic understanding of the internet, and had so far felt no need to learn more. She had told Elisabeth she was now studying human development, psychology and biochemistry and preferred to read books not computer screens.

"Where will you start?" Tanya asked, thinking she should try to learn.

"What say we try to find that town our mothers were supposedly born in? How do you spell it?"

Tanya supplied it and Elisabeth typed it into Google.

"I want a map," Elisabeth decided. She looked at a number of sites, found an old one and printed it out. "How do you say these names?"

Elisabeth listened carefully as Tanya pointed to different ones. "Let's see what we can find about the history of the place."

After some searching, she found a useful site. "So it is in Yugoslavia, or what used to be. It must have been in the way of Hitler's army when it invaded in April 1941. Then in 1945, it became communist – under Russian direction and stayed that way until the Iron Curtain came down."

"I remember that," Tanya said.

"Whoever took your Mother to Russia probably managed it easier than if they had tried to get to the west. I wonder how my mother got out, and if that third sister did get out," Elisabeth considered.

"Would they have lists of deaths as well as births?" Tanya suggested.

That proved unhelpful.

"What if you try looking in whatever country it is in now?"

They worked that out. It was in Serbia now. A further hour later they gave up that line of investigation.

Rowan Wallace found them, the following day, scanning old immigration registers, making notes of all Katrinas from 1957 onwards.

"We have clerks somewhere getting paid to do that," Rowan told them. "You don't need to."

"I had to do something," Elisabeth insisted.

"Give it a rest for a while. I have had more reports."

They sat in the office Wallace used when he was at the base.

"I've permission to tell you that we have had information from the British Military archive about Matthew Cassidy. It isn't much. He was apparently shot down over Yugoslavia in July 1940. They didn't say what he was doing there. He reappeared in allied territory some months later and was debriefed about conditions there. In March 1941 he was inserted covertly with a mission for the British Government – something about trying to prevent Yugoslavia from joining with axis powers. He was chosen because he had contacts there from the year before. You may not know that Germany made a push into Yugoslavia, bombed Belgrade – in 1941. Apparently Cassidy was injured again – badly – but was hidden and nursed back to health. He returned to England months later and was demobbed near the end of 1941. Then he went back home."

Elisabeth and Tanya exchanged looks.

"If he met Jai Ansuni there, her people must have been around there too. That Mosellan man was supposed to have come from around there," Elisabeth commented, more to Tanya.

"Did they mention any towns or people?" Tanya asked.

"Yes, but I can't pronounce them," Wallace admitted, handing Tanya the fax.

"Vrbas, Ruma," Tanya pronounced. "Is anyone looking there for records of the Mosellan guy?"

"Why?" Elisabeth asked.

"We look like the Mosellan man, you told me. If he was our grandfather, there might be a record," Tanya insisted.

"You mean him, rather than Tatarovich," Elisabeth asked.

"Or great grandfather then."

"Do you know if your mother had a birth certificate?" Elisabeth asked.

Tanya had to think. She sat still for a long time. "I am not sure."

"Could you ask your mother's family?" Rowan asked.

"Not exactly," Tanya admitted reluctantly. "I am not allowed to contact them. It's political." The last was added because of the question in Elisabeth's expression.

"We have people checking birth and death registers in Russia too," Rowan told them. "Nothing has come to light so far."

Tanya was thoughtful. "Dr Wallace, I have a friend who knows mother's family well. The Tatarovichs. I'm not allowed to contact him either, but maybe he could find out?"

Wallace considered the situation. "Tell me his name and anything you know about him. If you can tell us something we can use as a message that he would know came from you. I will talk to Magnus Goldman. Meanwhile – go find something active to do – scram!"

Elisabeth forced herself to get up early and exercise each day, knowing how important it was that she stay active. Tanya preferred to sleep in and then do some of her college work, since she still had to take it easy.

Early in the morning, Elisabeth had the gym to herself. Later the men training at the base came in. She was used to being unobserved, so the sense of being watched made her look around.

"I have seen Wanda almost flying around in here," Tanya commented as Elisabeth grabbed her towel and wiped her face as she came over.

"I like to keep fit – but not that fit," Elisabeth said. "But Wanda also likes dangling from ropes twelve stories up."

"Yes, I guess so." Tanya glanced up at some railing that was erected just below the high roof.

"What's up?" Elisabeth asked.

"Dr Wallace asked to speak to us."

Elisabeth considered going to change first, but decided against it. If Wallace had news, she wanted to know it.

Wallace smiled at the two young women as they entered the lab. He had one of the trainees walking on a treadmill, wired to machines.

"Another ten minutes at that speed, Stanford," Wallace told the man, the gestured for Tanya and Elisabeth to enter his office.

"Your friend came through," Wallace told Tanya. He found your mother's birth certificate, or a copy of it. It was amongst a pile of papers in a box on a bookshelf – right where you predicted. Attached to it was a death certificate for her mother and there were some scribbled notes on the back in a language he couldn't read. He had time to photograph them for us while he waited for your grandparents to return home. He also told our representative that they were glad to know you were well, even though they couldn't say so. They have agreed to post the original documents, or what they have, to the

US embassy."

"So what did it tell us?" Elisabeth asked eagerly.

Wallace handed a faxed copy of the document photos to Tanya to see if she could read it.

"The birth certificate isn't in Russian. I can read it though. Father Pieter Tatarovich, Mother Anneliese Mosellan," Tanya exclaimed. "There is a signature here that looks like Irena Malakova. It seems like midwife after it. There is another name that looks like Antov and one that might be Petrovich. They give the place as Vrbas and the date as 22nd February 1957. My mother's full name is Ivana Anna, and they have added below it sister to Katya Liesel and Katrina Olga. My great grandmother is Olga. My grandfather must have talked to Anneliese about her."

"Triplets!" Elisabeth marvelled. "Jim Phillips guessed right. What's the other stuff?"

"Serbian as you guessed," Tanya said as she read the spidery writing. "It's dated 24th February. Cause of death – something about childbirth. They had a priest in. I would not have expected that. He baptised the babies and the rest is a note that the midwife, Irena Malakova took Ivana, and the other two witnesses were going to adopt Katya and Katrina."

"I will have those names checked too," Wallace promised. He had been taking notes as Tanya had translated. "They didn't include Anneliese's parent's names?"

"No, they may not have known that."

"Well it's proof that we are related to that Mosellan guy," Elisabeth said carefully. "So if he is an alien he must be very like us. Perhaps that is where this weird genetic thing Wanda and I have comes from. Tanya – was your mother sick?"

"Sick? How?" Tanya asked.

Elisabeth outlined what symptoms might have been noticeable. Tanya shook her head. "I don't think so, why?"

"My mother died from it. How did your mother die?" Elisabeth asked.

Tanya looked as if she wouldn't answer.

Finally, "My mother was arrested for treason - supposedly for consorting with enemies of the state. Since coming here, I have learnt that she was talking to people at various embassies – asking about someone. I had thought that by then Russia and America were friends. Father and I were being watched too. Father's work colleagues were looking at him oddly. Some of my friends wouldn't talk to me. Father had just enough warning to leave. They were going to arrest him too. That's when your Mr. Phillips helped us. They tried to get mother from the prison, but they were too late."

Elisabeth took Tanya's hand and squeezed gently.

Wallace's phone rang, he listened, and gestured for Elisabeth. "For you, Henry Cassidy."

Elisabeth spoke into the phone, while Wallace went out to the trainee in the lab section.

"Hello, Mr Cassidy, its Elisabeth Willard. How can I help you?"

Tanya heard Elisabeth say, "Really? Yes please – I'd like that. I can come over this afternoon – about two o'clock."

Elisabeth replaced the receiver, her eyes glowed with excitement. "Henry Cassidy has found a diary of his father's from the war period. It was hidden in a place Henry only found by accident. He intends to show his family and then see if the military archives are interested in it. Henry's son thinks they should turn it into a book. Henry thought of me – since I claimed to be thinking of writing a history of the area. Some of the writing seems to be in a foreign language. Will you come with me?"

Tanya bit her lip – considering. "I probably shouldn't," she said.

Elisabeth refrained from asking why, at least for the moment. "I will tell you what I find."

Wallace returned and Elisabeth told him what she had told Tanya. "Could I get a driver to take me there?"

"I'll ask the General. It should be no problem," Wallace told her.

Elisabeth greeted the young private who was designated to drive her, and told him where she needed to go. He didn't try to keep chatting to her, which she appreciated, because she wanted to think.

Not about having alien blood – that would freak her – but about her mother. She had been a daughter of Tatarovich, had married a man called Antov – the same name as the people who had fostered her. She had lived in what was now Serbia, previously Yugoslavia. How and why she had walked or travelled from a place like Vrbas to wherever she had embarked from? Why had she come to America?

Why had Ivana, Tanya's mother, been talking to people at embassies? Had she wanted to leave Russia too? Did they know that they had sisters somewhere? Had they ever dreamed of each other like she and Wanda did?

"Katya came here," Elisabeth thought to herself. "But she never tried to find her sisters – or had she? Would her father know? No, he had thought she had no family.

What if she was pulled by a bond she didn't know and it was enough just to be here. If Ivana was trying to come here and Katya was already dead – did that mean her remaining sister was here?

Elisabeth was sure, in spite of having no proof, that Katrina Tatarovich was in America. That she had arrived before Katya. But they had checked the name and had found no records. Surely, Yugoslavian immigrants would be recorded. They were from a communist country.

"This the place, Mam?" the driver asked her as he slowed in front of the farmhouse.

"Yes, thanks. I don't know how long I'll be, but you can wait out here," Elisabeth told the spruce young soldier.

Henry Cassidy met her at the door. He smiled at her. "Your boss isn't with you?" he queried Jim's absence.

Elisabeth decided not to correct him.

"No, he was sent off on another job," Elisabeth claimed. "I hope I will do?"

"Of course, of course," he agreed. "Come through – we've left a few chairs in the old lounge."

"Still cleaning it out are you?" Elisabeth made conversation by stating the obvious. "Will you sell it or pull it down?"

"We are still deciding," Henry told her. "Had a young couple interested in it a while back – months. Didn't hear back from them. Probably scared off when that idiot brat of Eva's kidnapped a girl and brought her here."

Elisabeth decided not to tell him it had been herself – not if he didn't recognise her. Nor did she rise to ask questions about it.

"It looks emptier than on my last visit," she said instead, looking about the room. All the shelves, books, knick-knacks, pictures had gone as well as the curtains and the rest of the furniture.

"Yes, and that is how I found this."

Henry went over to the wall, where wallpaper was peeling off, and pressed on a floor board near the wall. One end lifted up.

From the hole, he took out a wrapped bundle.

"This is how I found it. I slipped and darn near twisted my ankle."

Elisabeth walked over and examined the hole. The board was hinged. "Did your father make this?"

"Musta done. I never knew about it."

Elisabeth felt it, moved it open and shut. For no reason she could think of, she put her hand in the hole and felt around. She felt something that might have been metal and drew it out.

"Well, I'll be..." Henry exclaimed. "It musta been further down than my big hand could reach."

He took the dirty, green tinted metal bracelet which looked so thin as to be brittle. It was about an inch wide and only big enough for a slender wrist. "Might clean up," he murmured. "Couldn't be worth much. Eva wouldn't want it."

"Can I look at it?" Elisabeth asked. Henry gave it back to her. She rubbed it with a damp finger. "I think it is copper. It is a bit like a bracelet that I have which helps with stiff joints."

"Well, perhaps you should have it. Won't fit me."

Elisabeth slipped it in her pocket and turned her attention to the pile of pocket sized notebooks that Henry had unwrapped.

"Did you know that your father kept a journal?" she asked, picking up one dated 1939.

"Never noticed so," Henry said. "But I read a bit. It's no wonder he hid 'em. I reckon he was one randy SOB. Seems like every chance he got, he had a woman. I probably have a dozen bastard siblings I don't know about."

"Apart from your sister, I wonder if you do."

Henry snorted. "I'll let you read a bit. You'll have to pardon his language. He kept a record of his ladies by name and place. I'm having second thoughts about letting my sibs and their kids read it. But I probably shouldn't hide it from them. Anyway, I have stuff to do here. Holler if you need me."

Henry shuffled off and Elisabeth looked at the first book. After glancing through it, she replaced it in favour of one marked 1941. Idly, she put her hand in the pocket with the bracelet, and it felt as if it had slipped onto her wrist. She drew her wrist out. For the merest microsecond, the bracelet looked to be shiny copper, etched exquisitely. Then once again it was old and dirty.

Elisabeth shrugged the odd vision off as imagination. She opened the book at the middle and began to read.

"I saw Jai today. I hadn't realised how lovely she was. The big, expressive brown eyes were like no others I have seen. She still seems so calm – in spite of the bombing. She did not recognise me at first, amongst the wounded. I watched her tend the worst of the others – until she finally came to me. As soon as she touched me, I felt a connection. And so did she for she looked closely at my face, as if she could see through the bandages. I wondered where her friend was – the beautiful one, Suzi.

"I wish I had not asked. Dead! The damn bombs had killed her. Her and a child. A child that could have been mine. Must have been mine. She had called her Anna Louise, like my mother. It hit me then, how irresponsible I had been, how selfish. Running off, leaving my wife, a baby of my own, my other children. I had had a good life. How easily it could have been me – dead."

The next entry was a week later.

"I swear Jai has the healing touch. When I was fevered, her hands cooled me. Those she tended seemed to get better faster. I joked of it. Better sooner, back to fighting sooner. Already, I was almost well enough. I had to get back to England to report. If the Germans came here, they would know I was a spy."

The entries were spaced in time, mostly about how he was keeping away from the Germans by staying with Yugoslavian partisans.

Then, about May, "It seems when I need her most, she's there. Jai. We'd been in an ambush. Yuri died, the others, like me, wounded. We thought the Germans would come and finish us – but they didn't. I saw them later, dead from knife wounds. I woke and she was there, tending us again.

"I wasn't so bad, this time. Yet Jai seemed more distant, as if thinking thoughts of death and horror. I had sworn that I would take no more women, that I had to live to return home to my family – but...

"She wanted a child, as a promise of hope. She wanted a child of mine. To love. To live after her. I would be gone soon, she knew that, but that was alright. I had a wife and couldn't marry her – but she understood. Would I do this for her? How could I refuse?

"Somehow, she knew that she had conceived from that encounter. I was assailed by guilt, and haunted by the death of Suzi and her baby. I wrote down my address in America for her and promised her any help she needed. Betsy would have plenty to say, but I will do my penance for her if I must."

The following entries were again, days apart, but for the next few, he still had Jai with him. She helped him avoid patrols and showed him a route to safety. Once he was safe, she had slipped away without a word.

Elisabeth had been so engrossed that it was only after a few moments of thought that something she had read had struck her as odd. The baby that had died – Anna Louise. If you said it quickly, it sounded like Anneliese. She found the book for 1940, and July, and skimmed through entries before and after, until she found what she wanted.

Matthew Cassidy, for the first time in his so far charmed life, was injured. He woke up – he had written – and saw an angel straight from heaven. She was blond; in the predominately dark and swarthy community. Her features seemed exotic. He couldn't decide if they were Nordic or something else. And he wanted her.

Elisabeth skipped over the erotic fantasies and finally found her name - Suzi Mosellan. Her friend, Jai had covered for her while they spent hurried moments together. It had been an experience like he had never had. He had been trucked out next day with another notch on his belt.

Elisabeth sat back, stunned. It all made sense. Wanda and this Jai Cassidy were linked – by blood and by friendship. Jai Cassidy was Jai Ansuni's child by Matthew Cassidy. Jai Ansuni had been close friends with Suzi Mosellan – who had also had a child by Matthew Cassidy. That child had been hers, Wanda's and Tanya's grandmother. Jai Ansuni had lied about it dying. Lied to protect it? Elisabeth was sure of it.

Henry returned to offer coffee, but Elisabeth declined.

"Mr Cassidy, I'd like to take these with me," Elisabeth asked with obvious desire.

Henry scratched his head.

"I will take very good care of them and ensure you get them back."

"You figgerin on makin a book of them?" he asked. "They just seem like a record of some old man's conquests."

Elisabeth blushed. "They are that, but they are also a frank look at conditions during the war and how the war affected people. I think these books also reveal how he finally grew up and realised life was sacred."

"I reckon my brothers will want to see them," Henry thought aloud. "Don't reckon Eva would like them – but they mean something to you, don't they, Miss?"

"Do you remember how you said that I was like that fellow, Mosellan? The one that took on your youngest sister?" Elisabeth asked, deciding to tell him what she had found.

Henry nodded.

"Well, John Masterton remarked on that too. So I began looking. I knew any link had to be on my mother's side. I learnt, just this morning, that her mother had been Anneleise Mosellan, and that she and her sisters had been born in the old Yugoslavia."

"Anna Louise? That was my Grandma's name."

He had made the same connection.

"Her name was the two, run together, but yes. So I went back to an earlier diary. Your father had a fling with a Suzi Mosellan, a friend of Jai. In that later entry Jai Ansuni told him that Suzi and her baby were dead. A baby she had called Anneliese."

Henry thought it through. "That would make you some sort of cousin. Well, I'll be... Are there any more of you?"

Elisabeth smiled. "My elder sister and I and a cousin I met recently and there may be more. I am still trying to find a third sister."

"So where does the Mosellan fella come in?"

"I'm guessing, but he was believed to have come from Europe – maybe a brother?"

"Could be?" Henry nodded. "Yes, you take the books. I can wait till they are back."

"I appreciate this, Mr Cassidy. And if I think I can turn it into a book – I'll let you know before I do anything."

"You'll do the right thing, Miss, I'm sure," Henry agreed. "And as for that bracelet thing – have it as a kin gift. Might clean up nice. I sure don't know where it came from though – musta been the war."

Elisabeth returned to the car, and pretended she didn't see the driver drop a cigarette and grind it under his heel. She couldn't wait to get back and tell Tanya what she had found. And Jim, and Magnus Goldman and Dr Wallace.

As the car took her back to the base, her hand felt over the surface of the odd bracelet. She closed her eyes and could almost feel etchings on the metal. It grew warm under her fingers and against her flesh. Some presence moved in her mind.

"Wanda," she thought strongly and hopefully. The feeling was like a skittering moth. It might have been Wanda – but there was a sense of desperation, despair, lost hope and emotions of all imaginable kinds. Then Elisabeth felt suddenly weak, as if something had sucked all her spare energy away. Something that had been starving and grabbed the first food it had seen.

"That's the link we were looking for," Jim Phillips told Elisabeth. He had returned whilst she was out.

"Aren't you freaked that I might be part alien?" she demanded.

Jim grinned at her. "You don't have green skin and antennae or whatever. In fact, you look perfectly American. Frankly, if that stranger's blood has made you such an intelligent person and your sister what she is, then I want more of you. And you know, there are laws these days about discrimination."

Elisabeth threw a cushion at him. "You'd like more trouble makers," she accused him in jest.

"You are not a trouble maker, and Tanya has settled down. So why do you think any unknown cousins might be trouble makers? Hunch?"

She shook her head, and then shrugged. "Have you heard anything more?"

"I only got back half an hour ago, and I am still trying to read through all these other reports. Goldman will have even more, soon. Can I read through those diaries?"

"Dr Wallace has them. They won't help find my mother's other sister."

"No, but they might reveal more clues about these two women in Matthew Cassidy's life," Jim said obliquely. "I wonder why they both chose him."

"Because he was a randy so and so," Elisabeth said tartly.

"It is surprising that the alien physiology mated so well with ours," Jim mused aloud. He shrugged. He had a lot of questions, like – could they be sure that no more of the aliens were still on Earth. And if they were – how could they be detected? And if they could assume that all left about when Jai Cassidy disappeared, how long before 1940 had they arrived?

He changed the subject. "Have you and Tanya together, tried to reach Wanda?"

"No," Elisabeth said at once, chagrined that she hadn't thought of it. "But..."

She mentioned the odd feeling she had experienced in the car. Jim asked to see the bracelet.

"Why don't you see if Rowan has a way to clean it up? Perhaps if it did do anything, it might work better if clean?"

Chapter 6

"My mother did what?" Elisabeth exclaimed at Magnus Goldman. She was meeting with him but Jim and Wallace were also there.

Jim glanced at her and she subsided. "Is that relevant?" she asked in her more usual polite fashion. "It happened nearly thirty years ago. And is your, Mr Secretary going to try and impeach my dad because of it?"

Goldman accepted Elisabeth's reaction as disbelief and went on to explain. "I am merely repeating what our embassy in Serbia was told. Katya Tatarovich was believed to have killed her husband, Rory Antov. The authorities wanted her found and questioned. This was in Ruma, which is quite some distance from Vrbas. It was also where the family that fostered Katrina Tatarovich went when they left Vrbas."

Elisabeth leant forward. "Did they meet?"

Goldman shook his head. "Five years before, that family, the Petrovich's had been accused of being foreign agents. Russian agents went into get them. The Petrovich family disappeared and the Russians were found dead."

"Do you think she had heard about her sister and gone looking for her?" Elisabeth asked.

"I doubt that we could find that out," Goldman told her.

"Well then, she - my mother – got there too late. They can't have found her..."

"No. Three months later, she arrives here," Goldman pointed out.

"She must have had help," Elisabeth stated. "She was from a communist country."

"Yes, indeed," Goldman agreed. "I have made a request for information on US agents active in Yugoslavia in 1975."

"So you think it is possible that US agents helped her? But why?"

Rowan Wallace, quiet so far, made a suggestion. "If – when Katrina's parents fled – their successors knew that their predecessor's adopted child was a Tatarovich. They might have recognised the name. They might have decided to help the girl."

"What if the others didn't survive? I assume that the Petrovich couple were US agents?"

"We will check that when we get the information I requested. Do you think they survived?"

Elisabeth fell into a moment of contemplation. She had no way of knowing, it would only be a guess...

"I want to believe they are here in the US."

Goldman glanced at Jim, but made no comment. He added, then, a thoughtful, "I know of several men who worked in Europe during the Cold War. I'll talk to them when I return to Washington."

For a moment, Elisabeth was sure that Goldman had had a revelation, but he had firmed his lips as if to withhold what he had thought.

Elisabeth sighed. "This is all very fascinating, but we're no closer to finding Katrina Tatarovich, and getting Wanda and the others back."

Rowan Wallace stood up and commented, "Why don't you go and find Tanya and come to the lab. You can try doing your thing to see if you can reach Wanda."

"Why not?" Elisabeth agreed, pushing herself up. "Thanks for the update. Am I allowed to talk to Dad?"

"I'll tell General Addison to let you have a secure outside line. But you will have to be discreet," Goldman warned.

"Of course, Mr Goldman," Elisabeth said demurely before she left the room.

Jim Phillips chose to follow her part of the way.

Wallace waited until she was gone before speaking to his colleague and long-time friend.

"What just occurred to you, Magnus?"

"Patrick Twomey. CIA. Served in Yugoslavia, returned with a teenage daughter. Pretty thing, fair, not dark like the Yugoslav's."

Wallace's expression turned contemplative. "Go on."

"She married, Edward Mason."

Both men had met Edward Mason's daughter.

"Is Twomey still alive?"

"No, but his wife is. She was too frail to get to Katrina Mason's funeral," Goldman said. "She is in a hospice out of Washington."

"Do you want me to go and see her," Wallace offered.

"If you have the time," Goldman accepted. "I have to fly back for an early meeting tomorrow."

"The Secretary?" Wallace asked.

Goldman nodded. "He has made it plain that I am wasting taxpayer's money chasing imaginary aliens, and the truth is, I can't really blame him for disbelieving it all. I doubt that I would, except that I saw Stev, Wanda and David disappear from right in front of me. And I can't be sure that even if we do find another cousin of Wanda, that it will be enough."

"I think I should come back with you, Magnus, and go and see Erin Mason. Last I heard, they had transferred her to a psychiatric facility."

"Then if her mother was Katrina Tatarovich, she may be no help to us at all?"

Wallace gave his friend a faint nod, before turning to head to his lab.

A dispirited Elisabeth and an equally frustrated Tanya trudged back to their shared cottage.

"It's no use, is it?" Elisabeth finally admitted. "I promised Wanda I would be here for her, but I must be too far away."

"She might be asleep," Tanya tried to infuse some hope. "How can we know what time it is there?"

"She might be dead," Elisabeth countered. "I think I want to go home. I miss Dad, and little Maddie, and the two little boys... I haven't been to lectures for two weeks. I must be so behind..."

"We had better eat – we may feel better," Tanya tried to convince herself.

"Yeah," Elisabeth agreed, unenthusiastically.

It was quite late when Jim Phillips knocked on the door. Tanya answered it and invited Jim in. He sensed their depression in their lack of enthusiasm.

"Those diaries are very interesting," Jim told them, by way of greeting. "We are having copies made so you can return the originals."

"Alright," Elisabeth agreed, dully.

"Did you find anything useful," Tanya asked, expecting nothing.

"Not really, but you might be able to read something for me." Jim pulled out a sheet of photocopy paper. It had on it a copy of part of one of the diaries.

Tanya looked at the tiny writing in the centre of the page. It was written by a different hand to the rest of the page.

"It isn't Russian, or Serbian," Tanya told Jim. "Yet the style of writing is a bit like my mother's."

Elisabeth was intrigued enough to come and look at the page. It was in no language she had learnt either. The date of the adjacent entries was about the time Jai Ansuni had been leading Matthew Cassidy to safety. She would have sworn that..."

"Jim, I'm sure I read that entry at the Cassidy place. I remember an entry that was directions on how to get to a rendezvous at the coast."

"When you read it – were you wearing that bracelet you found?" Jim asked in an uncanny echo of a thought she had just had.

"Yes," Elisabeth whispered, putting her hand into her pocket. She felt the thing slip onto her wrist again as if it were alive. She looked at the paper again. "How odd," she added absently.

"Can you read it?" Tanya asked.

"Yes. It says..." Elisabeth read it through. It was as she had said, instructions for a safe route. She wondered at the sight she was seeing. Her eyes saw glyphs that had no human meaning. Her mind recognized them and translated them. She, oddly, was feeling her energy returning.

Jim studied her as she read. When she finished reading, he didn't immediately retrieve the paper.

"Why don't you and Tanya try reaching for Wanda again?" he suggested.

"It didn't work before," Tanya complained, "We tried for two hours!"

"Wallace is a brilliant man," Jim told her. "But he is a scientist. He wants to see it, weigh it..."

Elisabeth leant forward. "I feel I can, Tanya. Here, hold my hand."

Tanya reached her hand out to her cousin. Both pictured Wanda in their minds and called out to her in their different ways.

In Elisabeth's mind, the picture of Wanda went dark. In the past, she sometimes had a glimpse of what Wanda saw. Was she in darkness? There was that skittering moth feeling in her mind again. A breath of a voice and a strong sense of desperation.

"Lishka?"

"Yes! Yes! We are here for you," Elisabeth thought more strongly. She started to feel weak again, and bunched her free hand into a fist, desperately trying for a stronger contact. Suddenly she felt energy flowing into her and out...flowing...somewhere.

"I've....got....to ...get...away."

"Wanda? Are you well?" Tanya added her thought.

"No..."

"Can you come here?" Elisabeth sent, putting all her longing and desperation into her thought.

"Not...strong...enough."

Elisabeth felt like a door had shut on her. She tried to drop Tanya's hand but her cousin kept holding tight, eyes closed with concentration. Instead, Elisabeth forced the tension and worries from her mind and emptied it. All at once her mind was assaulted by the same mix of emotions she had sensed earlier.

This wasn't from Wanda, but it was familiar. When her sister was in prison, Wanda had experienced pressing emotions, and sometimes they almost broke her spirit. Except that she, Elisabeth had shared it with her, calmly accepting the terror of them and thus had made her strong again.

Elisabeth reached for the mind she sensed, as she had for Wanda, and thought at it, "You are not alone, I am with you."

Tanya added, "And I. We are here for you."

"I have no one," Tanya heard in her mind. "Everyone I cared for is either dead or hates me. I'm horrid."

"We don't hate you," Tanya sent.

Elisabeth pictured hugging a dear friend, giving comfort.

"No, I can't stand it. The screaming – it feels like me."

"Is it?" Tanya asked, glancing at the intent face of Elisabeth. She heard her cousin sending, "It isn't you. I can tell it is not. You are not like that. You are on drugs."

"I...must be. They stop the anger, the confusion...until now. I didn't take them before...please, please stop the noise...please. No! NO! I don't want them...I can't think...I ...have...to...get...away. No! Don't tie me up... Nooooo!"

Tanya was trembling, tears streaming from her eyes. This time it was Elisabeth who would not let go. She imaged hugging Tanya too. "We can do this... together," she told both Tanya, and that other.

"Tell...me...what...to ...do."

"You have to get out of that place," Elisabeth thought and Tanya amplified it.

"Yes."

"Don't take the drugs. They will make you forget," Elisabeth sent.

"Yes."

"What you feel – is not you."

"No!"

"It is other people. Not you. It is confusing you. You are not crazy."

"Not crazy."

"No one must see you leave."

"No one."

"Where are you?"

"Know. Don't."

"Don't what?" Elisabeth asked.

"Don't want tablets. Drink."

"Don't take them!" Elisabeth thought urgently. "Pretend! Spit out!"

"Yes. Spit out. Get out."

The contact broke suddenly. Jim caught Tanya when she was slipping to the ground. Elisabeth caught the arms of the chair and pushed herself back.

Jim looked at Elisabeth, asking a question with his glance.

"Wanda is alive, Jim. But she's in darkness...and in trouble. Desperate. She doesn't think she will survive and come back." The fear showed in Elisabeth's face.

"Wanda taught herself to survive and she is too stubborn to give up. You know that," Jim said sharply.

Elisabeth shook her head. "You're right. I'm sorry. I feel so confused."

"What else did you sense?" Jim asked, guessing accurately.

"How did you know?" Elisabeth asked as Tanya began to stir in her chair.

"I watched your faces. Neither of you are any good at hiding your emotions."

"A girl, or woman, young anyway. She's amongst crazy people, and being drugged, I think."

Jim considered that answer. "Anything else?"

"I don't know for sure – but when we touched Wanda - I think we touched her too. Or that one and Wanda are linked somehow. Where ever Wanda is, she knew she had to get away. Where ever the other one is – she had to as well – for her sanity."

"Anymore?"

"No, that's all. I got mainly emotion. I think Tanya heard more thoughts – I felt echoes. I don't know who she was – I don't think she knew. Do you think she is another cousin?"

"If we find her and she can link with you two and Wanda, it doesn't matter," Jim said quietly. "I'll talk to Goldman in the morning. He and Wallace have gone back to Washington."

Tanya sat up but she was crying silently. Elisabeth went to her. "What's wrong?"

"Nothing,"

"Hardly," Elisabeth disagreed. "Tell me."

Tanya glanced at Jim. "I am sorry. I was thinking of my mother."

Elisabeth realised that Tanya had shared all the emotions too. "Tanya, I'm sorry. I didn't realise. But I needed you or I would have lost that other one."

"I know that. It is just that it felt like when...mama was in prison."

"I am sorry too, that I couldn't save her," Jim said quietly.

Tanya shook her head. "It was too late anyway. I knew it already. That's why I was acting so crazy then. I blamed myself. I thought they were blaming her for things I did. But I heard say she was a traitor."

"Was she," Jim asked gently.

"No!" Tanya almost yelled. "No, but they asked why she was talking to foreigners, and said she was going to sell out my father."

"Perhaps you should talk to John Stradbroke. He is the base psychologist," Jim suggested.

"I don't need him," Tanya protested.

"He could help you distance any distracting thoughts," Jim suggested obliquely, but Tanya didn't understand his subtle message.

Elisabeth put it another way, one that Tanya might accept. "We both need to be strong to help Wanda. If the negative thoughts and emotions we sense affect us too much, we won't be strong enough."

Goldman rose as the Secretary of State walked into his office, followed by the two secret service body guards.

"Mr Secretary. I was just about to leave to come to see you," Goldman greeted with all required respect.

Russell waved for his body guards to wait without.

"I wanted an unofficial chat," Russell said, walking around to take Goldman's chair and forcing him to use his guest chair.

"The President wants to know if you are any closer to finding Colonel Aldrin."

"I think so," Goldman said cautiously.

"Do you have anything I can take to the President or are you still wasting time and money on chasing dead people?"

Goldman considered his words carefully. "Am I to understand that the CIA has leads to his whereabouts, Mr Secretary?"

The man glowered. "I have them working on this, since my Office of Scientific Intelligence is working on a theory of abduction by alien, psychic or ghostly powers."

"If the evidence I have is in anyway faked, the most rigid examination is yet to prove it. I am still keeping an open mind."

"Your mind, Goldman, believes all this hocus-pocus," Stan Russell claimed, and Goldman didn't try to deny it. "Now, I am advising you to leave the investigation into Colonel Aldrin's whereabouts to the CIA. I want you to keep your attention on the DS-49-A report and the evaluation of the weapons proposal of that Russian professor. I have had reports that some of those weapons are in existence already – amongst less savoury Russian echelons. Which I might add, was where that Russian's daughter spent a lot of her time."

"Sir, with due respect, Colonel Aldrin is not only my employee, but a personal friend," Goldman felt he needed to say.

"I know that, Goldman. That is why I am telling you to back off and let experts handle things. You are personally involved."

"Are you questioning my objectivity, Mr Secretary?" Goldman challenged.

"I am saying - let the CIA do the work they are paid for. They won't get sentimental about criminal delinquents – Russian or American, or senator's daughters who are related to both. Have I made myself clear?"

"Very clear, Mr Secretary," Goldman said, face expression rigid.

"Now, perhaps you will explain why you needed to talk to Mrs Twomey?"

"Since you have made me drop investigations into Colonel Aldrin's whereabouts, I no longer need to."

"Good, because Martha Twomey is a very sick woman, on life support. It would be very un-American to hassle her."

"Hardly hassle, Mr Secretary," Goldman was ruffled enough to protest.

Goldman's secretary buzzed him. Russell indicated for him to tend to it. Goldman stood and leaned over his desk to reach the intercom button.

"What is it, Sandra?" Goldman asked. She had probably guessed he had company of some importance, if the body guards were just outside his door. She would have only just arrived.

"Dr Wallace and Simon Webster are here, Sir."

"Webster? I know him. Ex CIA. What's he here for?"

"I sent for him to see if he knew of anything that might relate to Colonel Aldrin. He may have retired but he still has contacts."

"Have him come in," Russell instructed.

Goldman rose again and stood beside his desk as he gave his secretary instructions.

Webster had a genial grin on his face as he entered. It vanished when he saw who Goldman had with him, but he didn't miss a step.

"Stan Russell. Long time and all that. Congratulations on your appointment." Webster came across and shook hands with Russell and then Goldman.

"Pleased to finally meet you, Mr Goldman. How can I help you this time?" Webster had a smile back on his face, but only Goldman knew he was dissembling.

The Secretary interrupted. "I require your knowledge, Webster. Are you aware that Colonel Stev Aldrin is missing?"

Webster was a past master at not betraying his thoughts. He made his brows rise as if in surprise. "No, I wasn't. What happened?"

"He went missing from a secure facility in California. He was last seen with two people, one of whom had Yugoslavian connections."

Webster knew where the Secretary was leading. He had been an agent in Yugoslavia after the war.

"If I can help, Mr Secretary," Webster stressed the title, but there was a sense of dislike between the two men.

"Who was it you wanted to find out about, Goldman?" Russell asked tersely.

"Katya and Katrina Tatarovich," Goldman said, meeting Webster's eyes, and then looking away. He took a folder from his desk and pretended to read the contents as he outlined what he already knew. He did not mention that Katya had married a US Senator, and stressed his ignorance of Katrina's whereabouts.

Webster nodded, stared at a point to one side of Goldman, as if memorising the details.

At no time did he reveal that he already had information for Goldman, and come to deliver it.

"Will that be all, Mr Secretary?" Again Webster stressed the title.

"Yes, and I don't need to remind you that anything you find is confidential. Report back to me."

Webster nodded to Goldman and left the room.

"Now, one last question. What is the interest of the OSI in Erin Mason?"

Goldman hid his surprise that the Secretary knew of it.

"To ensure her whereabouts are known," Goldman told her. "She was caught hacking into a sensitive Government website, and later was an instigator in a money-diverting scheme. She was gaoled for that."

"Yes, I remember. That abduction business with the Cubans. She was in that too," Russell's eyes glittered. "A dangerous social misfit, who had herself declared mentally unstable and transferred to a psychiatric facility. I cannot see why you would want to associate with her."

"Mr Secretary, she voluntarily educated the investigators as to how the money scheme worked. It was brilliant. She also solved a particularly difficult computing problem that had our experts wasting time for six months."

"Never the less, no one should trust one with such non-existent moral scruples," Russell dismissed Goldman's comment.

"Trust – probably not, make use of – perhaps. Now that she has had a rude awakening in prison," Goldman chose his words carefully.

"Trust – never!" Russell snapped. "Erin Mason has been placed on a list of dangerous criminals. She escaped from that secure psych facility last night. Perhaps you will propose that she left the way Aldrin and those others did?"

Goldman frowned to hide his sudden excitement. "Have you any information as to how she left, Sir?"

"Not yet. I have asked for a full report, ASAP." Russell didn't quite snarl. "If I learn that she was anywhere near a computer, heads will roll. And when she is found, she will be sent back to the federal women's prison, maximum security. She won't be able to pull that phony psych act again and I will personally make sure she is not eligible for parole."

Goldman kept a straight face, and didn't ask if all the authorities were notified.

The Secretary had one last comment. "I want those reports by 1600 hours tomorrow."

Stan Russell rose and strode from the room. He ignored Wallace and Goldman's secretary in the outer room. The body guards silently paced after him as he headed for the lift.

Wallace entered the office as Goldman was sitting back in his chair.

"What do you want, old friend," Magnus Goldman asked, relaxing now that the Secretary had left.

"You were right. Twomey's successor did sponsor Katya T into the country. He recognised the name and her likeness to Katrina, Twomey's adopted daughter. He also knew that the girl's maternal grandfather was American. Twomey told his successor that he had not killed the Russians that died about when he left. Allen, who followed him, heard that a young Yugoslav had done it – name of Antov. Everyone had clammed up to the Russians. They however, killed Antov and blamed his wife."

"Did Webster have anything else?"

"Yes, he found out she had married Charles Willard, but she was watched from the time she arrived. There was never any indication of her trying to contact foreign agents here, or of any contacting her. There is also no indication that she contacted Katrina Mason, either. She's clean."

Goldman was relieved. "Good news. Now the bad. Erin Mason slipped out of the psych facility last night. She's missing."

Wallace betrayed his concern. "She will be in a vulnerable state, coming off the medications so abruptly."

"We need to find her before anyone else does."

Rowan guessed what his friend did not say, and it was confirmed.

"And I am to have nothing more to do with her."

"Why did we have to be too late," Rowan growled, with frustration. "We finally trace the one we are looking for, but Katrina died a few months ago and her daughter escapes the very night before we confirm the link. What can I do, Magnus?"

Goldman smiled grimly. "You had better find a way to stay at Rockwater. Our hands are tied here. I will be here. If I hear she has been found...I will worry about that then."

"There's Jim Phillips," Wallace suggested.

"Yes, unless the Secretary gets to him too," Magnus noted. Then a faint smile relaxed his face. "Or maybe not. I understand that he has a mandate to act as he sees fit – under certain circumstances."

Rowan's face creased into a grin. "I'll call him and alert him. He had a report for you. The call came through while Webster was with you."

Magnus waited for Rowan to get to it.

"The gist of it is that Elisabeth and Tanya tried again to reach Wanda and believe they succeeded. She is alive, they say, but weak, desperate and in trouble. They lost the touch, but Tanya reached another mind. Young, female, confused – surrounded by madness. They told Jim that Wanda had realised she had to get away from somewhere, and this other mind realised something similar. He thinks there was a four way link for a bit."

"What do you think, Rowan?"

"I think it might work," Rowan summarised. "I think they reached Erin Mason, and somehow that is why she left."

Goldman nodded.

Chapter 8

A week went past with no news of Erin Mason.

Elisabeth told Jim she had flashes from the woman – like she'd had with Wanda, but she couldn't identify anywhere. The mental emotion was still of confusion.

She was feeling frustrated and useless when her step mother rang and told her that her father had been taken ill and asked her to come home. She promised to come at once and went to find Jim Phillips.

Tanya had asked permission to return to her studies, but was inexplicably refused. She sought out Elisabeth to complain as she was packing her bag.

"I'd stay, except for Dad. My stepmother is pregnant again, and with Dad sick and five young kids she isn't coping."

"I don't know why they won't let me go," Tanya continued her complaint.

Elisabeth said thoughtfully, "I am glad you will still be here. If something happens, and Wanda reaches out, at least one of us will be here. And that other one, that might be our missing cousin – if she comes here she'll need you."

Tanya grimaced an agreement. "It is odd that no one has reported seeing her. I have the sense that she is on the move. All I get, at odd intervals, is - I gotta get away. I gotta go west. Mustn't be seen."

"Here's my phone number. We'll keep in touch. When you can, you will be welcome to visit."

"I'd like that," Tanya said with a smile.

The two women hugged, and then Elisabeth went out to the car waiting to take her to the hired Lear jet waiting at the local airport.

The Third Generation Series

Book 9

Erin: The Call

By

Margaret Gregory

Table of Contents

Chapter 1

The sound of a gunshot nearby startled the woman who slept under a dense clump of bushes in the garden of the estate. She had little sense of herself, but like the deer that would startle at a noise, she awoke panicked. Some higher instinct kept her still, trembling in silence.

"Let no one find me," she whispered as a mantra to whatever power would listen to her.

Through a narrow gap between bushes, she looked out with fear of being found. She heard voices shouting orders, but no one was in her view. Then the woman heard something coming through the bushes. The noise suggested stealth, but whatever it was, was making more noise than the wind. Did someone know she was here? She retreated to be closer to the wall, sat and drew her knees up to her chin. "Don't let them see me," her mind thought again.

A picture came into her mind of black clad men with guns. No words came with the pictures, but she knew the men were dangerous. One had forced himself on her. Somehow he had not been affected by the strangeness that had protected her since she had begun running. His wallet was now in her pocket. With it she could buy food again.

The noise came closer. A man crawled into view, not wearing black. He had white hair and a tanned rakish face, twisted now in pain. One arm seemed weak and almost useless. Blood soaked through the sleeve of his jacket. He was crawling within inches of her and couldn't see her.

Now she knew it was his fear she had felt. She inched forward and touched him. He physically jerked, suddenly aware of her as if she had just appeared from nowhere. When she touched him, the pain in his arm throbbed in her own. It told her what she needed to do. Stop the bleeding. She didn't question this knowledge, just set to and began. She felt in the man's pocket and found a handkerchief and tied it over the wound.

The man accepted her help, realising she was not a danger to him. But if he stayed here she would be in danger. "Who are you?" he whispered urgently as he used his good arm to push himself up.

The woman placed a hand on her mouth, warning him to be silent.

They both heard, "He came this way. He can't get out except over the fence, and the top is electrified. Bring the dogs. I want him found."

The man tried to move away, but the woman grabbed his arm and curled herself back into a small ball. The man copied her, wondering why he believed she was helping him.

In the distance, dogs barked as if let out to hunt. The man briefly wondered if he was insane to remain. He had to get away.

Quivering brown snouts protruded from the bushes and sniffed the air. Any moment they would push through, bark, bite, and bring guards. They didn't, and the noses withdrew.

The handlers ordered them to search further on. The baying moved away.

"Over that way," someone ordered. The sound of running, booted feet moved away.

"Who are you?" the man asked again, but the woman stared back as if not comprehending the question.

She didn't answer, but she had known what she was doing when she had kept him still and bandaged the arm. It was feeling better already, but why had the dogs not sensed them?

"Will you help me?" he asked, taking the risk in trusting her. The woman nodded, not afraid of him.

"How did you get in here? Over the fence?"

She shook her head and gestured for him to follow. A few metres further on, she pointed to the base of the wall. There was a hole there, partly where the bricks had crumbled and partly where something had dug under the bricks.

The man sighed; he could not fit through there. The woman had, but she looked to be little more than a thin layer of flesh over bone. In fact, she looked more like one of those famine victims. Her belly appeared bloated.

The woman glanced from him to the hole and began using her hands to enlarge the hole. The man studied her. Her skin was tanned from exposure to the sun, her hands were well formed. Right now, the nails were broken and dirty. He heard more voices and moved closer to the hole to help dig using his good hand.

He stopped when the woman held up her hand. She crawled under the fence, stopping with just her head out the other side. Then the rest of her disappeared and a hand gestured to him from the hole.

The man commando crawled, slowly, under the fence. It was still a tight fit. The woman helped him stand up. His head swam, and for a moment he felt he would pass out. The woman might be nearly starved, but she was strong.

"I have a car – around the side – a white Pontiac with a thin red stripe."

The man pointed in the direction he needed to go. He was still weak and needed the woman's support.

They walked slowly, too slowly, towards the car – keeping close to the outer side of the bricked wall of the estate. His car was hidden in the thick woods.

Without warning, the woman slipped out from under his arm and shoved him off his feet. Before he could try to rise, he heard what she must have heard – the snuffling growl of a dog. Instinctively, he rolled under some low undergrowth and silently urged the woman to move. It was like she expected this dog to ignore her too.

The dog bounded into sight and sprang at her. It knocked her down and kept her there. Wisely she did not try to struggle. The dog was almost as big as she was.

"Effing bitch," was the comment of the handler when he examined his capture. "You aren't the bastard I'm looking for, but I have a score to settle with you. Down!"

The dog moved aside. "Guard!" The dog stood eying the woman.

The guard rolled the woman over onto her back, and slapped her face with vicious intent. "Where's my effing wallet, bitch!"

The woman made no sound. She may as well been mute. The guard struck her again. "I've been docked a week's pay for losing my ID and other things – because of you. And you pinched my effing trousers."

The man yanked them off the woman, revealing that she had nothing under them.

"Two hundred dollars you took from me. I'm going to get my money's worth – right now!" The guard began to unzip his trousers, his intention plain. He seemed convinced that the woman was too terrified to move. He was not aware of the other figure slowly standing up, risking further harm to stop the woman being raped. Neither man noticed the intent gaze of the dog. The guard exposed himself, and the woman simply stared at the enlarged proof of the guard's virility. As the man knelt and forced his hand between the woman's legs, the dog attacked. The man screamed.

The woman leapt up, grabbed the trousers and almost dragged the white haired man towards his car.

As they stumbled forward, the man removed his car keys from his pocket, using his good hand.

"Can you drive?" he asked. After a moment of thought the woman nodded, took the keys and ran forward to open the car. She tossed the trousers in, seeming to be unaware that she was practically indecent.

Her dress, the man now realised was torn, and he had glimpsed of pale bruised skin. He took in other details now – the tangled, matted hair, the shoes tied on with string and with holes in the soles. The dress had been white, now it was grey and brown. Oddly, her face was clean.

He climbed into the passenger seat, and the woman trotted around to the driver's side. She seemed more alive now than she had. Once in the driver's seat, she seemed to know what to do.

"This track goes back to the main road. Just drive, anywhere."

The white haired man kept checking behind them, and after a while relaxed. They had avoided further pursuit. He tried not to think of the guard they had left screaming, and probably neutered. What had the woman done?

More urgent, who was she?

She had no place in the house on the estate, but the guard had known her. Was she a prostitute? No, the man who owned the house would not let anyone like that on the estate. He was sure. He had made it his business to learn everything possible about the people there.

Somehow, though, he had slipped up and he dare not make another mistake.

The woman, although she had helped him, was an enigma and a distraction from the job in hand. Right now the job was to stay alive, now that his cover had been blown.

He studied the woman as she drove carefully, following his new directions. She had turned toward the town at the main road, and travelled through it until he had told her to turn around. Now he was taking her on a circuitous route to the safe house he was using. He had her turn at random, making doubly sure he was not being followed.

"Next street on the left, third house along. There! The brick fence. Drive into the garage."

The door opened automatically and closed again behind the car. The woman jumped when she heard the door closing and backed away from the man.

"It's automatic," he said, casually, as if he had not seen her wariness. He didn't ask for help, but the woman came around anyway and assisted him out. "Come through to the house," he invited, pointing to a closed door.

She opened it for him and shut it behind them. There was a wary, wild eyed look in her eyes.

"No one here will hurt you," the man promised, leading her down a passage to the room at the end. "I'll be fine now," the man said. "Thank you. I'm Jim. The bath room is next door, if you would like to clean up."

The woman nodded, and went in. Jim went and eased off the jacket, after untying the bandage. He looked at the damage and decided the bullet had only grazed the arm.

He came out to find the woman waiting, looking no cleaner than before, but with signs of having splashed water on her face.

"Do you want a drink?" he asked.

She nodded. "Water?"

The voice was so faint that he thought he had imagined it.

"Yes, and I think I had better stick to water too."

"Yes. I'll go."

"Through that door," Jim pointed, and followed her.

There was something about this woman that Jim thought he knew. Yet he could not place her face.

"What is your name?" Jim tried, when she handed him a glass of water. He turned and went to sit down, as a gesture that he meant her no harm. She took a second glass of water and perched on the edge of another chair. She didn't try to drink, just held it tightly as if she was thinking.

Here in the better light, he could see the vivid red patches where the man had slapped her.

"Drink," Jim urged, and she did.

"I don't know who I am," the woman finally volunteered.

"Why did you help me?" Jim tried. He needed to know that so he could put his mind back on the job.

"You were hurt. Afraid," she whispered.

"You have been hurt," Jim observed.

"It doesn't matter," the woman whispered.

Jim chose not to follow up with another question. He had a job to do and he had to warn his people.

"Could you make a telephone call for me?"

The woman nodded, looking around.

"By the passage door," Jim said.

When the woman was there he gave her the number. "When someone answers, ask for Henderson. Tell him..." Jim gave her the message.

The woman dialled the number and spoke as directed. She used slightly different phrasing, but kept the wording well enough that his man, posing as

Daniel Henderson had the correct coded message.

Her handling of his request and her speech was business like, and he wondered if it was initiative or reflexive memory. And she made no mistakes in the second and third part of the message – so she memorised things quickly.

"Thank you," Jim said when she had finished. "Are you hungry?"

"No."

Jim thought she must be used to eating very little.

"How about going into the next room and seeing if you can find something to wear? Tracey won't mind."

Or she wouldn't as soon as she saw the state of this woman.

His guest flushed as if only just realising her indecent state. "Your arm," she said instead.

"Get dressed. I will find something for bandages."

The woman moved from the room, taking the guard's trousers with her. Jim waited for her to go into Tracey's room before following, but he went past to a room where he was storing equipment. He always had a compact first aid kit, though rarely needed to use it.

When he emerged, he heard a minor scuffle from the living room where he had been. He was instantly wary, but relaxed when he recognised one of his men. "Let her go, Paul. She is no threat."

Paul released the woman and she scuttled over to the wall.

"She helped me get away from Dennard's Estate. Now you are here, I need help to bandage this arm."

Only then did Paul notice Jim's bloodstained sleeve and begrimed trousers. He glanced back at the woman before obeying.

"What happened?" Paul asked.

"I slipped somewhere," Jim admitted. "Dennard set his guards on me, but I got what we needed. Brendan is still there."

Paul shoulder shrugged to indicate the woman.

"I am sure she is not working against us."

"You willing to bet your life on it? This is a deep graze. You were lucky. I'll need to have the shirt off."

Paul was about to go for water, when he spotted some near the couch as well as a box of tissues. The woman didn't seem to be around. "Where is she?" Paul hissed.

"Don't worry, Paul. You probably frightened her. One of the guards was going to have a go at her, again, I think. She defended herself." Jim shuddered as the memory of what the dog had done returned.

"Sorry," Paul muttered thinking his ministrations had hurt.

Jim didn't correct him, instead he met the eyes of the woman now crouched by the wall with knees up to chin – trying to hide. And Paul couldn't see her – interesting. And a useful trick.

"Are you going to be able to drive, Jim? It looks like you lost a lot of blood."

"It will be fine, Paul. Can you pack everything into the car for me, and head off in yours to the next house. Paris should be there. I will be there by morning. As soon as Brendan leaves word, I'll be off."

Paul had gone again, and Jim was sitting back in a chair, washed and in clean clothes. He was mentally reviewing his job, trying to discover what had gone wrong. The light touch on his arm brought him to instant alertness.

"Who are you?" Jim tried again. He studied the still red cheeks, the blue eyes, and the dark blonde hair that was now brushed, but not any cleaner. It was longer than it had seemed at first.

She shook her head. Couldn't tell? Wouldn't?

Now she had his attention – she took something out of the pocket of the trousers borrowed from Tracey. She dropped it on his lap. It was a wallet.

Jim opened it up. In a clear covered inset was an ID – the guard's. Jim took it out and studied it. It looked the same as the fake one he had used at the estate. The woman was watching him intently. Did she know something? Jim reached, awkwardly, into the pocket of the clean shirt, and took out a similar card.

Reaction! His mind was slow! The guard had been angry about losing his wallet – docked a week's pay...Jim studied the ID more closely.

He spoke aloud, as if to himself, "What is so special about this one? Mine should have worked in the door."

The delicate fingers, now scrubbed clean, but still with broken nails, pointed to a spot on the edge of the plastic card. There was the faintest difference in colour there.

"Electronic?" Jim guessed aloud, watched his guest, who nodded.

Jim thought back to the day's events. Yes, his card had worked in several different electronic locks without a problem. It had only been that last lock – on Dennard's office. He glanced at the woman, wondering what she knew. She just kept watching his face. Jim thought of the guard's face, the owner of the ID and compared it to the guards he had seen inside the house. His photographic memory flicked images like a slide show. "Of course, he was one of the guards on Dennard's office. The lock there must be different."

"How does it work," he asked the woman, even though, thinking on it, he guessed.

"Two codes," she said in a whisper. "One you put on the number pad which is compared with the one on the black strip. The other is read from that corner. The door won't open if it is not there."

Jim nodded. It fit. He had been in Dennard's office three times. Twice

Dennard had let him in. The third time the guard had, believing the document Jim had produced. The last time, Dennard had not been there again. But this time the guard had made him use his own ID. Jim had spotted a flash of orange on the keypad a microsecond before the guard had attacked. He had dropped the guard and forced the door, entering to grab what he needed and was out before reinforcements had arrived.

"When did you take this? Last night?"

The woman nodded. So the guard couldn't have let him in – because he didn't have his ID-key. This woman who had helped him had taken it. The guard mustn't have told Dennard about it until after Jim had gone.

The woman seemed to shrink away from him as he connected events. Seeing the movement, Jim's concern for her surfaced.

"I'm going to put some soup on. We both need to eat. Then I need to get you somewhere safe."

There was real terror in the woman's eyes, and she began to back towards the door.

"You need medical help – you're nearly starved. You've been attacked..."

"No," she said, and he sensed resolve as strong as her unexpected strength.

"The police..." he began.

"NO! They hate me. I'm horrid!" The retort was unexpected. "I would rather die – free."

Jim stored that reaction for later thought. He couldn't deal with her now.

"Then would you let me help you?"

She nodded, relaxing a bit and stopping her backwards movement.

"Then sit down and eat the soup when it is ready."

Jim noticed the woman watching him warily as they both ate the soup. He refrained from further questions, and tried to think where he had seen her. He felt he should know.

Before they finished, another woman walked into the room.

"Jim! I heard you had been hurt..." Her voice trailed off as she saw the strange woman wearing her clothes.

"I am alright," Jim assured Tracey. "I told my guest that she could borrow something of yours to wear. Perhaps you could help her clean up and tidy up a bit more."

Tracey nodded, realising it was more of a request than a suggestion.

"What's your name?" Tracey asked, aiming to make friends. Some expression in the stranger's face when she didn't answer, gave Tracy an answer as to why Jim hadn't introduced her.

"Would it be alright if I call you Rose?" Tracey suggested. "Just for now, I mean. You remind me of a friend."

The stranger nodded.

"I will get some soap and stuff. You can have a shower – but don't take long. We have to leave here, but we don't know how soon."

The newly named Rose nodded.

"When you finish, I'll fix your hair and do your face and nails. If I have time."

Rose shook her head at first, but then nodded.

Tracey found soap and towels and shampoo and then directed Rose to the shower.

While the woman was occupied, Tracey reported to Jim. She heard in turn a brief summary of Jim's situation and how he'd found the woman. That was all they had time for before the woman was back, smelling clean, hair and all, and redressed in Tracey's spare pant suit.

Rose followed Tracey back to her room.

"Sit by the mirror. Will I brush your hair or do you want to?"

Rose accepted brush and comb and removed the tangles from her hair. Now it was apparent it was shoulder length and very shaggy.

"Wait a moment," Tracey told Rose, as she rummaged through a cosmetic case and brought out a hair dressing kit. After getting permission, she set about neatening the shaggy mess. First she evened it up to a short bob, and then styled the front to a fringe, leaving a long lock to either side of the face which she twirled to a curl.

"Like it?" Tracey asked and was rewarded by a slight smile. She helped Rose turn the chair around and opened up a make-up case.

Tracey talked as she worked the make-up on, first using a thick foundation to hide the reddened cheeks.

She felt Rose gradually relaxing back into the chair and wondered silently when Rose brought a hand up to rest on her belly.

When the new look was complete, Tracey touched Rose's shoulder gently and gestured to the mirror. She saw pleasure in the woman's eyes before the face turned back to blankness.

"Take a nap," Tracey suggested. "You can use this bed. I'll get you before we go."

Rose nodded and went over. It seemed she was asleep moments after lying down.

Tracey retreated and closed the door – returning to where Jim sat. He spoke first.

"What do you make of her?"

Tracey considered her observations and gut feelings. "She is in an awful state. It doesn't seem like she was caring for herself."

"Suicidal?" Jim asked, although he didn't read the stranger as being that way. But she didn't seem to think she deserved to live.

"Apathetic," Tracey countered. "At first I thought anorexic, but maybe she simply hasn't been eating much. And Jim, I think she is pregnant."

Jim stiffened.

Tracey went on. "Jim – she needs help."

"I know," Jim agreed. "But she was terrified when I mentioned police."

"Then she is probably trouble," Tracey predicted.

"Troubled," he corrected. "But she saved my life twice today. And thanks to her, I know how my cover was blown."

"Are you sure she's not a plant?"

"Yes. Eggleston hates all women – that's why all the servants at the estate are men. Dennard doesn't, but he only has one use for them."

Tracey shuddered. "Then keep Rose away from him. He'd fall for that innocent (in the biblical sense) facade she has."

"Rose?" Jim queried.

"Had to call her something," Tracey told him. "And I don't think she is biblically innocent."

Jim had no intention of putting "Rose" in any danger. But when the mission was over, he was going to find out what she had done, or thought she had done that made her neglect herself so.

Tracey woke Rose when they were ready to go, with everything in the car and nothing left at the house to identify them. Rose slipped into the back seat and let Jim and Tracey have the front. Tracey told Jim she would drive. When Jim glanced around a short time later, Rose seemed to be asleep again.

Rose roused when the car turned north, feeling a mental tugging to go west. She stayed in the car when it was stopped at a motel and made no comment when Jim returned to the car looking completely different. When the man, Paul, climbed in beside her and gave her a suspicious look, she turned her head to look out the window.

"What the latest?" Jim asked Paul. Paul scowled at the strange woman.

"Eggleston left last night to get to the resort. Dennard sent some servants ahead to look after him. Brendan was one. Dennard aims to arrive just before the meeting. We have a suite on the floor above Fuller's."

"Which other leaders are there?" Jim asked.

"All have been spotted by the watchers and all are using aliases. They all have laptops with them, except Eggleston. Dennard will have his."

"Karen?" Jim asked.

"Fuller is smitten – but still all business. However, Karen has what we need. Brendan will be ready well before the meeting."

"Paul, when we get there, we will take Eggleston out and I will replace him. Then you replace one of the guards acting as servants."

Rose listened, but did not show it. She didn't know or care what they were talking about. Images came into her mind, but she did not know if they were real or imagined. She didn't care.

The car stopped in the guest's parking area, in a position that was sheltered from the sun and convenient for a quick getaway.

"Stay here," Jim told Rose and he waited for her to nod. "We should be finished by two o'clock. There is water in the console between the seats and I will leave a window open a bit for air. The car shouldn't get too hot. Try to keep out of sight."

"I will," Rose said, and immediately curled up like a kitten on the back seat to go to sleep again.

Jim closed the car door, wondering if she would stay. He couldn't worry about her now. He gestured to the others to precede him, and he positioned a hat and glasses so his looks were obscured. He didn't want the real Eggleston to be warned.

Rose wasn't really sleeping. The sense of so many people around, often passing the car, made her wary. Like a cat, she opened her eye at the slightest sound. It wasn't the first time lately she had slept in someone's unlocked car, she remembered. Often she was chased away in the morning. For weeks, she had been surviving on cat naps.

An intense sense of danger roused Rose sometime later. She looked up slowly and glanced around the car. There was no one immediately near her, but the warning made her get out of the car and walk away. She came to a screen of trees and saw the pool beyond. She stopped there for she did not wish to be around all the sunning and swimming guests. Before she moved again, she tried to decide what had frightened her.

Into her mind came a picture of Jim meeting the one they knew as Dennard. Into her view walked the very man from that vision. Suddenly, she knew that if Dennard met Jim, Jim would die.

Chapter 3

The annoying voices in her head said she couldn't let Jim die. Jim had to bring her here. Here being somewhere near mountains but not the mountains where the resort was built.

Rose began running in the general direction of the man, but seemingly oblivious to him. "Let him follow me," she thought. "Let him forget where he is going and follow me."

Before she had returned to the car park, he had intercepted her.

"Please," Rose whispered. "You have to help me."

Dennard grabbed the woman gently. "Whoa, I'll help you. What is wrong?"

"I have to get away. Let me go. I have to leave here."

Dennard frowned. The woman was like a moth flittering in his hand, and that was already exciting him. He took one hand off her and checked his watch, he still had two hours.

"My car is over here. I will drive you down the hill." He picked up his lap top from the ground at his feet.

The woman came with him, always glancing over her shoulder.

Dennard's idea of help wasn't what he thought the woman meant. The woman was intent on not being seen, and seemed to have no idea of his flaunted charm. That was aggravating to his ego. He chatted to her, his usual patter that always had women panting after him. Either this one was immune or was ignoring him. She would soon learn.

In the car, he concentrated on getting out of the parking area. Once he was on the downhill road, he took his hand from the gear lever and placed it on her leg. She didn't seem to notice it. He moved it further in to press between her legs. She eased her position and trapped his hand between her thighs. He could feel her muscles contracting around it. He glanced at his passenger. The innocent damsel had gone. She was provocatively unbuttoning her blouse, and she had nothing under it. His mind pictured the rest.

The motel he had planned to go to was too far...

He turned off the road onto a forest track, just far enough to be hidden from the road. He got out of the car and raced around to the passenger side. She was getting out, slowly, breasts exposed – waiting...

Dennard lost all reasoning. He unzipped his fly and reached his hands into the woman's pants. Under the trousers she had nothing on. With both hands he pushed down the fabric and immediately thrust.

The woman grabbed him, moved with him, and began kissing him until he was breathless. He heard her cry out, and pull him closer as they rutted, standing up beside the car.

When he would have pulled away, satiated, he heard the woman say, "More." She began to do things to him that was rousing him again. She spun him around and pushed him into the car, across the seats. She climbed in and mounted him. Her hands moved behind his head, and she began to lick him on the chest. He could not with hold a moan of his own. His vision blurred as her hands spasmed on his neck.

Rose eased herself back off the man and stared at him, watching his chest move up and down. She tweaked his skin where it would hurt and he didn't react. Then, with very deliberate actions, found his watch and adjusted the time. While still astride him, she adjusted the clock in his car. She checked his pockets in case he had another timepiece, and debated interfering with the time on his computer. That she decided would not be vital.

"Well," she said to the temporarily unconscious man. "While that was thoroughly enjoyable for me, you are a right bastard, and I never want to see you again. So when you wake up, you'll get away from here as fast as you can and go about your business. Your mind will not be able to forget the sensations I made for you. You won't notice anything strange about anyone you know. You will remember the sensations but not my face and from this day on you will never be able to perform with any other woman again."

There was a questioning tendril of thought in her mind so she went on, "That's to pay you back for all the women you took who were barely old enough for this, or who were drugged, or had husbands they really didn't want to betray. Every single face flicked through your mind whilst I was rutting with you."

Three quarters of an hour later, although the clock in his car only showed a lapse of twenty minutes, Dennard stirred. His eyes feasted on the woman straddling him. He pushed her away.

"More!" Rose began to fondle him again, but he was spent. He had never had a woman like her before.

"Darling, I have a meeting," he checked the clock. "But if you come back with me – afterwards – anytime."

Rose put a finger to his lips. "Marry me."

Dennard flinched as if she had burnt him.

"Thought not," Rose pouted. She backed out of the car, still exposed.

She could see him rousing again in spite of himself. "Still there are plenty more like you." She began pulling up her trousers and buttoning her blouse, whilst Dennard did the same. She started walking up the hill without looking back. Dennard got back in his car, gave her one last glance and took off with wheels spinning.

Not until he was back on the road, did Dennard stop thinking of the woman. He accelerated, feeling a sense of urgency. When he saw a cruising police car he slowed down. He didn't need to get a speeding ticket. That would make him late.

He forced his mind back to the meeting, where he hoped to discredit Eggleston and take over his boss's operation. His review of plans morphed into fantasies of bringing that woman to Eggleston. He doubted that even a confirmed misogynist like Eric could have held out against her. He tried to picture the face, but he couldn't bring it to mind – just the memory of the best sex he had ever had. He let that memory occupy his mind as he drove.

Rose waited until the sound of the car was long gone before turning and walking back down to the road. There was no sense of guilt in her mind about what she had done. It had invigorated her. Anyway, the creep had wanted it as much as she had. The idea came to her mind that she had done similar acts before and a vaguer thought that she probably would again.

She cleared her mind of Dennard, and smiled knowing that Jim's plan, whatever it was, would now succeed. The criminal big wigs would be arrested, with all the evidence on them. All the money they had stolen or diverted would be found and returned. The men would go to gaol.

Rose stumbled, not from tripping, but from the overwhelming realisation of who she was and what she had done. She had embezzled money, like those men had. She had been caught and sent to prison – gone mad – put in that mad place – where they had drugged her and tied her to the bed.

She slumped to the ground in a heap, hugging her knees until a cool breeze on her face made her realise she was free. She didn't remember how she had got free.

A voice in her mind, made her begin walking again. It seemed that was all she had been doing. When she got back to the road, at the bottom of the hill, she had to go west.

For a time she walked without thinking, slipping back into the trancelike state she had been in. Until the image of Jim came into her mind. He was looking for her.

Of course he was, her mind said. He put people like her into gaol. If he knew what she had done he would hate her too.

"Please, don't let anyone see me."

She continued to walk, keeping off the road at the edge of the trees. A convoy of police cars went past. No one noticed her.

In her mind she sensed Jim calling her. She had a vision of Jim, Paul, a black man, a strange man and woman and Tracey who had called her Rose.

How appropriate. She was a pretty flower and Dennard had found the thorns. But it wasn't her name. Her name was Erin. Erin...

There was a blank in her mind when she tried to recall her surname. It didn't matter – she didn't deserve to still be alive. Everyone she loved died or was hurt. She had stolen money, given some to men who kidnapped innocent people, including a child. She had planted two bombs. She betrayed the people who had sheltered her. Her father... Her father never wanted to see her again. She was horrible, horrible, horrible.

But Jim and Tracey had helped her. Had been kind to her.

But if they knew, they would hate her. Resolutely, Erin kept walking, heading west, whispering her mantra, "Let no one see me."

Her mind was blank. She walked without seeing where she was going, instinctively picking her way on the rough ground. She didn't walk into the car, parked off the road, but only because she walked into the man first. He grabbed her. She was too weak to struggle.

Jim Phillips spotted the woman walking along the roadside and slowed his car. He honked softly several times but the woman never even looked around. Was she oblivious, or ignoring him?

He studied her gait, and his anger was replaced by concern. Up ahead was a side road, he would pull off and wait for her.

He expected her to see him and try to run, but she kept plodding forward. She walked right into him and only struggled weakly, until she looked into his eyes and the blank look changed to fear. Fear of him! Then she struggled, almost getting free, like a moth trapped in glass. There was almost nothing of her, except a smell.

She hadn't fouled herself, but...

Jim had a sudden revelation and bit down a surge of anger. Against his better nature, he clipped Rose behind the ear, but caught her as she dropped unconscious.

She was so light, that it was easy to hold her and open the door for the back seat. He lifted her in gently.

He thought he knew how she had come to be in this state. Dennard, he thought grimly. He had been seen going off with a woman, two hours before the meeting. And he had arrived late, in a less than immaculate state and smelling like the woman did now. And his mind had definitely not been on business. It had been easy to discredit him with Eggleston's co-conspirators. Jim had taken the real Eggleston's laptop from Dennard, before he was ousted from the meeting. The others wanted information from him, and he cursed Dennard when it could not be easily found. Sending the entire contents of the computer's memory to Brendan had been easy. When Dennard had pulled himself together and forced his way back in, to accuse his boss of being an imposter, no one believed him. Fuller's two heavies had evicted him again, into the hands of Paul in the passage, and onto the police.

Jim closed the door on the woman, and locked it. If she tried to get out he would have some warning.

With no other idea than the need to talk to the woman, he drove on in the direction she had been going. He would stop at the first motel he came to.

He watched the car as he booked a room and paid in cash. She hadn't stirred in his absence and he watched until he saw the slight movement of her breathing. He needed to get her a doctor, but before that he needed to know who she was and why the thought of police terrified her.

If Dennard had raped her, it might explain her condition now, especially after that incident with Dennard's guard.

Jim lifted the woman into the unit and placed her on the bed. He went to close the door, then returned and covered her with one of the spare blankets. He used his mobile phone to call Brendan Collins, one of his team.

"Brendan, I have her. Westhaven Motel, room 7. Tell the others they can disperse. I'll get in touch later. Can you come here, and bring your stuff?"

Rose was still unconscious or asleep, when Brendan arrived half an hour later. Jim let him in. They moved close enough to the bed to look at her face.

"Recognise her?" Jim asked quietly.

Brendan studied her, and then shook his head.

"Take a photo, and run it through the computer. Hook into the police and media photos. If we can't get a match, save anything that comes close." Then Jim had a thought. "I will have to get the make-up off her. She looked quite different before Tracey gave her a makeover."

"What about a doctor, Jim?"

Jim knew he should, especially if his suspicions were fact. "I'll call the desk from here and ask them to send someone. I am not sure how she will react to waking up in a strange place."

Brendan took a photo of the sleeping woman using a tiny digital camera. He transferred it to his laptop computer. He had noticed that the motel boasted a wireless hotspot, and he hooked into that to get on the internet. When he reached the police net, Jim gave him a user name and password to use. Brendan had soon accessed the national criminal register and provided search parameters.

The woman looked young, but that might be deceptive. She was so slight and short.

"Female, fifteen to forty years old, Caucasian, light hair," Brendan muttered, and pressed search. He would probably have to narrow it further.

"Can we get fingerprints?" Brendan suggested.

"Not yet. See what this turns up," Jim cautioned. "If we have prints and get a match, there will be a record on the system. This way it is only a general description query."

Brendan shrugged. It was Jim's call.

"What is she to you?" Brendan finally asked his friend.

"She saved my life yesterday when I had to get away from Dennard," Jim admitted. "And I saw her face when I mentioned police and doctors. It was more than fear, it was terror."

The search had already flicked up a number of possibilities. Jim glanced at each and deleted them.

After the first dozen, Brendan suggested, "She might have lost weight since these photos were taken."

"Yes," Jim agreed, but he didn't comment further.

He answered the discrete knock at the door, but gestured for Brendan to close the laptop, and keep back out of the way.

Jim invited the doctor in; glad he had heeded the suggestion to bring a nurse with him. Before taking him to the patient, Jim stopped him.

"A word, doctor," Jim said. "It is most imperative that information about this patient remains absolutely confidential. No mention of her is to be put into any kind of electronic files. If you deem it necessary to recommend police or other authorities to intervene, please speak to me first."

The doctor nodded. "And who might you be?" the doctor asked, scrutinising Jim.

Jim smiled faintly and produced a State Department ID. The doctor studied it with a faint look of annoyance, but he agreed. "Very well. Might I ask the circumstances of the woman's condition?"

Jim gave a very terse outline from when he found her walking along the road, until he had stopped at the motel. He then added, "A State Department operation has just concluded up at the resort. This woman fits the description of someone seen with one of the arrested men. I have arranged for two of the investigators to come and question her, if it is possible. However they won't be free until after they have processed the detainees. My concern is her present condition, and whether or not she is a victim, or accomplice of the man."

The doctor understood the implications.

Jim stepped back and let the doctor and nurse go to the patient. He kept an eye on them as he went to stand behind Brendan and review the backlog of possible matches. He closed the lap top again when he saw the doctor packing up his case. And he saw something the doctor missed. The patient opened one eye briefly, and closed it again.

"She's foxing," Jim murmured to Brendan, as the doctor walked over.

"I would prefer to have her in a hospital," he said bluntly. "She is showing signs of prolonged inadequate nutrition, old bruising, and dehydration and yes, I believe she is pregnant. I would estimate about four months. Though with her physical condition, the baby could be small for dates. I am worried about the baby. I have taken blood samples and a vaginal swab."

Jim murmured, "Do you think she was raped?"

The doctor hesitated. "From various signs, I would believe she had intercourse a short time ago – within hours. But there are no obvious signs she was forced. No fresh bruises or abrasions. The blood test should pick up if she was drugged. I am also concerned about your description of her behaviour."

"So am I. Any suggestion as to what caused it?"

"Trauma, shock, she may have been on drugs and come off them abruptly," the doctor proposed. "I would need to do a more thorough examination."

"Other than getting her to a hospital, what sort of treatment do you recommend?"

The doctor understood that that would not be an immediate option. "Most important, for her and her child, is to get proper nutrition and fluids into her. Start with soups and soft foods. I'll give you a prescription for a vitamin supplement...."

Jim listened to the doctor, asked questions to clarify points and thanked him for coming. Jim gave the name Rose, for his patient and a mobile number for the doctor to SMS the results of his tests.

The doctor, in turn, provided Jim with his contact details, in case the doctors who later tended the woman needed to speak to him. Or if the police required a report from him.

When the door closed behind the doctor and nurse, Brendan went to peer through the slit in the curtained window.

"They are gone," he reported shortly. "Do you think he will call the police?"

"Not right away," Jim said. "Could you have that prescription filled?"

Brendan nodded and glanced where Jim was looking. The woman seemed to be asleep. He slipped out the door and closed it after him.

"You can stop pretending now," Jim said bluntly. He was leaning against the door, making a statement of blocking her exit. He saw her eyes flick to the door of the en-suite. "Yes, there is a window in there, big enough for you to wriggle out of, but you may have heard me send my friend on an errand, but he knew where I was looking and will be standing where he can watch that window."

Rose stared at him without speaking.

"I told you to stay in the car," Jim stated, and he didn't take his eyes off her. He saw a flutter of emotions reflect on her face. "You agreed to let me help you, but instead you run off with a criminal, a man who has a reputation of being the worst kind of womaniser, and have sex with him."

"You are not my keeper," Erin told him defiantly.

"Well, from your actions, you need one," Jim snapped. "How long have you known Dennard?"

"I didn't know him until I saw him at that place."

"That is not what the surveillance camera showed. It shows you running right at him."

"It's not what you think," Erin protested. "I intended to get his attention."

"You did that alright. What happened?"

"I made out I was running from someone and was desperate to get away and wanted him to help me."

"And just like that, he offered you a lift?" Jim put scorn in his voice. "A perfect stranger. Did he rape you?"

"No!"

"Did you have sex with him?"

"So what if I did?"

"So, I am to believe that you deliberately lured him away from a meeting that he expected to give him a share of 20 million dollars? I can't see that happening."

"I wanted to distract him, and make him late to that meeting. Then he wouldn't be able to reveal you as a fake."

Jim asked the obvious question. "If you had never met him before – how could you know he could do that?"

"I just knew!" Erin stated, this time dropping her eyes. "Just like I know your arm is very painful right now."

"That would be a logical inference," Jim said coldly. "You will have to do better than that to convince me to keep helping you. I should take you to the police and let them look at you. They would put you in hospital for your own good. And I would insist on a psychiatric evaluation, because everything I have seen of your behaviour, suggests you are incapable of caring for yourself."

The terror was back in Rose's eyes. "I would stop short of saying you were suicidal, but I am not sure - since you let Dennard..." Jim took a breath and then told her all he knew of Dennard and his history with women.

He expected a reaction from Rose, as he was graphic in his descriptions. Instead the terror faded and satisfaction replaced it.

"I know that," Erin admitted.

"Did he brag about it?"

"No. I just knew. It didn't matter to me. And it didn't take much for me to get his brains to fall to his balls. In five minutes, I had him so horny, he couldn't think. He planned to come here, but he couldn't wait. He pulled off the road, just down the hill. By then, neither could I."

Jim hid his shock. "It was consensual?"

"I wanted it. I planned it and he couldn't help himself. You could say I seduced him and raped him. No one would believe that and he totally wanted it."

Jim was further shocked by her brazen claim. She was right though – no one would believe it. No one would believe that Dennard could be mastered by a woman. Tiny, petite, innocent...

Innocent? Definitely not.

After a pause, Erin added, "As we slaked our lust with each other, I had pictures in my mind of him and other women – as bad as what you told me. For that alone, I don't mind having used him. After me – he won't be able to perform with any other woman. If he tries his manhood will wither and the woman will laugh."

Jim liked the idea. "You know that too?"

"Yes," Erin hissed. "And when he was senseless, I changed the time on his clocks."

So that was why he was late, Jim thought. "You said you knew Dennard could tell I was a fake – how? He never saw me today until the meeting."

Erin recalled one of her visions. "I heard you mention him in the car. I had a picture of him then. When I saw him today, I had another – of you and him – somewhere. You had your normal face."

Jim shook his head, disbelieving her. "Surely he would have challenged me before I looked like Eggleston. He wanted to destroy his boss."

Trying to explain her visions was always hard. Erin closed her eyes and recalled that picture and looked for details. She described a room, in a building, some distinctive decorations, a snippet of conversation and the faces of two other people.

Half way through, Jim was convinced - recalled in detail the time and place and his mission there. He made no mention of that.

"You were right about Dennard. He did challenge me, but it was too late. The other men were convinced he was raving."

Erin nodded and relaxed a bit, but stayed under the blanket.

"So what other things do you just happen to know?" Jim asked. Once again, he saw a play of emotions on her face, until she rolled onto her side, looking away from him. "Nothing," she said.

Jim resisted a sigh and began to regret his impulse to help her. If she wouldn't co-operate with him, if she kept endangering herself – let her stew.

Brendan was taking a long time, Jim thought, when another twenty minutes had gone by. Almost at once there was a knock on the door. Jim opened it.

Brendan edged in laden with a suitcase and a shopping bag of food.

Jim's eyes glanced at the case and Brendan muttered, "Tracey."

"I'll boil the kettle for the soup – you have a choice of beef, chicken or tomato," Brendan said.

Jim took the case over to the side of the bed where Rose was facing.

"Tracey sent some things for you. There is a shower and toilet in the corner. Soup will be ready when you come out. If you want me to keep helping you, you come out by the door you go in – not the window."

He deliberately walked away and went back to the computer, to look at the pictures being saved by the search program. When Rose scuttled, with the case, into the bathroom, he and Brendan appeared not to notice.

Jim studied photos, erased most of them, but kept some, until he smelt soap and shampoo and saw Rose beside him, staring at the next picture that had come up. He glanced at the screen, and with a shock, recognised the woman.

"Do you know her?" Jim asked urgently.

Rose shook her head, but kept staring - almost like a deer in a spotlight.

"Have you met her?" Jim asked. If this woman knew Wanda Martin – it might be a clue about her. Not that he could get her to help him right now.

"No," Rose whispered. "No, she's a demon, in my dreams, staring, watching, telling me to move, when I can't because I am chained upside down to a wall in a dark place with faceless figures around me, touching me..."

"Someone who looks like Wanda Martin," Jim murmured.

"No!" Rose insisted. "It's her!"

Someone like Wanda Martin indeed, Jim said to himself and he was not thinking 'looks' now.

"Who are you?" Jim asked in a gentle voice. Rose walked forward to use the table as support.

"Erin," she admitted.

"Erin what?" Jim urged. He was aware that Brendan was including the name in his search.

Erin shook her head. "I don't remember."

Chapter 5

"Where are you from?" Jim tried.

Erin's hands clenched the edge of the table. "I don't have more than flashes of memory."

"Tell me what you do remember," Jim suggested. Brendan, seated near the computer, opened up a blank word document and was ready to take notes.

"I remember nightmares. People screaming – sometimes it was me. I remember trying to get free, and being drugged and restrained. I remember a deep dark place of silence. I can remember a bare room, brightly, too brightly, lit. I could feel hate, violence, lust, fear, terror, desperation, despair. Mostly, I remember being confused. All the time, I was afraid that I was mad."

Erin stopped speaking as if considering other memories. "The dreams were worst. It was like I was lying down and having dark shapes hurting me, or maybe it was someone else. I knew what they were going to do, but I couldn't help. I remember wanting to die, and recalling something and knowing I couldn't."

"Where did you come from – before you met me?" Jim asked.

"Confusion," Erin said trying to describe the blurred vision in her mind. "I don't know how I got to where you found me. I just remember having to get away from somewhere before I went insane. I kept saying, 'let no one see me' and no one did, except you. The voice in my head said you could help me. It knew you."

Erin clenched the table harder. Her gaze, already unfocussed, turned inward and she fainted.

Jim caught her and lifted her to the bed. She weighed virtually nothing. He removed the pillow from the head of the bed and raised her feet on it.

Brendan drew Jim's attention to a face in a police mug shot.

Jim studied it and went to study Erin's face. Without the make-up, it was obvious that the picture was of the woman he had rescued. Even allowing for the fact she had lost a lot of weight. But that fact made the resemblance to Wanda Martin unmistakable. He felt a rise in excitement. Brendan sensed it.

"Who is she, Jim?" Brendan asked. He knew her name and what she had done, but not why his friend was suddenly thinking furiously.

"Wanda Martin – remember her?" Jim asked.

"Of course," Brendan said at once. Wanda had impressed him. She had called climbing up the side of a five storey building – child's play.

"She and David have been missing nearly seven months, along with Colonel Aldrin of the OSI."

"And we have done nothing?" Brendan insisted.

"Not nothing," Jim assured him. "I am not allowed to discuss it, but every agency is looking. No one has found anything."

"It's like they disappeared off the face of the Earth," Brendan said. "Are you sure they are still alive?"

Jim made a 'hold that thought' gesture with his finger to his temple.

"Wanda's sister says she is. I believe her. Tanya Krinsky, who is Wanda's spitting image - says the same." Jim knew Brendan recognised the name. "They are related - first cousins."

Brendan waited, his face neutral, for more information.

"Tanya's mother and Wanda's mother were two of triplets. The third..." Jim glanced at Erin. "We can't stay here. Your enquiry may have triggered a reaction."

Brendan guessed at high level secrets and began packing up his computer. Jim cleaned up everything Erin had used, wiped everything she might have touched. The two of them were experts at this – leaving no clues.

When he lifted Erin out to the car, he took the blankets and sheets as well.

"This is one time when I want the Secretary to disavow any knowledge of my actions," Jim murmured. He did not mention that it was the Secretary's direct orders he was disobeying.

"Do you want me to stay and mislead anyone who comes?" Brendan offered.

"No," Jim said decisively. "They will know I was here and had an injured girl with me. Only the local nurse and the doctor saw her and she had make up on then. It changed the whole look of her bone structure. They only know her as Rose."

"What if they find you and ask you?"

"If I am asked about the query, I will say I was comparing the girl with police records. I don't have proof that she is Erin Mason."

"Where are you headed, then," Brendan asked.

"West," Jim said.

"I will follow a distance back, after I see if anyone turns up here."

Jim nodded to that idea. He got into the car and drove off at a casual pace. Brendan followed as far as a turn off to a lookout where he could overlook the town."

Erin stirred when the car wheels crunched on the gravel verge before the highway. She didn't speak, and after a few minutes of driving Jim glanced at her and saw silent tears running unchecked down her face.

"What are you running from" Jim asked gently, though he could guess.

"I'm not crazy," Erin burst out.

"I am, perhaps, the one person in a million that would believe you," Jim told her. "What did you do to make everyone mad at you?"

"Everyone?"

"Seems that way. I know you illegally accessed the computer at your father's company."

"I helped them fix it," Erin said, almost desperately.

"You were suspected of embezzling, like your colleague," Jim went on.

"They couldn't prove anything," Erin said.

Yet – Jim thought.

"You were involved with that group that abducted the Cuban ambassador," Jim said, glancing at his passenger. She was trying to hide in the blanket.

"The charges relating to that were dropped," Erin insisted. "And the Minister spoke up for me and ... Gerry died! I didn't want to be there, but Travis dobbed me in to the police and I had to hide there and do electronic things for him. And once he'd taken those people – I couldn't go then – they needed me."

"So, you are not all bad!" Jim told her.

"But I am. I'm horrid. You know what I did to Dennard. I did it to Travis too. I liked doing it."

"Both times you were doing it to help other people," Jim pointed out. But that did not explain the Secretary's furious desire to lock Erin up forever.

"Why did you interfere with the computers at Mason's?" Jim asked. "You made a mockery of their firewall."

"It knew me," Erin boasted. "I've been getting in and out through it since high school."

"And other places?" Jim probed, making a guess.

The blanket moved slightly where Erin's head was.

Jim continued to guess. "So you let your colleague embezzle money and covered it up."

The blanket movement indicated an affirmative nod.

"Didn't you want part of the money?"

This time the blanket moved side to side, vigorously.

Erin could not see Jim's thoughtful expression. His memory of the case told him that federal agents thought she had stashed millions away too. He let that pass. "So why did you do it? You were the programmer, weren't you?"

"Yes," was the verbal answer. "It was a challenge, and Nick...Nick knew things about me."

"Blackmail?"

"At first – but then – I had to. I couldn't help myself. The program just... excited me. It was a challenge to create."

"Didn't you think it wrong to steal money?"

"It wasn't real," Erin said. "It was just numbers in a program."

"So what happened to the rest of the money?"

Erin tried to explain. "It was never anywhere. It was just numbers. The companies only think they lost money."

"So, according to you, it is like me writing in my old passbook that I have a million dollars – and the bank will believe it?" Jim tried to follow her logic and failed.

"Yes," Erin said.

"Did you tell the investigators that?"

"No. They wouldn't have understood. They had irate companies on their back. I told them the money got lost in the ether."

Which, Jim decided, they would not believe either. They would be looking for an account somewhere. But millions of dollars out of nowhere? A skill like that could wreck the world's economy. Could it be true? Or was she really blind to how the real money world worked? Did she justify what she had done as a computing challenge and not a million dollar crime?

Even just wanting to recover that much money would keep people on her trail, and if the programming had been brilliant...

Perhaps that was all it was. He recalled that the judge had claimed - she lacked moral and ethical values and had no scruples when it came to using computers and programming.

He agreed with part of that. Erin's morals were ...quite different from his. Her ethics were questionable. But scruples? She had them. She couldn't bear others suffering and she wouldn't tolerate murder.

"They shouldn't have given me ten years in prison," Erin said from under the blankets. "I helped them. I told them everything."

Jim knew she hadn't lasted a month in prison. Had she, as they claimed, fooled the doctors into thinking her crazy? Had she suffered for the deception?

No, he decided. If she hadn't been fooling them, and wasn't deluded – could she sense emotions the way her cousin, Wanda, heard thoughts?

"Do you know why they made it so long?" Erin went on, her head emerging. "It was because I hacked into the OSI computer and fixed a program their expensive experts couldn't fix."

There was unmistakable pride in that statement.

And that detail had not been mentioned by Goldman when he had passed on information about this missing cousin of Wanda Martin. And that would explain the Secretary's attitude and the court ruling about her staying away from computers.

On whim, or perhaps a survival instinct, Jim turned off the highway onto a secondary road where there was a town only a few miles along. He stopped at the local garage, paid the owner to have the car undercover, and arranged for it to be driven back to where he had hired it. Since he still needed a car, he hired a less noticeable dark coloured car.

Into the new car, he transferred Erin's case and his own small overnight bag. The blankets and sheets were put in the boot and he took them to the local motel and slipped them into the laundry. He finally parked the car outside a small cafe and directed Erin inside.

"You need to eat," Jim told her, and he ordered something light for her and something more substantial for himself.

His mobile phone rang, and before answering it, he slipped the Bluetooth hands-free earpiece into his ear.

"Yes," was all he said on answering.

Erin watched his face, but his expression didn't change, nor was there any slight body reaction to what he was hearing.

Jim made no mention of the call, just returned to his food and considered what Brendan had told him.

From the speed and numbers of FBI that had raided the motel, the powers wanting Erin found were very desperate indeed. Brendan had listened to the radio traffic, and even to him, the reaction was excessive for someone who was not a serial killer.

One thing was sure – if that group had found Erin, she would have been back in prison so fast that they would not stop to notice the state she was in – or particularly care.

It meant he needed to change his plans. He had intended to hire a plane at the nearest airport, but if the FBI were in force in the area – the airport would be watched as a matter of routine. It would be safer to continue driving west, but he would have to be careful and stick to lesser roads, and keep out of sight himself.

"Eat as much of that as you can," he told Erin who had only picked at the food. "We need to keep going as soon as we finish."

"Why?" Erin asked with feigned casualness. She had started to relax.

"I need to get to a place called Rockwater, as soon as I can."

"Where's that?"

"West of here – California."

"West. Yes, I have to go west," Erin muttered to herself and began eating mechanically.

Then they became aware of the sound of a helicopter hovering over the town. Erin looked like a startled rabbit.

"They want me," she whispered.

"Yes," Jim said calmly. "So all you need to do is what I tell you. Finish your food."

The throbbing faded into the distance.

Jim drove along secondary roads; ever alert for cars that might be tailing him. He knew Brendan was following twenty minutes behind as a backup.

Erin, he noticed, was more relaxed in his company. Her face had lost some of the frightened look. Perhaps the food had put some colour back in her face.

After a while, be began asking her questions on neutral topics, to test her memory. She had no knowledge of recent news and current events, so he switched to asking her about computers. He was quickly certain that in that field her mind was genius level, and probably in electronics too. He decided that the Secretary's paranoia about her might be justified to a point. However, his attitude would also tend to alienate a person like Erin from being reformed. Jim paused his questions to wonder if Goldman wanted to use her genius after she had been reformed or learnt a lesson in prison. Perhaps that was why her unauthorised visits to the OSI computer network were not widely known. That was a better idea than turning a 'pissed off' hacker loose.

They reached a large town near dinner time. Jim had called ahead earlier to book a room for them at the motel. He pulled into the reception bay and glanced at Erin. He had thought she had gone to sleep, so he nudged her gently. He got no reaction and shook her arm.

"What's wrong," he asked bluntly. She seemed to be staring ahead of her. Jim glanced that way, saw nothing amiss and shook her a bit harder. "Erin!

Snap out of it."

She began to shake.

"What is it?" Jim asked, concerned by her manner.

"I think I was asleep," Erin said, her voice strained. "It was like the dreams I was getting before."

"When before?"

"Before the voice told me I had to get away."

"We are stopping here for the night, you can tell me about it after I get our room."

"No. Not here. I can feel them all around me here."

"Who?" Jim asked.

"They don't have faces, just hoods."

"Where are they?"

"All around me, touching me."

Jim's concerns for Erin's sanity returned again. Then he thought of Wanda Martin, and how she had been when her 'extra senses' had suddenly expanded.

"Ok," Jim decided aloud. "I know of a quiet retreat about an hour's drive from here. It is away from any large towns."

"Please..."

Chapter 6

Erin's tenseness eased as they got further away from the town. It made Jim thoughtful. When they arrived at the guest house, Jim cased the area from the roadway and then continued into the drive. It was more like an exclusive hotel than a motel. He knew from previous visits that it got very little of the one-night only traffic. Most of its custom was seasonal. He saw no other cars parked outside units.

Erin was happy to wait in the car whilst he arranged a two bedroom unit.

They checked out the room and brought in their few necessities before Jim took Erin to the on-site restaurant.

The manager had family members handling the catering. All spoke more Spanish than English. Jim was fluent in Spanish and discovered, after her initial period of shyness, that Erin was too. The manager's wife served at the table and was happy to talk. She knew exactly the thing for a recovering invalid, and chivvied Erin into eating a meal as big as Jim's own. She even succeeded in getting Erin to laugh, something that Jim had never yet heard from her.

Jim didn't comment on the sudden increase in appetite. He hoped it wouldn't make her sick, since the doctor had stressed increasing amounts more gradually.

He now believed that he knew how to keep Erin in a more normal state. He just needed to keep her away from large numbers of people. He was becoming sure that she was not faking her reactions. When he had time, he was going to try and see when her "madness" began. He had a feeling that it would be about the time that Wanda's had.

It was much later, well after Erin had succumbed to sleep, that Jim had a call from Brendan Collins.

As usual, he answered his phone with, "Yes?"

"Are you in Valley Grove?" Brendan asked, not needing to identify himself to Jim.

"No."

"It is saturated with officials."

"Get two secure phones," Jim said and abruptly disconnected.

He had told Brendan where he intended to stop, and only sent a text message to say he might go on.

Jim thought carefully. How had the FBI guessed where he was going to stop? He had booked the room, but he had not given his true name. Brendan knew, but he would not have betrayed it. Were they, as he had just thought, monitoring his cell phone?

It was the most likely scenario. Did it mean that he might have to move Erin from here? Maybe not.

Jim looked in on Erin, and then slipped out of the unit, locking the door behind him. He strode quickly over to the reception office. For a generous tip, the manager was more than willing to tell anyone that asked that the gentleman had stopped for a meal and then moved on.

Jim had only just finished getting the man's smiling agreement when the phone rang. From the owner's expression, Jim had acted just in time.

"No, Sir. There is no one of that name staying here tonight. Could you describe them to me?" the manager listened and caught Jim's gaze. "We had several guests like the gentleman at lunch, but no young ladies. I will have to check with my staff for this evening. I am in the office, might I call you back?"

The man wrote a number and hung up.

"That is good, Senor?"

"Gracias," Jim smiled, passing over further notes. "If you could ensure your staff know we are not here?"

"My pleasure, Senor."

Jim expected to see someone official come to check the report. He wasn't worried about them checking the register. He had not used his name, and had paid in cash. If the staff were shown a photograph, they would deny the likeness.

He did need to contact Brendan and tell him where to bring the secure phones. That was his first need at the moment. He still had to get Erin to Rockwater without being intercepted. He would have to break the trail, or the Secretary might just figure out where he was going and arrange a hot reception there.

Erin was still asleep when Jim saw the blue-red flash through the gap in the curtain. He moved to where he could watch the office. The car was a local sheriff department car, not FBI. The two figures that got out of the car looked around briefly then went into the reception office. After about ten minutes they emerged and went straight to their car and drove off. It didn't mean that he was in the clear – they might still watch the place, but he felt they were not about to raid it.

Jim watched the outside for five more minutes and then went to his bag and took out a dark coloured wool hat and a more casual shirt. With them on, and from a distance, he would seem to be a dark haired man, dressed much more casually than his normal appearance.

Jim strode back towards the office, and then paused near a partly overgrown ornamental garden. He paused and mimed trying to light a cigarette, then pretended his lighter didn't work, and headed for the office. In the process, his mobile phone landed behind a bush. There were no numbers stored in it, and he had cleared the incoming and outgoing calls and the memory. If the phone was found, it might be identified as his, but no more than that.

Jim continued to the office and asked the young lad sitting there if the motel had internet access.

"Si, in the restaurant foyer. Three dollar for half hour."

Jim paid and made his way there.

Working quickly, he accessed the site he wanted and through it sent an email to Brendan Collins's phone.

He included the web address of the motel, as that was on a sign near the computer and a number.

In less than a minute he got a reply, the screen changed to display a return message. "OK"

Jim logged off after clearing the browser's history listing

He returned quickly to the room, relieved that Erin had stayed asleep, even if she was now moving restlessly.

Brendan Collins was not alone when he arrived later that night. He had Tracey Randal with him. They both slipped quietly into the unit when he opened the door. Jim smiled at both of them.

Brendan got right to business, handing Jim one of the secure phones. He explained what Jim needed to know about them. "And they won't display the number at the other end," Brendan finished.

Jim nodded; now, anyone trying to use his previous number would be stopped.

Tracey spoke up. "They have Sherriff's cars at the road junction just down the road. They might have them at all ways out of the district."

"Have you been monitoring the radio?" Jim asked Brendan after hearing Tracey's report.

"They want our Rose very badly indeed. They think she is an escapee from a psychiatric facility, Erin Mason. They say she has been missing for four weeks and to treat her as dangerous."

Tracey had walked to the door of Erin's room and watched Erin for a while. She listened to the sounds Erin was making in her sleep. When she wandered back, she commented, "She looks better. But there is something else, Jim. Have you got cable here?"

At Jim's nod, she turned on the television and used the remote to switch it to a twenty-four hour news channel.

"I don't know if this is relevant, but Brendan said that our girl came from the Washington area."

Tracey flicked the interactive news buttons and scrolled down to a particular item of current news.

Jim watched the report and his face grew thoughtful. Zara Russell, daughter of the Secretary of State, was missing – abducted. The news had leaked to the press after someone had posted a video of the girl on the internet. The item showed the girl giving a message to her father. She looked battered and bruised. The report had gone on to say that she was last seen at a particular Washington night spot a week ago.

That would certainly put her father in a state, Jim knew.

Jim used the secure phone to make a call to a number he knew from memory. When it was answered, he only gave his surname.

"Jim," the voice sounded relieved. "I've been trying to reach you. What is this about you asking about Erin Mason?" It was the voice of the man that gave him his missions and the intermediary between him and the Secretary.

That was unexpected. "How did you know about that?"

"Goldman told the Secretary that you were hunting for her. He had been told to leave it to other agencies. There was a report that the national criminal database was queried about likenesses to her, and for a print of her record. They traced the computer that accessed it to a motel and the Secretary wanted to reach you, but I couldn't. He got the FBI to pull your mobile records. Do you have her?"

Jim was on the spot.

"I found a young woman, walking along a road, near the resort where a crime racket was broken up." Jim knew his listener would place that. It was a long way from Washington. So was Eggleston's place where he had really found her.

Jim went on, "She was in an extremely poor physical state and had possibly been raped. Her clothes were unwashed and ragged, her shoes in holes and she had amnesia. I did a search of police and media photos to try to identify her."

The man at the other end was silent – thinking.

"The Secretary does not believe that Erin Mason is a psychiatric case. He thinks she planned to escape from there and succeeded. With her genius at computing and the belief she has access to several million dollars of untraced funds, he has every agency working overtime to find her. Using tax-payers money."

Jim translated that as wasting money.

The voice continued after a pause. "He believes that Erin Mason is behind the disappearance of his daughter, either for revenge or as a means of ensuring her freedom."

"That is an interesting leap of logic," Jim said tactfully.

"If you have Erin Mason, Jim, you have to hand her over."

"If the woman I helped was her," Jim said carefully, admitting nothing, "She would have been in no condition and nowhere near Washington when Zara Russell disappeared."

"Bring her in, Jim, and we will let the medical experts decide."

"I had the woman looked at by a medical expert," Jim said carefully. "And what I said stands. Why is he convinced Mason is involved?"

The voice summarised the Secretary's logic, mostly based on Erin's previous activities. He had ignored the claims of her being forced to be involved. It was also based on the fact that the demands had come via computer and the internet.

However, the most damning evidence was the fact that CCT footage had shown the faces of Zara's two abductors, and they had been identified and were once known to be tight with Erin Mason at university.

It was Jim's turn to think quietly.

"Jim?"

"I'm here. What demands are the abductors making. Is it just the money figure shown in the clip on the news?"

"No," the voice on the phone admitted. "A second clip was withheld. They want Nick Bosley and Erin Mason freed."

"So, I assume it is believed that Erin Mason is behind it and that claim is to put us off the scent," Jim asked.

"It seems so," the voice agreed.

Jim was quiet, thinking furiously.

"Are there any leads to finding Colonel Aldrin?" Jim asked, seeming to change the subject. If this conversation got back to the Secretary of State, mentioning his protégé, Wanda Martin, would not help.

"Nothing," was the instant reply.

"If I were to say that I might have found a lead and needed to pursue it," Jim said carefully. "And to do it I needed a computer genius...could I have three days?"

The voice of his liaison spoke carefully in return. "The priority right now is finding Zara Russell. Colonel Aldrin is either dead already or his situation will not change in three days."

"Yes. You are right." Jim said, sounding agreeable. "I'll get my team together to help find Miss Russell, using whatever skills are needed. The police will be looking for Erin Mason – I will try to trace those videos. Is the FBI any closer to finding the site operators?"

"No the people who run the site are as hard to trace as those that post on it. If you are willing to help – do. If she is found, you can go and follow that other lead. Good Luck, Jim."

Jim smiled faintly. The liaison was an acquaintance of long standing, who had served under several different Secretary of State appointees. He had in effect given Jim a mission, although not in the usual manner. It was an 'out' so he could use Erin Mason to help find Colonel Aldrin. She might be able to help find Zara Russell. He believed, even if no one else did, that Erin had nothing to do with that abduction.

"Tracey, call Karen and Paul. See if they can meet us here. Do you have the means to make them look at a distance, like me and our Rose? Brendan, can you set up a secure internet connection – wireless or satellite?"

Both nodded, but Tracey asked, "Is she Erin Mason?"

Jim nodded, knowing he could trust both of them implicitly. He told them some of what his liaison had told him.

Tracey made the calls and got affirmative answers, and then she went to sit with Erin. When she saw the younger woman sitting up in bed, hugging her knees and staring in front of her, she went over and touched her arm. She was icy cold.

"Jim! Come here."

Startled, Jim strode into the room and took in Erin's state. "Find some blankets and turn on the heater in here. Boil the kettle and make tea or something hot."

Tracey set to work as Jim sat beside Erin and hugged her. When Tracey handed him the blanket, he wrapped that around Erin and went back to hugging her, to try to warm her up. He felt her trembling.

"Erin, wake up. Tell me what is wrong."

He repeated the question several times before he got a response.

Erin suddenly went limp and began to cry silently.

"Tell me what is wrong," Jim asked.

"I'm sorry," Erin whispered. "I know you want to help her, but I can't...I can't. I don't know how and..."

"Help who?" Jim wanted to know.

"That woman, on the computer screen," Erin whispered. "She matters to you, doesn't she?"

Jim nodded, and then realised Erin hadn't noticed that and said, "Yes."

"She haunts my dreams. I thought she was trying to hurt me, but those others are hurting her. I felt I was there. I couldn't get away – it felt like she was holding my hands so tightly. I was feeling what she was feeling and I wanted to scream, but couldn't. She was screaming at them, pleading with me to help her. And I can't. I don't know how. She called me horrible names. After a while, those others went away. She ... she said she was sorry, but she was crying. She'd rather be dead but people needed her and she couldn't walk out of where she was and I...I was...the only one she could reach out to..."

Erin tried to control her tears. "She knows I am with you. She knows you. She wants help. She kept saying she needs me to be somewhere she knows. How can I know where that is?"

Chapter 7

"I know where," Jim assured her. "I will get you there."

"Now," Erin pleaded. "Please. I don't want these dreams anymore. Why can she do that to me? Why can't someone else help her?"

"Lots of people are looking for her and her husband and Stev Aldrin. So far, no one has found any clues. I am hoping you can help me succeed. You won't be alone. There are others who deeply, truly want to get her back. I think I know why she can reach you, and I think that being able to reach you is helping her to persevere. To choose to live."

"Why? Why me?"

"From what you have said, you feel or sense emotions. Wanda hears what people think. I know she can hear thoughts from others – her sister most easily, and over a reasonable distance. Where she is now, I think is so far away that it takes too much effort to reach her sister. I think the emotions she is experiencing now, are so strong that they are seeking a mind that can share them – and they found you."

"Why are they so much worse now?"

"You are not drugged any more now," Jim told her.

"Did she cause me to freak out in prison?"

"I can't say about that," Jim mused. "But she woke you to the need to get away from the confusion place."

"Her need..." Erin started to say. "How come the day voices are telling me to go west?"

Jim decided he had better explain some things to Erin. "What do you know about your mother? I mean, where she came from?"

"Yugoslavia. She grew up there but was later adopted by American diplomats. She spoke some Russian-Slavic dialect."

Jim nodded. "That fits. I believe that you and Wanda Martin are cousins. That your respective mothers were sisters."

"Twins?" Erin guessed, losing the look of fixed staring.

"Two of triplets," Jim corrected. "There is another cousin, a Russian woman, who is the daughter of the third sister. I am hoping, now I have met you, that you, Tanya and Wanda's sister, Elisabeth, can help her."

"Is that the only reason you are helping me?" Erin asked bitterly.

"You found me," Jim reminded her. "I didn't know who you were then."

"So why did you help me?"

"You needed help," Jim said gently. "And you helped me."

"You could have taken me to a hospital."

"True, but I was grateful for your help." He wasn't going to mention he was in the middle of a mission.

"I am grateful to you," Erin admitted. "But you are asking for trouble hiding me."

She saw Jim's wry grin and decided he knew it. "Well, I want your help, so just hang in there and I will get you to Rockwater as soon as possible."

"Why can't we go now?"

"There are complications," Jim told her. "The police are looking for you and may be close to finding you."

Erin seemed to shrink under the blanket.

"And not just because you escaped."

Erin's head reappeared. "What do you mean?"

"How well do you know Zara Russell?" Jim asked, watching her face as she answered.

"That prig? I haven't seen her since Uni – three, four years ago? Why?" Erin was surprised at the reference.

"She was abducted a week ago," Jim told her still watching her reactions.

"What has that got to do with me?"

"I don't think you are involved," Jim assured her first. "However, two men have been identified as being involved." He mentioned the two names and saw Erin's recognition. "They sent demands via the internet – from an untraceable site. One of the demands was the release of you and Nick Bosley from prison."

"Of all the fatuous fardling idiots," Erin cursed. "So everyone thinks I put them up to it. I'd never..."

"Easy," Jim warned. "I don't believe it, and if you are willing, we can use this to your advantage. Just listen to a few facts. Zara Russell is the daughter of Stan Russell, the Secretary of State. So naturally there is an all-out effort to find her. Stan Russell knows of your talents and does not like you."

"An understatement, I gather," Erin said bitterly.

"Quite," Jim agreed. "However, I know what condition you were in a week ago. The Doctor who examined you will be able to state that you didn't get that way in a day or two. Also, you were found a long way from Washington."

"What can you do?" Erin slumped as if in defeat. "No one is ever going to believe I am not a violent monster."

"Tell me about those friends of yours."

Erin thought for a moment and began to speak. Brendan and Tracey came into the room to listen and take notes.

Jim asked questions to clarify points. "Do you think them smart enough to hide their internet tracks completely?"

"No," Erin said at once. "They are smart, and computer savvy, but not innovative. They can only use what someone else has done before. What way did they send the message?"

Jim explained and Erin nodded.

"Do you think you could track them?" Jim asked.

"Yeah. I know how those imbeciles think."

"Do you think they will hurt Miss Russell?"

"They didn't like her back then," Erin considered. "I don't think they will do more than make things unpleasant for her."

"What if they are cornered?"

Erin shrugged. "They think they can't be found, so I don't know."

"I'll arrange a computer and internet access," Jim said, starting to rise.

"I can't! They said I wasn't to be allowed near either, or I would be kept in prison longer."

"I'm supervising you," Jim assured her. "I'll be responsible. What else will you need?"

"I'll let you know," Erin promised. She looked a lot more alert than Jim had yet seen her. "Let me access that message site for a start."

Erin got out of bed and walked to sit in a chair next to the table where Brendan had the computer. Before long she was totally engrossed. Jim left Brendan watching her and planned his next move. That was to have Karen and Paul lead the police way from the motel in a direction away from Rockwater. He would need to recover his phone. Meanwhile, he needed to work out the fastest way to the base in California.

Jim prepared a mug of soup for Erin and put some bread rolls on a plate, and put them beside her. She drank and ate without seeming to notice that she had. Her fingers seemed to be flying over the keypad, as she tapped out keywords or passwords or commands. She was equally oblivious of the arrival and after a while the departure of Karen and Paul. They had been long gone when Erin suddenly laughed.

Jim came over.

"I'm almost on to them," Erin said smugly. "You wondered if they were the owners of that site? Well, I don't think so, but I think I know who is."

Erin told Jim a name. "He was a senior at WU the first year I was there.

He did a thesis on firewall specifications. I know his work."

"Can you get around it?" Brendan asked, having followed most of her workings with awed appreciation. He saw Erin's feral smile and had his answer.

"I have a direct link to their web cam," she stated.

Jim came over to watch. "Can you send them a message?"

"Easy," Erin claimed. "I would like to tell them what I think of their little demands."

"Could they trace your message?" Jim asked.

Erin snorted. "They are infants at this. I am surprised the FBI experts haven't cracked them yet."

"What would you say," Jim asked.

"Why the hell did they drag me into this? I got free without their help and don't appreciate the heat."

"Go on then. We need to lure them into the open. See if you can get a lead on their location."

Erin sat thinking for a moment before her fingers got busy again. She kept one eye on the webcam as she worked but it gave her little information except the faces of the suspects.

"Can you get voice?" Jim asked, noticing that Brendan was setting up a recorder attached to a second laptop. It had a direct feed from the one Erin was using.

There wasn't much sound at first – the two men were simply lounging around. They jerked up as the message tone on their computer pinged.

"Can you remotely adjust the view of the webcam?" Brendan suggested, as the men reacted to the unflattering message Erin had sent.

"Ask her where she is?" the voice of one of the men came over the speaker.

"I'll ask how she ruddy well got onto us," the other voice spoke – rattled.

The picture on the web cam widened to include a window. Erin tried to focus it on the scene outside.

A return message came through via the expedient of reply to message.

It came through the front website Jim had used to send the message to Brendan.

Erin replied with, "Why would I tell you idiots that? Every bit of heat below the President is looking for you. I don't need them looking for me, but they are. No thanks to you."

While she waited for the next reply, Erin asked, "Did my disappearance make the newspapers?"

"A brief mention in the papers in the Capital. Nothing full scale," Jim told her.

"And Zara went off after that?" Erin asked further.

"Yes," Jim agreed, wondering what Erin was thinking.

"If you assume that I didn't organise to have her taken – what is the point?"

"Money," Brendan said at once. "All that money that everyone thinks you took and no one has found."

"But – Nick had his accounts frozen and the assets seized," Erin pointed out. "So they might think I still have hidden accounts, so why Nick."

"The two of you worked the scam together," Tracey suggested.

Erin winced at the term "scam". "That might make sense. But taking Zara Russell – they can't really think they can force the powers to free us could they?"

"Some people don't think sense," Tracey commented.

A ping heralded the arrival of a message. Erin looked at it in a small window in front of the view from the web cam.

"We were trying to help you," was the claim.

Erin typed rapidly. "Bull shit. I was out three weeks before you took that stuck up bitch. Ok, you have my attention – what do you really want?"

Erin started doing something else before pressing the send key.

"Can you save a picture from the webcam with a date and time stamp?" she asked Brendan. She let him at the keypad for a moment. When had had saved the picture she adjusted the field of the webcam again and sent her reply.

A window popped up with a lot of computer jargon. Erin saved it and waited for the next reply.

Jim spotted movement in the webcam view. "Can you widen that again? I saw something off to the right."

Erin did, but only the two men she knew were in sight. One of them was reading out her reply. A woman's voice, out of webcam range, spoke angrily. "Stuck up bitch am I - she's only a whore!"

"One with a brain, Zar. We need her skill, remember."

Erin looked up at Jim.

"Well, does that mean Miss Russell is a part of this?" Tracey asked aloud.

Another window popped up with more jargon, again Erin read it.

"I can identify the repeater that there computer modem is using, its Wi-Fi so I haven't got an exact location," Erin said.

"Give me what you have got," Jim asked, as he opened his secure mobile phone. Erin told him the locations. He spoke quickly, listened then closed the phone.

"The FBI experts will have that soon," Jim assured Erin. "They were not that close yet."

The camera view showed one of the men typing. Zara Russell moved into view, unrestrained and with no evidence of the damage seen on the video.

Brendan saved another shot from the webcam.

"Where is..." Erin asked.

"This side of DC." Jim supplied. In fact it was well outside of the Capital and not all that far from where Erin was found. "Do you think they are mobile?"

"I can't tell." Erin admitted. "Just that they aren't moving around at the moment. Why?"

"Try to arrange a place to meet," Jim directed. "Let me think..."

A message arrived. "Secrets. Worth millions. Solve a snag = rich," Erin read out. "So that's it. How could they have got hold of some secret project stuff?"

"Do you think that's it?" Jim asked intently. Erin knew the men well enough.

"At least part of it. They know me as well as Nick Bosley. I like a computing challenge – even if it's not legal – that's my problem. But I don't know how they could have got hold of such a thing. They aren't thieves, and not that clever at hacking."

Erin started typing again. When the window popped up, she glanced at it.

"They just sent an email to...." she read out the address. "I think there is something else behind this."

"Okay," Jim said aloud, as he thought furiously. "Tell them to let Zara Russell go unharmed and to meet you at Cosgrove Park, Westchester tomorrow after three pm. I know there is an internet place there with a wireless hotspot. Tell them that if there is any sign of the police you won't be there. Do it quickly. If the FBI act – those men will be alerted soon."

Erin typed quickly. "Ditch the bitch, unharmed or no deal. Cosgrove Park Westchester >3pm No Heat Email me if I am not visible."

Erin looked up in time to see the webcam go blank.

"They are moving." Brendan deduced. "They may not have got that message."

"No matter. They'll get it when they set up again. I think we can be sure Zara Russell won't get hurt."

"Even if cornered?" Jim asked.

"They are not violent, just cowards. That's why they are using the net to contact people. Do we have to move too?"

Jim nodded to Tracey. "Pack up everything, put it in the car. We can't go yet. Paul and Karen are leading the FBI away from here."

Erin suddenly realised what no one had told her. "They are that close?"

"In the last town we went through. The one that scared you witless. They checked here but the office people kept quiet."

Erin went pale. Jim distracted her, "Will you have trouble contacting them if they have moved."

"No and neither should the FBI."

"The operator of that website, is he likely to be able to access restricted sites?"

Erin nodded.

"Did you get a line on his location?"

 Erin brought up the last two saved popups. "His email address ids like theirs – it goes through the website. Tell the FBI that and send those two pages of jargon. They should be able to do something with that."

Jim nodded and made another call. He spoke an email address to Brendan, who sent off the data. Then he told whoever he was talking to the details of the proposed meeting place.

"What now?" Erin asked.

"We wait to hear if Zara Russell is released." Jim said.

"What if she is up to her neck in it?" Erin asked.

"I will have Brendan send those two pictures to Goldman. The FBI can look into it. My concern ends when Miss Russell is free."

"Mine doesn't," Erin muttered. "I was meant to help her be released unharmed so her daddy will like me. If she is involved in something illegal, he won't like me. He will still want me locked up for life."

"We don't know all the facts, but with what Brendan recorded, we can prove you were not involved – except in finding Miss Russell. We will have to wait to see if we helped plug a security leak and to recover stolen secrets."

"We were only guessing about that," Erin muttered.

"Perhaps," Jim hedged. "But don't worry, we're safe here."

Jim turned to Tracey, and checked that everything was in the car. "See about some food, will you."

Jim went over to Brendan who had headphones on. Erin watched, and her fingers seemed to itch with the wish for a reason to use the computer again. She hadn't realised how alive she felt, having her fingers flying over the keyboard, her mind intuiting the electronic pathways that the data used. And then, while her mind was occupied, those insidious mind voices had been pushed from her awareness. Now they were back, more urgently than before.

She only vaguely heard Brendan saying that the police and FBI had given up following Paul and Karen and been redeployed to Westchester and the probable location of Zara Russell's abductors. All she was aware of was the urgent need to be somewhere – she didn't know the place – and of a cramping sick feeling in her stomach.

She didn't understand why she felt the urgency, or why the mental voices were so frantic.

Jim's phone rang and from his replies she guessed it was the Paul she had met some days ago. Jim only gave single word answers.

Then Erin felt him shaking her gently.

"Erin? Are you alright?"

"No, I think I need to eat something. My stomach feels like it is trying to eat itself."

"Tracey won't be long. Is that all?"

"No. Those voices in my head are at it again. Jim, wherever it is that you think I need to be – I need to be there now. If I thought I could get there faster on my own, I'd start running."

Jim put a hand on her shoulder. "I will get you there tonight," he promised, rapidly reviewing the arrangements he had made. "Brendan, you and Tracey will have to see this business through. Erin, tell Brendan everything you can. I'm going to have to reorganise the transport arrangements."

Erin forced her mind back to the hacking she had done and began to explain how she did it. Brendan listened intently with every sign of having understood what she said and meant. She didn't notice his fascination with how she worked computers – just the shared sense of needing to finish the job.

When Tracey arrived back with pizzas, Erin ate a whole one by herself. When the voices began again, she fought to keep it down.

Less than half an hour later, Jim was ready to go. Erin more ran than walked out to the car, and sat in the front seat. She could only think of the need to be somewhere and that she was getting there.

After a while, the voices reduced their urgency. Erin found herself wanting to sleep, but she feared sleep because then that other – that face – her cousin – gripped her into her nightmare.

Chapter 8

Erin sensed it coming on and fought to ignore it. The face was in her mind, screaming at her to help. She still didn't know how to help, or how to get to that somewhere, any faster.

She didn't know what special importance that mountain clearing had for that other.

"Jim, where are we going? Rockwater was it?"

"Yes," Jim answered while still watching the road.

"Is that near mountains?"

"Yes, why?"

"There's a clearing. She wants me there."

Jim knew where Erin meant, but did know how long it would take to get there. He still had a half hour's drive to get to the airport where a hired jet was waiting. Then an hour's flight west to where a helicopter was waiting at the airport nearest Rockwater – to take them to the base. The helicopter could not land in the clearing, even if he knew the exact coordinates, even if it was daylight. The clearing was a two hour walk from the base of the mountain. He didn't think Erin was fit enough for the climb. It was remote.

"Does it have to be there," Jim asked, more to himself. He didn't expect the answer he got.

"Because no one is there," Erin tried to explain. "I'm not the person she thought she could reach – but I am the only one. But I am a stranger to her, so she has to know the place. She thinks they are going to kill her soon. And she can't walk out. So she said she had to try to go half way and hope she can spring back somewhere else. She can't come back. Not without ... it's a face. I don't know him. What does she mean?"

"I'm not sure," Jim admitted. "But I have an idea. She knows Rockwater – she was living on the base. Surely there..."

"No!" Erin almost yelled. "There are too many people – too many minds – too much confusion."

"I can have the base evacuated," Jim proposed. "If that would do?"

Erin was hunched over. "Yes. Yes. It will have to. It will take too long to get to the clearing."

"What else?" Jim asked.

"I...I just need to be there," Erin said. "But I'm so far away and she hasn't much time. What was her name?"

"Wanda," Jim said "What..."

"Stop the car! Let me out! NOW!"

Intuition was one of Jim's most important talents. He braked and pulled off the road. It was an open deserted stretch.

Erin almost fell out of the car. Jim got out and raced around to help her. He caught her as she stumbled. She was staring at something in the near total darkness. She reached out, stretched and stumbled towards something. Nothing that Jim could see. He supported Erin, and then, for an instant, like the flash of a torch – someone was there. A faint glowing outline. It touched Erin. It touched him and a wave of faintness came over him along with a sense of "Wanda". He felt that someone had recognised him. Then it seemed to back away and was gone.

Erin collapsed in his grip. He lowered her to the ground, just before she fell. She hadn't fainted for her could feel her shaking.

"Erin?"

He heard her gulp, and a moment later retch, and finally to throw up. He went to the car and returned with a bottle of water. He passed it to her when the heaving eased.

"Are you able to get back to the car," Jim asked with concern.

"I really don't think I can move," Erin managed to say, but her voice was weak. "I just want to sleep."

Jim leant over and lifted Erin in his arms. She felt lighter than when he had first seen her. Inexplicably, he felt weak too, and he feared he might drop her.

He forced himself to stay upright, hold onto her and get to the car.

He settled Erin into the passenger seat, and fastened the seat belt. She slumped back. In the interior car lighting he saw she was crying. He took a packet of tissues from the glove compartment and laid them on her lap. Then he closed the door and walked carefully around to the driver's side and got in.

He remembered then, the bag Tracey had pressed into his hand. "Snacks for the journey," she had said.

He needed something now, to give him energy and to wake him up.

He pulled out an energy snack bar and began to eat. Erin made a faint sound. She was watching him. Jim felt in the bag and drew out a chocolate bar, opened it and passed it to her. He didn't think it was a good idea, since she had just been sick, but maybe she needed it too.

After a while, she reached into the bag for another.

He felt impelled to ask her if it was a good idea.

"I have to. I am so hungry," she told him.

"But you have been sick."

"No. That was something else. Food is helping."

"What do you mean? What did you see?"

"I don't want to talk about it," Erin said. "But – she was here – almost here – enough to touch me. She knows me now."

"Was it enough?"

"For now," Erin said. "But she is not out of the darkness. She's weak too – but now she's not chained up... she ..."

"What?" Jim prompted.

Erin described what she had seen in her mind, as if she had actually done what she knew this Wanda person had done.

"It was like I was strangling them with the chain, and enjoying it. She dragged one of the bodies over to where there was a faint light. She dragged off the face covering and whatever it was – it wasn't human. Then she stripped it, took a knife and something else. While she was doing that, another one found her and she swung around and got it in the throat..."

Erin's stomach roiled again, "All she did was get free of the chains – but she isn't free, just hiding."

Jim started the car again. "At least she is still alive, still fighting. She is at her smartest when the danger is greatest."

"This was plan 'z'," Erin blurted. "And it didn't work."

"Maybe it was enough," Jim tried to sound hopeful.

Erin said nothing, the sense of what she had received was not optimistic.

Jim returned the car to the road and gradually increased speed. He knew he needed to concentrate on his driving, because he was tired. He glanced at Erin after a short time and realised she was asleep.

She was still asleep when he drove through the gates of the local airport and around to the side of the building where two marines stood waiting.

Jim shook Erin gently. She woke with a start. The darkness disorientated her. "Where are we?"

"Airport. Do you need the ladies room?"

"Yes. Where is it?"

They got out of the car and one of the marines approached. It was a woman. Jim asked her the question of where the facilities were. She led them through the side door of the otherwise deserted building.

Erin eyed the woman warily, and then dived into the ladies room. On her return, the woman simply said, "This way. The plane is ready to go. Your stuff is loaded."

Erin nodded, realising with relief that this woman was not acting as if she was going to call the police to arrest her. Did she know who she was escorting? Two more marines joined them at the plane and when all were seated the plane began to move.

Erin slept again - waking as the plane landed. They had only a very short walk from the plane to a waiting helicopter. Its rotors were rotating slowly. This was to take them the final distance.

"How did you arrange this?" Erin asked Jim in a whisper. "What are you? Some kind of policeman?"

"Police? No. I do have some influence in certain circles. I am a kind of trouble shooter." He was not about to tell Erin what he actually did.

"You haven't shot me yet," Erin muttered.

"That's because you can help me and I hope I can help you," Jim reminded her. "Now – when we get to Rockwater we will discuss what to do next. The people there are expecting us and even if they recognise you – they will not be turning you in. You are there on my authority. And having said that, you won't be free to leave the grounds. It is a State Department facility and you will be restricted to only part of it. If you leave, I have no authority to stop any policeman who sees you from taking you in."

"After I help you, then what?" Erin asked in a small voice.

"I don't know, yet. We will see how things are when Wanda is back."

The sudden increase in noise from the rotors effectively stopped further conversation. Jim helped Erin up into the passenger compartment and climbed in after her. Two marines followed and showed her how to strap in.

Erin was thankful for the noise. It meant that she couldn't hear the mental voices. However, she still felt an overwhelming fear and knew that wherever this Wanda was, it was coming from her.

The noise also kept her awake, in spite of wanting to collapse into sleep. With Jim's help, she disembarked from the helicopter and, with her head down and eyes shut against the dust being raised by the rotors, she let him guide her. She stumbled across to a building as the helicopter lifted off. The two marines went with it. She was barely aware of meeting other people and being led to a bed. The last thing she recalled was someone removing her shoes and placing a rug over her.

Chapter 9

When Erin awoke she realised that she was in a totally unfamiliar place. She looked around and saw the stand by the bed with a drip bag hanging from it. A portable screen gave her privacy from the rest of the room. A table beside the bed held a covered tray and a sipper bottle of water. All that made her think of a hospital but without the overwhelming sense of sickness.

There was no policeman sitting beside her and that gave her a sense of relief. If only she knew where she was. She sat up and had a better look around. She remembered Jim telling her a name – Rockwater - and his telling her what the place was and that she would be safe here. For a little while anyway, she added mentally.

It was well that she remembered that because moments later a man appeared around the screen and she knew him from her past.

"What are you doing here?" she demanded rudely.

Rowan Wallace merely smiled at her. "It is good to see you are awake and with a bit more life in you," he said neutrally "There is food on the tray if you are up to it."

"Why am I here?" Erin asked a bit less rudely. "With this drip thing in my arm?"

"That is because you were dehydrated and exhausted. It is potassium with glucose. This is the base infirmary. I will be keeping you here until I have completed a full examination of you and the results of various blood tests come back. If you had neglected yourself much longer – you would have put that child you are carrying at risk."

Erin visibly started. Not once since she had met Jim had she thought of the child. Now, the thought of losing that precious link to Gerry brought back all the emotion of losing him. In her current depleted state, she could not control them. She looked down at her lap and tried to stop the tears.

Wallace let her be for a few minutes and then spoke casually. "You slept for over twenty four hours so you should be feeling like getting up and walking around. It would be better if you did."

Erin didn't respond.

"Are you up to a visitor?"

"Who? Your friend Goldman?"

"No, though he will be coming here."

"I don't want to see him," Erin blurted.

Rowan didn't react. "Do you know why Jim brought you here?"

"More or less. Something about a missing cousin that I don't even know." Erin quickly wiped her eyes on the sheet and looked up. "Why does that matter to you?"

"It matters because a very good friend of mine, and of Magnus Goldman, is missing too. Wanda and David Martin and Stev Aldrin were on a mission together. We want them all back safely."

"Oh, so Goldman doesn't want to throw me back into prison yet."

Rowan chuckled. "Not yet. What happened when Jim was driving you here to deplete you so?"

The unexpected question jolted Erin. "You won't believe me," she told him.

"Try me. I know Wanda Martin, and what she can do."

Erin told him what she had told Jim Phillips. He nodded, seeming to understand. It added detail to what Jim had told him. When she came to the part that still had the power to make her retch, he suggested she take long, slow deep breaths.

"I slept a whole day. She might be dead by now," Erin thought aloud, once her stomach was under control. "Those things, those creatures might have got to her by now. And you don't know where on Earth they are? You can't let those things stay loose."

"No," Rowan agreed. "As for Wanda – she's too stubborn to let them kill her. And she won't let them win. Think on it – she reached out over an unknown distance and succeeded."

"She only partly succeeded. And she had to kill..."

"Perhaps she did what she intended," Rowan suggested. "And, if, as you suggested, she knows you now and that will make her return easier."

"But how will she return? Where is she?" Erin asked, but a realisation dawned.

"Oh no – It isn't possible. People just can't move from place to place like that. You must be insane to even consider it. No, I must be. I saw it."

"It is possible," Rowan stated. "We have proof that Wanda can do it." He did not mention that he believed Erin herself had done it when getting out of the psych facility. "And I think that she needs you to get back. So you will need to be much stronger. Eat what is on your tray and I will send in your visitor."

Erin reached for the tray and lifted the lid. The savoury aroma made her instantly hungry and she found the fork needed to eat the stew like food. She was so hungry that she couldn't eat it fast enough.

"You will make yourself sick eating like that," a voice with an accent so familiar said.

Erin looked up, somehow expecting to see her mother, even though she was dead. Instead, she saw the image of the face from her nightmares - the face of the apparition of the previous night.

Rowan Wallace returned at a run when the screams began.

He found Tanya Krinsky trying to calm Erin.

"I'm Tanya. Tanya Krinsky," she was saying. "I'm not Wanda. We are alike – like twins, but are cousins. You are my cousin. Please, I'm not going to hurt you."

Tanya looked pleadingly at Rowan Wallace. "I didn't do anything. She just looked at me and began screaming."

Rowan disappeared for a moment and returned with a hypodermic, and injected the contents into the drip. A few minutes later, the screams turned to sobs that were just as unstoppable. Erin finally collapsed back onto her pillows, quiet, but with tears still running down her face.

Tanya stood back a bit trying to send calming thoughts at her new found cousin.

She jerked when a voice in her head snapped at her. "Get out of my mind. I'm here dammit. Leave me alone."

"You heard me," Tanya said, looking at Erin who had her eyes shut. Erin opened them at stared back.

"Leave me alone," Erin said aloud.

"We were just trying to help," Tanya said contritely. "We needed you and you were confused."

"We?" Erin snarled. "You and who else?"

"Er – Elisabeth. We are both cousins."

"Well, tell her to keep away too." Erin turned her head away, closed her eyes and ignored all further attempts at conversation.

Rowan gestured for Tanya to leave, and then went to perch on the end of Erin's bed.

"What upset you? Was it just that Tanya looked like the face in your dreams?"

He thought Erin wouldn't answer.

"I did think it was her, at first. And I was afraid those creatures were around here and likely to come for me."

"At first? Then what?"

"Her voice. Her accent. It sounded just like my mother. She's dead. She killed herself because of what I had done."

"Ah," Rowan breathed. "I do not think that all the blame is yours. But you can't change things. However, at the time, you were trying to help others and if she could have known that – it might have been different."

Erin shook her head. "I saved them – those foreigners, but Gerry died. My mother died. My father hates me. I destroy what is close to me. I dare not try to help this Wanda."

Rowan seemed to change the subject. "Wanda told me that she had felt her mother's illness – felt her die." Erin turned to stare at him. He continued. "She turned to anti-social behaviour when she felt herself becoming sick. It was her way of fighting it. I wondered if you were the same - if you sensed your mother's sickness."

"Dad said – my being around – once I was a teenager – made mum worse. I had to move out. I thought they hated me. I thought it was my fault."

"And..." Rowan prompted.

"And I started hacking Dad's computer. I did it to feel I was getting back at him. But when I lost myself in cyberspace, I forgot them."

"When did you start feeling emotions?" Rowan asked. He tried to make it sound like an everyday matter.

"When I was a teenager," Erin said. "I thought it was all my emotions."

"And since then?"

"It didn't go away. In that prison – I couldn't block it all out. There were too many minds, all broadcasting the darker emotions. I really wasn't pretending. The other place was worse. With the drugs they gave me. I could only mirror the emotions and confusion around me."

"I see." Rowan Wallace did understand. "Have you found anything that helps?"

Erin glanced at Rowan as she answered. "Yes. Computers – which have no emotions and...sex, which blots everything else out."

He grinned wryly. That candid statement explained a lot of what he had heard about her.

"It should not be too bad here. We redeployed all non-essential personnel."

"It's okay here," Erin agreed. "Is there anymore to eat?"

Rowan grinned and stood up. "I'll organise it. And I will also arrange time with the base psychologist."

"I hate shrinks."

"John is a top man at what he does. He has helped many battle scarred soldiers to recover."

"Do I have a choice?"

"No. But think of it this way, with his experience – his diagnosis will carry a lot of weight."

"And if he decides I am a dangerous, anti-social whatever, that needs to be locked up for the good of society…"

"Are you?" Rowan asked mildly.

Erin sighed. "I don't know anymore."

Rowan nodded, though Erin didn't see it. He was satisfied if Erin was questioning her motives. He doubted that she had done that before. Moral ethics aside, her sexual behaviour might shock a lot of people. If he could persuade the powers that her computing genius could be channelled into a proper usage…that she could be trusted to be patriotic…that he and Magnus Goldman could keep her mind challenged…what an asset she could be.

"We will see what happens," Rowan suggested. "For now, I will send the food message and ask about things to keep your mind busy. Should I send Tanya back?"

"No offense, but – not just yet."

Rowan accepted that and left the room.

The combination of the sedative and the food and her generally poor condition, caused Erin to sleep again. When she awoke, it was evening and for a long while she did not realise that there was someone dozing in the chair beside the bed. There was still enough light for Erin to study the blond woman's face. The bone structure resembled her own and that of the Russian girl she had met briefly.

"You must be Elisabeth," Erin said aloud and the woman woke suddenly.

"What?" the woman said, moving in the chair.

Erin repeated her comment.

"Yes, I am. Sorry." Elisabeth yawned. "Long day, but I wanted to meet you. At least you didn't start screaming at me."

Erin felt herself flushing red. "Who were you speaking to?"

"Well, Tanya of course. But Rowan Wallace let me sneak in. I knew I wouldn't be welcome at the tele-conference the powers here are having with Washington."

"What about? Me?" Erin asked.

"How would I know? Senator's daughters don't have a need to know. But

Jim Phillips was there. He came in with me. He told me you were here."

Erin suddenly realised she had forgotten him. What was her mind doing to her?

"I didn't realise he had gone off again." Then the details of the past few days returned. "Have they found Zara Russell yet?"

Elisabeth leapt to a conclusion. "Was that what Jim was doing?"

Erin nodded.

"Yes, the FBI went to a place and found her tied up. The men were long gone. At least that is what they said on the news."

"Tied up? Yeah, well, I suppose so."

"Why wouldn't she be?" Elisabeth asked.

"Because I hacked into the webcam of the so called abductors and had a glimpse of her walking around."

"Ah," Elisabeth said thoughtfully. "Now wouldn't that throw a spanner in things? I wouldn't have picked her to be involved with men like the news claimed those men were."

"Me either, to be honest. She's too prudish, goody-goody and stuck up," Erin summarised.

Elisabeth sorted in amusement. "I agree with stuck up. She gave me the 'my father is the secretary and yours is only a senator' routine." She was suddenly serious. "You know, I have to feel sorry for her father."

"What do you mean?"

"Even though I don't really like him, I suppose he is trying to do a good job and all, but he had a go at Dad a while back. He found out that Wanda was his daughter. My sister has a rather impressive criminal record but because she helped put the Franklin family in prison has been allowed free. Now it is his daughter doing illegal things."

"Serves him right," Erin muttered. "He's the one insisting that I be sent back to prison and left there to rot."

"I wouldn't be surprised if he thinks the same about Wanda," Elisabeth admitted. "Anyway, I am keeping out of the Zara Russell discussion. Let the FBI and police figure it out."

"Easy for you to say – but I think her father is still convinced I am involved with the men who took his daughter," Erin argued.

"Were you?"

"Not for years. Not since I left Uni," Erin admitted. "Except Nick Bosley was one of that crowd and he is the one that got me into the mess I am in."

"Interesting. I wonder if there is a connection."

"What? Hardly – except that those two wanted me to make them rich – like Nick was until he got caught."

"Could Nick have done the things by himself?" Elisabeth asked.

"No."

"Well, he was using you. These two were trying to use you."

"Manipulate me," Erin hissed. "Nick did that. Yes, it's similar. Those two who had Zara – were trying to make people think I was involved and trying to misdirect the police. And..." She shook her head.

"What?"

"Never mind," Erin muttered. "Just say that it took those two bumbling idiots to make me realise how people have been manipulating me for years."

Elisabeth saw the flow of emotions on Erin's face. "Harrison Franklin did that to Wanda – but she let him."

"Well, I guess, I let them too. But no more! Did Wanda get to that point too?"

Elisabeth nodded.

They both fell silent, neither feeling the need to make further conversation.

"I should apologise to Tanya," Erin said finally. "I wasn't myself."

"I think she knows that," Elisabeth assured her. "It must have been a shock, seeing her."

"It was more than that. She spoke like my mother...who overdosed a few months ago."

Elisabeth reached out and took Erin's hand. "I am glad you got here safely. And when Rowan lets you out of here there is an extra bed in the cottage they gave us to use."

Chapter 10

Erin wasn't sleeping well. It wasn't the bed for that was better than the one in the infirmary. Nor was it the company for she had to admit she was feeling comfortable with her newly discovered cousins. They were both noticeably non-critical about her past activities. Also, Elisabeth was an unusually calm presence even if Tanya was a jittery one.

Even while awake at night, Erin felt the 'dreams' in her mind. And they had started to be more alarming again. She spent much of the night awake, trying to banish the dream by occupying her mind with mathematical progressions.

She was aware of Elisabeth moaning softly in her sleep. Perhaps she was having bad dreams too. Maybe it was not surprising if she was a full sister to the Wanda person.

That made her recall what her cousins had told her – about how they had traced her. That they had sensed her panic/fear/confusion in much the same way as it felt that Wanda's emotions could be felt by herself.

Too much had been happening to herself for her to be able to really consider that.

Now, in the quiet of the night – with all the nearby people asleep or concentrating on guarding the base – the realisation of what it meant made her shiver.

She had accepted that she sensed her mother's erratic emotions but had considered that be more like a subtle reading of her body language. But with her cousins - she had heard their thoughts in her mind. There was no doubt of it. The logic loving part of her mind wanted to deny it – to prove psychic powers could not exist.

Elisabeth cried out in her sleep and Erin got out of bed to wake her.

Yet Elisabeth was awake and sobbing quietly. Erin went and hugged her, wordlessly.

"I felt I could almost reach her."

"I thought you were dreaming," Erin told her.

"No, I was trying to call her with my mind. We have always been able to know what the other as doing," Elisabeth said in a small fearful voice.

Erin thought of the horror images trying to invade her own mind and contrasted them to the sense of innocence about Elisabeth.

"Right now, you don't want to know."

"Why?" Elisabeth demanded urgently.

"You don't," Erin insisted.

"I do! I promised her I would be here for her. All the time she was in prison, when horrid things were done to her – I was there. I shared it with her – helped her."

Not so innocent, Erin realised.

"Even if she is killing living creatures?" Erin said softly. "Murdering them."

Erin felt Elisabeth shudder. "Yes."

Erin sensed Tanya joining them on the other side of Elisabeth. They joined in a three way hug and the sense of Wanda grew so strong it was almost like they were there sharing her desperation and the sickness at the killing.

"Wanda?" Erin heard Elisabeth's mind voice.

"Lishka?" She heard, and sensed desperate hope. "I'm here. We're here. What can we do?"

"I don't know," the desperate thought came to them. "I can't see in this darkness. I can't find my way out. I have been wandering for days."

Some of her memory of the darkness seemed to seep into Erin's mind, even as she tried to block out the contact that so elated her cousins. With the emotion it was hard to think. Yet Erin seemed to know where Wanda had moved in that darkness – even without her unmet cousin thinking consciously of it.

The memory of her movements began to form a pattern – began to take on a logic – like a circuit diagram, like the pathways of a computer – tantalisingly familiar.

Something wrenched Wanda's mind to a different problem – the warning of danger. Another alien was stalking her – no stalking Wanda. Erin knew she was about to kill again.

Erin moved deliberately away from Elisabeth – breaking the link.

Tanya protested.

"I wonder if our mothers could do this," Erin said to distract her cousins.

"No," Elisabeth forced herself to say. "They were split up soon after birth. I don't know if they knew each other existed."

Tanya made a sound like a sigh. "I think my mother was searching for someone. She spoke to many foreigners. I think that was why they arrested her. I think they thought she was a spy or traitor."

"I don't remember my mother," Elisabeth said. "But from what we learnt, once she came here and met my father, she didn't seem to be looking for anyone. I think she just wanted to be loved. What about yours Erin?"

"I don't know. I think she only cared about herself. She was jealous of my father's affection and begrudged what he gave to me – as if I would take him from her."

"My mother died a couple of years ago, September," Tanya said sadly. "Just before I came here."

Erin shivered. Her mother's major blow-up had come about then. "I am cold and tired," she said. "I think we should all try to get back to sleep."

The others agreed, but Erin thought none of them probably would.

Erin sat in the deserted mess hall eating a second breakfast while waiting for it to be time for her appointment with the base psychologist, John Stradbroke.

The appointment had been made by Rowan Wallace which was the only reason she had agreed to go and see him. She liked the brilliant doctor, and he really seemed to care about her – in spite of her crimes. She hoped he would be an ally against his friend Goldman – whom she still feared.

The lack of lots of minds around her was relaxing. Jim, it seemed had indeed been able to have the base evacuated. She didn't know why she was so important. Well, in terms of getting this Wanda back and the others, yes, but really, why coddle her and send nearly everyone away?

Secrecy? About her? Erin snorted at the idea.

"What's funny?" Tanya asked from behind her.

"Nothing really," Erin claimed. "I thought you were jogging?"

"I was," Tanya admitted. "But General Addison has put guards on this quadrant of the base and I am not allowed to go all the way around."

"How long has that been happening?" Erin asked. "Since I got here?"

"About then," Tanya agreed. "Elisabeth thinks that now you are up and about we will be expected to try and get Wanda back."

"Where is Elisabeth?" Erin asked between mouthfuls of cereal liberally sprinkled with sugar.

"In the gym, doing exercises. If she doesn't keep exercising every day, she could get sick."

"Oh. I have to see the psych guy later," Erin said.

"He's not bad," Tanya told her.

"I don't like shrinks of any kind," Erin said. "I can imagine what he will think if I told him I heard voices in my head telling me to escape from where I was."

"I don't think he will think you crazy," Tanya assured her. "Wanda and I proved we could think at each other and that she could reach Elisabeth from here to Los Angeles."

A sense of unreality invaded Erin's mind. "I just wish that we can find where ever it is on Earth that Wanda is so they can send someone to get her and let me go."

Erin knew they wouldn't let her go, but she might be able to forget the freaky things she was hearing. But they would send her back to prison. That thought paralysed her mind and she didn't react to what Tanya was saying. She pushed the rest of the cereal away and stood up. "I have to go."

She was at the door of the mess hall when the sense of Tanya's words got to her.

"What do you mean - it isn't that simple? That she is not on Earth."

Tanya had started to follow Erin, but stopped when her cousin swung around.

"If she is dead – we can't bring her back. And if she is a ghost, then so are you," Erin said loudly.

"No, not dead. On another world," Tanya blurted.

Erin stared at her. "I am not crazy. You are!" She turned again and hurried away.

Rowan Wallace found her sitting on the bed in the infirmary, hugging her knees. It was half an hour after she should have been seeing Stradbroke. He notified the psychologist before letting Erin know he had found her.

Erin expected anger or sharp words about not going to her appointment. Instead, Rowan simply said, "Oh. Here you are. We have been looking for you."

Erin turned away; well aware she had not made a good impression by running off.

"So, you don't share the pet theory of Elisabeth and Tanya that Wanda isn't on Earth?"

She returned her gaze to watch Wallace and waited for him to continue.

"You are not the only one," Wallace assured her. "The Secretary flatly refuses to consider it."

"Do you?" Erin challenged.

"I'm keeping an open mind," Rowan admitted. "Perhaps you could come over to John's office and look at some film, and listen to some tape. Of Wanda."

Erin agreed, but only because she wanted to see if the person in her head really was Wanda.

Erin felt herself go cold all over, as she listened to the tape taken when Wanda was under hypnosis.

Aliens? This was getting weirder and weirder.

The tape finished and Rowan told her some of what Tanya and Elisabeth had discovered. To her mind, it did not prove that aliens had existed here, bred here, on Earth. Nor that Wanda Martin wasn't still on Earth. She said as much.

Then Rowan darkened the room and showed her the security tape showing Wanda, disappearing and reappearing.

"I can think of lots of ways that could be faked" Erin blurted.

"In real time?" Rowan asked.

"Several," Erin amended. "I suppose your experts went over the film?"

"Thoroughly," Rowan assured her. He went on to explain where Wanda had been found after she had disappeared one night.

That fact alone convinced her, but she did not want to be convinced. As Erin mulled over what Rowan had told her, a call came for Wallace.

"Erin, you and John can talk this over – now, if you would. John will organise a NS-16 form."

Something in Rowan's manner made Erin agree to his implied command. As the door closed behind her, she heard him greeting "Mr Secretary" and "Magnus."

Stradbroke explained first what the paperwork was for and Erin did not object to not discussing this totally insane situation with other people. It did not mean she couldn't talk about it to Stradbroke. That is what he talked about next before moving to other subjects.

Erin slipped back to the house after the two hour session – mentally and emotionally worn out. A short time later, Tanya brought over a covered tray. "I thought you could use this," she said.

"Yes, thanks," Erin told her.

"He's thorough," Tanya commented, without asking questions. "And you had best stay out of sight. The Secretary is here having a meeting with Dr Wallace and the others."

"Does he know I am here?"

Tanya shrugged.

Much later, Jim Phillips knocked and came in. He greeted Tanya and Elisabeth but went over to Erin.

"Stan Russell would like to talk to you."

"As Zara Russell's father or the Secretary?" Erin asked with a grimace.

"I think the first, and possibly that will influence the second," Jim warned her. "I think this is a good idea."

"All right," Erin agreed dubiously, and went to check her appearance.

Erin felt Russell's scrutiny as soon as she walked into the room. She felt also, his antipathy until he really took in what he saw. Then his emotion turned to uncertainty. She recalled her business training, took the initiative.

"Good afternoon, Mr Russell. I'm Erin Mason and I am glad your daughter was found safe."

Russell scowled, but he tried to sound civil. "I am told your help made it possible."

"I was happy to do it, Sir," Erin tried to make him feel her sincerity. "And I was pissed off at those two for involving me. I will admit I never really like Zara at Uni, but she didn't deserve to be used by them either."

"I believe you know those men quite well," Russell asked her.

"Used to, yeah," Erin admitted. "Have they been caught?"

"Yes," Russell admitted. "But they are refusing to talk. Why do you think they wanted you?"

"I hadn't had anything to do with them since I left Uni, but Nick Bosley was one of that group too. I expect they wanted to use me again to – perhaps to get rich."

"So is that your story? They used you?" Russell challenged her.

"I think they were – but back then I thought I was using them."

"Really?" Russell was sceptical.

"Yes, really. But this – I can't understand why they thought you would free me for them. From what Jim told me – I had got out of where I was a week before Zara disappeared."

"Those two men have only made one statement – that it was your idea," Russell told her coldly.

"No!" Erin retorted. "When do they say I had this idea?"

"They haven't said anything else," Russell admitted, impressed by the fact that Erin kept meeting his gaze.

"Did Zara overhear anything significant?" Erin asked. She wondered if he had been shown the webcam.

"She is under sedation," Russell said with a slight tensing of face muscles.

Erin suddenly blurted, "Don't be angry with her, Sir."

His expression became more rigid. Erin was sure he knew of the webcam shot.

"Sir, you don't have to believe me in this, but these men thought that they could get me to do something. I think it was to work on some secret program to fix it up so they could sell it and get rich. They knew me well enough to know I like a computing challenge. Once I might have been tempted but..."

Russell's expression indicated that whatever she said he wouldn't believe it.

"Go on, Erin," Jim encouraged.

Erin shook her head. It would be no use.

"No, do go on," Russell insisted.

"Well, their approach was exactly like Nick used. He got me thinking of it only as a computing challenge and then got me too involved to back out. When I tried, he threatened to tell people about some things I'd done. And somehow, I found myself doing what he wanted, but really only covering his tracks."

"And what might this have to do with Zara?"

"It is possible they got her involved without her realising what she was getting into. When she got reluctant, threatened to reveal something questionable she'd done. Perhaps she didn't want it to come out and reflect badly on you."

Erin studied Russell's expression and then looked away. She was beginning to feel an unwanted pressure on her mind.

"Miss Mason," Russell spoke. Erin didn't look around. She couldn't. She felt exactly has she had in the car coming here.

Russell repeated his words more sharply. He got Erin's attention.

"I hope you realise that you will not be permitted to stay here. You will be going back to the Washington Women's Prison. And your sentence will be extended because you escaped."

Chapter 11

Erin shuddered involuntarily and began to feel very weak. "I don't know how I got out and I didn't aim to come here. I know I am a prisoner here but the people here seem to think I can help find your Colonel Aldrin and my cousin."

"And can you?" Russell asked her.

Erin turned to face him. "I think they are all crazy."

Erin walked quickly from the room and into the hands of John Stradbroke.

"Come to my office, this way," Stradbroke urged.

"I need air," Erin protested, feeling awful.

"Tanya and Elisabeth are there," Stradbroke continued to urge her on.

"This is crazy," Erin insisted, trying to get free, but too weak to struggle much.

Jim excused himself as soon as he had reminded Russell that Erin was currently his responsibility. He added that if his daughter had chosen to associate with unsuitable people, then he shouldn't take his anger out on Erin Mason.

Russell glared at Jim Phillips but didn't retort. Instead he let General Addison lead him to where refreshments were prepared for him.

Erin stumbled between Jim Phillips and John Stradbroke, vaguely hearing the psychologist explaining, "Tanya and Elisabeth are nearly hysterical. They came to me and said I had to get Erin, now."

"Not again," Erin moaned. "Not again."

She could not see. It was like she had gone blind. The sense of terror pressured her mind. She seemed to be having trouble breathing.

She entered Stradbroke's office where it seemed stiflingly hot.

The hysteria of her cousins was like a spear in her mind, she began to scream.

Rowan Wallace arrived moments later, took in the scene, and shepherded Tanya and Elisabeth out of the room; neither wanted to leave.

"Get control of yourselves," he told them sharply. "When you have, then you can go back in."

Elisabeth removed a bracelet from her wrist and put it in her pocket. Then she began taking deep breaths. Tanya kept babbling away in a language Elisabeth only partly understood. She stopped when Elisabeth shook her.

"So, what is the matter?" Rowan asked more gently.

Elisabeth gulped. "It's Wanda. They…I think they are torturing her. I can feel it, but I can't help her, like I always could before. I had this bracelet on. The one I found at the Cassidy place and she felt me in her mind, but threw me out."

"So what do you think Erin can do?" Rowan asked, urgently.

Elisabeth glanced at Tanya before speaking. "I don't know, but together, last night, we could speak to her. I need to do that."

Rowan allowed the two women to return to Stradbroke's office, only to see Erin being given air through a face mask and lying on the floor.

Erin pushed the mask aside when her cousins returned and closed her eyes, using mathematical problems to calm herself. She wondered why she had never tried it before. It took her mind right away from the volatile emotions still emanating from her cousins. She would have to give at least an outward impression of calm and her business training helped her. She stood up unsteadily.

Elisabeth sensed what she was doing and recalled how her father had explained about a poker face and practiced that. Tanya saw her cousins acting calm and she relaxed.

Erin reached out and clasped hands with her cousins, joining as she had the previous night. Elisabeth momentarily released one hand to reach into her pocket for the bracelet. When she had it on, it brushed against her and she felt a jolt. Suddenly, it was like she was inside Wanda's skin – feeling everything she felt. That was how she realised that the incoherent behaviour of her cousins mirrored Wanda's thoughts.

Erin closed her eyes. The logical part of her mind told her that the pain was not hers. That same part of her said, "I've had enough."

Enough of being used, pushed around, locked up, manipulated, having emotions shoved in her face. Anger blossomed in her mind, overcoming the sense of the pain.

Elisabeth and Tanya felt the anger, as if it were directed at them. It had the effect of a slap in the face and stopped their frantic thoughts.

Far away, the sense of Wanda reacted to the anger. "Why? What have I done to you?"

Erin ignored the voice and concentrated on damping the pain she felt. It was not hers; she should not be feeling it.

"Wanda, you are not alone," Elisabeth and Tanya sent together.

"I am," a mental voice wailed. Memories of terror and despair filled their minds, but Erin ruthlessly blanked them with memories of drugged oblivion.

Erin spoke aloud for Elisabeth to hear. "Tell her they are playing mind games with her. The darkness is a mind game. Tell her." She heard the mental message and felt Wanda's reaction. "Tell her she is the rat in the maze. Except that she is smart enough to work out the plan – if she could see."

Hope! Erin sensed it. "Tell her to clear her mind." When she felt Wanda was calmer, she imaged the view she had sensed from the previous contact. The plan of the maze.

"Where is she?" Elisabeth asked. She was seeing the maze through Wanda's mind.

"It doesn't matter," Erin told her. "If she 'walks' to the centre, and then keeps following the left hand wall, she will come to the way out. Warn her that there are life forms guarding the portal."

The sense of Wanda vanished for a moment – then returned more confident. Erin sensed a roar of rage from an alien mind. "Tell her that they have lost her for the moment."

Elisabeth and Tanya tried to hold a fading contact. It was a while before they realised that the hand they gripped was limp and Erin was no longer standing.

Erin roused some hours later, once again in the infirmary with a drip in her arm. This time she also felt the pressure on her finger of a monitor of some kind. On her wrist, she felt an unfamiliar presence of a bracelet. Elisabeth must have slipped it on to her. She tried to remove it but it seemed stuck to her skin.

Lying flat seemed like the only thing she felt like doing. Not even the mixture of agitation, anger and anxiety that she could sense seemed to affect her. She had no strength at all. None of the emotions seemed close and she could hear no sounds of people in the room with her. It relieved one worry. She could not be in too bad a way even if she was hooked up to things. And no doubt, they had ways to watch her. Zara Russell's father really hated her and he wouldn't want her to have any chance to escape.

Erin finally realised why she seemed so unaffected by the anger. She recognised the floating effect of a sedative drug. Only a mild dose, for she could still think, though her mind wandered from subject to subject. The sedative let her think calmly about the things that might be hallucinations that she had been seeing, hearing, and doing. Nothing like the mathematical beauty of computers, the perfect logic of an electric circuit.

The contrast between that and the psychic manifestations made her feel like two people. The sedative stopped her switching from one to the other and in spite of it she couldn't stop thinking she was really, truly going mad. That they would find out and keep her locked up. She could stay calm while thinking of being locked up for a long time but she felt her eyes watering at the hopelessness of it. Then she began to think of the child within her, of the kind of life it would have. Would her father love her child if she couldn't be with it? Would the child be better off dying before birth? A vague memory surfaced of Rowan Wallace telling someone that if Erin was exhausted like this much more – the child would be at risk. A surge of protectiveness filled her. That child was all she had left of Gerry, who had loved her with all her faults. She wanted this child. She would do nothing more to risk it.

The first thing she needed to do was eat.

Erin was allowed to leave the infirmary next morning but only if she wore a bio-monitor of a hush-hush kind.

"It will alert us if you get ill," Rowan told her. "You really should still be resting, and eating."

Erin had promised to do both and had returned to the house which she had been sharing with Elisabeth and Tanya. However, she only stayed long enough to gather her few possessions before heading out to go to another of the unassigned cottages.

"No offence," she apologised to her cousins, "But you two feel as twitchy as dying blowflies and I need to rest."

They had conceded, reluctantly.

But Erin herself was too twitchy to rest. She put it down to the sense of being watched, and not being trusted. And perhaps from knowing that people wanted her back in jail without a key to let her out. She wished the Secretary would go back to Washington. He really made her angry, particularly as he had issued further restrictions on where she was allowed to go and it was feeling like she was in prison.

Tanya found Jim Phillips and Elisabeth found Rowan Wallace in the early hours of the following morning.

"Something is going to happen," Tanya told Jim. She was wild eyed; half dressed in pyjamas, half in a hastily donned pair of jeans. "Where is Erin? We can't find her."

Elisabeth found Rowan Wallace in General Addison's office, talking with Magnus Goldman, who had flown in late the previous night. Stan Russell was also in the room. She was glad she had put a track suit over her night clothes. He would not be impressed by a distraught senator's daughter in pyjamas.

"Sir, we can't find Erin and we really need to."

Russell began his tirade about Erin, likened her behaviour to Wanda's, and wasn't describing either in diplomatic terms.

Goldman silenced him. "Mr Secretary, you are needed in Washington. The helicopter is on the way to take you to the airport. If you wait here you will be summoned."

Goldman followed Addison to a room off his office where the base security was overseen. Wallace spoke to Elisabeth, who tried to be clear but even to herself, sounded to be raving.

"Something is going to happen. I don't know what. It's Wanda – I feel her. But I can't hear her. We need Erin."

"Wait here," Wallace ordered, and he followed Goldman into the security office. He could be heard saying, "Check for the bio-monitor."

Jim arrived soon after with Tanya in his wake. He had been asleep and had dressed hastily. They both greeted Elisabeth, and then heard Russell bellow, "How did she get into the high security section? Send someone to bring her here."

Jim slipped into the room and saw where the light flashing indicated Erin's position.

"Send a squad in there," Russell demanded. He made a strangled sound when Addison told him that the base only had a skeleton staff and those on duty could not leave their posts. He would rouse the off duty staff. He set the klaxons off throughout the base.

Erin heard the noise but ignored it. She sat on a patch of dirt, huddled into a small ball – fighting a battle to ignore the voice in her head, and the pressure for her to do something.

"No! Not again. You will kill my baby," Erin screamed in her head.

The pressure increased. Erin knew she could not resist it much longer, but the fear for her child had become paramount. Already, the pressure had forced her from her cabin, through three security gates that had been criminally easy to get through. The voice in her head had told her exactly where to go and the numbers to use on the keypads to get there. Once in the restricted area the voice and the pressure had made her go to this isolated corner and hunt around in the dark for some trinket that the voice knew about and needed.

"I dropped my watch there," the voice had told her. "I need you to put it on."

Erin had protested and tried to ignore the voice, but the watch was now on her wrist – the one not wearing the bracelet.

"I have to do this," the voice was currently saying, trying to force Erin to listen and obey.

"Why do you want to kill my baby?" Erin pleaded.

"Erin! Erin, I don't, but I need your help. That watch is old, very old. It was my mother's, and I think it will let you get energy from the aura of the Earth. I need the bracelet, it belongs to this world. I think it will let me get energy from the aura of Korvu. Then I will be less likely to hurt you unwittingly."

"No! Leave me alone."

The voice got desperate – she sensed it – but the words were almost calm. "They know I'm in here. They know I know their secrets, their weaknesses. If they find me again, they will kill me. I have to get out or thousands more will die. Touch the watch to the ground and think of getting strong."

There was a lessening of the desperation when Erin touched the watch to the ground. She felt herself stop trembling with bone deep fatigue.

"It is going to work," the mind voice sounded exultant. "Where are you? At the base? Show me where you are."

Erin opened her eyes – lights were on everywhere and the space in front of her was well lit.

"Please, don't fight me," the voice pleaded, as Erin baulked at what she knew was going to happen next.

A hazy ghost like outline formed in front of her, and it turned around and crouched down. Erin felt a fierce cramping in her belly and moved her hand over it. The ethereal figure reached out and grabbed the wrist with the bracelet. The object, which had until now clung to her skin, fell loosely and the ghost figure moved it along to her fingers and took it. Then the ghost figure stepped back. "I'm sorry," it seemed to say, as the voice in her head. "But you are the only one I can reach and you are so far away."

The figure faded into the brilliance of the lights. Erin suddenly lost every bit of food left in her stomach. The cramping pain continued, until Erin curled into a tighter ball. It was only luck that kept the watch touching the ground.

When Jim reached her, moments ahead of the hastily roused marines, she was almost bloodless in colour, had tears streaming down her face and was as limp as a fabric dummy.

Chapter 12

Magnus Goldman, Jim Phillips, Rowan Wallace and General Addison all stared at the security footage for the fifth time. Not one of them wanted to verbalise what they had seen.

As soon as Erin had been located, additional security devices had been activated in her area. Infra-red cameras had picked up a presence suddenly appearing in front of Erin. Visuals had shown Erin handing something to someone seen only by infra-red, and that had disappeared a short time later. Then Erin being sick and curling into a ball.

They had requested tapes from various cameras from just prior to the alarm being raised.

Passive IR sensors in Erin's cottage placed her there seconds before she appeared in a visual at the first of three security gates. It showed her pressing the keys on the lock pad. The new cameras in the garden had shown her scrabbling around and finding something.

What none of them spoke of was the certainty that Erin had 'walked' from inside her cottage to the first of the fences in the same way that Wanda had – even if she did not realise it.

Erin had wanted to protest when Jim had pried her fingers out of the dirt, but she was still too weak. Yet clinging to the earth had stopped the spinning and drawn warmth into her centre where her child lay dreaming.

The feeling of spinning had begun again as soon as Jim carried her. Erin thought about what Wanda had said – that the watch might help her draw energy from the aura of the earth – whatever that was. She couldn't see it or feel it, unless it was that feeling of drifting...

Elisabeth and Tanya watched as Jim placed Erin on a stretcher that was then slid into a truck by two marines. The truck roared back towards the infirmary building.

Tanya reached for her cousin's mind. "She seems to be fading out," she said, worried.

"Erin!" Elisabeth called mentally.

"Leave me alone," was the almost dreamlike response.

The voices shattered the feeling of relaxation. Erin was jolted back to awareness, irritated by the voices, and wanting the felling of relaxation to return. Her chest hurt, her head ached.

"Leave me alone," Erin said, or thought she said.

"Vital signs are stabilising," Erin heard. To quieten the voices she began to count by threes.

Jim walked over to Tanya and Elisabeth as they sat, slowly eating a meal prepared in the base canteen.

"How is she," Elisabeth blurted.

Jim sat down. "She will be fine – if she rests, eats and doesn't try to do anything," he assured them. "And her baby is fine too."

Elisabeth let out a sigh of relief. "It was meant to be me," she said. "I promised Wanda I would be here for her. It should have been me."

"Does it matter?" Jim asked quietly. "If between you we get Wanda, David and Stev back."

"It matters to me. Erin is pregnant. I would never forgive myself if she loses the baby."

"You can't blame yourself," Jim stressed. "Nor can you blame Wanda. We have to accept what is and be glad of the contact we have."

"When can we see Erin?" Tanya asked. "Dr Wallace said we can't visit."

"She needs rest and quiet for now," Jim confirmed. "They had to resuscitate her twice and they want to keep monitoring her."

Erin stirred, woke and lay still, realising that yet again, she was in the infirmary. But the silence was a relief, both mental and physical silence – well except for the muted beeping of the monitoring machines. She had no desire to move as all her muscles felt like lead weights on her bones.

Sometime later a nurse walked into her line of view and then to the end of her bed. When she lifted Erin's wrist, she realised her patient was awake.

"Awake, I see," she commented.

"Yes," Erin tried to say but the result was a barely audible croak.

The nurse finished taking Erin's pulse and then offered her water from a glass with a straw.

"Thanks," Erin managed to say. Then she saw the watch she had found, sitting on the table next to her.

"Watch," Erin asked.

"There is a clock on the wall," the nurse commented.

"Too hard to move," Erin managed to say.

Without comment, the nurse reached for the watch and helped her put it on.

"I wound it up for you and reset the time," the nurse told her. "It's an old one isn't it?"

Erin nodded.

"Now, do you think you might stay awake long enough to eat something?"

"Try," Erin promised.

"Good. Then you can have your medication and you will probably sleep again. You need rest and food."

Erin made no answer to that comment, but her stomach growled at the mention of food.

When the nurse had gone and she was alone again, Erin realised that part of the way she felt was familiar. The blankness in her mind and the lethargy was from being drugged. Part of her was angry, part relieved not to be sensing emotions – or the thoughts of her cousins. Only a tiny fraction of her conscience was worried that she was not hearing Wanda. She, Erin, had done enough, hadn't she?"

When the food tray arrived, Erin woke from a light doze and realised that she wasn't feeling quite as leaden as before. She assumed it was the drugs wearing off. Just how long had she been asleep anyway?

The food, though it was only pureed vegetables, made her feel more alert. But by the time she finished eating her arm was cramping with tiredness.

She looked at her watch and saw it was seven o'clock. She assumed it was evening, and was proved right when the nurse wheeled in a portable TV which she tuned to a satellite TV news channel before placing the TV remote control near Erin's hand.

Erin watched the news for a while, feeling detached from all events – until she took in the mention of Zara Russell and forced her mind to concentrate.

The gist of the news item, besides rehashing past events, was that Zara Russell was not to be charged for helping to fake her abduction – and thanks to her information and information from an unnamed source – several men had been arrested. Apart from the two she had stayed with, one was the person Erin had suggested as being the owner of the website Zara's abductors had used. The other was claimed to be a foreign agent.

The news presenter went on to mention that some stolen state secrets had been recovered and a spy ring broken.

Erin felt a trace of anger. Zara Russell was luckier than she deserved to be – luckier than Erin herself had been.

"Lucky bitch," Erin said aloud, not realising that she was no longer alone.

"That may be a matter of opinion," Rowan Wallace answered her comment. "She has to attend counselling. She has lost a lot of influential friends and she is on a kind of probation for two years. Not to mention, she has to live with her father."

"Whatever," Erin replied. "Do you have to drug me again?"

Rowan considered. "Yes, for a while, until you are more rested and restored. How are you feeling?"

"I am not hearing things that normal people can't, but I feel like spread fertiliser and I don't like the sluggish feeling when I try to think."

"If you can get up and walk around, that should help the sluggish feeling. I will reduce the dose a bit. Do you want visitors?"

"No," Erin said, but was expecting to be overruled by Wallace.

"As I expected," Rowan agreed. "Your cousins have been asking about you. They are fidgeting like fleas but since they aren't also hysterical – I will presume that Wanda, wherever she is – is fine for now. Let me know if you change your mind."

When Wallace had gone, Erin switched TV channels but found nothing to keep her attention, so she turned it off. She tried to concentrate on easing the sluggish feeling in her mind. She tried counting but soon realised she was even doing that wrong. She thought she would prefer to be outside but it was night now and would be getting cold out there. Besides she was hooked up to machines and drips. Maybe the next day?

Magnus Goldman listened to his friend report on his patient.

"Yes, it has been almost a week. I have reduced the medication to a minimum but she still says she is tired and has no energy. She doesn't want visitors and I am sure she is not hearing from Wanda. Her vital signs are improving, so I am expecting her to be feeling better than she is."

"Could she be foxing?" Goldman asked.

"Possibly," Rowan agreed. "But resting is what I want her to do, and she is beginning to eat very large meals."

"I am convinced that she is the key to getting Stev back," Goldman confided.

"And I believe that she thinks she has done enough. And I wouldn't be surprised if part of her reluctance to do more is because once Stev and the others are back she will be sent back to prison."

Goldman sighed. "I am working on the Secretary, but he is somewhat sensitive on the subject at the moment. He does not want to see the parallels between Erin Mason and his daughter."

"It is the differences that matter," Rowan reminded his friend. "Erin was operating longer and her crimes became public and provable. Zara is only suspected on the word of two criminals. But, saying that, Erin did a lot more than Zara to break up that spy ring and she has a genius we can use. Zara Russell is little more than a flighty socialite."

"What are you saying, old friend?"

"Not just me. Stradbroke agrees that Erin is refusing to help further because she doesn't want to return to prison. We think that if you want her to help further, she needs to have some hope. And she needs to keep her mind off the weird psychic things she has learnt about herself – which freak her out. When she isn't thinking of that, she eats hugely, which I think is an indication that she is still reacting to psychic stimuli – to prepare for the next need. At the other times she is tense, apathetic, not hungry and uncooperative."

Magnus considered that. "I have something that can give her a distracting challenge, and a chance to test her to Russell's satisfaction."

At the suggestion of Jim Phillips, Tanya and Elisabeth refrained from discussing Wanda and her situation with Erin. They were both upset by Erin's flat denial that anything extraordinary had happened. When Elisabeth had remarked about the absence of the bracelet, Erin simply said she had misplaced the bracelet and found the watch. She also insisted that her fainting fits and hallucinations were due to her poor physical condition and being pregnant.

So for the periods when Erin was ordered to take a break from the task Goldman had set for her, she sat with her cousins outside in the small garden near the infirmary and talked of their mothers and what they still wished they knew about them. No mention was made of likely alien antecedents.

They talked about their own growing up, and Elisabeth naturally included Wanda in her narration. Erin listened with interest as if she had never heard of Wanda before. They were becoming fast friends, and that Jim said, would be important. They needed to trust each other.

Finally, Tanya asked Erin what she was doing when she was working.

"I can't tell you much," Erin said truthfully. "Mr Goldman told me it was hush-hush but to see what I could make of it. Trouble is – I can't quite figure what it is meant to do. I need a computer with the program on – not just a print out."

"Ask him to let you use one," Elisabeth said logically. "Tanya and I are – that's how we did a lot of searching about our mothers."

"I am a different case," Erin said resentfully. "I am not to be allowed near one – or the internet or anything without supervision. I think it was Goldman who insisted on that."

"Ask him anyway," Tanya suggested with a sly look. "If you are doing a job for him – let him supervise you!"

Erin visibly shuddered. Goldman still overawed her. "He'll say no," she predicted. "Besides, he's too important to do that himself."

Tanya shrugged, and turned to Elisabeth. "Isn't it time you went and exercised – before you stiffen up?"

"Not yet," Elisabeth acknowledged. "Sitting out here in the sun – I am feeling great. Even Erin looks better."

Erin looked at Elisabeth in surprise. "You're right. I do feel better out here. It's not just being in the sun – the first time I came out it was threatening rain."

"Fresh air," was Tanya's opinion. "Not that I have noticed anything."

"That's because your dancing keeps you fit and healthy," Elisabeth decided. "Not like us sickies."

"You don't look sick," Erin protested.

"Not at the moment, thank the powers, but both Wanda and I have to keep active if we don't want to relapse."

She lapsed into silence, feeling the tug of her sister and not able to respond. After a bit, she said, "Perhaps we should do what Jim suggested – join the marine team hiking up the hill."

"What hike?" Tanya asked, although she did know.

"There is a marine team going to do an exercise – something about building an observation post. You should come, Erin, in case they need help with the electronics."

"As if they will let me! Anyway, they will have their own experts."

"Actually," Tanya broke in. "Most of the people who were here were sent off just before you came."

"Yes," Elisabeth added thoughtfully. "They must only have a skeleton crew here. Jim said he was thinking of going."

"I couldn't keep up with marines. I'm pregnant. And that is assuming they will let me."

"They won't be going fast," Elisabeth smiled faintly. "They will be carrying everything they need to build the post. Besides, most of them are good looking and single."

Elisabeth watched Erin whose expression suggested she was considering it. "Are you in Tanya?"

"It would be good to leave here for a bit. Did Jim really suggest it?"

She got an affirmative nod. "Yes then."

Tanya turned to Erin and explained, "I'm not usually allowed off the base either. I am not sure if it is they don't trust me or if they think agents of Russia will try to get me as a means to make my father go back."

"I thought it was just me," Erin said.

"No, it's not just you," Tanya sighed.

"In that case, I'm game if they let me go," Erin decided. A day of freedom appealed to her. "When are they going?"

"I will find out," Elisabeth promised, dashing off.

"I had better ask about that computer," Erin said, pushing herself up.

Chapter 13

Erin lost herself in the program that Goldman had downloaded onto the laptop. It had been a battle to get him to agree to her having the program on a computer. The laptop was a compromise. He told her that it could not connect to the internet.

She was so involved in the program that she ate the food she found beside her without knowing who had delivered it. It did not take her long to find the section of code causing the glitches that were causing concern to Goldman and had almost debugged it – when she paused it to open another window to do a search through the program.

It took her a moment to realise that the search had somehow jumped to the internet and that the page she saw was not a cached page.

Her fingers hovered over the keypad, her mind battling between the command, 'thou shalt not' and the opportunity to go on-line when no one knew about it.

There were things, personal things, she wanted to check on-line, but a deep rooted caution said, "Not on someone else's computer".

Closing her eyes to temptation, she exited the browser and deduced another method to check what she needed to check.

"She has eaten five platefuls of food," Tanya told Jim.

"And two jugs full of that horribly sweet energy drink Rowan concocted," Elisabeth added. "She never even saw us come in. I have never seen anyone so focussed. Are you sure she will open up to Wanda once we are up the hill?"

Jim smiled grimly. "If my reading of her is correct, we have the decks stacked in our favour. She wants to forget all the psychic stuff – this little project of Goldman's is doing that. He is very pleased with her work. And the pair of you manipulated her like experts. The hike idea is a big day out from supervision, even if she won't be alone. It will be like freedom to her. Mentioning the electronics was brilliant – she will be thinking about that and therefore be relaxed. They will let her help if need be, because only one of the team knows anything. Two are medics and the other three are merely extra hands."

"And she may not realise that the clearing where we are going is the one Wanda mentioned," Elisabeth added.

"Are you sure Wanda will try to return soon?" Jim asked. Both Tanya and Elisabeth nodded.

"Ok – we will head off tomorrow – after Goldman vets Erin's work. Actually, just in case, we will have the necessities for a camp. And I will talk to the marine team about possible reasons to delay."

Erin was elated. Goldman had praised her work and she sensed his sincerity. He hadn't promised to help her appeal her sentence, but, he had advised her to behave appropriately whilst on the hike, if she went off on her own, without permission she would be in bad trouble.

Erin did not need a definition of bad trouble. Jim had already spelt it out. The secretary's attitude had made it explicitly obvious. The fact that she should have been sent back to Washington under high security guard, was being quietly ignored. She had no illusions though that if she did decide to run off that the marines had orders to bring her back.

In spite of that, the prospect of the hike excited her as it was like a forbidden treat. It might be a long time before she could pretend to be free again. She squashed the idea of having to go back to prison, before it led her to think of the reason why she was still in California. She had managed to completely suppress the memory of having been driven there by another mind. Any time such thoughts began to intrude, she switched to considering the elegant programming of the work she had done for Goldman.

Twice on the drive to the foot of the hill, Elisabeth had to tell Erin to stop wriggling. Jim glanced in the rear-view mirror each time. He was driving them in a hired car, following the two army vehicles.

When Jim parked at the side of the road, Erin was the first one out and impatient to get going, and she objected to Jim's fussing to be sure her hiking pack was fitted properly and not too heavy for her. She missed the significant glances her cousins exchanged with Jim. All of them were wondering if Erin was reacting to the same sensations Tanya and Elisabeth were feeling.

The full group set off at an easy walking pace, until the track began to climb. The pace slowed, but the marines made no comment. Three led the way and the others followed behind Jim's group.

Tanya allowed herself to stay in-rapport with Erin's unguarded thoughts. She sensed when Erin relaxed the barrier she had built to block out emotions. Even with the base almost deserted, there were still over two dozen people there. Up on the hill, it was only nine and six of those were focussed on a mission of their own. Tanya felt it safe to relax her own barriers.

Elisabeth was trying to sense Wanda as she walked towards the clearing where Wanda had been drawn that night months ago.

Jim called a halt for a water break, but Erin didn't seem to hear him and kept walking, seeming to be lost in thought. He trotted after her and caught her gently. He did not expect the start of fear in her expression.

"Have a drink," he suggested, passing a bottle to her.

Erin took a drink, but her feet kept shuffling as if she needed to be off again. Jim made no comment, just continued to keep observing her involuntary body language.

Then Jim glanced at Elisabeth, already putting her pack back on and edging toward the path. He met Tanya's gaze, then moved his eyes onto Erin and back. She shrugged. She wasn't receiving anything.

"Tell me if you sense anything," Jim whispered to Tanya as they set off again.

Tanya tried to talk to Erin but her cousin just continued doggedly up the path, seeming to be focussed simply on getting to the top of the mountain and recalling complicated formulas in her mind.

The path widened again Elisabeth and Tanya quickened their pace to walk abreast with Erin. Just as she got there, Elisabeth put her foot down awkwardly on a protruding rock and had to grab Erin to keep her balance.

In that moment, with the pain in Elisabeth's ankle so powerful and close, her concentration on blocking other sensations weakened. Her barriers to emotions had been almost down, but she had still been blocking the thoughts she sometimes received with them.

"Open up your mind you stupid bitch," Tanya heard as clearly as if spoken. "I need you. I can't reach the others. We need to leave, now. That she-devil can't get to us…"

Erin slammed down a tight mental barrier – startling Tanya who had only heard it through Erin's mind. The thoughts that had to be from Wanda were cut of mid-sentence.

Tanya reached for Erin, but Erin shoved her away, unaware that there was a rocky down slope at the edge of the path. She stubbornly focussed on the path in front of her feet and kept moving up the track.

Tanya yelled out in pain as she began to slip down the hill. Erin sprang around, reacting to her pain, and moving to help her.

Jim held her back from the edge, and let two of the marines help Tanya. Fortunately she had not slipped far. It was too much. Erin dropped to the ground, hunched into a ball, hands over her ears in a futile attempt to block out the insistent mental voice. Her own arm throbbed, echoing the pain in Tanya's arm – that felt broken. She resisted Jim's attempt to get her to her feet.

"I can't do this. I can't!" Erin said to Jim. Elisabeth limped over.

"Erin, please, we are here to help. Wanda needs to come back. I can feel it. You have to help us to help her. Her, David and Stev – please."

Erin seemed to ignore Elisabeth but tears were streaming down her face. "I can't do this."

Elisabeth looked helplessly at Jim as the two marines carried Tanya up the slope to the path. One of the others had a field first aid kit ready.

Jim shrugged a shoulder at Tanya. Elisabeth took the hint and left Jim alone with Erin.

"What has you so freaked out? Are you hearing Wanda in your head?"

Erin took a deep breath and nodded.

"I see. The mind to mind thing does take some getting used to," Jim murmured, admitting his own sense of unreality.

"Can you hear her too?" Erin asked. "Right now?"

"No. It takes her a lot of effort to get through to me – but she has done it several times – and saved my life."

"I couldn't before, why now?"

"I don't know, but I suspect that desperation is fuelling her sending. I think you are receiving it with the emotion."

"She wants me to bring them home," Erin admitted to Jim. "I want to help – but I have no idea how to do it."

"And it is not logical, not mathematical or even believable," Jim murmured.

Erin said nothing, just stared off across the track.

"I have known Wanda for quite a long time. I found her again after she had become a highly skilled thief and infiltrator. Some said she was extremely amoral. This was when she had decided to be a witness against the Franklin family - which was a suicidal thing to do since she had been working faithfully for them for years. She – like you – drew a line at murder. She didn't expect to survive that treason, and purposefully did not ask for consideration or reduced sentence or to be put in witness protection. I think that same stubbornness is what is helping her to survive. I think, even then, she had latent psychic abilities."

Erin turned her head to listen to Jim.

"Then something happened. She claimed some alien being called her

– up here – and opened those latent talents. She began to hear everyone's thoughts, amongst other odd abilities. I think that whoever called her was also calling to anyone who was sensitive to him. Wanda was probably nearest and heard clearest.

"You are more of an empath, open to emotions. I think though that you blossomed even before Wanda, but you couldn't hear the thoughts and know what to do. That is where Tanya and Elisabeth come in. Three of you together, not just one."

"I'm a freak and she is a freak!"

"And most people would agree with you. I certainly hope there are not many, if any, others like Wanda around. Nothing would be secret. Because of the work she does for me, she has a level six security clearance. Her abilities are classified at the highest level of need to know. Only eight people, and that includes you now, know what she can do. It scares me. I am not surprised that it scares you."

"What can I do?' Erin pleaded.

"What Wanda had to do was find an analogy that would give her an image of how to control her power. I think you need to do the same. Hearing Wanda's voice in my head is like having a tiny microphone implant in my ear. It is tuned to Wanda's frequency, and only I can hear it."

"But they say she is on another planet!"

"Another planet? Another country? Another state – next door?" Jim shrugged. "Think of it as a transporter, like on that space fiction show. It does not exist in reality but it is believable in the context of the show. It needs someone at one end to operate it. You."

"But how?" Erin insisted.

Elisabeth had been listening and finally came over. "Erin, Wanda knows what to do. All she needs is a target to aim for, an anchor at this end, a line to follow to get here, you are not alone. Tanya and I are part of it. Those that helped her get there, know the place where we are going. They will help send her to us."

Jim sensed Erin tensing further. He remembered her talking about a clearing in the hills. Was she remembering that now?

"I will only believe it when I see them," Erin said, pushing herself up. "If all this is real – that will be very soon. I have been hearing her on and off for the last few days. I've tried to ignore it. She started up again back there. I blocked her out until Tanya tripped. I had finally thought it was safe to drop some of my mental shields. I reacted to her pain and couldn't concentrate.

She – Wanda – hit me with a mental thought to open up. Hell, I was wide open. She is in dire straits, Jim. She is with the others again, I think. And they are cornered. The aliens there know they were behind the native's successful fight and are after them. They are hiding, but the aliens will find them soon. Wanda has to try this, but she hasn't the help she had to get there – so it is just her. But she isn't telling the others that she doesn't think she is strong enough to bring them all back."

"What do you mean?" Elisabeth demanded, gripping Erin urgently.

"I sensed her saying – they will come back – not we will come back. Tonight when the rotation of that place and this is closest," Erin whispered.

Erin's face betrayed the wild eyed look Jim had seen before. She jerked loose from Elisabeth.

"Jim, we have to move," Elisabeth urged.

"No! You don't understand. Last time she tried it – for just her – I almost died."

"Just let's get to the clearing first," Elisabeth said, feigning calm. Erin had to come; she was the key to it all.

Erin began to stalk off, uphill. Jim gestured to two of the marines to follow her.

Tanya, pale but with her injured arm immobilised, walked unsteadily over to Jim. The remaining marines packed up the first aid gear or stood guard.

"She will do it, Jim," Tanya said quietly. "She is thinking very loudly, shouting...I'll do it damn you...well I won't repeat those words...but you will probably kill me."

Jim felt a lessening of tension. He had not been wrong. Erin did have a sense of responsibility and courage.

"Not courage, Jim," Tanya spoke, not realising she was answering Jim's thoughts. "Fatalism. She thinks it would be better to be dead than back in prison – or locked up for believing all this crap. And – I don't know who Gerry is – but she thinks that dead, she will be with him."

Chapter 14

Erin had found a fallen tree trunk to sit on and watch the marines begin to set up their observation post. They were erecting it at the edge of the clearing where they could overlook the valley below. She couldn't see the use of the military having a post here – unless it would also be used for fire spotting in the summer.

When the last of the marines arrived, assisting Elisabeth and Tanya, they set to in earnest. It amazed Erin how they had fit all they needed into six backpacks. The 'building', though, was really a large tent with a framework for solar collectors to charge the batteries of the equipment.

The whole works was coordinated from a laptop computer.

Erin lost interest in the marines and their mindless activity until she saw two of them selecting and cutting long slender branches to be slipped into a fabric envelope to make rough beds. She saw Tanya follow one of the marines into the post and stay there. She declined the offer of another to rest on, choosing to stay where she was. Later, she slipped down to sit on the ground and rest her back against the trunk. She fell asleep.

Elisabeth was not tired yet. She wandered around the clearing, looked inside the post and studied the changing pictures on the laptop; saw the beds and the small camp kitchen which already had water on to boil. She went back outside and saw two marines digging a trench and erecting a small tent over it.

She came upon Jim Phillips unexpectedly. He was talking on his mobile phone, but finished his call abruptly when he saw her.

"Sorry," Elisabeth apologised. "I didn't mean to creep up on you. Tanya is asleep in the tent, and Erin is almost asleep outside. I wondered where you were."

"Making sure everything is ready," Jim told her.

"And that the observation post is ready to watch us – and not the scenery," Elisabeth commented dryly.

Jim nodded slightly. "Orders," was all he said.

Elisabeth nodded, not needing an explanation.

"Medical help is available for when Wanda, David and Stev return. If it is needed."

"That makes me feel better," Elisabeth admitted. "Assuming they get back."

"Have you any feelings about that?" Jim asked.

Elisabeth shrugged. "Not really. Just a sense – probably only wild hope – that something will happen."

Jim nodded. "Will you sit where you can keep an eye on Erin?"

"Do you think she will run off?" Elisabeth asked, alarmed.

Jim glanced back at where Erin sat, seeming to be staring at nothing. He shrugged slightly. "Not if she keeps her nerve."

Elisabeth studied Erin for a while. "Alright, Jim. I will watch her for you."

Erin thought she was dreaming, and yet she was aware of the tree behind her. In her dream, she was following two men, strangers to her, though one seemed familiar from somewhere. They were traversing a dry arid area, approaching a cleft in a wall of sandstone. The men had weapons – guns of some kind, and knives strapped to their legs. Looking down, she saw she had a gun too, and knives strapped to her legs as well. They were like no knives she had ever seen.

In this dream, she heard a sound like a horn. Her view spun around. Approaching at a terrifying rate were three air vehicles. They were flying at a height of less than a metre from the ground. Someone yelled at her to run. She turned again, racing after one of the men. The second man stood and fired calmly at the approaching vehicles. An explosion behind her made her stumble, but she kept running. She was more prepared for the second explosion. Someone yelled, "Down!" and she fell immediately, and the third vehicle roared above her and something dropped onto her. She twisted in instinctive self-defence and saw one of the cowled aliens – claw-like hands reaching for her neck. In the corner of her eye, she saw one of the men fighting off two more aliens in a frenzy of fighting. The cowl of the alien on her came loose and she could clearly see the alien features. Her hand reached down for the knife strapped to her leg, felt it in her hand, and she plunged it into the unprotected groin of the alien. At almost the same moment, another knife slashed the alien's throat and sent a spurt of garish blue blood over her face. Where it touched her, it seemed to burn, but there was no time to stop, only to throw the alien aside and run again.

She reached the canyon, the man with her pointed to a cave, high up on one wall. She scrambled up a narrow trail after the other man.

In the relative safety of the darkness, she felt the man hug her tightly. All too soon he stopped as another figure blocked the light from the opening.

"I have removed our tracks," that person said. "I couldn't do much about the debris and bodies except bury them roughly. More of the bastards will be here shortly. If we are to get out of this, Wanda, you will have to try soon."

Erin felt as if she were the one swallowing bile. "I know," she seemed to be saying. "But I need some rest. And that blue stuff they bleed is burning my face."

"How long?" the almost familiar man asked harshly, as the other one began to dab at her face with a damp cloth.

"Until tonight," Erin felt herself say. "That is when contact is easiest. I think it is when our rotation here is closest to that at home."

"Very well," the man agreed. "Rest. David and I will give you that time."

The two men moved to the cave entrance. Erin watched them and felt overwhelming despair. For a moment she wanted to cry with helplessness.

The squawk of some bird roused Erin slightly. Not enough to fully rouse her, just enough to let her realise she was on Earth, not in some arid alien wasteland.

The realisation let her feel the odd sense of strength that had filled her since sitting on the ground and the sense of weakness from her dream. Once again she was Wanda, or sharing her mind.

"Wanda!" Erin thought strongly, but the dream self didn't hear it.

Erin closed her eyes and moved her right hand to close over the watch on her left wrist. In her mind, dream, her hand did the same, but covered the odd bracelet. She concentrated on the feeling of strength flowing into the watch and out through the bracelet. The dream self tensed, Erin pictured her hand reaching out to that dream self. "Peace," she tried to project. "We are here for you."

Suddenly Erin wanted to sob with desperation, but it wasn't her emotion. She herself would welcome death, but later, she had one last task to do. The dream self seemed to sense that and consider it.

"Yes." It was an agreement. Death would be welcome, but first she must get David and Stev back home. A moment of resolution, then the despair returned again and the thought, "I don't know if I can do this – I am not strong enough."

Erin shared that sense, but anger gave her a surge of energy. "Dammit, dream woman, if I have to do this, you can do it!"

Once again the dream self tensed.

"Relax," Erin sent – forcing her real self to do that. She returned to the image of the hand on the bracelet and the sense of strength. The dream self was not feeling it. The dream self brought her knees up to her chin and clasped them with hand joined to wrist. In the dream, Erin saw her feet had boots on, but her real ones were bare, though she did not remember removing her boots.

No sooner than she thought that, than the dream self took her boots off. And for a fleeting moment, Erin felt a slight pressure on top of the hand on the watch. It might have been a breeze…

Elisabeth took a packet of sandwiches and a bottle of water over to Erin.

"How are you," she asked. "Have you been asleep or staring at nothing?"

"I'm good," Erin told her cousin, once she was aware of her. "I'm feeling quite rested."

"Why have you got your shoes off? Aren't you afraid or getting insect bites or something?"

Erin shook her head. "I think I am getting stronger, by touching the Earth directly."

"That's crazy," Elisabeth blurted. Then she cursed herself for being tactless. "Sorry, but that makes no sense."

"No more than any of this," Erin told her. "But try it. We should get Tanya to try it too. I don't understand it, but – trust me."

Something about this new calmness in Erin, alerted Elisabeth, but it did not worry her. Almost as if the calmness was contagious. Elisabeth removed her boots and socks and sat next to and just touching Erin.

There was no sudden surge of energy, but after half an hour, she realised that she felt well. Better than she had felt for years, and peaceful.

She stood up and said, "I will get Tanya out here."

Elisabeth saw the signs of pain that Tanya was trying to hide, but did not mention it.

"Come out side and sit with Erin and me. I think you will begin to feel better."

Tanya glanced at the medic.

"Won't hurt you – just be careful of the arm. Let me know if you need more pain relief."

Elisabeth helped Tanya stand up. "My shoes," Tanya reminded her cousin.

"Leave them," Elisabeth directed. Tanya stared in surprise when she realised her cousin was barefoot.

"Trust me," Elisabeth said quietly, pulling on her cousin's good arm to get her moving.

The same sense of calm infected Tanya as she walked towards Erin. She sat down next to Erin so her sore arm would not be jostled. Elisabeth sat on the other side of Erin.

Tanya glanced at Erin and noticed the faraway look.

"Is she okay?" Tanya asked of Elisabeth.

"I think so," Elisabeth guessed. "Just sit back and relax. We need to be strong and rested."

A while later, Tanya spoke. "What is happening? My arm was throbbing, but now it has eased right off."

Erin answered. "It is the aura of the Earth."

"What?" came two voices at once.

"The aura. It knows what we need to do and it is giving us strength."

"And calm," Elisabeth added quietly.

Jim watched the three women and wondered what was happening.

"Major, are you recording everything?" Jim asked of the marine at the electronics monitors.

"Yes Sir," was the crisp reply. The man was too much of a professional to ask, "Why?"

Instead he asked, "Are you expecting any trouble?"

Jim shrugged. "No trouble and I am not expecting anything in particular. I am hoping that something will happen. Sorry, Major, I am not able to tell you anything more."

Jim moved away and took out his mobile phone to check if he had signal. He did. He left the tent and walked down the hill, far enough not to be overheard but close enough if he was needed. He rang Magnus Goldman, via the Rockwater base and reported events up until then.

"Yes," he answered in response to a question. "All sensors are working at optimal. I am told that a flea couldn't jump without being detected."

After several more questions and answers, Goldman had the final word.

"Everyone involved in this must return directly here to the base for debriefing. Call me as soon as there is a positive outcome so that I can call Washington."

Jim agreed and ended the call. He walked slowly back up the trail. The only person in the group that he was not completely sure of was Erin Mason. She was calm enough now, but later? Still, if she ran away afterwards, a second ring of marines – called in from other bases – had formed a perimeter down the hill.

Jim hoped Erin wouldn't run because that would ruin any chance of a successful appeal from her sentence. He hadn't mentioned his intentions to her yet. He also hoped that she would not collapse as dangerously as last time. If that happened, the marine medics would have to depend on portable defibrillators to revive her. Then she would have to be evacuated by foot.

The afternoon wore on. The three women maintained their sitting positions until evening when the marine allocated to cooking called a meal break. Erin nudged her cousins and stood up. She helped Tanya and Elisabeth rise. They both seemed stiff, but soon loosened up. Jim gestured for them to sit with him.

"How is the arm, Tanya," he asked, as she sat down and thanked the marine for the plate of stew he delivered.

They were using camp stools and used their laps for a table.

"Its fine, Jim. It has stopped hurting."

"What about you, Elisabeth? I didn't think you could sit so long without trouble."

"I'm fine Jim. The fresh air must be good for me."

"Erin?" Jim turned his attention to her.

"I'm fine." It seemed though that her mind was elsewhere, until she said, suddenly, "Jim, could you see that there is plenty of that energy drink available? Warmed to body temperature?"

Surprised, Jim assured her he would. "Anything else?"

Erin seemed to be thinking. "Warm blankets?"

Jim nodded to the hovering major. The man had already told him that they expected the temperature to drop to near freezing that night. A gust of cold wind seemed to confirm it.

The sky darkened as the last of the sun's rays lighted the clearing. Erin, after being chivvied to eat her meal, was pacing around the clearing, watched by alert marines as well as Jim and her cousins.

Jim decided that her restlessness was a sign that something would happen. He walked over to intercept her and then kept pace with her.

Erin was aware of him and stopped when she was in the centre of the clearing. She looked at Jim to be sure she had his attention, and then pointed at a patch of sky just above the tree tops.

"There, Jim. They are coming from there." She pointed to a star cluster, just visible. "When that is directly overhead, that's when she will try."

Jim gestured to a shadowy marine guard. Erin ignored the whispered,

"Identify that star cluster, would you? And predict when it will be directly overhead."

Erin kept pacing, but Jim went to his pack for a jumper and then re-joined the other women. When he suggested that they should get jumpers, they just echoed each other. "We're fine."

Jim moved a hand to feel their faces. To his surprise, they both felt warm, almost feverish. His intuition told him that Erin would feel the same.

At an hour before midnight, right at the time the marine had estimated the star cluster would be at zenith. Erin stopped pacing and called to her cousins.

"Now!" she directed, and the three of them joined hands to form a circle.

Erin seemed totally focussed on something only she could sense. Tanya slipped into rapport with both Erin and Elisabeth, but could only sense the picture in Erin's mind of them, as if seem from above. Somewhere, vaguely, she could sense Wanda.

"Now! Grip hard."

Chapter 15

Tanya saw an image in her mind of something streaking at them and of Erin swinging on a trapeze, swinging towards the something, grabbing it and swinging downwards. In the next instant, she felt someone with in the circle of hands. That someone collapsed onto her and Elisabeth, and dragged them free of Erin.

Marines moved quickly as Erin called, "Help here."

Light from carefully placed lamps began to illuminate the clearing. They were as bright as LED torches.

The unconscious man was lifted off the two women and carried into the tent. Jim helped Tanya up and asked about her arm, only to get another, "Its fine."

"Can those lights be angled down," Elisabeth asked. "Erin can't concentrate on whatever analogy she is using, she is getting frantic."

Jim called out the order and was obeyed. Elisabeth and Tanya went and joined Erin.

"Take deep even breaths," Elisabeth told Erin. "We have one back, Colonel Aldrin. How are you?"

Erin was gulping air, but was trying to steady herself. "I'm still right to go." She did not tell them how nauseous she was feeling.

"Jim," Elisabeth called. "Some of that energy drink, quick."

In moments, Elisabeth had a cup of it in her hand and was urging Erin to drink it. She was relieved when Erin obeyed her. Jim brought two more cups and told the others to drink as well.

They only had time to have half of it when Erin dropped her cup and grabbed for her cousins. They responded to the urgency Erin felt. As soon as the circle joined again, they felt it too. They also sensed Wanda and her relief that David would be safe, and her desolation at his going.

"Be ready," Erin warned. "He's coming."

This time they all braced themselves for the sudden weight, and gently lowered David Martin to the ground. Once again the marines approached and the women parted to let them in.

As David was carried away, Jim brought more drink over. Erin was crying silently, ignoring Jim's concern.

"What did she mean, Jim," Tanya asked. "I heard Wanda thinking that she can't come herself unless some devil turns up. Isn't a devil an evil creature?"

Elisabeth analysed what she had experienced. "It's Jai Cassidy. Wanda hopes she will turn up. Her title is she-devil. But I don't know why she can't come now."

Erin answered that. "She can't. Not anymore."

"Why?" Elisabeth insisted.

"I think she has lost the ability to move herself. I think she hid that fact from the others. She sacrificed her chances to get them back."

Erin still had tears streaming down her face, but she wasn't saying all she had sensed.

"What can we do?" Elisabeth demanded. "Surely we can do something? Can we can feed her more energy?"

Tanya suddenly slapped Erin hard. "Stop it! Wanda doesn't need your self-pity right now! She needs to be strong. Stop thinking of yourself! So, she thinks she has sacrificed herself, so the others will live, David is alive. She is alive. There is still a chance, but if she thinks David is dead, she'll give up. So stop thinking of whoever it was that died!"

Tanya pushed one of Erin's hands into Elisabeth's and took the other, and then reformed the circle. Erin's hands were limp in their grip. Nothing was happening. Elisabeth sent a wordless call to Wanda, trying to feel the power flowing through them again so she could send it with her desperation.

"Wanda?"

The power began to flow outward.

"Lishka?" It was a very faint whisper.

"Wanda!" Elisabeth yelled with her mind. Erin's hands gripped hers with more force as she reacted to Elisabeth's desperation.

"David is dead?" Wanda's mind voice was heard by all three. Erin felt Wanda's despair and fought her own.

"David is ALIVE!" Elisabeth shouted mentally. "ALIVE!"

She did not dare think that it might not be true, for she didn't know for sure.

"I am so weak," Elisabeth heard.

Erin spoke aloud. "Those aliens are closing in on her again. She is weak and confused. She can't stay there."

"Wanda! You have to get away," Tanya yelled in her mind.

The words echoed in Erin's mind. Provoking a forgotten memory of the instant when she, weak and confused in the psych hospital – experienced a moment of clarity and acted.

A second memory followed it - the short period of exquisite relief from the pressure of so many minds when the medicines kicked in. She concentrated on that moment in time.

"She's calm," Elisabeth reported.

To Tanya, Erin said, "Tell her to think of darkness – empty darkness. Tell her to dig her fingers into the dirt where she is, or clutch the bedrock. Tell her to feel the aura giving her energy."

Erin thought of calm and silence as Tanya repeated the words over and over.

All of them experienced the sudden surge of panic, but Erin's soothing emanation quelled it.

"What are those things," Elisabeth suddenly blurted.

"There is no one there!" Erin said urgently. Elisabeth gulped and pictured an empty cave, with armed aliens walking around in it. Slowly, she became aware of the sense of a breeze blowing through her and the faint warmth of another hand on hers. She relaxed.

"They can't see her," Tanya whispered. "Those things are walking all around her as if she were a lump of rock."

Erin began to smile faintly. This was what she had done during those weeks she could not remember. She had convinced any police or authority that they could not see her. She hadn't known how she had done it until now.

"They have gone," Tanya said finally.

"Tell Wanda to continue thinking of darkness but with a rope of light winding its way towards her, and to catch it."

Elisabeth sensed the moment when Wanda 'caught' that image of rope. The breeze she felt picked up in force and Wanda's thoughts grew stronger. Erin sensed relief, tempered with resignation and the knowledge that she had to fight on. That the aliens would not give up on their efforts to find her and that she, Wanda, had no food and little water and the day was searing hot and dry.

"What now?" Erin asked. "What more can we do? Hope that the devil woman turns up in time?"

"We have brought her time," Tanya said.

"She can't show herself. The aura won't hide her if she is moving. She'll run out of water soon. Half her trouble now is dehydration."

"Wait a minute," Elisabeth said, trying to think logically. "Erin, what happened to that bracelet – really? The one I had. It belonged to Jai Cassidy, I think."

Erin looked blankly at her cousin, but absently touched the watch.

"I..." Erin couldn't remember.

A minor scuffle, loud in the night's stillness, distracted Tanya and Elisabeth. A figure erupted from the tent and ran towards them. A second figure followed and soon caught the first.

"Let me go, Stev! Let me go! I want Wanda back."

Elisabeth left her cousins and met the struggling man. "David!"

David stopped struggling and Stev Aldrin eased his grip. Elisabeth ignored Stev and gave David a hug.

"We are trying everything, David. Really trying."

"Where is she?" David cried out, sobs erupting so his next words were garbled.

"David, she is still alive. Hear me! She's still alive. She just needs to regain some energy."

David forced himself to control his anger. "She said...she could pull it from the aura or something. The bracelet thing she found – helped her."

Elisabeth turned to Erin. "How could she know about the bracelet? I didn't find it until after she had gone."

"I have no idea, but it made it easier for us to hear her. Perhaps she sensed it on you?"

"What are you talking about," David demanded.

"The bracelet," Elisabeth explained. "I found it at the old Cassidy place – or rather it found me. Then it found Erin and..."

"I don't remember," Erin admitted.

Tanya spoke up. "You went into the restricted area and spoke to someone."

Erin had flashes then – of having the numbers for the security locks come into her mind and having to find some old watch. The one she still wore.

"She had the bracelet when we found her," David said. "It wasn't the one she found before we left. If you had it – how did she get it?"

Erin was looking ill. Elisabeth glanced at her then spoke to David. "Sometimes, the three of us together can reach her. We are all cousins. I am not sure Wanda knows that."

David glanced around and recognised Tanya but not Erin.

"Wanda seems to be able to reach Erin easiest. She feels emotions and Jim thinks her sendings are emotion driven."

"What about the bracelet?" David persisted.

"I felt it at the Cassidy place – like I said. It was hidden in a secret place. I think it found me because I...we...have traces of Cassidy blood."

David shook his head. "That she-devil is Jai Cassidy."

"I guessed that," Elisabeth admitted. "She's Atapi, isn't she?"

"Half human, half of those lizard folk. Are you?"

"No. There was another group of people from there, here for a while. One was a friend of Jai Cassidy's mother." Elisabeth decided not to mention their relationship to her.

"Kumatan," David deduced. "How did Wanda get it?"

Erin finally spoke. "Wanda couldn't reach you or anyone else where you were. She was desperate and reached me. She used me to escape from someplace, by walking here, but not quite arriving and then going back elsewhere. The last time, she took the bracelet."

David sagged, dropping to the ground before Stev could catch him. He buried his head in his hands.

"David?" Elisabeth crouched beside him. "Can you tell us anything that might help?"

He shook his head.

"Get him some of that drink," Erin suggested to Jim who was standing close by.

"What about you?" Erin demanded of Stev. "Can you tell us anything?"

Aldrin answered. "Not much. We encountered the lizard folk. To them, we are as alien as the others, but at least they did not try to kill us first. We were told to leave and they were not pleased when we said we needed Wanda to do that. They might have told that Jai-devil about us."

Erin said, "Wanda knows of her - she mentioned her and is hoping she will come."

David reached up and gripped Erin's arm. "Why?"

Erin couldn't lie. David would know.

"I think she is not able to move herself anymore."

David moaned, and Stev moved closer to support him.

Aldrin spoke thoughtfully. "Apart from building resistance to those alien invaders, we went because they thought that we, being human, Jai might sense us and get word to us. The Kumatan admit that the Atapi are most finely in tune with the aura of Korvu as well as being fierce warriors. I don't understand where they were believed to be hiding – some here but not here place."

Elisabeth nodded as if she understood,

"David, drink that stuff and rest," Elisabeth told her brother in law. "Erin, Tanya and I need to talk. We will want you when we try to reach Wanda again." Elisabeth gestured to her cousins to move to the edge of the clearing.

"What have you thought of, Elisabeth?" Tanya asked. "Have you a plan?"

"Maybe an inkling of one. My thoughts are not clear, so I will give you the bare ideas. One, Wanda said that bracelet was native to that other place and could be used to draw on the aura. Two, I found it at the Cassidy place, where Jai was born and grew up. She can't have made it – it had to have been her mother's. That is where I start to lose grasp of the idea. It's something like – Wanda ought to be able to use that bracelet to call/contact this Jai-devil through the aura. And that bracelet found me, then it seemed to choose to go to Erin, and then it chose to go to Wanda…"

"As if it is making its way back to Jai?" Tanya suggested.

Elisabeth shrugged.

"Why you in the first place," Erin asked an obvious question.

Elisabeth started to speak then shut her mouth.

"What?" Erin demanded.

"There are things we found out that we didn't tell you because, well, you weren't exactly handling the idea of Wanda on another planet."

"Go on – I have just had two people materialise out of nowhere into my arms – what could be worse?"

"When Tanya and I were trying to find out how we were related, we discovered our mothers were two of triplets – that's how we got onto you."

Elisabeth paused, considering her words.

"I know that – what's your point?"

"Our grandmother was Anneleise Mosellan, her mother was Suzi Mosellan. The father mentioned on her birth certificate was Matthew Cassidy."

Erin stared at her intently, suspecting that her cousin still had not got to the point.

"Matthew Cassidy is Jai Cassidy's father. Her mother was part of an Atapi colony that was on Earth for about two decades. She and Suzi Mosellan were friends and the Mosellans were part of a Kumatan colony that was trying to remove the Atapi from here."

"Really," Erin managed to say calmly though she was far from it. "So, something about that relationship makes us able to feel the Earth aura? And all the rest?"

Elisabeth thought about that and nodded.

"Does Wanda know this?"

"No, we only found it out after she was gone."

"Then we need to tell her. It might give her ideas," Erin suggested. "God,

I knew I was a freak."

"Speak for yourself!" Tanya retorted. "I think that bit of foreign blood makes us better than others. We certainly don't look like monsters."

They all fell silent, trying to think of a plan.

Erin, feeling freaked, suggested, "How about we try to reach Wanda. We tell her what you just told me. We say she should try to make a stir in the aura there, hoping Jai will sense it , investigate, see the bracelet, give Wanda a chance to say 'Hi cousin' and Jai will help send her home – if not to get rid of another alien, then to help kinfolk."

"Something like that," Elisabeth agreed, not seeming to notice the sarcasm.

"A lot of if's," Tanya pointed out.

"Considering we are working blind and we don't know what is happening there," Erin said with more veiled sarcasm. "Well, if you think it will work, we had better do it soon."

Before I lose my nerve, Erin thought to herself.

As soon as Erin touched David's hand she knew he had enough desperation to push his call to Wanda by himself. Except that David had no scrap of broadcasting telepathy. His hand was icy cold and he was wavering in his concentration. Erin thought of the aura and thought of David being needed to focus on Wanda. She thought that they all needed strength for what might be a long night's vigil.

"Wanda!" both David and Tanya called mentally. Elisabeth added her own call to theirs, and Erin projected all the desperation in David's soul.

They did not think they had reached her until Erin said aloud, "It's cold. There. She's cold. No – petrified."

Their combined efforts to get a response had no effect. Wanda was not 'hearing'.

Erin felt a tremor – Wanda was dehydrated and suffering from hypothermia – she had to move. Very deliberately, Erin pictured herself standing in front of a curled up Wanda as she had often seen Wanda watching her in her dreams. Then she imagined her hand slapping Wanda hard. One, twice, three times before she got a weak response. She ignored David's sudden anger – Elisabeth gripped his arm to stop him taking his desperation out on Erin.

"Get up you stupid cow," Erin sent along with a wave of disgust. "After all you have put me through, all the trouble I am in because of you, and don't you dare sit there and die! I told you before – stop feeling sorry for yourself. You need to get up and move – remember? You have to keep active. And if you just sit there that devil-woman won't find you either."

They all felt the overwhelming despair.

"Stop that!" Erin pictured another slapping action. "Listen! The bracelet can help you. It is tuned to the aura where you are – remember? You need to think of what you need help with."

"I don't know."

"Listen! You need to make a big stir in the aura," Erin sent, speaking aloud all this time for the others to hear. "The Atapi should sense it and come."

"How?"

David, muttered, "We left guns there. She could shoot a few aliens."

"Too dangerous – they already searched the cave she is in without finding her – we don't want them returning," Erin countered.

"Could she throw it away from the cave and kill a few if they were set to overload?" David tried.

Erin considered. "How would she do that?"

David explained, but Erin saw it as pictures. "That might work," she agreed.

"Tanya, can you repeat all that, I'll think the pictures."

Elisabeth sent encouragement.

They waited, nothing seemed to change.

"Move you stupid bitch," Erin returned to her mental anger. "Find the damn gun – it's in a crevice above the opening." Erin was repeating what she heard David muttering.

The movement was very slow and sluggish.

"It's not good," Elisabeth muttered. "She is suffering from more than cold. She must keep moving."

"Heat!" David suggested. "It is hot outside there. Get her to move near the entrance."

It was like watching a glacier move. Erin kept up her swearing and Elisabeth pleaded and David added his own encouragement.

An hour later, Wanda reached the gun and the entrance. Then they waited until she had warmed up enough to overload the gun.

"This won't work, you hell demon," Wanda finally sent back." They are too spread out."

"Tell her to touch the bracelet and imagine herself in the open and where the goblins can see her. Not to go there, just picture it," Erin directed.

"I don't believe it!" Wanda's amazement was clear to all of the listeners on Earth. "They are coming from everywhere!"

"Get the thing ready to overload, and throw it into that crowd of goblins," Erin sent, with the others reinforcing the message. "Picture it going there but not being visible."

Erin sensed that Wanda was a bit more animated. The panic was once again under control.

"They are shooting and hitting each other!" Wanda sounded both amazed and satisfied.

"Hurry and throw the thing!" Tanya and Erin sent.

They all saw the result, sent through Wanda's mind - a massive explosion, bodies flying everywhere and the survivors buzzing angrily, having no idea where the threat came from.

"How did I do that?" Wanda wondered.

"It is the aura working through the bracelet," Tanya sent, echoing Erin's comment. The answer seemed to make sense.

"But how? I am no sorceress like Jai Cassidy."

"No, but you are related to Jenha Mosellan. We all are."

"Mikha's father?"

"Who?"

"Jai's son."

"Probably. How would I know?" Erin sent.

"The Traegers can do some magic," Wanda thought. "How can I be related?"

Tanya was the best one to try to send the explanation, and she summarised what Erin had been told.

"Tell her to try calling to Jai Cassidy," Elisabeth suggested. "The Atapi should have felt that disturbance, surely."

Erin felt Wanda obeying and also trying to work her muscles loose, but it was like they were leaden.

To Elisabeth she said, "How should she fix that problem you have?"

"Keep moving, hot water, the aura helped me, I think."

"Then think at her," Erin told her. "Remind her of what to do. She is not really thinking for herself."

David slumped into unconsciousness. Erin glanced at the tall Stev Aldrin, who moved forward and lifted David like he was a child. Erin wondered at the man's endurance and how someone with artificial limbs could be so strong and agile. She had sensed those things when he had arrived back into their arms.

Erin let her mind wander from the three way link and began to feel very tired. It was the longest they had managed to stay linked to Wanda. She was jerked back to the link when Elisabeth screamed. She caught a vision from Wanda, and then darkness.

"Damn!" Tanya swore. "Where did those lizards come from?"

"What happened," Erin asked. "I wasn't concentrating."

"Wanda was watching from the cavern entrance, in the sun, calling for that Jai Cassidy," Tanya revealed. "Then a winged lizard appeared, right in front of her. It said something, but Wanda couldn't understand it. It grabbed her, and I think it bit her, then – nothing."

Erin felt nothing either. "She couldn't move fast enough and the aura didn't hide her," Elisabeth said. "They must be Atapi."

"Where's David? He might know what they might do," Tanya asked, looking around.

It was Stev Aldrin who answered. His voice sounded tired.

"They are reputed to be barbaric," Stev told them. "Most Kumatan have stories of atrocities done to kin. But, they have been absent for over a generation. Traeger Mosellan claims that Jai can control them, and I have seen evidence of that. The devils, the winged ones, liked us as little as the other aliens and they warned us to leave."

Erin shivered. "I don't think she is dead, but I can't concentrate on nothing." She shook her hands free from Elisabeth and Tanya, and dropped to a sitting position. She was almost asleep when Jim shook her and insisted she have some of the energy drink. The marine medics were doing the same for Tanya and Elisabeth.

When Jim lifted her, Erin struggled feebly. She was asleep as soon as Jim laid her on one of the beds, and did not feel the warmed blankets being tucked around her. Sometime during the remainder of the night, her hand dropped to touch the dirt floor of the tent. She began to dream.

She dreamt that the lizard-like folk were surrounding her and she was suspended on some sort of net. Pointed sticks were poking her and spinning her around. She couldn't speak, due to being gagged by some pungent tasting vine. It felt like her legs and wrists were tied behind her. She couldn't seem to think.

The poking stopped abruptly, and the lizards backed off. By twisting her head a bit she saw the winged devil bow to another winged one and a human woman dressed in clothing as rich as that of the just arrived devil.

Oddly, she could understand their speech.

The woman stayed silent. The newcomer asked for an account of the manner of prisoner that had been caught.

"It was warned to leave and did not," the first devil proclaimed. "It was fair prey."

"What reason did it give for staying?" the woman asked sharply.

"That it could not leave."

"Where did you find it?" the other devil asked. He seemed to be much older than the first one.

"Where the hated ones were converging."

"Do you know it, She-devil?" the older devil asked.

The woman made a show of examining the prisoner.

"Yes. This is the one that visited us. Though it looks to be starving now. I smell the stench of the hated ones on it."

"You warned it to leave?"

"Yes. Were the other two, the males, with it?" the woman asked.

"No," the young devil told her. "Just this one."

"Hardly worthy prey," the woman said derisively. "Cut it down. I will deal with this one. She is not our enemy."

The young devil made no move to comply. "It is alien. It does not belong here."

"Cut it down. This one is mine." The woman walked forward towards the young Devil and whispered a name. The devil obeyed then and slashed at the ropes holding the net with a careless slash.

Erin felt as if it were herself that fell heavily.

"It cannot stay," the older devil stated. His tone indicated that he meant what he said and would see that the order was obeyed.

"No," the woman agreed. She cut the bindings on her prisoner's wrists and legs.

Erin, in her dream, seemed unable to move. She could only watch as the woman walked away to a seat that faced her prisoner. She waited until all the other Atapi had left before speaking.

"I warned you to go," the woman, Erin seemed to know her name was Jai Cassidy, stated as fact.

"I can't," Erin felt herself to say. "I have sent David and Stev back, but I can't go. I tried."

Jai stood and walked to her, and circled her, and the squatted beside her.

"How long have you had the stiffening sickness?"

"Years," Erin felt herself say.

"How can a human from Earth have that? It is a Kumatan disease."

"I'm kin to them."

"What!" Jai exclaimed. "You didn't tell me that before."

Chapter 16

"I didn't know then," Wanda admitted.

"So how?"

"Before Matthew Cassidy fathered you, he fathered a child on Suzi Mosellan," Erin felt herself say.

Jai hissed softly. "Yes, I know that. It died."

"No, your mother thought it died. Anneliese Mosellan had triplets."

"Anne Elise, like my grandmother." Jai's tone had softened to curious. "And triplets! Blessed Larcia. I would bet that Jenha does not know this."

"Probably not. I only just found out. I am a granddaughter of Anneliese Mosellan."

"There are others?" Jai asked sharply.

"Three others. My sister and two cousins."

Jai sat back on her heels. "So that was why Jahni could reach you. I am sure that move was not sanctioned by the Kimh."

"Did you ask Kaer that?" Erin heard herself ask.

"No, I kept my visit as short as possible. The Kimh don't trust me. They think I am dangerous," Jai admitted.

"Janhi doesn't," Erin seemed to say.

"Nor his father, but as Traeger, Jenha must obey the Kimh. Jahni is not one of them and has a little more freedom. Why did he even try, though?"

"I think he thought that other humans might be like you."

"Hybrids? No, the Atapi usually killed such abominations at birth. But surely he was pleading with the wind."

"Maybe, but he caused me to have a lot of freakish abilities, though he said he couldn't help me master them. One of them was the ability to walk across planes."

Jai nodded. "Traeger abilities. Members of Jenha's family have held that rank for centuries. I don't recall him mentioning Suzi, but my mother's brother met her. He said that if she had been male, she would have been a Traeger too. You got here, so why can't you leave?"

"We had help from Jahni and others to get here, but it isn't that. I can't seem to move myself anymore."

Jai studied her again.

"It is not just the stiffening sickness. I can help you with that. I think, perhaps that the evil ones have damaged you."

"If it stops me having all the freakish talents, I don't care. Can you help me get home?"

Jai considered. "Can your kin help you?"

"I don't know. I can sometimes feel their minds but how? None of them, as far as I know, can cross planes deliberately. And they are so far away."

"I must think on this, Little Sister. I cannot take you. I am now bound to this world, and I must help rid it of those evil ones. They are like a rash on my skin." Jai was quiet for some moments, and then said, decisively, "Stay here! I will send healers. They won't like you, but they will obey me. Don't leave until I call you. The male devils will not warn you again."

Erin jerked awake. She heard voices speaking outside of the tent.

"...orders, Sir. This post is to be dismantled and all personnel to be returned for debriefing."

That was enough. Erin didn't need to hear more. Wanda wasn't back, but whoever had issued the orders did not care. That meant that they would ensure she went too.

It was equal parts reasoned thinking, sheer panic and anger that moved her. In spite of still feeling tired, she went over to Elisabeth and Tanya and woke them. She whispered a warning to be quiet, and then told them what she had heard. Both of her cousins were alarmed and upset.

"We can't leave yet!" Elisabeth said, turning pale.

"That's why I am getting away from here," Erin said. "I hope, that while they are hunting me, they won't insist that you two leave. I won't be far."

"They will think you are trying to escape," Elisabeth was alarmed for her now.

"I really don't think it will matter if I do or if I act like a docile lamb. I know who is behind this and it is the only way I can think of to stay. Tell Jim will you."

Erin slipped away, heading towards the latrine tent. No one followed her. The two sentries were both intent on the argument between Colonel Aldrin and the government agents. They must have had to climb up here in the dark. She thought rudely that the suited types were lucky to find them. The two men were wearing expensive, jogging suits.

Erin hoped she understood the way she had hidden from the police during the first few weeks after her escape. Her plan depended on it. And what she intended to do had worked for Wanda.

From a screened position on the edge of the camp, Erin sat perfectly still, watching the activity as equipment was packed and the tent was dismantled. She knew that more marines from somewhere were looking for her. Her disappearance had caused a big stir.

The government reps had been livid, but they declined to stay and help search for her. They had escorted Colonel Aldrin and David Martin down the hill. David had been carried on a stretcher toted by two marines.

Now, Erin watched Jim, Tanya and Elisabeth who were standing around with four packs and blankets. She had heard Jim ask if there were specific orders for them to return immediately. There had not been; only general ones that said they were to return to the base for debriefing.

One of the marine searchers reported briefly to Jim and went off again. Since he was not one of the six that had escorted them up the hill, she had wondered where he had come from. Later she had heard about the perimeter that had been established half a mile down the hill. That was when she realised she was glad the reasoning part of her mind had won out over panic. All that had really set the balance was her anger.

Jim had been doing an excellent imitation of a worried guardian. His contention was that Erin might have slipped down the hill in the dark and was lying injured somewhere. He insisted that she had given her word not to run off, etc,etc,etc.

After a while, Tanya and Elisabeth had sat down on their packs, and Jim had started pacing. Jim had been on his phone a bit too. One call had been to Goldman, protesting at the action taken, but apparently told that Goldman was unable to interfere. However, he had said to Goldman not to worry about her. She had seen the faint smile on Jim's face at that point as he had casually turned around. She was quite sure Jim knew what she was doing and approved.

When the last of the marines that were leaving disappeared down the track, the two that were staying came over to Jim Phillips.

"We are your escorts, Sir. How long do you intend to stay?"

"Until Erin is found. She cannot have got away from here. You had experienced marines forming the lower perimeter. Therefore, she must be lying injured somewhere. I am responsible for her. Find her and we will be able to leave."

"No," Tanya and Elisabeth said in unison. The marine Major simply nodded and turned back to coordinating the search.

The same suggestion was repeated a few hours later, when a group of men - a civilian and three uniformed marine non-coms arrived.

The civilian didn't seem particularly pleased to have had to hike up the hill. He had taken Jim aside and spoken harshly about his 'losing' Erin Mason. He had tried to get the two women to leave, but Elisabeth had glared at him and warned, "Just try it! Erin is my cousin and my friend."

The man glared back but held his tongue. She didn't need to read his mind to tell that his opinion of her had just fallen to the ground. Instead, he had spoken loudly when he advised the Marine Major that Erin Mason was to be apprehended by any means possible.

As the civilian had stalked off, Jim spoke quietly to Tanya and Elisabeth. "Stay calm. Stay here."

Jim pulled out his phone again and appeared to make a call. He seemed to wander casually away from the women and towards the edge of the clearing. It just happened that he walked directly towards where Erin was hiding. He spoke in a voice audible only to Erin.

"How are you?"

Jim watched the bush where he had decided Erin was. A branch moved slightly.

"Do you need anything?"

Faintly, Jim heard, "No."

"Anything I need to know?"

"Not yet."

"I will be watching here. If you need to talk, hold down the lowest branch - the one with the flowers on."

"Ok," Erin promised. What she really wanted to do was use the latrine. She was intending to try to go when one of her cousins did. In the meantime she was trying to keep her mind open and think of nothing. Especially not of the angry people searching for her.

Elisabeth hummed, just loud enough to cover the whispering as Erin told her of the dream she'd had just before the invasion, early that morning.

"I hope Jai doesn't wait too long," Elisabeth whispered, rustling her clothes to cover the sound. Erin didn't answer. There was no need. Both wondered how long Erin could hide. The sun was up now, and the day growing warm, but it would be near freezing again if they had to wait the night up here in the open.

"I will distract anyone while you get out," Elisabeth promised. She had an inkling of what Erin was doing and decided to try some manipulation of her own.

A marine was waiting for her to finish. As he made to move toward the tent, Elisabeth thought at him, "You don't need to go here yet."

He checked his movement, and Elisabeth greeted him casually, and began some small talk. The man was quite young and without superiors around, happy to talk to her for a few moments. As he did, Elisabeth thought of the aura, and thought at the man, "There is no sign of Erin here."

Elisabeth caught a fleeting glimpse of movement, but the marine didn't. When she thought Erin well away, Elisabeth apologised for taking up the marine's time and walked back to Jim to report.

"What can we do, Jim?" Tanya asked. She rubbed her bandaged arm. It was aching only a little, which amazed her, since she had only had the one dose of pain relief. It couldn't have been broken after all.

"Stay receptive," Jim told her. "We are still ahead of the game. I think there is something here still working to help us."

Erin dozed off. Almost at once the dreams began and Erin felt a rush of adrenalin. Once again it was as if she were Wanda. Part of her mind realised that her muscles were no longer stiff. The rest was telling her to dodge the snaking line of light. The tip barely touched her arm, but the pain was terrible. Erin knew it was not in her arm and damped the sensation. It seemed to have the same effect on Wanda, who faltered for a moment, but was quickly dodging again and trying to run for the cave entrance. The winged lizard with the light weapon was suddenly blocking it – intent on tormenting her.

It spoke, but neither she nor Wanda understood it. Then the creature leapt at her, knocking her backwards to the hard stone floor. There was no doubt from its expression that it hated Wanda. It held her down and examined her, turning its head at odd angles. Then it leapt off her with a downstroke of its wings. When it spoke again, its words were understandable, "Run vermin!"

It moved back, and Erin's view rose slowly from ground height as, Wanda, in that faraway place pushed herself up – cautiously. Her eyes never left this unexpected enemy. Her mind was calling for Jai Cassidy, the one Atapi she knew she could trust.

The creature raised the glowing line again, his intention clear.

"Run vermin!"

Wanda had been told to stay in that place but she was being forced out. She had no choice. The power in that force whip was formidable. Wanda ducked and ran, but not quickly enough. The glowing line struck her back, making her stumble. Once again, Erin damped the shared pain, and Wanda scrambled to her feet and ran. Shock that she could move at all, slowed the creature from following her.

Erin's dream view changed to a narrow canyon of sandstone, shaded from the sun's glare. A glance behind her showed the winged lizard striding after her.

At the end of the canyon, the sun's glare off the desert sand was blinding. Wanda used her hand to shade her eyes, enough to spot a rocky gully not too far away. She glanced around, saw no other creatures and raced for it.

Erin's mind heard buzzing. Wanda's mind recognized the sound. Aliens! She began to run faster; the rough track to the gully came closer several times as Wanda tripped. One time the buzzing came close, just as she tripped. Wanda recognised that the alien's weapon had narrowly missed hitting her.

She ran on, heading for the shadows, hoping for shelter, and still deathly afraid, because the aliens could see just as well in the dark.

Erin was suddenly overwhelmed by fear. Alien fear!

"What the...?" Erin heard Wanda's mind shriek, as something strong and clinging enveloped her. She struggled helplessly.

"Little sister?"

"Jai!" Wanda's mind screamed.

"I told you to stay," a woman's voice spoke in Earth English.

"Couldn't."

"Stop struggling," the same voice sounded resigned.

Wanda had to stop. There was too little air to breathe. Erin too, fought the sensation to black out, by reminding herself to breathe. She felt she had dropped when the muffling folds of wings released her.

"Yours, I believe, Jai-devil," Erin understood the words.

"Yes, and kin to me in fact."

"No wonder it did not stay. It reeks of the hated ones. Are you sure you can trust it?"

"She escaped from them. And somehow killed thirty of their number."

"Still, it did not obey you. You should punish it."

"Look closer, Master."

Erin felt a powerful hand seize her and lift her until her feet dangled a foot from the ground. The lizard face sniffed her, and licked her face.

"It tastes of Traeger. Smells of alien and ... Sotak."

Wanda was put on her feet. Jai put a supportive arm around her. "Come back to where you were."

"What's happening?" Wanda asked.

"Nothing to worry you. Atapi business. You, however, have impressed the Old One and that is no small matter. So while I am not allowed to discuss what is intended, you would be wise to betray nothing."

Wanda struggled free from Jai, turned to the Old One and bowed as she had seen the other lizards do.

"Thank you for protecting me."

Jai translated and the snarl on the lizard face could have been a smile.

The cave was empty when they returned. The Old One had not followed them.

"Why didn't that other winged lizard like me?" Wanda asked, finding a place to sit. "I didn't do anything to him."

"Old prejudices," Jai said. "The newest sorcerers, I hope, will have none. Sotak, was one of the first to become a full sorcerer after I hid the tribes. He still had memories of before, when things were being stirred up by others of the aliens' kind. You are alien, humanoid like me, and as such like enough to the Kumatan to interbreed. Three reasons for him to hate you."

"Oh," was all Wanda could think of to say.

"When this matter is dealt with," Jai said quietly. "Stay with the Old One. He will protect you, for my sake. Sotak is an arrogant one, but he will not dare challenge the Old One. I must go and roust out the Kumatan and the Kimh. Now that the aliens are retreating, it should be safe enough."

"Can one of them get me home?"

Jai chuckled. "I think, of all the choices, it should be Jenha who returns you. This news I have of his kinship to you will shock him as nothing about me did. This is delicious. You are of the blood of his line, and of Cassidy." She seemed to savour the notion. "I really like you, little sister, like I could never like my siblings. It is a pity I cannot meet the others you mentioned. She who is in your mind is a strong protector."

Erin twitched as if someone had physically touched her.

"It seems like, even back there, troubles dog you."

"What's new?" Wanda muttered. "I was trouble and in trouble since I could walk."

Jai laughed. "So was I, but I had thought it was only my Atapi blood."

From one moment to the next, two figures appeared in the cave – both winged Atapi. Jai was suddenly back to her formal manner.

One of the arrivals hissed, angrily.

As a courtesy to Wanda, Jai spoke both in English and Atapi. She challenged the younger sorcerer as to why he had attacked one who was under her protection. The Old One watched as the younger looked around as if trying for an escape route.

"Were you trying to challenge me, Sotak?" Jai asked.

After that, the conversation was unintelligible, but with Jai speaking calmly and the young sorcerer angrily trying to justify himself. Finally, the Old One spoke sharply and the young one stopped speaking and drew himself up arrogantly.

Jai stepped back, placed a hand on Wanda's shoulder, and whispered. "Do and say nothing."

She produced a device from her robes that was identical to the weapon the younger sorcerer had used. She treated the younger sorcerer to exact equivalent of what he had done to Wanda.

It was clear that the effect on the Atapi was much worse than he had expected. He bit off a cry of agony, not wanting to lower himself further by screaming aloud and betraying more suffering than a mere human female.

In her dream, back on earth, Erin seemed to feel someone grasp her hand in thanks.

Jai deactivated the line of light and hid the weapon. She saw the Old One gesture to her and bowed slightly before walking away and vanishing on the second step.

Wanda slipped off the rock she sat on, and rested her back against it, with knees tucked up to her chin. She watched the Old One walk around the younger sorcerer who had dropped to the floor. His manner showed no sympathy, and he leant down and sniffed.

"You reek of alien, Sotak," the Old One challenged. Wanda understood that.

"That one reeks," Sotak growled angrily, trying to look like he wasn't hurting as he stood up. "I found it with the aliens. It consorted with them."

"I know she was their prisoner and won free with their secrets. What did you do?"

The spate of Atapi was unintelligible until, "What did they pay you Sotak?"

The younger Atapi fell silent. The Old One went over and placed his hand over the other's face, and what he did caused the other to moan. Then with deliberate movements, the Old One removed his hand, and in a frighteningly fast move, jumped behind the moaning Atapi and twisted the others wings. The younger collapsed completely.

The Old One walked away and found an outcrop of rock to sit on. He gestured for Wanda to sit at his feet.

Erin sensed no free will in Wanda, and that worried her. She seemed to lapse into something akin to sleep. Erin couldn't tell if she was tired or the lizard man was controlling her.

Her mind drifted back to awareness of her own surroundings. She looked through the screening leaves. The marine Major was talking to Jim.

"...dogs..." Erin caught the word and tried to focus her attention on the conversation.

She shivered. They were going to bring dogs up here to look for her. Keeping them from finding her would take constant concentration to influence them, and they would be more intelligent than the ones she had encountered before. They would find her, even if they couldn't see her, and that would ruin everything.

All she could do was think at the distant presence and urge, "Hurry."

Chapter 17

The dogs had run straight at her and the concentration needed to redirect them was giving her a headache. She had nothing to spare to sense Wanda. Twice the handlers had checked the bushes and dragged the dogs away. After the second time, she began to feel a pressure on her mind.

"Now, Erin. Now!"

Elisabeth yelled. Erin stopped her attempts to hide and stumbled out of the bushes and to her feet. The dogs began barking furiously, and she stopped moving. Tanya and Elisabeth ignored the dogs, who were well restrained, and Jim gestured for the handlers to take them away.

Easily, so easily, the three women linked their minds and reached out to Wanda.

Erin expected to sense Wanda's chaotic thoughts, not a calm ordered presence. With that was the surprise of the one she had seen as Jai Cassidy.

"I know that place," surprise coloured Jai's mind voice. "Jenha, so do you."

"Yes, indeed." That mind voice was unfamiliar to her, but fit with the calm competent presence.

"Little sister, reach out to your friends...we need a tighter link."

Erin sought for Wanda's mind and couldn't find it. She sensed the same failure from Tanya and Elisabeth. Then in her mind, she heard, "Coming at you, kin-sibs."

Where? Where? Erin felt panic rising and didn't realise she was crying until someone slapped her.

"Focus, Erin! Don't go to pieces." It was Jim, and his faith in her was a solid anchor.

Erin thought of the first image that came to her mind – of a catcher in a trapeze act, swinging out, timing his swing to catch hands at the exact moment.

Erin felt more than just her cousin's hands. It was like she had caught someone and grabbed them just in time. She could see nothing, but could feel the drag on her shoulders.

The hands released her. Tanya and Elisabeth released her and were exclaiming in relief at having Wanda back.

Erin sat down abruptly, and heard a roaring noise in her ears. Wanda was back! There was no need for her now. She felt herself blacking out.

Erin's next feeling was the hand on the back of her head, pushing it down between her knees. She struggled, but the hand remained firm.

"Calm!" came a voice in her head. It had to be there, the blood was pounding a drumbeat in her ears. Her head was pulsing pain in time with it. Struggling was futile.

"Calm!" The command came again. The pounding in her head and ears subsided, enough for her to hear voices.

Jim was arguing with someone. Erin recognised the voice of the officious civilian of the early morning.

"I have orders to take her into custody," the civilian was saying.

"Not until she has had medical attention," Jim was saying.

Erin found she couldn't breathe as panic flared in her.

"Calm!" The command was more forceful this time.

Someone tucked a blanket around her and the hand holding her down, lifted.

Jim put her hand around a mug of drink, but she didn't feel like drinking.

"Drink!" came the command in her mind and she seemed to have no choice but to obey.

Her head cleared and the pounding eased off more. She looked up and around in her line of vision. Two armed marines were staring at her, weapons ready, but not yet aimed. The civilian, exuding righteous authority, was explaining that his orders came from the highest level. He drew out the written orders and presented them to Jim.

Erin glanced away and saw, crouched beside her, a fair haired stranger. He stood up. And Erin felt she should know him.

She heard the civilian demand, "And who are you?"

"My name is Jenhari Mosellan, and I will be representing this young woman."

Jim had been surprised to see the man materialise with Wanda in his arms, but he had made no comment. Wanda had said he could trust him, before she had passed out. That he could speak English with only a trace of accent, gave him a clue as to who he was. They had only managed a few cautious words together in the short time between the marines that had been here leaving with Wanda, and the reinforcements arriving from the perimeter down the hill.

"How did you get here?" the civilian demanded.

Mosellan spoke quietly but with no deference. He acted as if he had every right to be there.

"I walked."

"Impossible! How did you get past the guards?"

"I was unaware that there were any," Mosellan countered calmly.

"How did you find this place," was the next question.

"I knew where I needed to be, and I have hiked these hills for many years. I probably know them better than you do. However, your questions are wasting time. I would like this young woman to have medical attention."

Erin had the oddest feeling that his wording was a repetition of what Jim had said. She wanted to stay cowering in the blanket, but it would not help. She put the empty mug aside, and threw off the blanket. The civilian's eyes were on her as she stood up, very unsteadily.

She looked at Jim and asked, "How is Wanda?"

"On the way down to the base. Tanya and Elisabeth are with her. How are you?"

Erin shrugged, swaying a bit.

"We might as well go down, then. I am not needed here anymore." It didn't answer Jim's question, but he would know she was lying if she had said, "Fine."

The civilian gave orders and the two marines watching her, shouldered their weapons. Erin felt her hands being forced behind her and handcuffs applied.

Jim protested. "Is that wise? The track down is quite steep and it is going to be getting dark very soon. And I can see that Erin is still not very steady on her feet."

Erin wished Jim would drop it. "I'll be okay if we keep it slow," Erin claimed, sounding calm.

The civilian was quick to accept her claim and gave the orders to move out.

Erin seemed to prove her statement, as the two marines held her arms to steady her.

Twice, she apparently slipped on a loose rock and nearly fell in their grasp. It was enough to test their reactions, and to sense that they did not think her dangerous.

Erin didn't try to talk to them, and acted very docile until she was level with the point where Tanya had slipped.

Without warning, she struggled and threw herself at the drop off. The marine on that side fell, pulling her with him. The other, not expecting such a move, had been holding her loosely, lost his grip.

Jim was bringing up the rear, and was too far away to act. Mosellan was not. He reached out and grabbed Erin, who fell awkwardly to the ground, and not down the hill. The marine managed to find footing and climb back up to the track.

Jim saw Mosellan help Erin to her feet and something like fear crossed her face. For the rest of the way down, Erin walked with deliberate care.

At the civilian's direction, the marines passed Erin into the custody of two dark clad men, with FBI on their jackets. They took her to a black SUV and assisted her into it. They were given orders to take her to the regional police station and into the detention cells.

Jim strode over and reiterated his insistence that Erin should be looked at by a doctor.

"She is no longer your responsibility," the man's look implied it should never have been. "A police doctor will look at her." The word, 'eventually', seemed to hover unspoken.

The civilian didn't wait for further discussion. He entered a second SUV and both cars drove away.

The marines waited.

Jim glanced at them. "I will follow you back," he told them. They saluted and walked to the waiting army car. It did a u-turn to head back in the direction of the base.

Jim then turned his attention to the stranger who had arrived carrying Wanda.

"Wanda said I could trust you. Do you know her well?" Jim asked.

"I probably know her best of any of my people and enough to have a great deal of respect for her."

Jim accepted that. "Would you prefer to walk and talk, or drive somewhere to talk?"

"It is your home ground, Sir. I bow to your judgement," Mosellan said quietly. He stood very still.

"We will drive then. It is getting quite cold," Jim decided.

Jenha walked to the passenger side of the car. He had observed the other cars and imitated what he had seen others do, but the car door didn't open.

Jim spoke across the top of the car, "Press a bit more firmly. You need to move the lever under your fingers towards the other part."

Jenha smiled at the courtesy, and followed the advice. He was soon settled in the passenger seat.

In the same neutrally matter of fact tone, Jim explained the use and purpose of the seat belt.

"We will get going in a minute, if you will just bear with me for a moment."

Jim used his mobile phone to make two calls. The first was to Goldman reporting that Wanda was on her way back down to the base, and Erin to the detention facility. To Goldman's statement of concern, he explained, "Nothing I could do at the time, and no I do not think it wise. If you have any options, you can try them."

The second call was to Brendan Collins, his trusted friend and team member. To Brendan, he quickly explained the situation and what he needed.

When he turned to regard his passenger, Mosellan was smiling.

"That did not sound like 'nothing'," Jenha murmured.

"It isn't much," Jim admitted.

"But if an opportunity arises..."Jenha asked suggestively.

"No, in this case, it would not help Erin to remove her from custody by unauthorised means."

Jim wondered how much he should tell this stranger. This alien stranger.

Jenha seemed to sense his thoughts. "I think you know some things about me. Perhaps it might help if you told me and I will correct any important details."

Jim summarised what he knew.

Jenha was impressed, but alarmed enough to ask, "How many people know this, do you know?"

"No more than a dozen. Twelve." Jim added the number quickly, since he was not sure of the stranger's grasp of idiom. "Many of them resist the idea that you came from further away than Central Europe."

Unspoken, was the tacit acknowledgement that Jenha did not come from Earth.

"Your information is correct in outline," Jenha admitted. "How did you discover that Atapi and Kumatan were here?"

"Wanda asked for more idea of what she would be getting into if she went. It was what she was told."

Jenha nodded. "My son acted without authority, but he acted with wisdom. He is now considered the saviour of our world, even if it was three humans from here who did more for us than anyone could have expected. I knew what he intended, but I did not believe that he would succeed, so I said nothing. I think he hoped to find another like Jai Cassidy. Instead, he found out that I had failed to finish my duty here."

Jim listened thoughtfully. "Perhaps you could tell me what that duty is now?"

It was Jenha's turn to be thoughtful. "To speak simply, and not wanting to get into a philosophical discussion – it is this. When I left here, many years ago, it was on the understanding that everything that had come from home was taken back – except for what the Earth had claimed. And all that the Earth had claimed would have no changing effect on it."

Jim nodded. That careful statement confirmed his own intuition that Jenha Mosellan was not a danger.

"My sister insisted on coming with us when my father was sent here. She had made friends with Jai Ansuni, the mother of Jai Cassidy and the daughter of Stacion Ansuni, the sorcerer that fled here with his tribe. Stacion discovered, once he was here that he could not draw power from the aura of this world, as he had been able to do on Korvu. He did discover that he could harvest it from death. I believe he had a part in prolonging the war occurring at that time."

Jim prompted him when he fell silent.

"And it was your duty to stop him?"

"Yes, and to protect the innocents of this world from him. When my father was killed, it became my task. I had been here, training to be his successor. But in coming here the normal training for one such as I was interrupted. I should have spent years more being trained by the Kimh before taking up the work of a Traeger."

"The Kimh. I didn't hear about them," Jim murmured.

"They are..." Jenha paused to find the right words. "Probably the closest you have here would be politicians and priests."

"Hmmm." Jim decided he would have to think about that combination, later.

"To continue, my family have been Traegers for many generations. One of the few bloodlines that breed the trait predictably. Because of this, we have high responsibility and are..."

"Watched and controlled?" Jim suggested into the long pause.

"That will do as a basic idea," Jenha agreed. "Having your young friend act every bit as efficiently as the men was an affront to many. They accepted it on the basis that she was from elsewhere. Human, not Kumatan."

Jim intuited much and asked, "No one knew, or everyone assumed that the women of your family could not be as talented as the men?"

"Yes," Jenha admitted. "In short, an untrained Traeger could prove to be as dangerous as an uncontrolled Atapi sorcerer. I am here because I must examine the young women, evaluate them and take appropriate action."

Jim could envision a wide range of things that might be considered appropriate.

"Let's travel and find somewhere we can eat and talk," Jim decided. He needed time to think on all he was learning.

Chapter 18

Jim drove to an exclusive restaurant that he knew of and paid to use a private parlour. Once the meal had been served, they were assured of absolute privacy.

"You will, no doubt, notice many changes from your last visit," Jim said to re-open the conversation. "Yet you seem to have a knack for fitting in."

"As I should. It is part of what a fully trained Traeger should be," Jenha explained.

"Erin worries you," Jim said then, getting to the point.

"The one who was taken away in the car? Yes. You are worried too? May I ask in what way?"

Jim studied the stranger. "She feels emotions. At least that is what I believe. Where they will take her is full of dark, unpleasant ones. Would you be able to help her?"

Jenha nodded. "I would need to know more about her, and the other young women."

They spoke quietly, for some hours, first about Jenha's newfound kin, and then about how the actions of each had previously affected the wider society. Jim knew, intuitively, that the stranger's culture was quite different to what he knew, and he would see things in a different perspective based on that and on what he had previously learnt about Earth. Earth had changed a lot since the war.

Jim tied to be factual, and speak neutrally about how things were viewed. It seemed that Mosellan was equally perceptive and intuitive.

They both eventually fell into a contemplative silence – comfortable in each other's presence.

"If I am able, I would like to talk to the three women at this base first. Then I will need to spend time with Erin," Jenha proposed.

"I assume you will not wish the full details of your qualifications to be known?" Jim suggested with a faint smile.

"That would be both wise and in line with the commands laid on me," Jenha admitted.

"I can arrange for identification, letters of introduction and letters of authority, and anything else you need," Jim offered. Then he considered a moment.

"There are two people that I think you should meet as yourself," Jim said carefully. He mentioned them and explained who Rowan Wallace and

Magnus Goldman were in terms of position and association with Stev Aldrin, David and Wanda Martin.

"Yes, I agree that would be wise," Jenha agreed. "Tell me about this man who does not wish Erin well."

Jim could not give a lot of information about the Secretary of State, so he stuck to the facts that he knew.

"How do you think Erin will fare until I am able to speak to her? Do you think she will attempt to end her life again?"

Jim sensed his distaste for that prospect.

"No, I think that was an opportunity taken in a moment of weakness," Jim decided. "Even though it seemed accidental, I don't think Michaels, the civilian, was deceived. They will ensure she is watched to prevent a repeat. Once she has slept, I don't think she will try."

"That pleases me," Jenha admitted. "I am glad that you insisted on having her looked at by a healer."

"I do have doubts that a doctor will be called," Jim had to admit. "I am sure Michaels has been told that she has only ever pretended to be sick or unstable. I know better. You did a lot to calm her down. How long should that effect last?"

"In her case, I am uncertain. She should not have even considered killing herself."

Jim tried to present his beliefs in how Erin was thinking and behaving in a logical manner. His ability to read people was usually excellent.

"So – she is with child," Jenha said with wonder. "Have you information on the father?"

"Erin thinks he is dead, but I have a name and some details. I have people checking."

Jim found accommodation for Jenha Mosellan and left him to his privacy. He had made sure the stranger had the means to contact him and knew how to get to the base.

Before Jim left, Jenha had a warning. "You will need to be prepared for Wanda to be unstable. I did not have any time to examine her before we left to come here. I did sense a deep psychic trauma. It will be more complicated because she appears to be mind-linked to Erin. To help with that, I will need to learn of previous contacts between them."

"I know of some," Jim admitted. "Tanya and Elisabeth will probably know more."

Jim achieved a lot more before he arrived back at Rockwater. He had confirmed Erin's location through Brendan Collins, organised documents, activated a lawyer member of his team to look into Erin's case for appeal and sent orders for a police doctor to see Erin first thing in the morning.

It was dawn when Jim finally allowed himself to sleep and he permitted himself four hours.

At nine o'clock he sought out Dr Wallace and found him in the infirmary, where Wanda lay on her front, and a nurse was changing a dressing on what looked like a burn.

Rowan shepherded Jim to the room he used as an office.

"Thought you would be around," Rowan indicated a seat. "David is fine, he just needs to sleep for a week – so he will probably be up tomorrow. Stev has finally agreed to rest. Wanda is in a poor state, although her vital signs are improving. She looks malnourished and dehydrated, has several injuries that look like burns, numerous inch wide bruises, and what looks like a bite on her neck. Those are the worst, but there are signs of older injuries. And, since I don't know better, it looks like she was tortured."

"Erin implied as much," Jim said with sympathy.

"How?" Rowan asked.

"Erin, Elisabeth and Tanya were having intermittent contact with Wanda - Erin more so, and for longer periods. This is in addition to those fainting fits she had."

"She really needs to be here for the debrief," Rowan said worriedly.

"I agree," Jim told the doctor. "However I could not go against a direct presidential order – not then."

Rowan picked up on the qualification and grinned slightly. "What happened up there?"

Jim told him what he could and added at last, "Wanda didn't return alone."

That got Rowan's interest. "I will introduce him to you when I have some identification for him. That should be here now, or very soon. He has familial interest in Wanda and the others."

Rowan nodded. "That, I hope, will be helpful. Tanya and Elisabeth have been told not to appear until tomorrow."

Jim sat back in the chair. "I am doing what I can to get Erin back here."

A crash from the other room made them both jump up and trot to the door to the infirmary.

Wanda was standing, or rather trying to. The IV stand had fallen over, dragging the drip out of Wanda's arm. She was clad only in the basic hospital gown and was scarcely decent. She was trying to get to the door, and there was no trace of intelligence in her eyes.

The nurse seemed to be unconscious on the floor.

Jim immediately stepped over the obstructions and went to Wanda. Rowan went to the nurse, who had a vivid red mark on her face.

Jim picked Wanda up and carried her two steps back to the bed. As soon as he laid her down, she began to struggle to get upright. Jim let her, and held her in an embrace.

"Wanda! It's me, Jim. You are home, and safe."

After a fifth repetition, Wanda seemed to understand and collapsed in his arms. He continued to hold her until the drip line was reinserted. He felt his shirt growing wet and knew Wanda was crying.

Jim had just finished settling Wanda, when his mobile phone rang.

"It's Julian. We are taking Erin to the emergency hospital. When I got there, that officious secret service guy was trying to get Erin up for questioning. I've put the fear of hell into him for not having her checked last night. He claimed she had been well enough to walk down the hill and try to kill one of the marines."

"What's the status?" Jim asked urgently.

"Hypothermia, dehydration. Her shoulder is swollen and I couldn't hear a foetal heartbeat."

"Keep me advised, Julian," Jim ordered, ringing off. He knew he could trust Julian to see that Erin had the best treatment.

He had a further call as he was returning to the cottage. This one was from Brendan.

"That civilian? He put a call through to Washington – to Stan Russell, on his private number. He requested a security guard for the emergency hospital."

"Julian is taking Erin there. He didn't get her looked at last night. Russell must be obsessed. Local police would have been reasonable. Keep a watch on things will you?"

The next call came as soon as Brendan rang off. This time it was the security guard at the gate, telling him that a Professor Mosellan was there by appointment. Jim smiled and changed direction. He had collected the express delivery of the needed identification on his way from the infirmary.

"I would talk first with those you trust in authority," Jenha advised Jim. "You would perhaps introduce me?"

"Certainly," Jim agreed.

"How are the women today?"

"Elisabeth and Tanya are tired but will be fine after they rest. Wanda has been sedated to ensure she does."

"Was there an incident?"

Jim described what he had observed.

"And the other one? Erin."

Jim told him what he knew.

"Your agent? Is he extremely concerned?"

"Concerned, yes, but I believe he feels he arrived in time. He was more concerned for the baby."

"How difficult will it be for me to see her?" Jenha asked with some urgency.

"There will be guards," Jim predicted. "Probably both inside and outside of the room, due to her action on the way back. However, they should not be a problem since the doctor treating her is my agent."

Jim was glad Magnus Goldman was with Rowan Wallace when he arrived. Jim made the introduction, only mentioning Jenha by name and the claim that he could assist the recovery of Wanda and the others.

Goldman instantly recognised the name, and his eyes narrowed slightly, but he admitted nothing. After giving his own name and position, he invited his guest to be seated.

A short time later, while Goldman and his guest were cautiously getting to know each other, Stev Aldrin was announced and given permission to enter.

Aldrin recognised Jenha immediately, and welcomed him warmly. His greeting reassured Goldman.

"I thought my eyes were deceiving me," Aldrin said. "I am both surprised and delighted. Did you bring Wanda here? We were worried when she did not come after David."

Jenha nodded. "Your young friend needed my help."

"And you will have no trouble returning?" Aldrin queried.

"There will be no problem," Jenha assured him. "However I have duties to perform here. Some members of the council were unsettled by the loose ends I left here on my last visit."

Aldrin didn't need a further explanation.

"I have already related much of the events of my visit with you," Aldrin told Jenha. "I think I have portrayed the reactions of your Government correctly."

Jenha waved that concern aside. "Discussing events will need to wait until all participants are able to contribute. I am here today to arrange to acquaint myself with those who know young Wanda and her kin the best, so I can help them."

Rowan explained to Aldrin, "Tanya is Wanda's cousin as we guessed, and as well as Elisabeth, Wanda's sister, there is another cousin, Erin. She was with them when you returned."

"The four women are the loose ends I mentioned. I discovered, mere hours before I was sent here, that they are the great-grandchildren of my sister. She came with us here, and died here."

Stev glanced at Goldman, who nodded.

"Are there any others?" Aldrin asked.

"I was not aware of these ..." Jenha admitted. His pleasant manner slightly ruffled. "However of the women with our group, my sister was the only one who wandered, and she did so for weeks on end."

"Having met your people, Jenha, and having the chance to help them, I think I am glad of your sister's ... foresight."

"Your first thought of 'indiscretion' seems more appropriate," Jenha told Aldrin. "And I must agree, even if those who I serve tolerated your young friend's brazen ways only because she was human. Now that they have discovered differently, they refer to her by fancy euphemisms that mean 'mongrel female'."

Jim inserted a question. "What do you want to do first?"

Jenha was quick to answer. "I wish to see young Wanda first. I had little time to evaluate her before we left. I did however see some injuries that concerned me. She will, however, need some time to recover before I can finish my assessment. I wish also to meet Erin again under less stressful circumstances. I hope to spend some time with her before you try to get Wanda to talk to you about her ordeal. Then I would like to meet the other young women who helped."

Goldman nodded. "I am very pleased to have you here. I will be able to supply identification to give you free access here."

Jenha acknowledged the offer, and rose to his feet to indicate the meeting was over.

Rowan stood up and gestured to the passage that led to the infirmary.

Jenha spoke in a low tone to Jim as they walked after Rowan. "Am I correct in saying that my having free access here may not be popular?"

"Until you have the ID any that might object are not here and can be dealt with. They will only know you as an important medical specialist."

The nurse tending Wanda accepted the presence of the specialist and made no fuss about assisting him.

Jim waited out of the way, whilst Rowan and Jenha discussed Wanda's condition in low tones. When they were finished, Rowan dictated notes for the nurse to put on Wanda's chart based on Jenha's suggestions. He apologised then for needing to be elsewhere.

Jim led Jenha back outside to where his hire car was parked. They were driving to the hospital before Jim spoke. "I have told my doctor that you are coming. He has left word with the ward sister to admit you. The guards should not be a problem."

"You are most efficient," Jenha commended him.

"That's part of my job," Jim answered, then asked, "What concerned you about Wanda, if I might ask?"

"Your concern is great. May I ask what she is to you?"

"Fair question. Though you sound just like a doctor! We are friends. She works for me, often doing dangerous things needed to achieve an expedient end."

"Ah! That explains a great deal."

Jim suspected that Jenha must also have some degree of telepathy.

"I had sensed that in her when she first arrived. Did you train her?"

"For the most part, Wanda trained herself. Or rather some unpleasant people did. When she decided to change her focus from criminal activities, I was able to redirect her purpose."

"When I return home," Jenha said shaking his head slowly, "I will never underestimate a woman again. She saved my people, but they would be scandalised by what she has done. She is magnificent."

"The wounds," Jim reminded his passenger.

Jenha finally decided to answer. "They were made by some particularly nasty Atapi weapons. The burn marks were from a force whip and the bruises from pressure prods, which are like a stick that can punch. The burns look to be healing, but the danger with them is of infection. It may be that being mainly human that the infectious agents on Korvu will not affect her or it may be that they are more virulent. I should be told if an infection does not respond to your local treatment."

"What about the greenish tinge to the skin?" Jim asked.

"That, I believe comes from an Atapi remedy for muscle ailments. Does Wanda suffer from such?"

Jim described Wanda's ongoing problem.

"The stiffening sickness," Jenha identified. "The Atapi remedy seems to have worked well. I must remember to advise our healers. How do your people treat it?"

"Some infusion of a particular protein," Jim tried to describe it so this stranger would understand. "They discovered Wanda could produce it, but not always in sufficient amount. They used it to treat Elisabeth and made a synthetic form to help Wanda, Generally they both need to keep active. Wanda fights it by doing dangerous things."

"Ah," Jenha suddenly understood. "Then I would reduce her health and ...usefulness...if I wished to make her more...law-abiding."

Jim saw what Jenha might have been intending. "We are a lot alike, and you feel to me like a friend, but I sense our cultures look at things in different ways. I would only wish to be assured of Wanda's mental equilibrium, and not have some controller of morals and ethics placed on her."

"I understand what you are saying, my friend, I do. And perhaps it will reassure you when I say that I contrived that my son was not trained as I was. There are many unpleasant, expedient things a Traeger must do, and when I choose to view the intended result differently – then I must abide the consequences."

"As must I," Jim told him. "As must Wanda. Erin is still learning that lesson. It is the basis of her current situation."

Chapter 19

They met unexpected resistance at the hospital. The normal security let them through, but the guards on the ward had been changed. The officious civilian was giving these guards instructions. He spotted, and recognised Jim and Jenha and moved to block their way. From beyond the civilian, Julian, Jim's agent, moved to intervene.

Julian Ackerman was fully ratified as a police doctor, and often also called on by the FBI. As he was apparently not associated with Jim, the civilian treated him with more courtesy.

"May I see you orders, Mr Michaels?" Julian asked, holding out his hand.

Michaels, the civilian, handed him a faxed transcript. Julian read it carefully and handed it back.

"Yes, Mr Michaels, it does authorise you to oversee Miss Mason. However, it does not supersede my jurisdiction as physician in charge of Miss Mason, nor countermand the instruction I received to consult with Professor Mosellan about her case. Mr Phillips kindly agreed to bring the professor here. I have been led to understand that I have encountered a particularly sensitive case that must be handled 'by the book' and that the professor is the expert on the science of the mind. I'm sure his credentials will prove to be perfectly correct and if you wish to discuss this further, I am willing to do so in the office I am using. As the Professor does not accept just any case, I would prefer not to waste his valuable time."

Since Julian had covered every objection that Michaels had thought to make – he moved aside and let Julian escort Jenha into the private ward. Michaels glared at Jim who ignored his hostility.

When Julian emerged a short time later, he gestured to Michaels and told Jim he could wait near the nurse's station. His dismissal of Jim mollified Michaels, and so did the comment Julian made in Jim's hearing. "You can be quite reassured that Miss Mason will not fool the Professor and that I think is the important issue here."

Jim turned to hide his smile.

Jenha was not familiar with the machines to which Erin seemed to be attached. Julian had quickly explained their purpose, telling Jenha that Jim had briefed this doctor very well.

The machines were not things he had encountered on this Earth planet during his previous time here. That though, had been half a century earlier.

Traegers on his world often had some healing ability too, more in the realms of healing the mind.

His first impression, apart from the strange machines, was the absence of the planet's aura. It was not surprising, but it meant that this child of his bloodline could not use it to heal herself – if she had realised that she could.

This one had already realised that the aura existed and some of the ways to use it. That showed that she had tremendous potential – in spite of being a female – and untrained.

His people had not seen the same potential in his sister, Suzi. He hadn't thought of her for a long time, and tried not to now. The woman, lying on the bed as if dead, was the image of her.

Having studied the ambience around Erin, he touched her face, gently. Some awareness flitted away from him.

Clever! She was indeed not as dangerously ill as it seemed. Yet her face was cold to touch, in spite of the warm blankets around her.

He glanced at the graphs being produced by the machines. The one Julian had called a foetal heartbeat monitor was strong and regular. The one for the mother was weaker.

He placed a hand under the blanket where the bulge indicated the baby within.

"At least, young woman, you have one priority correct." He spoke softly and felt a faint tensing of muscles.

He removed his hand. "However, now that your child is well, you should stop draining your own life force to give to it. To her! You need to be well enough to take advantage of plans being made by your friends to get you back to where you are needed."

He watched Erin's face and caught the rapid glance.

"Wanda must be made to talk about her experiences and you are the key to helping her."

Jenha was aware that Erin was listening.

"You WILL do NOTHING to jeopardise those plans."

Touching Erin's hand as he spoke, told him that his coercive command had been recognised as such by Erin. He felt her instinctive reaction. That command should hold for now - until she got stronger physically and that chance led to the likelihood of going back to the prison Jim mentioned. Time would reveal if it would hold longer than that.

If she had been a woman of his people, from birth, she would never have become what she was, as she was. Had she been a male, she would have been marked to be trained as a Traeger, and again never have come to be in the state she was in. A commoner of his people in this state would be easy to treat. This woman would be a challenge.

Tanya was sleeping and Elisabeth was ready for bed when the knock came at the door. She went to the door to open it. She had expected Jim. But her mouth dropped open at the sight of the other.

"Come in," she managed to say.

"I don't think you have been properly introduced," Jim smiled at her. "Jenha Mosellan, this is Elisabeth Willard."

Elisabeth seemed lost for words, an unusual situation. Jenha smiled and gestured to the chair she had vacated.

"It seems that you know who I am," Jenha suggested.

Elisabeth nodded. "You don't look any older than my father," she blurted, and then blushed.

Jenha pretended not to notice her embarrassment. "Jim tells me you did an exceptional job of piecing information together. I had not realised I had left so many traces behind." He adroitly confirmed he was the same man that Elisabeth had discovered. "I must admit that learning that my sister had left behind such a legacy was unexpected."

Elisabeth's attention was so thoroughly caught that she did not notice Jim slipping out of the room to give Jenha the privacy to do his evaluation.

Jenha sat in a second chair and asked, "Tell me what you discovered."

It was easy to talk to him, Elisabeth discovered. He was like a long-time friend, and she wanted to keep talking to him and feeling his approval. She told him about her search to find if Tanya was related to her and where it had led and how other people had given her parts of the answer. It moved naturally to talking about Wanda, and her own thoughts and feelings about her actions. When she came to mention when Wanda had been in prison and it began upsetting her, it felt natural to be comforted by this great-great-uncle. When she felt she had talked enough, she fell silent.

"I would like to meet your cousin," Jenha suggested. "You could perhaps visit with Jim," Jenha suggested with the lightest trace of coercion. He stood and offered his hand to help her up.

Unexpectedly, Jenha found himself being hugged by Elisabeth and didn't know what to do.

"I have never had a grandfather and now I know what it must be like.

And you brought Wanda back, didn't you and then disappeared like Erin did. Thank you! I don't know how I would have managed without Wanda."

"Very well, I suspect," Jenha assured her, "Wanda helped you to blossom, and you have, splendidly. Now, you have a chance to help her."

"I will! I promised to always be there for her. Just as she was always there for me. She said she needed me to be her conscience."

Jenha marvelled. This woman was one such as even the Kimh would approve. Perhaps it was because she had so little of the Traeger's power that she was so serene and deceptively strong – not physically – but in spirit. And steadfast in being her sister's conscience. That was a comment that opened a vast new insight into her sister.

Jenha gently eased Elisabeth away from him with some reluctance. Almost at once, she trotted off to wake her cousin.

Her excited chattering was audible from the other room. In a while, she re-emerged bringing her cousin, who, Jenha could sense was wary of strangers.

"He brought Wanda back," Elisabeth said.

"Yes, I saw him there," Tanya said, but she met Jenha's gaze. "What did you do to Erin? I felt you do something."

"There was a need for calm. I supplied it," Jenha told her, keeping her gaze.

Tanya shook her head, trying to break free of that compelling gaze. Elisabeth suddenly realised that she wanted to talk to Jim.

"You are doing to me what you did to Erin," Tanya accused.

"You do not like the feeling of being coerced," Jenha murmured. "Is that because you grew up in Russia?"

Tanya thought back to before she came to America and her relative freedom now.

"Probably, I guess."

"Tell me about it," Jenha suggested and he gestured her to the seat her cousin had vacated, before sitting himself.

Soon Tanya was talking as freely about her earlier life, her mother, her guilt that she had caused her mother's arrest and eventual death. She told him things she had never even wanted to admit to herself. Her understanding listener then told her how she need not bear all the guilt and quietly erased the memory of how she had learnt to manipulate her friends into doing things for her. Wrong things. A small beginning that might have led to a dictator.

Tanya finally ran out of things to say. She was no longer resisting Jenha's coercive suggestions of moral and ethical behaviour. That she now trusted him was evidenced by her grip on his hand.

Jenha was satisfied to let it stay there as she sat thinking on what she had said. He considered her to have little more of the Traeger's power than Elisabeth, though both had enough to respond to his son's call. Tanya had enough telepathy to sense his calmimg of Erin. Enough to have begun to use it, but fortunately not for long in that repressed country or she would likely have been incarcerated like her mother. She had been fortunate that Jim had rescued her.

Now, in ways that would stay in her mind, she knew what might have been and why what she had done was wrong.

Jenha left her sitting quietly in the chair, eased of a burden of guilt but with much to think on. He left, satisfied with his work and with more insights into Wanda, and glimpses of Erin's past.

He was walking back to the main building when he recognised another figure, leaning against one of the few trees, in the dark. He slowed. David had fought for his world, even though he had no ties to Korvu. The young man was seemingly oblivious to everything around him. It was not his place to interfere with the people wholly of this world, and yet...

He walked closer. "David?"

David seemed to jump, had turned in the direction of the voice. "Jenha?" he sounded incredulous, but moved quickly to where he could make out the shape of a person.

"You are here!" David greeted, his face betraying hope. He reached out a hand to shake hands, but bowed instead when he recalled the protocol of Korvu. He was surprised when Jenha returned a similar bow. That made it a greeting of equals.

"Have you recovered, David?"

"The past months are not something a night's sleep can cure. But, I have some of my energy back."

"Do you want to forget them?" Jenha asked.

"No. They are part of me. They have changed me and it will take time to – how would you say it – integrate the changes?"

"Well said, David. Is that what is on your mind now?"

"No." David said tersely. "I assume the powers around here, know you are here?"

"Yes, your friend Jim has been very helpful. Few, however, truly know who and what I am."

"Just as well," David commented neutrally, turning to stare some distance away.

"Did you know that Jai Cassidy insisted that I bring Wanda back?"

David returned his attention to Jenha. "No. I can vaguely recall the girls saying Wanda couldn't move herself anymore and hoping that Jai would come and help. Did she do it because of her relationship to you?"

"I was the logical choice," Jenha admitted. "And she enjoyed the chance to shock me."

"I suppose because you had been here before..."

"That of course, but Jai informed me that I had unfinished business here, namely some great-great nieces."

"Wanda was one! And Tanya and Elisabeth?" David stated in sudden understanding. "So that is how Jahni could reach her."

"Yes. Do you regret being involved?"

"No."

"Except?"

"Except that I wasn't able to protect her, and because of that, those aliens tortured her, and I couldn't find her, or hear from her, or help her. And she was all alone," David blurted.

"She was not entirely alone," Jenha told him.

David stared at him.

"It seems that Tanya, Elisabeth and particularly Erin, could reach her at times. I think they did help her a little."

"I don't know Erin," David said thoughtfully. "Was she the one I saw yesterday? Is she here?"

"Unfortunately not. Jim is trying to get her here."

"I have no doubt that he will succeed," David assured him.

"Perhaps you would like to walk a while? You could tell me more about Wanda."

"Can you help her?" David asked, trying not to sound desperate. "I don't know how."

"I will do all I can," Jenha promised, "What worries you?"

"Distance and darkness," David said. "I don't know her anymore and she is my life."

"Tell me about her and then we will go to see her."

Erin let herself wake up and groaned. Her whole body seemed to be suffering from the pins and needles feeling as her blood began to flow at normal speed. She felt cold, is spite of the blankets around her.

A nurse came into the room and noticed she was awake. She checked the monitors that Erin was only just becoming aware of. She bustled around, making notes of blood pressure and pulse from the machines and putting a thermometer into Erin's mouth. When it beeped, she looked at it and frowned.

"I think we will remove some of those hot packs," she said aloud.

"Cold! I feel cold." Erin's voice came out as a croak.

The nurse felt her forehead, and drew her wrist from under the blankets.

"I will get the doctor to look at you. Your temperature is way up."

The nurse walked out and Erin raised herself slightly to look around. She was relieved that the room did not look like the prison cell she remembered being hustled into. It wasn't hard to guess what had happened. As soon as she had been put in there, she had probably passed out. She had been awake out of sheer stubbornness. In that place, the subtle breeze she called the aura did not reach her in the cell. Had she had to be resuscitated again? She thought not, but she was in a hospital...She extended her senses a bit and sensed guards outside her door. She sought a bit further and felt the familiar sense of damped illness. Why had they brought her here? Had she freaked out again? No. There were no restraints on her.

She sighed. This then was only a temporary respite. She would be sent back to prison, and her sentence extended for escaping...

Chapter 20

The nurse returned with the doctor, and Erin saw another man follow them. She tensed, identifying him as the one that had insisted on the handcuffs and enjoyed her helplessness as he had pushed her into the cell. Erin expected to feel panic, but didn't.

She lay quietly while the doctor examined her. He listened to her breathing, checked her ears and the glands around her neck, and all sorts of other things as well as asked questions. He was baffled by the fever.

"You were brought in with dehydration and hypothermia," the doctor explained to Erin. "What were you doing yesterday?"

She was not going to tell him everything. "Just sitting out in the fresh air. I didn't feel cold."

Her suspicion was confirmed. The civilian guy snorted in contempt. No way would she admit to the freaky thing she had been part of.

The doctor seemed annoyed by the man too. He ignored him and directed the nurse to give her a dose of a general antibiotic, while he arranged for a series of x-rays.

"We will need to get in quickly. Emergency is preparing for patients from a multiple MVA," the doctor told the nurse. He turned to the civilian and seemed to be polite, "Mr Michaels, you will need to leave the room."

The doctor used the phone in the room to organise the scans and orderlies to get her to the x-ray department. The nurse began to remove the monitors from Erin.

Erin enjoyed the fact that Michaels had not enjoyed being ordered out. As she was wheeled out, she saw Michaels on his phone, and the guards from outside her door followed them.

David yelled for Rowan Wallace. The doctor came quickly, and didn't ask why David was there. That was obvious, Wanda was his wife.

"She's burning up," David said. "Feel her. I've tried using cool cloths, but it isn't helping."

"How long ago did you notice this," Wallace asked, quickly checking the chart.

"Ten minutes," David guessed.

Wallace checked Wanda over, and then had David support her while he checked the marks on her back. They were looking red and inflamed now, when they had seemed to be healing. He eased Wanda down and went to fetch the nurse.

Jim Phillips received the call from Julian after seeing Goldman and Jenha off on a flight to Washington. The visitor had requested a chance to talk to the fathers of Tanya and Erin, Elisabeth had already called her father and asked him to come to the base, but not why. It was not yet generally known that the missing Aldrin and associates were back.

Julian reported Erin as being awake, lucid calm but with a very high fever. He reported what he was doing, and admitted his complete absence of probable cause. Jim had given him a layman's version of what Erin and the others had done, and how Erin had been after previous incidents, so the original symptoms were explainable, but not this fever.

Jim abruptly told him that he would call back. He called the infirmary and David answered.

"Jim? Wanda? She's burning hot. The marks on her back – they think are infected. They are taking specimens for analysis. They have her packed in ice..."

Jim now had a very good idea what Erin's problem was. He assured David that Wallace would have the problem in hand, and rang off so he could speak to his doctor, Julian.

"Psychosomatic?" Julian echoed thoughtfully. "That is what Michaels is claiming, only that Erin is causing it herself."

"It is not deliberate," Jim insisted. "Mosellan warned that something like this was possible. He says their minds are linked at a very deep level."

"I will need to think on that. However, you will have to get rid of Michaels before his presence unsettles my patient. I am surprised it hasn't already, from what you have told me. Even I can feel his malevolence towards her."

"I am working on it, although it may not be a fast solution."

Michaels waited until the gurney transporting Erin Mason had moved out of sight into the patient lift. He hurried then to the nearest public lifts. He was not going to let his prisoner out of his sight for a moment longer than necessary. He didn't trust her, not at all. A fever! He didn't know how she had done it, but if the doctor couldn't fathom a cause...

He caught up with Erin outside the x-ray cubicles. She had seen him, glared at him and then pretended he wasn't there. He moved slightly so he could study her face. If he didn't know better – he would say she was frightened. Good! She was a criminal – she did not deserve to be coddled. She should have been sent back to prison as soon as she had been found.

That Jim Phillips, whoever and whatever he was, should be charged with harbouring a wanted fugitive. He would see to it.

Erin wasn't frightened, and that surprised her, but she had another problem. One she had not learnt to overcome. The sensitivity to people who were sick or in pain. On the upper floor where she had been, the sense had been distant, muted. When she had first woken, her own discomfort had blocked it. It wasn't so now. The x-ray department was right next to the emergency ward and she was feeling, full strength, the pain and emotions from there. She tried blocking the sensations by her usual means, but she was still too weak and felt too sick to concentrate.

Somewhere close by were two minds full of violence and hate, being restrained by police so that their knife wounds could be treated. She had to keep telling herself that they could not get to her.

Michaels was excluded from the x-ray chamber, but he knew it only had one entrance. So he turned his attention to the surge of activity in the emergency room. Six ambulances, he had heard, were arriving with at least that many victims of a major car accident. The staff were doing triage on them as they arrived.

He pulled his attention away, somewhat reluctantly when Erin was wheeled back out. She was as white as the sheets she was on, when only a short time ago her face was flushed red with fever. And what was she doing struggling? The orderlies were having trouble trying to wheel the gurney and keep her still. He would see about that!

Erin couldn't help herself. She had to get away from there. The pain she sensed was too intense. It was overwhelming her mind. She felt she was losing all control and knew she could not afford to.

Michaels had no qualms about pushing her down and holding her. He was too strong for her to fight against. It was his hatred and the sense that he was enjoying watching her struggle helplessly that was the final straw.

Her 'episode' brought staff running to see what the screaming was about. Michaels was pushed away as the orderlies took over trying to restrain her until restraints could be put on her. Julian was paged.

Against the instructions of Professor Mosellan, he felt his only option was to sedate her. He held her until her screams abated and the struggling stopped. When he released her, Erin gripped his hand as she seemed to be struggling to breathe.

"Oxygen, here," Julian called. Erin batted the mask away from her face. Instead, she pulled Julian's arm to get his attention.

"Woman," Erin managed to say. "Came in. Blue...blue jumper. Minor wounds. Can't breathe."

Julian took a moment to make sense of it.

"What crap?" Michaels exploded. He shoved Erin back, not caring that she hit her head on the rail. "It's a trick to distract us so she can get free."

Julian suddenly stalked away towards the emergency room where injured people seemed to be everywhere. He looked around, and then headed straight for a trolley parked near the wall. A woman, in a blue jumper, stared up at him in panic – unable to breathe deeply. Julian summoned help.

Erin was back in her room before Julian was able to leave the woman he had gone to help. When he returned to check on her, he had two policemen with him. Erin was barely conscious, and no longer had such a high fever. Michaels was staring at her with hate filled eyes.

"Michaels, if you touch my patient again, I will have you charged with assault and arrested."

"You can't do that! I have a job to do and I outrank the local police!"

Julian was ready. "You are not above the law. However, these men are not here to arrest you, yet. Nor to evict you from the hospital. They need to talk to you."

"In private, Sir," one officer suggested.

Michaels followed that one out the door, the other followed.

Julian wondered what the man would say when he found his wife was downstairs being prepared for an operation to repair a crushed lung. And she had been the woman in the blue jumper.

Jim rang off after hearing Julian's report of the part solution to their problems and of Erin's condition. He was able to feel more relaxed again now that both Erin and Wanda were improving again. What Julian had told him explained why Wanda now passive once again had been struggling and swearing. He thought to call Goldman, leaving a message for him to call back as soon as he got to Washington. Jenha Mosellan needed to know what had been going on.

Chapter 21

Magnus Goldman walked through the hallowed halls of the Whitehouse following a presidential aide. The Secretary of State had agreed to a meeting, but due to the pressures of his job, needed to fit them in between other meetings. They were led to a small room and asked to wait.

Goldman had a case containing a laptop and other documents prepared for this presentation. On the way, he had explained to Jenha some of the normal roles of the Secretary of State and the line he proposed to take to present Erin's case. He had warned Jenha that they might have to wait some time – as on a national scale, Erin Mason simply wasn't that important. It was a great concession that he had agreed to the meeting.

While they were alone in the waiting room, Magnus explained more about the significance of the White House, how the leaders were chosen, some of the protocols and at Jenha's question, how Goldman was wanting to use Erin.

As soon as their assigned aide announced the Secretary, both men rose to their feet. Before they could sit again, the aide announced another, the President, William Walters.

Jenha followed Magnus's lead when greeting and being introduced to the nation's leader.

The unexpected presence of the President required Goldman to quickly adjust his approach and how he was going to present his argument.

Before he could say more than the outline of his contention, Goldman was interrupted by Russell.

"With all due respect, Mr President," Russell stated, "It will take a great deal to convince me that Mason should receive any consideration. Even if she did somehow help Colonel Aldrin return."

"I have read to your reports, Stan, and I would like to hear what Goldman has to say. I have not heard where Aldrin was being held."

Goldman kept his briefing terse. He did not know how the President would react to the facts he had to present. He began with the outline of the existence of Atapi and Kumatan on Earth fifty years before, followed the genealogy that led to Erin and Wanda. He continued with facts of Wanda's sudden increase in psychic abilities and of Erin's different ones, offering video proof. Then he talked of the situation that Colonel Aldrin and his team had landed in, and what he knew of the circumstances of their return – clearly stating Erin's part in it and how it had affected her. He back tracked and summarised from when Jim had found her, her condition then, and how she had helped find Zara Russell.

The Secretary kept his face impassive, except for the twitch in a cheek muscle. Walters already knew the details about Russell's daughter. The press had given them both some heat about it.

The President asked the important question of Goldman. "You are here because of the Mason woman. What importance has she to you? The rest of your report is much more thought provoking."

It was the opening that Goldman wanted, so he could present the need to use and not stifle her computing genius, and to ensure it was used for the benefit of the United States and not by a foreign power.

Stan Russell was asked for his opinion. He rebutted most of what Goldman wanted. The gist of his disagreement was that she was an unpredictable maverick.

"Undisciplined, I think, Mr Secretary," Goldman suggested. "And vulnerable to unscrupulous influences."

He had an idea he wanted to propose, but hoped to have Russell think of it on his own. He was carefully inserting certain keywords into his briefing; hoping Russell would subconsciously connect them.

Goldman went on quickly to bring Jenha into the conversation, referring to his expertise in the science of the mind. He asked permission for Jenha to explain how he believed he could help Erin Mason.

Jenha was very experienced in dealing with the rulers of his own world, and noted that this man was not much different. His questions were intelligent and to the point. He first stated how he could help Erin Mason, and made no secret of his off world origin, and relationship to Wanda and Erin. He, like Goldman was intentionally leaving the other two women out of the spotlight.

Finally, the President spoke, "When I first heard about this I was not convinced, but I feel there is too much evidence for this to be an enormous fraud. I am convinced that all that you have told me is the truth, but it is a truth that will not be made public knowledge. We will simply have to tell the press that Aldrin's whereabouts these past months is classified. So, Goldman, what is it that you propose to do with Miss Mason?"

Goldman had no difficulty in being blunt. "I will make no secret of the fact that I want to use her genius, once I am satisfied of her trustworthiness. Twice, she has been able to study a section of computer code and not only determine why it did not work but to correct the code – in a matter of hours, when my own people had already spent weeks on it."

"Impressive," the President agreed. "You have a plan to overcome your reservations?"

"Yes, Mr President," Goldman answered at once. "I have heard that there is a lawyer looking into grounds for an appeal of her sentence – based on the grounds of being coerced into it. I believe along the lines of Miss Russell's case." From the corner of his eye he saw Stan Russell suppress a scowl. "I have no wish to have her released but still be vulnerable in the future. I would like to see her assigned to Professor Mosellan for therapy and only after she has satisfied his criteria to be considered for release."

"Stan?" the President asked his advisors opinion.

"I don't think we should set a precedent here." Russell aired his view. "The court sentence was correct."

"With due respect, Mr President," Goldman added quickly. "The decision may have been correct but the circumstance is unique. Erin Mason is too sensitive to be kept in the normal prison system. She survived less than two weeks in prison before she had a break down and at the psych facility she needed high doses of strong drugs to maintain a level of sanity. This is a situation that would only lead to either drug dependence or a major mental disorder. The idea of prison is to reform and rehabilitate offenders, not to destroy them."

"Professor, do you agree with this statement?" the President asked.

Jenha had no hesitation in replying.

"It is far better to train the mind to be less sensitive than to rely on medications. This is true for those with depression, anxiety and a range of other disorders."

"You are not saying that a person, like Miss Mason, won't reoffend again," the President queried.

"No, I am saying that should the person have no wish to be in a certain condition – once they recognise the symptoms they will have strategies to fight it," Jenha clarified.

Stan Russell picked up what had not been said. "So if such a person – like Miss Mason – sees she is being used and decides to let herself be used, she will be treated like anyone else?"

"Unless she can prove coercion," Goldman countered.

"No, I don't agree, that woman is smart enough to make it look like coercion," Russell objected.

The President sat back, listening to Goldman and Russell producing counter views. He occasionally glanced at the professor and saw the man was listening with equal interest.

"I would not like her to be let free without strict conditions placed on her," Russell argued. "I do not fancy a genius, as you claim, without scruples or discipline."

"Do you have a suggestion, Stan?" the President asked.

"Yes." Russell was interrupted by his mobile phone. "Excuse me, Mr President." Russell rose and walked away from the group. He spoke into the phone, keeping his comments neutral and uninformative. He was very thoughtful when he returned and sat down.

"Your thoughts Stan," the President prompted, aware he had other important meetings.

"Mr President, I agree that psychiatric therapy should be given to Miss Mason, as a priority. Then, rather than being released, I would suggest a period of national service, to replace the remaining portion of her sentence."

Before the President could respond, Goldman did. "Mr Secretary, that is a very intuitive suggestion. The army or marines would teach her discipline and to think in terms of the nation and not herself."

The President invited Jenha to add his opinion. "Mr President, I cannot see a problem with the idea. I have had only a very brief introductory session with Miss Mason, but I am aware that the shock of prison has left a deep impression on her. She is extremely loathe to return. I need to evaluate her further before I decide if her behaviour in prison was self-induced or inevitable. However, the discipline of prison is more negative than that in a military training situation. I do not know how Miss Mason will feel about that condition but from those I have spoken to, that know something about her, she will now, try to obey the conditions. The final point is that any military training will need to wait until her child is born and able to be passed into the care of her family."

The President suddenly stood up. "That sounds like a plan, gentlemen. Stan, contact the department of justice – have them speak to Miss Mason's lawyer and invite him to state his case and apply for a confidential ruling. Have your recommendation sent to Mark Joletti – include the recommendation of having Mason placed on detached duty with the OSI after completion of basic training."

The President breezed out and Goldman breathed a silent sigh of relief.

Stan Russell sank back into his chair. He did not seem as belligerent as before.

"Have you heard from your people out west, Goldman?" Russell asked.

"Mr Secretary?"

"You haven't," he stated. He explained the bizarre matter of Erin sensing the critical state of the wife of the confirmed sceptic that he had put in charge of her security. "There is no way that could have been rigged," Russell admitted.

Tacitly, he was saying he would not obstruct the proposition just discussed. "What else did you want, Goldman?"

"It was a request of mine," Jenha inserted smoothly. "I feel that it is of extreme importance that I have Miss Mason closer to Mrs Martin. The two currently share a link – stronger than that believed to exist between twins. In the short term it is vital if we are to get Mrs Martin to talk about her experiences. In the long term it will not be healthy for either of them. I need to work with both of them."

"And when will you have finished debriefing them, Goldman?"

"I would like it concluded as soon as possible, but Mrs Martin is suffering from an unidentified infection and Miss Mason has not recovered from her part of bringing the team back."

Russell, jerked as if suddenly recalling the unbelievable return of Aldrin and the two Martin's. Either he had forgotten it until now, or he had accepted the truth of it.

"I will be travelling back to the Rockwater base tonight, Mr Secretary," Jenha advised. "I will begin Miss Mason's therapy as soon as I can. Perhaps you would be able to be there on Thursday, to attend the debriefing?"

Russell mentally considered his schedule. "Yes, I can clear time then." He looked thoughtfully at Jenha and asked, "Have you any advice about dealing with recalcitrant young women? I have a daughter and…"

Jenha permitted a smile. "Young women are not as complex as they think they are. Perhaps you would invite her to come with you to Rockwater. I will make time to evaluate her."

Russell smiled and seemed to relax. "I will hold you to that. If I thought she would agree to it I would make her join the marines."

Jenha nodded. "It is one way of giving a purpose that is acceptable, rather than the wrong purposes finding her."

"Thank you for your time, Mr Secretary," Goldman stood up as Russell did.

Russell nodded, "I will authorise Michaels to release Mason into General Addison's custody." He departed the room first.

Goldman and Jenha summoned the aide to escort them out.

Chapter 22

Goldman took the first opportunity to ring Jim Phillips with the results of his meeting. This was when he was being driven away from the White House. He made a second call to Erin's father, Edward Mason, who was also a personal friend of his. They arranged to meet at Mason's home.

Goldman introduced Jenha as a colleague.

"So Magnus, old friend, what brings you away from your busy schedule? More news of my wayward daughter?"

"As it happens, Ed, Yes," Magnus admitted, accepting the invitation to be seated.

Mason wore an expression of resignation. "So where is she and what are they going to do now?"

"The what is reconsider her case. There is a lawyer preparing an appeal on her behalf. The where is a Defence Department base in California."

Mason sat himself down abruptly.

"The how and why is a longer story and part of that is the reason I have Professor Mosellan with me."

Mason took a better look at the other man. "Do you really think you can straighten out that little idiot of mine?"

"I have every reason to believe that I can." Jenha didn't miss the sudden look of hope in Mason's eyes.

"And no doubt that is the reason why Magnus brought an eminent psychiatrist to see me," Mason surmised.

"Make yourselves comfortable. Can I get you anything? Coffee? Something stronger?"

"Not for me, Ed," Magnus declined. Jenha followed his example.

"I read in the paper that she was supposed to be involved with the abduction of Zara Russell. Is that true?" Mason asked.

Magnus shook his head. "No, we can conclusively prove that she wasn't. It was not made public, but Erin had been found a week before Zara disappeared, and was in the custody of an agent of the State Department. She had been wandering in the vicinity of Gainsville, with amnesia. And, however it was that she left the psych facility it was not to go and collect the millions she is supposed to have hidden away. When she was found, she was malnourished and unable to recall who she was."

"So how would they think she was involved?"

"The men involved, used the fact that she had escaped to blame her. They had in fact known her at university and wanted her to do some work for them."

"Them again," Mason sighed.

"This time," Magnus gently corrected him. "She helped capture them by infiltrating their computer. She had by then remembered who she was."

Mason winced at hearing Erin had been hacking again.

"So why hasn't she been dragged back? Was it because of that?" Ed Mason was staring at Magnus.

"No, there are other complications. Rather interesting ones. What do you know about Katrina's family?"

Mason stared harder at his friend, wondering what he was leading to.

"I wasn't aware she had any. You know she was adopted from Yugoslavia by American diplomats."

"Well, it turns out she did have family and from some research that was done, that she was one of triplets – three girls. One of the sisters was raised in Russia. She died a couple of years ago, and her husband and daughter recently arrived in America. The other sister fled from Yugoslavia and came here. That one had two daughters. One of those daughters works for the State Department and was assigned to work with Colonel Aldrin."

Mason's expression betrayed interest. "The astronaut, the one that has been missing?"

"Yes. The reason that Erin is being detained in California is that she and the other two cousins seem to have a psychic link with the other. We will soon be announcing that Colonel Aldrin and his team have been found."

Ed Mason fell back in his chair. "And she helped find them?"

Jenha answered that. "Mr Mason, she played a very important role in their return. However, it has not been a very easy time for your daughter. She is what I call an empath, able to feel the emotions of those around her. You would have noticed this. I think?"

Mason nodded. If that was true, it explained a lot of things.

"I can help her deal with this, without using drugs. It would help me to do this if you would be prepared to talk to me about your daughter and your late wife."

"Of course," Mason agreed, eagerly. "Will this also help with her tendency to poke her nose into restricted websites?" This was said with a glance at Magnus.

Goldman gave him a surprising answer. "I would like to use that skill of hers, and yes, I think the Professor might help with that too. I had it reported to me that she claimed that the only things that blocked out all outside emotions were sex and losing herself in cyberspace."

Goldman was in a position to observe both men. His comment caused startled understanding in his friend and what might have been a fleeting look of distaste in the Professor. He would have left when Mosellan began his gentle questioning, but Mason gestured for him to stay.

Without seeming to listen to the conversation, Goldman began to get a new perspective on why Erin Mason behaved as she did. He also admired the skill of this stranger, who he could easily forget was not a native of Earth.

Not only was he learning about Erin, but he was gently easing the guilt Mason felt about Erin, his late wife and the new woman in his life.

Jenha's final suggestion was that he arrange to come out to California and talk with his daughter. Ed Mason seemed undecided.

"Erin is pregnant, Ed," Magnus told him gently. "Which is not helping either. I think you might find that she would welcome the idea that you had found someone."

Mason's head swivelled to let him look at Magnus.

"Pregnant!" Mason was probably doing sums in his head. "Who is the father?"

"Rand, she claims," Magnus told him.

"It could easily have been that other bastard," Mason snarled. "How is she to look after a baby, if she is sent back to prison?"

"Perhaps that is a reason to talk to her?" Jenha suggested.

They left Ed Mason to his thoughts and let themselves out.

Later, Goldman took Jenha to speak to Stefan Krinsky, the father of Tanya. He discovered to his surprise that the stranger was able to converse in fluent Russian. He could not be sure, but Goldman thought that Jenha was doing what he had for Ed Mason and talking Krinsky through a tangle of emotions and guilt and easing their hold on the man.

Jenha asked about Wanda's father. Goldman made a call to find out if Senator Willard was in Washington or his home state.

"Apparently, the Senator cancelled his appointments here for this week due to a family emergency. I think he may well be at Rockwater when we return."

"Ah yes. Miss Willard is Wanda's sister. You did not mention that to your friend."

"No. You won't be aware that Wanda, once known as Gwenda Willard, walked out on her family and changed her name. She deliberately distanced herself from them before she gained a very bad reputation as a thief. However, after she helped put some major criminals in prison, she was put into witness protection for a while, and it is believed that she died. After that she became an agent of the State Department."

Jenha betrayed his distaste at the reminder that his great-great-niece was a criminal. "It is perhaps well that she did not grow up on my world. Such behaviour would shock everyone. Erin too would shock them, I think. My people revere truth and honesty. I must keep remembering that I should not judge humans by the beliefs of my culture. And I dare not consider the ways of my people from the views of this, when it was the imperfect humans who saved us and my own leaders ran and hid."

Goldman was not shocked. He said, gently, "Should war come to us here, the President and others of importance would be taken to secure bunkers. The fighting would be done by those who are trained to stay alive. It is no benefit to send those who cannot fight, into battle. We are not that different. From what Stev, Colonel Aldrin, has told me, your Atapi are born warriors."

"Yes," Jenha agreed and he said no more for a while. "I think, perhaps, we should return to Rockwater as soon as possible."

Erin was relieved to be back at Rockwater and the enthusiastic welcome by her cousins made her feel less hard done by. She didn't have to ask how Wanda was – both were full of the fact that she was in the infirmary and David was refusing to leave her and that Rowan Wallace had Colonel Aldrin sequestered for observation. They were both fine, though still tired. Erin told then she was okay, but had been ordered to rest still.

That was as much as she learnt before Jim Phillips emerged and sent her to the cottage she had used before. Erin shrugged and obeyed, not at all displeased to leave the company of her cousins who sounded too well compared to how she felt.

Later, as she tried to read a magazine on her bed, Erin heard Jim moving around the other room of the cottage. She guessed he was playing nurse, though surely he had better things to do. It was very late, almost midnight but Erin had been unable to sleep She felt hot, so when simply removing blankets didn't help, she got up and went to get some water from the fridge.

Jim stirred in the chair he was dozing in and asked her how she was. Erin told him and he stood up to come and feel her forehead.

"You are hot," he agreed, but his first thought was that he might be still mimicking Wanda's symptoms, as it seemed she had done before. "Are you up to walking across to the infirmary? There is a night nurse on duty. We can talk to her."

"Alright," Erin agreed but she refused the suggestion of putting a light jacket over her sleeping things.

Jim had Erin wait in a little anteroom off the infirmary while he went in search of the nurse. He returned to find her gone and a disturbance coming from within the infirmary.

What had disturbed Erin hadn't been strong enough to overcome the 'calm' compulsion that Jenha had put on her. Not that she realised what he had done. That was until she walked into where Wanda lay and sensed David's state. He was distraught of the point of tears. It had been his misery that dragged her from her seat and into the room.

The dimly lit room, the figure on the bed, David leaning anxiously over it – threw memories of nightmares into her mind. No. Not memories, they were Wanda's nightmares – and she was screaming silently as if her voice had been used too much. She was screaming for David but couldn't sense him right there with her. And David desperately wanted to help her but she wouldn't wake to see him.

Erin stepped closer, went to the nearer side of the bed, opposite David and took Wanda's hand. It was hotter than her own, but it gripped hers as if to a lifeline. Erin had never sensed Wanda's mind like it was – it was an almost overwhelming mix of fear, terror, yearning, despair all mixed with a feeling of illness.

It was building up in Erin too, threatening to engulf her. In that realisation, Erin did as she had before – realised that it was not her own emotions she was sensing and projected the sense of how her own mind felt, back in that place she had been in, when the drugs had numbed her mind.

Just holding her hand was not enough. Erin sat on the bed and lifted Wanda into a hug.

Slowly, the emotion storm subsided, until Erin was aware David was sobbing. She spared a hand for him, hoping to ease his distress, which was adding to Wanda's. Jim found her there.

"You shouldn't be here Erin," he said quietly. "We don't know what is making her sick."

"Jim, she was screaming in my mind. Terrified of being alone. David was frantic too. I had to be here. She is quietening down now and David really needs to rest."

Jim decided to seek a medical opinion, and went out.

Rowan Wallace, roused from sleep, arrived wearing a robe over pyjamas, instead of his day suit. He took in the scene and called for the night duty nurse. She was already on the way with medication that Jim had asked about for Erin. He told her to hold off giving it to her until he had checked her.

He went first to David and lifted him away from the bed. He allowed himself to be moved, but only so far, before he tried to struggle back to Wanda.

"David, if you don't get any rest, you will be of no use to anyone. If you collapse, you won't be able to help Wanda. Jim, can you take him back to his bed and see he has that medication?"

Jim nodded, and began to steer a weakly struggling David out of the room.

Rowan studied Wanda's chart as the nurse took a new set of vital sign readings. Over the past few hours, Wanda had not improved, but had not worsened. The new readings showed an improvement. Then Rowan told the nurse to check Erin. She protested, but to no avail. The nurse soon learnt that her temperature was up.

"Erin, you will need to keep away from Wanda. We don't want you getting sick too," Rowan told her.

"But Wanda needs me! She doesn't want to be alone."

"She isn't alone. David was here. The nurse is here."

Erin shook her head. "She couldn't sense them – not even David. But she knows I am here. When I got here, it looked like she was screaming silently."

"She is calm now," Rowan said gently. "Let her sleep, it is what she needs now."

Erin could feel Wanda's grip increase as her concentration on the mental numbness was interrupted. "She still wants me here."

Rowan nodded to the nurse, who moved to remove Erin, only to discover how firmly Wanda was gripping. In a no nonsense manner, she began trying to loosen the grip, and commented on it to Rowan.

"She is almost due for more sedative. I think we can give that now."

"No," Erin protested. "It isn't working. That's the problem. If she could wake up, she would be able to see she was not alone, and not still in the middle of some horror. She would be able to control this a bit. The drug is stopping that and she is caught up in nightmares. That is why she couldn't even sense David. She should have been able to."

Rowan repeated his instruction and sent the nurse off. Erin continued to protest.

"I think perhaps that Miss Mason is correct," Jenha Mosellan said quietly. He had just arrived back with Goldman and had come directly to the infirmary. He looked at Erin and she stopped protesting in mid-sentence.

He walked over to Wanda, and gently removed her grip on Erin. He made it look easy. Erin, who could feel the strength of the grip, was distracted and didn't struggle against the nurse who was firmly pulling her off the bed. But that same distraction caused her to stop projecting a calming numbness to Wanda who began to thrash around.

The nurse stopped Erin from going back. Once again, Mosellan met Erin's gaze and she stopped struggling. He eased Wanda back onto the pillows, and she had stopped fighting.

Rowan told the nurse to take Erin back to her cottage and to see she had something for her fever.

With Wanda quiet again, Erin realised how tired she was and how much she needed sleep.

Goldman, standing back out of the way, watched and was impressed by Mosellan's effortless control of the situation. Rowan was happy to leave Wanda to him and came over to Goldman. In a whispered conversation he filled his friend in on what had happened while he had been away. Goldman chose not to speak of his trip just then.

Wanda began moaning, and his attention returned to her.

Mosellan was speaking quietly – though it didn't seem like Wanda was listening. Her moaning was getting louder.

The nurse walking Erin to her cottage suddenly found she was alone. She spun around and could not see her charge anywhere. Since she was almost at the cottage, she checked there first and finding it deserted, ran back to the infirmary.

Chapter 23

Goldman saw Erin suddenly appear and didn't smother a mild oath. He glanced immediately at Mosellan and caught a fleeting glimpse of annoyance before the calm purpose returned. Erin had seen it too, for her movement towards Wanda was halted.

Mosellan looked over at Rowan Wallace and asked, "Would you keep talking to Wanda to reassure her that she is home again?"

Rowan took his place. For a moment, Wanda began to thrash again, but it seemed that she did recognise his voice.

Mosellan went over to Erin and took her arm in a gentle grip and spoke very quietly. He gave her a gentle tug to get her walking. It was obvious though that Erin didn't want to leave, as she kept looking back at Wanda.

Once they were alone, Jenha continued his quiet talk. "You can safely leave the care of your cousin to me." Erin felt as well as heard his words.

"Yes but she needs me," Erin protested. "She recognised you, but she still thinks she is wherever you came from."

"Indeed," Jenha agreed. "Because it is as you surmised – that her higher mind functions are neutralised by the chemicals your well-meaning doctor has given her. However, I do not wish Wanda to form a grasping dependence on you. I am trained in what needs to be done and you are not. I am also able to induce her body to metabolise those chemicals at a faster rate, and you cannot."

"But..."

"There will be no buts!" Jenha commanded.

Jenha felt Erin's resistance and rebellion to his commands. It was not unexpected, but a complication he needed to deal with now.

Once inside Erin's cottage, away from the prying of mechanical eyes, and before Erin realised what he was doing, Jenha Mosellan had placed a round metallic disc on each of her wrists. He spoke a few sentences in his own language. Erin watched, too amazed to speak, as the metal flowed into a bracelet circling each wrist, flattened and faded almost to invisibility.

However, as soon as the metal faded, Erin realised she was trapped. It was a simple thing – she tried to pull her wrists free of Jenha's gentle grip – and couldn't. No matter how much she tried, she couldn't.

"Be calm," Jenha said quietly, and Erin felt the force of the command in her mind.

"Come and sit down," Jenha instructed Erin. "And you will listen to me."

Erin continued to stand where she was, angry at herself, and at Jenha. He waited quietly for her to come. He sat himself, but did not force her. Eventually she came quietly to perch on the edge of a chair to watch him, warily.

"What have you done to me?" Erin asked in an unsteady voice.

"I have merely applied a mild restraint," Jenha told her. "It is not intended as a means of control, although it can be used for that."

"You had no right!" Erin hissed at him.

"On the contrary. As someone older and more experienced than you, as related to your psychic gifts, I have a right and a duty to teach you. As I am related to you, and there is no one else here who can teach you, I must."

"Wanda found someone to help her!"

"Perhaps. However, at this moment, I have not the time to teach you some basic control. You are extremely vulnerable. If you think of how you have been you will realise this. Also, I do not think it wise, for your sake, for people to realise that you can walk across planes."

A picture of what she had done entered her mind. Erin felt the blood rush from her head. Jenha reached forward and gently touched one wrist. Erin felt less faint.

"The bands will prevent you from doing that inadvertently."

"How...how often have I done that?" Erin whispered.

"Twice that I am sure of, possibly three times," Jenha told her.

"When?"

"Once, just now when you were told to come back here and you went back. One time when you were found in a place forbidden to you. Those who watch around here have a recording."

"And the third time," Erin asked still in a whisper.

"Of this I am not sure, but it is likely since no other explanation has been proposed, when you left that place amongst sick minds."

Erin swallowed hard, to settle a very nauseous feeling.

"I still want to help Wanda," she said stubbornly.

"And you are needed for that, but not until Wanda is stronger and not until you have some control of your emotions."

"I can, a bit." Erin claimed. "When I think of mathematical equations and computer algorithms."

Jenha sensed her meaning, though his culture had no direct correlation. He also knew her other 'cure' for intense emotion and carefully controlled his reaction to that.

"Blocking incoming emotion is not the same as controlling your own. Your method, while effective in blocking, does not permit you to do anything else constructive at the same time."

"What would I need to do?" Erin asked.

"If you are to help your cousin, you will need to accept all of her terrors, deal with them, without them awakening your own. If you do not – your terrors will in turn feed hers."

"Oh!" Erin flopped back.

Jenha stood, sure now that Erin would be obedient to his suggestions, without needing coercions. "You need sleep, Erin."

Sleep was far from her mind. "Should I feel buzzing from where these things are?"

"Perhaps at first," Jenha suggested. He knew that the sensation she had described was a sign that she had not yet accepted the implied constraints.

Erin removed the watch from her left wrist. "Then you had better give this to Wanda to wear. And take off that Atapi made bracelet if she still has it."

She did not look at Jenha as she said it. He tested her emotional state. There was none of the resentment he expected to feel.

"What is the provenance of this object?" Jenha asked.

"It's a watch. It keeps track of time. Wanda said it was her mother's."

"And when did she tell you this?"

Erin didn't answer.

"A question for later," Jenha said, more to himself. "What then, will this do for Wanda?"

"She said it should help me to draw on the aura of the Earth and the bracelet I had would help her where she was."

"You could use this object?" Jenha asked, a bit more sharply than he intended, due to surprise.

"Yes," Erin admitted, without explanation.

"And the bracelet?"

"I...don't think it will help here. It wanted to get back to your world." Erin surprised him again.

"Do you know that this object will help Wanda?"

"Yes."

"How?"

"I just know!" Erin snapped. Jenha saw in her mind other times when she 'just knew'.

He placed a hand on her shoulder. "Rest, Erin, and sleep." He kept his hand there long enough to sense her reaction. She was tired, over tired, and compliant without the impetus of Wanda's terror. It was as he had thought, and shielding her until she relaxed had worked. She was almost asleep already. He sensed Jim Phillips returning and knew that his friend would watch Erin.

As he walked back to his main charge, he was thoughtful. He had not expected the women to be aware of the aura. That was something they should all be trained to use – if they could prove to be sufficiently ethical. And there were more questions he had to ask about things he had assumed – wrongly.

Jenha Mosellan sat with Jim Phillips having breakfast. The former was listening to what Jim knew about the four cousins, even though he had heard most of it before. The subject changed from Erin to Wanda when they heard Erin moving about.

"I had expected to see Senator Willard here," Jenha said. "Goldman was told he had cancelled appointments in Washington due to a family emergency."

"He might be driving down," Jim suggested. He saw Erin enter the room.

"Good morning Erin. How do you feel?" Jim asked.

Jenha copied Jim's greeting.

"Hello," was her reply, as she busied herself making a hot drink.

Jim rose, knowing that Jenha wanted to talk to Erin. "I will just check on David. He will be glad to hear Wanda is doing better."

Erin dragged out the coffee making as long as she dared, then finally took the seat Jim had vacated.

"Why aren't you still with Wanda?" Erin challenged.

"She's sleeping easily at the moment," Jenha told her. "Are you planning on having breakfast?"

Erin shrugged. "I'll get some later. Aren't you going to get some sleep?"

"I'll get some later," Jenha copied her answer, realizing that her verbal fencing was due to nerves.

"Who are you, really?" Erin demanded.

"I believe Jai Cassidy mentioned me to Wanda and through her to you?"

Erin tried to recall that 'dream'.

"Yes," she remembered. "And you said you were related to me. Elisabeth said...we had alien blood. Where do you fit in? Were you Suzi Mosellan's husband?"

"No, I was her brother." Jenha watched Erin's reaction.

"You don't look that old," Erin said, sounding calm enough, but Jenha was aware that her apparent control was fragile and that she was on the verge of what Jim called, 'freaked out'.

From the way she was rubbing at her wrists, Jenha knew they were 'buzzing' as Erin described it. They reacted to muscle tension and he was going to have to teach Erin to recognise that.

"What unsettles you about what I am?" Jenha asked. "Or is it who you are?"

"Nothing."

"If you want your empathy to be a useful tool, Erin, honesty is essential," Jenha told her softly.

Erin wasn't ready for honesty.

This man, this relative, could look at her – touch her – and make her behave. It felt like manipulation and she'd had enough of that. It felt like having no free will.

"I will be teaching you control," Jenha said with a trace of coercion, and he knew Erin felt it. "It is necessary, and I will be a tough task master. I will insist on honesty, no matter the personal cost. We do not have the luxury of years to learn this. Already you are an adult and expected to behave in a mature fashion and that is the standard I will expect of you."

"And if I can't reach that standard?" Erin asked, diffidently.

"I will teach you until you can."

Jenha touched her mind lightly to understand why the bracelets were humming. In her mind, teaching meant punishment. That warned him that he needed to proceed carefully. He leant over and placed a hand on one of the bracelets.

"They will buzz or hum when you are emitting emotion," he explained, meeting her eyes. "They will also limit that emission to below the point where you would affect other people."

"Who are you, an alien, to judge me?" Erin said, very deliberately.

"I am the only one on Earth qualified to do so," Jenha stated with the same deliberation.

"And if I don't choose to co-operate?" Erin challenged.

"You should be more concerned about me not wanting to teach you," Jenha countered.

"I've managed so far!"

With his hand still on Erin's wrist, he drew out of her memory one of the strongest emotion storms she had sensed – from her first time in prison. He held her in that moment.

"Stop it!" Erin screamed. "Take these things off!"

Jenha let the memory fade out. "That is the level you are at now. You must do much better if you are to help Wanda."

"What if I can't?"

"Then I will have to take control for you," he told her unequivocally. "And that is not what I want to do. I would not even consider forcing your training, except that you have such high intelligence. I believe you will quickly understand the exercises I set you."

The appeal to her intelligence worked.

"Empathy has its own logic," Jenha told her. "It is just that not all people do."

"Prove it," Erin muttered.

That was the opening Jenha wanted.

"Relax, then," he suggested. She didn't fight him as he calmed her mind, relaxed it into a trancelike state and asked her to return to her earliest memory.

Images flowed and Erin marvelled – it was like watching a video she had taken as in infant. But she felt, what her long ago self had felt; only now, she understood those emotions – hunger, discomfort, thirst, happiness. Simple uncomplicated emotions.

Was the woman she saw her mother? It didn't look like her. She saw her father; much younger – sensed his delight and wonder in her. Images flashed by. There! That was her mother – where had she been until then?

Jenha paused her mind on that image and murmured, "After you were born, your mother was quite sick. Nothing the doctors could identify. It took her over a year to recover."

The images continued. Erin's view was, at first, the roof of rooms, or the walls over people's shoulders. It moved to the floor and feet, then the furniture at a low level.

Always, when she saw her father's face, it was delighted – with her. The other faces varied. Nurses, Erin realised. Very seldom did she see her mother. When she did, it was amongst a crowd of people like at a party.

Jenha paused her mind at that realisation – giving her time to consider it.

Erin's eyes began to water, they hadn't then. Then it was just the way things were. She wrenched her mind from that moment and considered what her adult mind now understood. Her mother had not exactly hated her, but had resented her, Erin's birth had made her sickly, had meant that she could not do as she wanted any more, had distorted her figure and she had to share her husband's attention. And at times forced her to act as if she liked being a mother. Her prominent thought was of handing her back to her nurse to take out of sight.

The emotion was overwhelming, she wasn't aware of the buzzing of the bands at her wrists, growing louder, vibrating until finally producing something like an electric shock.

Jenha felt it, since he was still lightly touching her wrist. He sensed the memory go dark and carefully reduced the level of emotion until Erin's sobbing subsided and she could listen again.

"I did everything she told me to," Erin said, forcing the words out. "But I was never good enough, never!"

"It is a memory, nothing more. The problem was not you, it was her. Accept it, put it aside, and move on."

"Why are you putting me through this?" Erin asked, still crying, but now it was silently.

"So that you can understand yourself," Jenha told her. "To learn what is you, learn to understand your emotions."

"Is this how you learnt?" Erin asked to distract herself.

"In a way. But I was younger, my teachers would bring dreams, like your memories, for us to experience and as we got older our perceptions of them would change. In this way we learnt, were instructed. We experienced more emotions than just our own."

Erin had a fleeting sense of a younger person, like herself, reacting naturally to those dreams then being instructed on other ways to view them. When Jenha realised this he tightened up the controls on his own mind. There were conflicts in his mind that he did not want his pupil to sense.

"Are you ready to continue or would you like to talk about it?"

"Why should I react like that," Erin asked. "I'd figured out that I was a rival for Dad's affections."

"Now you have. Then you hadn't."

Erin cautiously recalled that memory. "I knew – I just hadn't got the words for it."

After a moment she asked, "Is this like taking me back to when I first felt an emotion?"

Jenha nodded.

"But because I am older, I perceive it more fully?"

Erin bit her lip and tried to withdraw her hand from Jenha's light grip. He took her other hand and held both just firmly enough to stop her.

"You are not going to let me stop, are you?"

"No," Jenha stated.

Erin sat thinking. This time Jenha did not intrude.

"Is...Wanda receiving from me?"

"Yes."

"Right now?" Erin clarified.

"No, she will sleep quietly for a time." Jenha was pleased that she was considering that point.

"You...ensured...that?"

"Yes. It was necessary."

"And you have ensured that I accept what I am?" Erin needed to know.

"Yes. That too is necessary – for now. Does that make you angry?"

"No. For now." She made her admission sound like an oblique warning.

"We will proceed," Jenha directed. Erin took a deep breath and nodded.

The dream images resumed. Erin sensed her younger self, the misery at being dragged away from the glittering party, even though her older self knew it was no place for a child. That misery swelled, causing an upset stomach and as she was dragged along by her mother she was sick.

"You rotten little brat! What did you do that for? I'll be a laughing stock. I'll make you clean it up! And my dress! You got it all over my dress!"

Erin felt herself shrinking into a ball. Then others had appeared and her mother had managed to say, "I'm sorry, we didn't quite make it back to the room."

Another voice, "We'll fix things. You take your daughter and pop her into bed."

Erin's mother had picked her up, holding her breath against the smell.

And in the room, a hotel room, Erin recalled, she was handed to her nurse and the woman was told to clean her up because, "I'll have to do something about this dress before it is ruined. Thanks to her, I won't be able to go back to the party."

Jenha stopped the flow of images there and asked softly, "What were you feeling?"

Erin considered. Her adult self was analysing the feelings of her child self who was still too young, at about four years old, to have a name for the concepts.

"Miserable and confused. I could not understand what I had done to be dragged from the party. Lots of people had liked me and I didn't mean to be sick. I was still feeling sick and my stomach was in knots."

"What about your mother?" Jenha asked. "What were you getting from her?"

Again Erin considered. "Anger was the most obvious emotion. Disgust and fear. No concern for me, only herself."

The memory sequence continued briefly before halting again. The young Erin was watching her mother carefully and fastidiously removing her dress, whilst the nurse carried her away.

"How are you now?" Jenha asked her.

"Happier. The nurse always treated me as special. I felt relieved to be away from my mother and my stomach felt better."

"And?" Jenha prompted.

"I think that must have been the first time that my mother spoke to me, not at me. And I think I felt a bit like I had been rewarded."

As Jenha's reading of the events agreed with hers, the memories began to flow again.

Erin realised that she had, at that age, started to subtly annoy her mother. At the same time she had been enjoying having her mother's attention. She now realised how she had been provoking her mother and had enjoyed doing it.

The memories stopped. Jenha asked, gently, "How do you look at this now?"

"I was only a child!"

"Then! And Now?" Jenha was feeling buzzing from the bands. What he sensed was satisfaction at how cleverly she had annoyed her mother and got away with it. And even now, in given circumstances – she would do it again.

Four years old, Jenha marvelled. She had been something of an empath, even then. And that unacceptable behaviour pattern had started then. Twenty years was a long time and now, Erin didn't even realise that manipulating people with her empathy was not ethical. He had spent enough time on Earth to be sure that was also true here.

Well, there were times when it would be acceptable, but she could learn those exceptions later. This was not going to be an easy lesson.

Chapter 24

Jenha let Erin stalk out of the room. The wrist bands were buzzing, loud enough that the humans might even hear it. They hadn't reacted to her emotional state, so she still maintained some control. That was a promising sign. Not so promising was that she had overcome the 'calm' compulsion. In her current state of awareness, she would sense him and fight him if he tried to replace it.

Still, she needed time to integrate the lesson. Time alone.

Jim realised that Erin hadn't even sensed him and he said nothing until he saw Jenha walk out after her.

It wasn't hard to see the lines of strain on his face.

"I brought over some lunch," Jim told him. "And some for Erin when she decides to be sociable again."

Jenha nodded and gestured for Jim to come in. They sat together at the table inside.

"She is neither the most difficult nor the easiest person I have had to deal with," Jenha commented in response to Jim's unspoken question. "I have ensured she cannot 'walk' out of here. I assume your people have ways to keep an eye on her?"

Jim nodded and they both began to eat.

"Charles Willard is here," Jim told his strange friend. "He and David are sitting with Wanda out in that little area of garden near the infirmary. Wanda is looking better and her temperature is going down."

"Good! I would like to meet Wanda's father."

Elisabeth found Erin in the mess hall kitchen, washing dishes. "Some new form of therapy," she asked lightly.

"I thought you were with Wanda," Erin said a little rudely.

"Yeah, well, Dad arrived, which was nice, but he got talking to David. Now they sound like they are doing some father-in-law son-in-law bonding thing ..."

"And Tanya?"

"In the gym. She decided she had neglected her dancing exercises for far too long."

"Have you been doing your exercising?" Erin asked, deciding to quit indulging in self-pity.

"I haven't actually felt I needed to today," Elisabeth admitted with surprise. "Anyway – why the dishes?"

"I went out looking for trouble and found it," Erin admitted. "They did not appreciate me trying to get through a few gates. The code numbers were in my head – so I used them."

Erin shrugged at Elisabeth's look.

"It was the closest I could get to using a computer keyboard. Anyway, I had fun wrestling with a couple of young marines. General Addison bawled someone out for not changing the codes after the last time – which I don't remember, really. Then he told me to go wash dishes."

"So why did you go looking for trouble? Aren't you in enough already?"

"This was fun trouble," Erin muttered, going back to washing plates.

"Jim said you had been talking to that nice Professor Mosellan. Isn't he sweet? It's like having a grandfather."

Erin turned around, dripping plate in hand and stared at her cousin.

"Well, he is!" Elisabeth insisted, and then made an informed guess. "Okay, so maybe it depends on how naughty we've been in our previous life. Tanya was a bit testy with me after her chat."

"Yeah, well, something like that," Erin admitted, turning back to the sink.

Elisabeth moved to lean against the bench next to her.

"Bad?"

Erin shrugged. "No, it's just me. I have stopped being angry with him. I've stopped kicking myself. I'm into telling myself I am a coward for not wanting to go back for more of the same. I know he is not going to yell and scream at me. He doesn't have to. I know what he is trying to do for me and I agree I need to learn things but..."

"You don't like being told you are wrong," Elisabeth finished for her.

"In a way I can't forget," Erin finished.

"Wanda didn't like being told either." Elisabeth said glancing at Erin. "She kicked herself out of home. The night she left, she and Dad had such a foul row. You probably haven't heard half of the vile things she said. Dad didn't argue about her leaving, nor did I. She was upsetting the whole family. The boys cried for hours afterwards."

"Do you think she had empathy?" Erin asked, putting the last plate into a rack to dry.

"If she did, she stifled it when Mum died," Elisabeth said softly.

"I wonder what our nice great relative will make of her when she is well enough for a chat?" Erin said.

Elisabeth shrugged. "I am more concerned about whether you will be ready for the debrief in three days."

"Three days!" Erin echoed, suddenly petrified.

"Yes, and Dad intends to be gone by then, so that Mr Secretary Russell doesn't see him and Wanda together. Though I have heard that he will be bringing Zara and I will have to keep her company."

"I wonder why that is?" Erin smirked. "I wonder if it so the famous professor can 'chat' with her."

Erin imagined Zara in her own position and enjoyed the thought immensely. For half a minute and then she felt a jolt through her wrist bands.

Elisabeth saw the sudden jerk and the stillness that followed. She studied Erin's face until she moved.

"What was that?"

Erin spoke carefully, "Just some reinforcement of a lesson."

"He is being tough on you," Elisabeth said with sympathy.

"He doesn't have years in which to teach me."

Elisabeth gave her a hug. "I know you will be able to do what you have to."

"What is your Dad like," Erin asked to distract herself.

"Come and meet him. After all, he is your uncle."

"So he is," Erin realised. "I've inherited a great-great-uncle, but I have never had a regular uncle. Yeah, I'll come."

They found Charles Willard talking to Mosellan, still out in the garden. Wanda must have been taken back inside, and no doubt David was with her. The two men stopped talking when Erin and Elisabeth appeared.

Erin liked her uncle as soon as she shook hands with him. He seemed to be as calm a presence as Elisabeth. However, after a few minutes of social niceties, she knew she could not put off her lessons any longer. She walked over to where Jenha was and stood behind him, holding onto his chair.

"Charles, it has been pleasant talking to you. Perhaps we can continue this tomorrow?" Jenha invited, standing up.

Willard nodded easily and put an arm out to hug his daughter.

Erin glanced at them, felt the bond between them, pride of a father in his daughter. She glanced at the door of the room where Wanda was and felt David willing Wanda to wake up. She squashed another memory of Gerry.

Settled once again in a chair in her cottage, Erin waited for Jenha to speak. When he didn't, she finally said, "I am sorry I acted like an idiot."

"The reaction was not entirely unexpected," Jenha told her. "Your solution was effective. Would you however share with me the reason you were upset?"

Erin had known he would ask. "Could my little annoyances, the things I did to my mother, have pushed her over the line? Made her crazy?"

"On their own, I do not think so. Except that your mother might have been tending towards mental problems and you helped reveal them sooner."

"Do you think she was like me? Exactly like me?" Erin asked.

"It is possible," Jenha agreed. "My sister was very like you. I taught her some things but no one would teach a girl as I was taught."

"Yet you are teaching me."

"We should return to it," Jenha reminded her, but this time he did not put on the 'calm' compulsion.

For a while, the dream visions continued. Erin's mother appeared more often, seeming much more relaxed, and more interested in her daughter. The younger Erin didn't need to be annoying.

When she was about six years old, the last of her nurses left. Erin started to go to the local school, usually driven by a friend's mother as Katrina did not drive.

The next incident that caused Jenha to pause the flow of images was when Erin was about seven years old and she had slipped into her mother's room and played with her makeup. Her mother had returned and found her there, and 'angry' was too mild a word for her reaction.

She kept Erin home from school for two days because Erin could not have sat down without wriggling. During those two days she had kept Erin shut up in a room under the stairs. The remembered initial terror, and sobbing, had brought her mother to drag her out and tell her...

"It is a memory," Jenha said as Erin's mind froze in that moment. "She is dead now. She can no longer command you."

Shuddering, Erin opened her eyes.

"She did that command thing that you do, didn't she?" Erin asked.

"Yes," Jenha kept his voice calm. He had his own feelings very well shielded. What Katrina Mason had said and done was unacceptable. "And you never mentioned this to your father?"

"No," Erin confirmed, still feeling ill from the memory. "Nor did I provoke her anymore."

"How long did this go on for?"

"Years," Erin said. "On and off. When Dad was away, which was fairly often, if I wasn't in school or meant to be in bed – she would make me go there. I couldn't fight her. When Dad was home, he started taking me to school and I would study in the library until he picked me up. I avoided my mother as much as possible. The best part of the day was the hour I had with Dad while Mum prepared dinner. After dinner I was not allowed near him."

Jenha moved the memories forward again and stopped at one of the cupboard memories.

"I see you improved your conditions," Jenha remarked. "A clever evasion of the obey command."

"I hated it in there until I found the power point and an old laptop of Dad's in there. I gave myself light and there were some games on the computer. Dad showed me when he and I had that hour together. I learnt other things from him too. Sometimes he had work to do, so I watched what he did. He, being the boss, had access to everything. Then I discovered that the old lap top had a wireless connection to the internet."

Jenha had heard some about computers, but he didn't really understand the ethics there so he let it pass. He halted the memory review when Erin was almost a teenager.

"You have done well, this time," he praised Erin.

"That's because you stopped me before..."

"Before?"

"I started being a total brat!" Erin finished. "Do we really have to keep doing this?"

"Yes. It is giving you a chance to experience these very subjective memories from a more enlightened viewpoint. The emotions will be the same but you are now different. This is the basis for learning how to deal with new ones."

"Oh! Then on a scale of one to ten – how am I doing?"

Jenha didn't fully understand the question. "The science you are learning cannot be quantified by numbers."

Erin made a brief laugh. "I thought you might say that. What now?"

Jenha stood up. "Why don't you fetch us a drink and run over to organise some food, whilst I look in on Wanda?"

Without thinking, Erin said, "Are you keeping Wanda asleep until I get some control of myself?"

Jenha did not answer at once, and Erin glanced at him, thinking that she might have been rude. Jenha went and sat down again.

"Yes, as it happens," Jenha told her. "It is also so that her body has a chance to heal and for her to gain strength. Why is that a point that needs to be mentioned?"

"It's just that David is frantic. He is begging her to wake up. He is almost as bad as he was when he was back and Wanda wasn't."

"I will reassure David," Jenha promised. He leant forward and took Erin's hands. "Why is that affecting you so?"

As hard as she tried, Erin could not stifle her memories of Gerry. Not when she felt the soothing ripples coming from Jenha and felt his genuine concern.

Wordlessly, she allowed herself to remember the first time she and Gerry had met. She had come from a violent argument with her mother. Her father, for once in his life was overcome with emotion and needing to deal with her mother and with her. He had chosen to deal with her mother and had told her to get out and calm down. Erin had felt rejection piled on top of anger and the maelstrom that was her mother's mind. Erin had walked, close to mindlessly, ending up in a district that was dangerous.

A small part of Erin's mind noticed details that she had missed before - various men who might have propositioned her, or taken her to use, except that they saw something in her face or her manner and they veered off.

She herself did not know where she was going, until she felt a need as great as her own.

In this review, Erin saw Gerry as he had been – filthy clothes like a vagrant, drunk but not blind drunk and tending to suicidal. It had been his burning need for sexual release that had attracted her. It was the one thing that Erin knew that would blanket everything in her mind.

She had maintained enough sense to drag him into an alley but little more. That they had rutted more violently than any animals amid the rubbish and trash – Erin only now realised.

Yet after they had both sated themselves and had finally looked at each other...

Gerry had held her, gently, like something precious. "Are you sorry?"

"No," Erin had said.

"Neither am I," Gerry had admitted. He had passed her a bottle of very strong liquor. So that when the police had found them, in their state of partial dress, they were perfectly willing to think her drunk. When they realised that she was underage and claiming she had accosted Gerry and did not want to have any charges pressed against him, they gave her a stern lecture and dragged her home. As she was taken off, Gerry had said, "I'll find you girl."

Erin almost resented the feeling of calm Jenha projected to her. She wanted to cling to the memory but it vanished into a picture of ripples on a pond.

After a while, she began to hear what Jenha was saying and to feel totally relaxed for the first time that she could remember. It was a jolt when the image vanished and she was eager to restore it. Jenha worked her through it.

"Well done," Jenha praised her. "Now, can you keep that image in mind and go and organise that food?"

Jenha followed more slowly, considering what Erin had just revealed. Taken by itself, his people would consider it obscene. He had seen more in that incident than mere mutual passion. It was a joining of souls and Erin didn't recognise it. No wonder the separation affected her. He must talk to Jim, and see what he had found out.

Erin had eaten, while waiting for Jenha to return. When he hadn't arrived before she had finished, she went outside and sat on the ground in the sun. After a while, she removed her shoes and hid in the aura. When she began to feel normal, she opened her eyes and found Jenha sitting opposite her.

"Could you see me?" she asked.

"Not till just now," Jenha admitted. "But the mechanical eyes were giving an anomalous reading here and your shoes were here."

"Oh! Have you eaten?"

"I have," Jenha told her.

"Ok. Back to it, right?"

"Indeed," Jenha agreed. He stood up with graceful ease and bent down to offer his hand to help her up."

"I swear, this baby has doubled in size in the past few days," Erin commented, feeling awkward.

"Perhaps it is that you are now eating well and taking better care of yourself."

"Then I had better make the most of it," she said, squatting to collect her shoes before walking into her cottage.

Chapter 25

It was late, well after midnight. Jim Phillips moved quietly into the room where Jenha and Erin had been all afternoon and evening. Erin seemed asleep, but Jenha was awake. Jim could see his eyes reflecting the light coming from outside. They looked odd, almost as if they had their own faint luminescence. It was the first time he had really thought of this friend as alien.

Jenha turned the lamp to a low setting and the effect vanished.

"Can I get you anything," Jim offered. "A drink?"

"No thank you, friend Jim," Jenha declined. "Would you care to join me? I am feeling particularly alien."

"I'd noticed," Jim admitted. He dragged a third chair nearer. Jenha covered his eyes for a moment, and then took his hand away. "I must be tired. You and I are a lot alike, we both bleed red. But in spite of that we are two different species of humanoid. I am honoured by your trust."

"You seem to be having success with your patients. They are both calmer." Jim offered this as a reason for his trust.

"I am waiting to see if that is still the case with this one," Jenha admitted. "I have had to be a very hard task master and for the most part, she has obeyed the lessons. It helps that she is so intelligent and eager to learn."

"Eager or desperate," Jim asked.

"Both in truth," Jenha admitted. "And I cannot but agree that putting one like her in a 'prison' is like the worst Atapi atrocities I have witnessed."

Jim accepted the censure. "It isn't a perfect system but it is a means to keep the worst of the antisocial elements where they can't affect the majority of innocents."

"I tell myself, many times that I cannot judge Earth humans by the beliefs of my people. But, I can only teach in the way I was taught."

"Will she be ready by Thursday?" Jim asked.

"In any normal situation I would say impossible. I was trained for years."

"Erin doesn't need to do all that you do," Jim suggested.

"No, but if I am right, the link that exists between Erin and Wanda is very deep. It is linked to emotions, not to thought. I have been forcing Erin to remember particularly emotional moments from her life. This serves more than one purpose – to learn what emotions are hers and to be able to deal with them and to stop herself from sending them out. I have also been teaching her ways to accept external emotions and deal with them without them awakening her own. This is where we are now but..."

"It is hard on her," Jim finished.

"Yes, but she is trying earnestly, and her own emotions are the closest I could come to what she might expect to feel from Wanda. Not the content, but the feel. I know that she has received from Wanda and realised that what she was getting was not hers and damped it. She can do it instinctively, but she needs to do it consciously."

"And the present," Jim glanced at the oblivious Erin.

"When she controls her anger, at me, and integrates the lesson, she will rouse."

"If Erin cannot do what is necessary for Wanda, can you do it?"

"Yes, though it is preferable that I do not. I do not think it wise to be present at the questioning when all the mechanical ears and eyes are watching. I do not understand how they 'see' and as you noticed, some things about me are alien. To control Wanda, I would need to be in contact."

"Would Elisabeth and Tanya be able to help?" Jim suggested. "Like when Wanda was still on your world."

"Not in this," Jenha considered. "In fact it would be kinder to both of them, not to know too closely, what Wanda experienced. It is not that either is innocent to the less pleasant realities, but they are naive as to the depths such realities can reach."

"Surely their part should be included?" Jim said.

"I am not saying it should not, only perhaps they add their part later when I can be present to maintain their calm."

"Would it be better to have only a very small group present for the debrief?" Jim asked.

"Yes, though others could listen from another room. Then I could be present to enforce calm on the reactions. It will be enough for Erin to deal with only Wanda."

"Who do you suggest?" Jim asked.

"My choice would be Dr Wallace and Dr Stradbroke to lead the questions, Stev, David, Wanda, Erin and..." Jenha stopped, debating whether he should interfere further in human affairs.

"And?" Jim prompted.

"You may tell me if you think this will be unacceptable ... the man Erin always thinks of when she sees Wanda and David together."

It was Jim who needed to think.

"Gerry Rand," Jim finally recalled. "That's the name Erin knew him by.

He is alive. Erin thinks he is dead. I don't know if she had any access to newspapers – but if she did, she may not have realised that Reginald Anderson was the person she knew."

"Is he able to be brought here?"

"It would help me if I knew what purpose it would serve," Jim asked.

"It is not something I can explain. It is not a logical deduction based on fact, but I believe that this 'Gerry' is to Erin, what David is to Wanda."

Jim considered that. "A stabilising influence?"

"That description will serve," Jenha agreed.

"If it is possible," Jim said carefully. "I will get him here. The concern will be that he will be privy to confidential matters."

Jenha understood. "I am already interacting more than some of my people think advisable – another instance will make little difference."

"I think, that I too, will get little sleep tonight," Jim commented.

Sometime near morning, Erin stirred and woke enough to realise she was still sitting in the chair, although Jenha was not still holding her hands. Instead he was leaning back, perhaps dozing. Erin didn't try to move, she ached all over. That had been the worst lesson yet. Necessary, but horrible. If she hadn't been so stubborn, so thick headed, so angry...

Erin felt tears and was glad it was dark still. She felt like a sock must when washed in a washing machine full of other clothes. She didn't know what was worse, having to re-experience that time in prison over and over or the effect of the 'mild restraints' when she had lost control.

"You are a strong young woman," Jenha said quietly.

Erin glanced at him and saw his odd looking eyes, but then Jenha blinked and the oddness vanished.

"Stubborn little bitch," Erin corrected.

"You have no need to chastise yourself," Jenha told her. "You have achieved more in a short time than I dared hope."

"Is it enough?" Erin asked.

"It is a start. Do you think, now, you could deal with being in prison?"

Erin said nothing for a moment. "Yes, damn you. The mere thought of going back there, and I know I will have to, isn't paralysing me anymore. But do you think I can handle Wanda yet?"

"That's the next stage. But now, you need sleep."

"I feel quite rested." Erin realised with surprise that the aches had gone.

"Well, I need sleep," Jenha admitted, standing up. Erin pushed herself up then.

"There's something else..." Erin said walking closer to him. He waited for her to finish her statement, but was astounded when Erin suddenly hugged him.

"This is thank you," Erin said, feeling Jenha relax. "Not patient to doctor, or student to teacher, but me to esteemed great-great-uncle. I just wanted to say it in case I didn't get another chance."

Just then, she felt her baby kick. From the slight tensing in Jenha, he had too.

"Well...she...wanted to say hello too," Erin said, awed.

"I must say, as uncle to niece, I am proud of your strength and courage." Jenha admitted.

"But as doctor and teacher, I'd better sleep and eat, etc., because there is more to come," Erin said, cutting off what he might have said. "Tell them, they have no hope at the moment."

Erin drew away from Jenha and with a hand on her stomach, walked off in a delighted daze as the baby kicked again.

Jenha permitted himself a smile. He hadn't been a grandfather for long before the aliens on his world had killed his grandson, but here was his sister's great grandchild carrying yet another generation. It was awe inspiring to realise he had kin on two worlds.

"Good Afternoon," Jim greeted Erin as she finally emerged from her bedroom. It was a minute past twelve.

"You just have time to have a quick breakfast. Magnus Goldman wants to see you at twelve-thirty and you will need to stay away from here until I let you know you can come back."

"How come?" Erin asked. "Or is it a big secret?"

"Jenha Mosellan will be having a meeting here," Jim explained. "The other party hasn't the clearance for the more restricted areas."

Erin was curious, but had enough on her mind not to want to pry. It was a boost to her ego that in spite of her record, she had access to more of the base.

Erin had ten minutes before her meeting with Goldman. She had no idea what he wanted to see her about and felt some apprehension. However, it was minor compared to the delightful tickling inside her.

She was concentrating on the baby's kicking as she walked across, when she glanced up and saw one of the marines escorting someone in her direction. When they were closer, recognition was mutual.

"What are you doing here without a keeper, bitch?" Zara Russell greeted her.

"What are you?" Erin countered immediately. She deliberately glanced at the marine escort.

"I thought you would be back in prison," Zara went on maliciously.

"Perhaps they haven't fixed up adjoining cells for us yet," Erin retorted. "Though, in case you haven't noticed, this isn't some Florida millionaire's resort. I'm not free to leave."

Hanging unspoken was the obvious, "Neither are you."

Zara's face was turning pinker.

"Father hates your guts. He'll see you get an extra twenty years for putting your friends on me."

"Really? I do think he might have changed his mind since I suggested how you might have been used."

"Rot! You were behind it all. They said that," Zara hissed.

"They?" Erin queried that with lifted eyebrows and feigned surprise. "I don't know what bilge you swallowed from your friends, but I was in State Department custody a week before you faked your own abduction. And once they weaned me off the drugs I had been given, I hacked into the computer of those bumbling amateurs and their webcam and saw you walking around, making out with them."

"Liar!" Zara hissed. "If I found out you told such vile lies..."

"Pleeeese," Erin drawled. "I didn't have to say a word – one way or the other."

Let Zara think on that, Erin thought.

"But you aren't allowed to use computers or the internet," Zara accused.

"Before you think to try and cause trouble, Zara Russell, the stipulation was – without supervision. I was supervised. And it isn't my skills they hate. Just my ...guts."

"At least mine are better than yours," Zara claimed. "Isn't that Nick Bosley's baby you've got?"

Erin noticed the secretary approaching. "I am a bit choosier about who I rut with," Erin said sweetly.

"That's not what I heard," Zara implied lots, and Erin had to admit, this time she was probably correct. Still...

"I can't help it if you heard wrong. Or if you chose to better my reputation," Erin said over her shoulder as she walked off.

The Secretary and his escort arrived.

"Miss Mason," the secretary acknowledged her tersely. He immediately turned his attention to his daughter. "Zara, we have a meeting."

"Yes, Daddy," she said meekly. Her eyes, still fixed on Erin showed hate.

As the Secretary began to steer Zara onward, Erin glanced over her shoulder at her cottage and returned Zara's glare with one of 'I know where you are going and why'.

She caught a wink from the young marine escort. Considering this was the one she had tried to push down the hill, she concluded that Zara was acting like a spoilt rotten...something.

Erin knocked on the door of the room Goldman was using as his office, and heard him call, "Come in."

Her euphoric mood of moments before turned into apprehension when she realised that he had two other people with him. A man and a woman.

The man had his back to her. She entered and closed the door behind her, trying to maintain calm.

When she looked up, the man had turned around.

"Dad!" she exclaimed involuntarily, and then didn't know what to say or do.

Edward Mason had no such problem. He strode across the intervening space and took her into a bear hug. After a momentary delay, she returned it. When he released his daughter, he held her at arm's length and looked at her.

"You look better than I had heard," Mason told Erin.

"I am making the most of a brief respite," Erin said, calmly. Then she turned the conversation away from her. "You look well."

Erin noticed Goldman leaving the room with a faint smile on his face.

"Why are you here?" Erin asked awkwardly.

"To see you of course, you little idiot," Mason said, hugging her again to prove he wasn't still angry with her. "And to meet some nieces I have just heard about."

"What about the grandchild?" Erin looked at his face to see his reaction.

"I am going to wait a bit for that, aren't I," Mason said. "That young Rand the father?"

Erin's face felt tense as she nodded.

Mason changed the subject after that and managed to get Erin talking some more, and the so far silent woman began to add comments or observations.

"Oh, how remiss of me," Mason finally said. "Erin, this is Loren Turner, a ...friend of mine." He almost seemed to be embarrassed, or expecting an emotional outburst from her.

Erin turned her attention to the woman, who was keeping her face neutral. Then she looked back to her father.

"Dad, if she makes you feel this relaxed, don't lose her."

Mason hugged Erin again, but she turned her head to Loren. "Are you sure you still want him now you have met the skeleton in his closet?"

The woman smiled. "More than ever."

"Are you planning on having some new improved model children?" Erin asked without thinking and suddenly sensed it had been a tactless thing to say and admitted it.

"I'm sorry," Erin said looking at Loren, and still sensing her anguish at being unable to have children.

"Ed knows I can't have children," she said with quiet dignity. She kept meeting Erin's eyes as she kept staring back.

"I am sorry," Erin said again. "I am a bit full of myself at the moment, but ...I am going to have a problem in three or four months and..."

"And what, Erin? What do you need?" Mason asked.

"I...I didn't think I had the right to ask..."

"What is it Erin?" Mason encouraged.

"Would you take her?"

"Her?"

"My baby, take her and love her... I didn't see how you could...before...but..."

Mason hugged her again. "Of course I will."

"We will," Loren clarified. "Until you can..."

"No!" Erin struggled free. "Take her, adopt her. So she doesn't have to live under the cloud of being born in prison – having a criminal for a mother."

This time Erin looked at Loren. "Please?"

"Erin, are you sure?" Mason asked.

"Yes, I am sure," Erin insisted. "Dad, you did okay with me, I think, mostly. And I am not saying I will have no regrets – I'll have thousands. And I am not saying I want nothing to do with her – I do. But I know that this is the better way."

"What of the father?" Loren asked. She could not believe that a long regretted dream was within her grasp.

"He is not around to have a say," Erin managed to say calmly enough, but Mason knew his daughter well enough to see through it. But he also knew something he wasn't allowed to mention yet.

"If he was?" Mason asked gently.

Erin looked down at her just bulging belly. "He'd understand."

"And if you were offered freedom tomorrow?" Mason asked.

"As if!" Erin said derisively. "It won't change things. I still know I have made the right decision, so you had better get the paperwork drawn up by your solicitor."

Loren came and hugged both Erin and her father together. She was in the right place to feel a hefty kick.

"Are you sure that is a girl?" she asked.

Erin wriggled free. "I think I know where Tanya and Elisabeth will be – if you want to meet them. Wanda is still out to it but Elisabeth's Dad is with her if you would like to meet him too."

Chapter 26

Erin wandered into the mess room and found Tanya and Elisabeth having an afternoon snack.

"I liked your father," Tanya told Erin. "It feels odd to have an American uncle. Two uncles!"

"He has gone, has he?" Elisabeth asked.

"Yeah. I never expected to see him here. I thought he never wanted to see me again."

"So, aren't you meant to be doing something now?" Tanya asked.

"I think I am free until Professor Mosellan finishes with his current meeting," Erin said.

Elisabeth smirked. "How long has it been? Four hours?"

"Wipe the smirk, cuz," Erin advised. "She is not leaving until after the debrief, and they might decide to have her bunking in with you two."

"So she is likely to be major bitchy," Elisabeth grimaced. "And she isn't to know why we are here."

"Tell her you are having special training for a job with the State Department," Erin suggested. "As for me, she thinks she knows why I am here."

"And since we know better, how are things going? You seem calmer." Elisabeth said.

"So far," Erin agreed. "The real test will be when Wanda wakes up."

Erin waited in Rowan's office, eyeing the computer with an addicts longing but keeping away with a stoic's determination. She was concentrating on that so that she didn't go running down the hall to the infirmary.

It wasn't that Wanda was dragging her there, like last time. It was the 'nothingness' – the sense of something wrong.

Yet, if Rowan could sense nothing, nor Jenha – she was not likely to do better. And if David, Elisabeth, Tanya and Uncle Charles couldn't reach Wanda – why should she have more success?

There was nothing there! In fact, if Wanda had not been 'there' earlier, Erin might have thought Wanda's mind was left between this place and where she had been.

Tanya and Elisabeth wandered into the room, looking dejected.

"They sent us out," Tanya said. "We can't get through to her. David is still there, and Uncle Charles. Can't we do anything?"

"It is not that stiffening sickness is it?" Erin asked. "She has been lying still for days."

"No, Rowan has been having the nurse massage her twice a day. And he has been talking to our doctor," Elisabeth assured her.

"Professor Mosellan says that all the drugs are out of her system – though how he can tell I don't know," Tanya commented. "We tried to suggest taking her outside, like before, but they say it is too cold."

"Does she still have that Atapi bracelet?" Erin asked, idly. She did remember telling Jenha to remove it. "And your mum's watch?"

"She is wearing the watch," Elisabeth said. "I don't recall seeing the bracelet since she got back. Why?"

"I don't know," Erin admitted, but she thought she needed to.

"Is it important?" Elisabeth asked.

"I don't know," Erin admitted again.

Tanya slipped out of the room and went to talk to Jenha Mosellan. He returned with her.

"What concerns you about the bracelet?" he asked Erin.

"I feel like I should know something," Erin said. "It is like I am just seeing something out of the corner of my eye."

"Perhaps we will take things from the start," Jenha suggested. "Tell me again everything you know about it."

Elisabeth began by telling how and where she had found it. Jenha held her hands during this and envisioned her memories. Then Erin took over, telling and recalling her memories of it.

Jenha sat back in a chair and thought about it. He looked at the three young women waiting for an answer. He stared longest at Erin.

"It is indeed an Atapi artefact, either made on Korvu, or made here of only Korvu material. I remember seeing it – here – a long time ago."

"Is it dangerous?" Elisabeth asked.

Jenha shook his head in the Earth style of negation. "It shouldn't be. It was made by Jai Ansuni for her friend – my sister, Suzelaine. It was sorcery made – call it magic, but made by using natural forces."

"Could it have gone bad with age?" Tanya asked.

"No."

"Wanda was sure it would help her," Erin said. "I don't know how she knew about it. She had it on her wrist – not long before she sent Stev and David back."

Jenha reached for Erin's hand. "Show me!"

Erin recalled her dream.

"What else did you dream?" Jenha asked. "After that."

Erin recalled the dreams and shared them with him.

"That's the last - when Jai Cassidy sent you and Wanda. I couldn't see you – I had to trust I would catch you."

"Your instincts were excellent," Jenha murmured.

"Is all that important?" Erin asked.

"It may be," Jenha said thoughtfully. "The lizard man with wings is an Atapi sorcerer – Sotak. From what was said, that you probably didn't understand – he disobeyed the Old One's command to leave Wanda alone."

"Was he the one that gave her those burns?" Erin asked.

"Yes. Sotak was judged by the Old One and neutralised."

"Killed?" Tanya asked.

"No."

But Erin recalled what the older sorcerer had done – twisted the other's wings. "Are sorcerers are the only ones with wings?"

Jenha nodded.

Erin spared no mercy for the 'neutralised' sorcerer. "I think Wanda was unconscious for a while with him. Could that, Sotak, have tampered with the bracelet?"

Jenha pushed himself up. "It is an idea I never considered, and should have."

He guided Erin out of the room after telling the others to wait. "I did not observe the bracelet on her," he said quietly to Erin.

In the infirmary, he requested all to leave. Rowan Wallace gave him a strange look as he departed last.

Jenha spoke quietly, so only Erin could hear. "Where are the mechanical eyes in this room?"

Erin looked around for the security cameras and told him where they were. Jenha positioned himself so his back was to one and he directed Erin to stand so she blocked the other.

"I should not be showing you this," he told Erin, softly.

At first she didn't know what he meant, but then she saw his eyes change and that odd glow that she had seen in the dark returned.

She shivered, but felt linked to Jenha and seeing what he saw. He spoke in her mind, explaining what he saw. "The bluish areas are where the aliens touched her, the purple where the Atapi had."

The blue was all over Wanda, but the purple was most obvious at the healing burn marks.

Jenha examined Wanda minutely, starting with both arms, the torso, and working down to the legs. He stopped at the ankle and foot, but he didn't touch there.

He spoke words in his own language, and two narrow copper bands were revealed on Wanda's ankles. The bands were ornate, with green gems set in them.

"Are the stones familiar?"

Erin nodded. "Yes, they look like ones on the bracelet, but the bracelet was wider. What are those things?"

"Slave bands," Jenha murmured. "Or at least they are now. Atapi sorcerers put them on captured sorcerers to neutralise them."

Jenha said something else in his language and the bands became visible to normal sight. His eyes returned to a more normal – in human terms – look.

Then he spoke, or perhaps chanted another series of words and reached for the bands.

The jolt that went through Jenha was obvious. "Don't touch..." he warned, before he slumped unconscious – his hands still touching the bands.

Erin pulled them away – feeling a minor jolt herself. Erin felt for a pulse and found none.

"Help! Doctor Wallace, help!" she screamed.

Rowan rushed back in, followed by the nurse and he took in the scene. He too checked for a pulse and called for a defibrillator.

Erin was feeling too shocked to move as she watched Rowan working to resuscitate Jenha. She realised that she was holding her breath, only when Rowan announced he had a pulse again.

"What happened," Rowan asked. He had to shake Erin a bit to get her attention. She moved aside and pointed to the now visible metal bands, with the inset greenish gems.

"He called them slave bands. An Atapi sorcery thing. He was about to take them off. I don't think he expected trouble. When he touched them, they jolted him. He said – don't touch."

"Please stay here, Erin," Rowan told her. "We will look after him. Are you alright?"

Erin nodded, but she wasn't. She felt a gaping hole where Jenha should be. As soon as Rowan had transferred him to a stretcher and with the nurse's aide taken him to another room, she couldn't stop tears flowing.

It was with considerable disbelief when she saw him walk back in, ten minutes later. She ran to him and hugged him. He didn't push her away.

"I am alright," Jenha told her, but it was a lie – she felt it. But he needed to appear so to her people.

Rowan Wallace checked Wanda, but her condition was unchanged.

Jenha studied the slave bands, without touching them, until Rowan asked, "Can you remove them?"

"I cannot try again now," Jenha admitted. "I must study them. Erin may stay – but may we have privacy?"

When they were alone again, Erin asked, "What happened. You were not expecting trouble."

"No, I wasn't. They were 'trapped' and I wonder why."

Erin considered what she knew, aware of gaps in her knowledge.

"Can I assume Sotak did this?" Erin asked. After a moment, Jenha nodded. "I think he knew Wanda should have gone. He tried to convince the others that she had consorted with those aliens – when it was actually him. I can sort of understand him wanting to kill Wanda – but that is where I lose the plot."

Jenha tried to continue her logic.

"He knew Wanda was related to Jai, and he must have realised that Wanda had some of the power of the Traegers – for the slave bands would not affect those without a sorcerer's or Traeger's power."

"What effect would those things have on a sorcerer's power?" Erin asked.

"Like I said, it neutralises it."

"Would it have reacted if another sorcerer tried to remove the bands?"

"It is likely, however..." Jenha lapsed into thought. "The green gems are not usually part of slave bands. If he used the metal of the bracelet, he left the gems there for a reason. The bracelet was made by Jai Ansuni, given to Suzi, and passed down to Jai Cassidy. Elisabeth found it, then you had it, and then Wanda. He may have been hoping to kill the She-devil. The stones would recognise her, I think. But I don't think Jai Cassidy ever wore that bracelet."

"If what you said is possible, would it recognise you as Suzi's brother?"

"It is possible."

"What about me?" Erin asked. "If the stones could recognise people – I wasn't wearing it long."

"You would be wise not to touch it."

Erin ignored that and her mind hopped to another point. "Those bands – if someone had put them on you, what would have happened?"

"They would drain my life force unless I could use the aura to sustain me. Here, I cannot."

"Do you think that is what it is doing to Wanda?"

"Yes, but slowly. As you surmised earlier, the watch is drawing on the aura."

"Could the fact that we are only one-eighth Kumatan, even if we have some of your power, be an advantage?"

"I would not like to assume so," Jenha warned. "We do not know Sotak's intention."

"Could he have sensed your bloodline in Wanda?"

Jenha nodded. "In that though, you are identical to Wanda."

Erin knew that. "How do you remove them? Could you use insulated gloves?"

She thought Jenha wouldn't answer.

The machines monitoring Wanda started to change their tone. Rowan hurried in, and Erin heard him comment that Wanda's vital signs were beginning to decline.

"An application of magic," Jenha said softly.

"Could I do it? Would it have to be Korvu aura, like you use or could Earth aura work it?"

In a barely audible whisper, Jenha said, "Yes, you could do it, and I do not think the Earth aura would set it off. But you cannot use gloves to remove them."

"Ok," Erin breathed deeply. "Teach me."

The three line chant came into her mind and Erin spoke it aloud, repeating it until she had the intonation right. She took a deep breath and mentally thought of the power that had kept her invisible – there was the faintest of stirrings. She should try this outside. She murmured that suggestion to Jenha, and he passed it on to Rowan Wallace.

He was reluctant to remove Wanda from the machines, and to take her out into the cold. Still, he did not know what else to do, so he organised a trolley, portable monitoring equipment and more blankets. He summoned Stev Aldrin to lift her from the bed to the trolley.

Erin had removed her shoes and gone outside, taking the time to draw on the aura to give her strength. She thought of the breeze that she had felt and hidden within and pictured it filling her. She thought of what she needed to do and what she feared would happen.

Jenha had not mentioned what she was going to try. He came out with Wanda, and Erin moved next to him, taking his hand and sharing some of the breeze with him. She touched Wanda and imaged the breeze filling her.

"We need her to be lower," Erin said. "So the watch can touch the ground."

"What are you going to do?" Wallace demanded. He glared at Jenha, as if he should stop Erin doing what she planned.

"I can get those things off her," Erin told him, sounding confident. To do it she had to be.

"You know what they did before!" Wallace insisted.

"Yes. But I know I can do this. They reacted to Jenha because he is from Korvu. I'm not." Erin told him. It wasn't quite true, but it sounded logical.

Rowan sent the nurse for the defibrillator.

Erin approached Wanda's ankles and studied the bands of metal. She turned them, without ill effect so that the narrow line of the join was uppermost. Then she held them loosely and spoke the words Jenha had taught her. In the next microsecond, she saw the bands fly open. Then the bands moved as if with a life of their own. Light blazed from them and around her wrists, she was blinded by it.

Something pushed her backwards, away from Wanda. The fiery light was clinging to her hands and wrists. It was burning her. She felt herself screaming, "Pull it off!"

Aldrin acted before anyone else. Using his artificial hand, he wrenched the fiery objects away and threw them away from everyone. The light pulsed once, and then faded out.

Jenha stumbled to Erin and held her close to him. He was speaking quietly, more to her mind than aloud, telling her the words to use to get the aura to heal herself.

"Are you hurt," Rowan asked.

"I'm okay. Check Wanda," Erin told him. That she sounded well enough, allowed him to do as she suggested. Erin could have told him that Wanda was immensely better, because she could once again sense her dreaming mind. However, she wanted some time to heal her hands a bit before Rowan looked at them.

Aldrin asked the important question. "What do we do about those things?"

Jenha knew two solutions. The better one was to lose the pernicious things in the space between planes, but he could not do that in his depleted state; nor could Erin, even if he took the restraints off her. She had the ability to cross planes, but it was instinct. To do what was needed, she would have to pause mid 'walk' and return without being disorientated. Wanda had done it, it seemed, but Erin was in no condition to try it either.

"Extreme heat," Jenha said. "That will destroy them and the – call it a spell – on it. Stev, you should not be affected by them, but to be safe, keep them away from other people."

"Done!" Stev Aldrin said. "I'll deal with these." He strode over to the deceptively innocent looking metal and picked them up. Then he vanished into the darkness.

Rowan had organised taking Wanda back inside, and checked her condition. It was improving. He returned outside where Jenha still seemed to be comforting Erin. "Coming inside?"

Jenha nodded, and shepherded Erin before him. He was feeling much stronger now, for the healing energy Erin had summoned, she had shared with him. Neither of them was completely healed, but it would not do for Erin to be seen with no adverse effect.

Rowan indicated a chair near a bench, with glass cupboards behind it. Erin sat where he pointed, cradling her hands under her light jumper. Rowan drew them out and said simply, "You, child, are definitely not okay."

Erin said nothing. Her hands were still hurting, but not like they had been. And although the burns looked bad, they were not the black, ugly looking burns she had glimpsed.

Rowan examined her hands, gently. He was surprised by the narrow space that was unaffected.

Jenha said nothing, so Erin offered, "I had some bracelets there. I guess they melted and came off with those things." She could still see the restraints there, but Rowan couldn't.

Jenha squeezed her shoulder gently, and stayed with her until Rowan had finished treating and bandaging her hands and wrists. When he had finished and moved away, Erin became aware of someone else near her. She glanced up. Charles Willard looked at her with sympathy.

"I am not sure exactly what you did," he admitted. "But I wanted you to know that I am deeply grateful. I may not, now, be able to admit Wanda is my daughter, but I would have no hesitation in admitting you are my niece. You must visit sometime and meet your other cousins."

"I appreciate that," Erin told him. "Cousins are proving to be very interesting."

Charles reached out and offered Jenha his hand. "And you too, Sir, are welcome at my home, anytime."

Jenha shook the offered hand. "You are very generous."

Willard smiled. "Now I had better disappear before Stan Russell knows I am here. It is not that I dislike the man, I'm not saying that, but for the sake of peace."

Jenha returned the smile and said, "If it is any help, I believe that Magnus Goldman is currently receiving his wisdom."

David stood up from beside Wanda. "I'll walk you out, Sir."

Erin distracted Rowan by saying, "I'm tired."

"Well, I think you should stay here tonight," he glanced around.

"Can I use the stretcher," Erin suggested. "I just want to collapse."

Within minutes, the nurse had produced a pillow and blankets. Erin proved her statement by falling asleep as soon as she was lying down.

Jenha turned to leave, but Rowan stopped him. "You are not going anywhere until I check you out."

Chapter 27

Wanda awoke, going in an instant from asleep to alert. It was dark – when she had been dreaming of daylight. She tensed in that same instant, fearing she was back in the noisome place of the blue aliens. Then she realised that she couldn't be. She felt peace, not despair and death. And it really wasn't completely dark. There was light, coming from instruments? And faint light coming from a window. An Earth type window?

She pushed back the blankets and stood up. Only then did she realise she had a drip in her arm. Without a thought, she ripped it out, so that she could walk to the window. Looking outside gave her the most glorious view she had ever seen. Tears of relief and joy fell unheeded.

"Wanda?" David said, suddenly, waking from a doze and seeing the bed empty.

Wanda spun around, hearing his voice. She couldn't get to him fast enough. She bumped into the sleeping stretcher, waking Erin but unaware of her.

David met her half way and their mutual joy was painful to witness.

Erin covered her head with the blanket and thought of ripples on a pool.

"I'm back?" Wanda breathed. "I'm really back?"

"You are," David assured her. "Are you alright?" Wanda asked, running her hands over him to be sure.

"Tired at first. Stev is okay too. He managed better than me."

"And Tanya and Elisabeth?" Wanda asked. "I felt them. And..." Wanda seemed to be searching for a name.

"Erin," David supplied. "They are all fine." He glanced at where he knew Erin was sleeping.

Wanda followed his gaze. "Who's that?"

"Erin. Did you know she is also your cousin?"

"Also? I don't have any cousins," Wanda said, confused.

"Tanya is another cousin," David told her.

"She is? I think I knew that. I can't seem to remember anything."

Erin pushed herself up. "I'll head back to my place," Erin told David. He nodded but Wanda asked, "Do I know you?"

Erin shook her head. "Not really." She backed away. She wanted to be out of the way for a while. Whatever was between Wanda and David was strong, even if Wanda was too emotionally numb to feel it. She, Erin, wasn't and it was tearing at her. Even the pond image couldn't contain it.

"I can't sense you," Wanda said, confused.

"Can you sense David?" Erin asked, keeping her distance.

"Of course I can. Why?"

"Well, there is an awful lot of something you need to deal with first, and then you will have room to sense other people."

"I feel I should know you," Wanda insisted, staring at Erin. She was still, numb, still not alarmed.

"We have met, briefly, and in an unconventional way," Erin finally admitted.

Wanda moved forward, hand out to touch Erin, who continued to back off. Erin sensed the start of a desperate need to know. A need to remember.

Erin stopped moving, because she had no more room behind her. Wanda touched her, and her body went rigid. All of her memories returned and they were all muddled up.

"You!" Wanda challenged, her eyes were full of insane hate and terror.

Erin shrugged, letting the memories and the emotions flow past her into the rippled pool.

"You're one of them," she said loudly. "Keep away from me! David! She's one of them. You have to kill her, now!"

David had hold of Wanda or she might have tried to kill Erin herself.

"Erin is not one of them," David told her calmly. "She is your cousin. She helped you get back."

Wanda screamed and struggled, breaking free of David and diving to grapple Erin. Erin tried to duck sideways, but a stool almost tripped her. Wanda grabbed her and punched hard.

"Stop it!" Erin thought at her. "You will hurt my baby!"

Erin doubled up, part in pain, part from nausea and breathlessness and part from an instinct to protect her unborn child.

Anger fuelled her reply. "Stop it! Pull yourself together. Concentrate on David and let the memories sort themselves out."

Erin sensed that Wanda recognised the tone, and recognised her mind, at least. Wanda backed off, less tense, but still wary. Erin breathed in and out carefully. "I'll be going," she told them.

"No! Stay! I need you," Wanda's mind screamed.

Erin projected calm. "You have David. You are safe."

Erin knew the memories were swirling in Wanda's mind, making her physically dizzy. Erin felt the need to go to her, but until she got her own pain and nausea under control, she didn't dare.

David was frantic, not knowing what to do.

Erin stumbled forward, still unsteady, and grabbed Wanda. She thought of the drug induced blankness. Wanda clung to her, body and mind. The swirling memories slowed.

"David is here." Erin thought at Wanda. She didn't seem to understand. Erin projected a hint of what she had sensed earlier and Wanda reacted to it. She started kissing David like it would be the last chance she had.

Erin took a breath to calm herself, and to try to block memories of Gerry. She tried to leave again, but the sense of need was still too strong.

At least, Wanda knew she was home, but the memories threatened to engulf her, and she knew Erin was holding them at bay. Finally, Wanda left off kissing David and seemed almost sane again – outwardly. She sensed a presence behind her and spun around, and saw Erin, really saw her – and screamed.

Jenha arrived at the same time as Rowan Wallace. Rowan went to Erin who was pale and sweating. Jenha went to Wanda and began speaking in what Erin recognised as a commanding tone.

"Come and sit down, Erin," Rowan directed.

"Not just now," Erin told him, distracted. She was still holding memories of numbness on Wanda, with only partial success. Wanda had stopped screaming, but she wasn't really hearing Jenha yet.

"Can you make her think I'm not here, or I am someone else?" Erin said aloud.

Jenha seemed to understand and something he said then seemed to work. Erin breathed a deep breath and hissed in pain. Some of the desperate need for her eased, and the fear/terror/hate/revulsion, that Wanda was directing at her. Erin started heading for the door. Rowan stopped her.

"Please, I need to go outside, into the fresh air." Erin struggled to get free.

Rowan went with her and helped her sit in a chair.

"What happened?" he asked, pulling over a second chair.

"Wanda is confused," Erin told him. "She thought I was some kind of enemy, and swung one at me, before I convinced her I was a friend."

"It didn't look like that to me. Where did she hit you?"

Erin put her bandaged hand over the spot, which was about her diaphragm.

"I'll need to check you out," Rowan said standing.

"I'll be alright," Erin told him. She did not want to go back inside the infirmary. "The baby will be alright too. I just need to stay out here a while. I will call you if I feel worse."

Rowan settled for that and returned inside.

After a while, Jenha came out. Erin thought he looked older and tireder. He sat down where Rowan had been. "Are you alright," Erin asked.

He nodded and smiled at her. "Yes, dear child, I'm well enough. Tell me what happened."

Erin did, as well as she could. Jenha nodded at each point.

"And you still feel her clinging to you?"

Erin nodded.

"Will that bother you?" Jenha asked. "I am not yet ready to touch that line of sanity."

"No, it is okay – now that she isn't also screaming at me."

"Yes," Jenha murmured. "That was unexpected. You told me she had seen you, when she came here and took the bracelet."

"She is confused. If she sorts those memories into sequence, it might be okay. I think, when I was seeing her in my drug induced nightmares, she was seeing me. I think, but I am not sure, that in those early contacts, when I wasn't very aware – she'd see my face and I would do nothing. Now she has linked me to those robed blue aliens. She called me one of them."

Jenha nodded, accepting her surmise. Erin sensed that their relationship had changed, she didn't feel like his student anymore, nearer his equal, but she couldn't be that.

"I don't think I handled things very well," Erin admitted.

"You did well enough, young one," he assured her. "You kept your emotions from her and that may have helped to fuel her confusion. I will spend time with her and David. Would you like to go back to your place?"

Erin nodded, but Jenha looked at her and asked, "Are you well? You feel edgy."

Erin shook her head. "Spoiling for a fight perhaps. It's just having Wanda both holding me there and reviling me at the same time – it was too much like me and mum having a fight. I was so helpless."

Jenha smiled again. "We will talk later. I have convinced Dr Wallace that if you say you are well, you are. So if you would put some distance between you and Wanda..."

"Delighted," Erin agreed, feeling well enough to get up.

Erin didn't rush back. She was feeling the breeze that was the aura, and it was revitalising her. It was daylight now, but still early.

"Erin!" Elisabeth called out, and she and Tanya detoured to talk to her. "What happened?" They were both looking at the bandaged hands.

"Later," Erin promised. "I need to go get more sleep and you two seem to be going somewhere."

"Prof Mosellan wants us," Tanya said. "Any idea why?"

"Wanda is back with us, not completely in her right senses. She thinks I am her lifeline and prime ally as well as her worst enemy at the same time," Erin summarised.

"Oh! Do you think she will know me?" Elisabeth asked.

"I sure hope so," Erin said.

"We'd better get there," Tanya reminded Elisabeth. "Oh, Erin, watch out for Zara, she's ropable."

Erin heard Zara before she saw her.

"Get your hands off me or I will have you up on charges," Zara was saying shrilly.

"Sorry, Mam, orders. This section is restricted."

"But you let them in," Zara argued, loudly.

"Yes, Mam. I must ask you to return to your accommodation and stay there."

Erin caught sight of Zara trying to walk past the marine guards and being restrained by one of them. She was struggling and swearing. To Erin, it seemed that a second guard was using his radio. She guessed he would be requesting an escort for her.

Zara spotted her, and shrugged the guard off. "Never mind. I'll go."

"Ran into some trouble, did you?" Zara asked as she caught up to Erin. "Or was it a bit of biblical justice – you know – like they used to cut the hand off a thief? You couldn't use a keyboard now, could you?"

"Grow up, Russell," Erin suggested. "You're talking nonsense."

"It looks like you have been crying. Was it you screaming earlier?" Zara suggested.

"Whatever turns you on, Russell," Erin said as if bored. "If it makes you happy thinking I was being bashed up, then ok, I was beaten up and was screaming."

"What's going on?" Zara demanded."

"If you haven't been told, it's no business of yours," Erin told her.

"But you know!"

"You've got that right," Erin agreed.

"But you are a criminal!" Zara protested.

"And there but for the grace of I, stand you," Erin misquoted.

"What do you mean?"

"That you are one lucky bitch," Erin told her.

Zara seemed to guess where Erin was going.

"Hey! Have they sent you to that Prof fellow too?"

"Not at the moment," Erin told her. "I'm going back to my cottage,"

"Your cottage? But that's where..."

"I know. He used it because you weren't allowed in the area where I have been. But, if you must know – I have been receiving the attention of the Prof and from what I have seen, the after effects of such meetings really depend on how honest you are and how naughty we've been in our past life."

Zara smirked.

"So I suggest that you calm down and grow up before I whop you one," Erin warned.

"You wouldn't!" Zara dared.

"Try me! I was pissed off enough after the first time to take on two marines."

"What happened?"

"They whopped me one – so don't think they won't."

Zara felt the truth in Erin's voice and backed off. She had the sudden urge to be in the cottage she and her father were staying in.

"You have been stirring up Miss Russell," Jenha said mildly, as a greeting when he returned late in the evening to find Erin seated outside.

"I was just telling her what I thought she needed to hear, and puncturing her balloon sized ego," Erin admitted. "Isn't that what Elisabeth did when you sent her to find me?"

"Your technique was quite rough," Jenha murmured.

"She's a spoilt brat! Anyway, her timing was lousy. I needed to let off steam. And those restraint things didn't even twitch."

Jenha smiled. "We will forget about that difficult young woman for a time. I believe her father has plans to get her involved in something productive."

Erin shrugged, not caring.

"I have decided on a different approach to our problem," Jenha said, gesturing to Erin to return inside.

"What?" Erin asked, going to a chair to sit down.

"I will explain it to you in a moment," Jenha promised. "First, Wanda is now aware of David, Tanya and Elisabeth, Goldman, Wallace and Aldrin.

She has all of her memories up to the point of departure from here. I have blocked the memories from that time, until a short time ago."

"Okay," Erin said waiting for him to say more.

"I plan to reintroduce you to her, and look at those dream/nightmare images."

"Get her to trust me at that point?" Erin guessed.

"Exactly. David will be an asset there. He will be supporting Wanda. I must warn you that the memories at this point will be traumatic."

"Worse than mine?" Erin asked.

"They might be," Jenha warned. He didn't mention that he hoped there would be support for her. He had heard nothing from Jim Phillips.

"Tell me what to do," Erin said, resigned.

Chapter 28

Erin opened her door, late the following evening, and saw Wanda standing there, calm and collected.

"Uh, hi," Wanda said. "Can I come in? Dave said Jim wasn't around so I wouldn't be disturbing him?"

Erin shrugged. "Yeah, Ok." She moved aside to let Wanda in. She hadn't been expecting to talk to her until the morning, and then, not alone.

"Have a seat," Erin invited. "Want a drink?"

"Water," Wanda suggested, and Erin went to fetch some.

"I suppose you are wondering why I was here," Wanda said when Erin had returned and taken a seat herself."

"I know who you are," Erin admitted cautiously.

"Well, David said you were my cousin."

"Apparently," Erin agreed.

"I always thought Tanya and I had to be related, but you were a surprise."

"I am no famous relative," Erin said mildly.

"That's what David said. He told me you were more like me – infamous."

Erin smothered a laugh. "What else did he say?"

"That you, as well as Tanya and Elisabeth would help me remember what happened to me."

"I hope we can, but don't feel pressured. I am only here until you do. Then they will be dragging me back to prison."

"You poor thing!" Wanda sympathised.

"Poor thing yourself!" Erin retorted. "I brought it on myself and it is only for another couple of years."

"You are like me! What did you do?"

Jenha received David's report. "They are chatting away like old friends – definitely two of a kind."

"Good. You may tell friend Jim that the way is clear."

David pulled out his phone and dialled, and told Jim to come onto the base.

"It would be an idea if you were to greet him," Jenha suggested.

David waited with the marine guards. Then he spotted Tanya loitering where she wasn't meant to be. He moved away from the entrance to talk to her. "You were sent to bed two hours ago."

"We want to see what he is like." Tanya whispered.

"I won't ask how you found out," David told her. "Just keep out of sight. You shouldn't be here, and we don't want Russell hearing of this yet."

"He's busy nursing Zara. Elisabeth slipped something in her drink to make her sick. She is staying there to be helpful."

David chuckled and went back to his position.

The black SUV drove in and stopped at the door to the admin block. General Addison stepped forward to meet the driver and his passengers.

Tanya held her breath. First out was Jim, and then a uniformed cop. The last passenger was clad in bright orange coveralls, and handcuffed. She studied the man's back. His hair was shaggy, and when he turned, looking around, his bearded face looked gaunt. He seemed like a nobody.

She risked trying to read his surface thoughts, and was startled when he twisted around and seemed to stare right at her. The man straightened his stance.

"What is this place, Haroldson?" the man asked. "I thought I was going to some parole hearing, not being transferred to nowhere. Does my lawyer know about this? Military guards! What's...?"

"This is the man Anderson?" General Addison asked, cutting the man short.

His escort, Haroldson, confirmed it in clipped tones. The General looked Anderson up and down, but made no comment to the prisoner. "David, find him something else to wear. He's about your size."

David was reluctant to leave just yet. It was quite obvious from the man's body language that he was very wary.

"Anderson, you will be told why you are here in due course. It comes under need to know. You will be expected to be honour bound not to escape. I won't pretend that you have a chance. I can tell you that this is a State Department facility and there are parts to which you are not permitted. The guards will advise you. If you obey all commands during your stay here, it will mean a favourable report when you do come up for parole. Lieutenant, you can remove the handcuffs. I don't think they will be needed."

Anderson rubbed his wrists and shrugged a few times to loosen stiff muscles.

"It sounds like I can follow that," Anderson agreed. He had a pleasant sounding voice.

"Very well, and since David is still hovering, I'll get him to take you where you need to go."

David didn't waste a moment. He beckoned Anderson, who paused to thank his escort before following the indicated young man, who was not wearing a uniform. That fact eased some of his worries.

Anderson waited until he was out of earshot to quiz David. "What can you tell me?"

"Not much yet," David grinned. "I can tell you that you are not going to be sent on a potentially lethal secret mission."

"Well, that cancels that worry," Anderson said wryly. "But since I have no family or friends, or skills to speak of – I can't understand why I am here."

"Trust me – you have a very important qualification, and the job you are needed for is very important. I don't think you will object to your part. And afterwards, if all goes well, I will be very grateful to you."

"It sounds like something totally illegal. What's the take?" Anderson said warily.

"Not money! Not official secrets – though the matter is highly classified," David warned.

"Sorry I asked," Anderson said wryly. They had reached David's cottage.

"First things first. You can shower and change here, in my place. My wife won't be here tonight, so I have a spare bed. Are you hungry?"

"Very," Anderson agreed.

"Ok, I'll fix something," David agreed, as a knock sounded on the door.

He opened it again to see Tanya with a tray of food and coffee. David glared at her.

"There are mind readers around here," David said as if joking. He took the tray and gave Tanya a 'get lost' stare.

"Your wife?" Anderson asked, taking a long look at Tanya.

"No, merely a friend. My wife is in the infirmary at the moment, and Tanya thinks I need looking after."

"Well, somebody has to keep an eye on you. After all, look at you; the minute your wife's back is turned you bring your mates in," Tanya teased.

"Get out of here," David growled. He waited for Tanya to go and shut the door behind her.

"Bathroom is through there," David led the way. "You can use that bedroom. I'll put out some non-orange clothes for you. The food should stay hot for long enough."

David walked off and left Anderson to himself, and wondered at the odd look Anderson had given Tanya. Did he suspect? Tanya and Erin were not all that alike – except for the bone structure.

Anderson, who still preferred to be called Gerry Rand, felt strange – suddenly on his own. He was still confused as to why he was at this State Department place. He stared after David, who hadn't even given his whole name or anything about himself. He stopped worrying. The thought of a shower and civilian clothes was more important.

After washing thoroughly to remove the stink of several days travel and the long months of prison, he began to feel almost free. He thought of the woman he'd seen and realised that it was a long time since he had enjoyed one. He allowed himself to fantasize, but the woman's face kept turning to Erin's face and that was the doorway to despair. He didn't even know where she was, how she was. He regretted every day, getting her involved with Travis. If they ever met again, would she ever forgive him?

Jim Phillips waited until Anderson had been in David's place long enough, and then walked to the cottage he shared with Erin. He acted surprised to see Wanda there.

"Good to see you up and about," he said. "But I don't think you are meant to be here."

Wanda grinned as if caught out. "I'll sneak back to the infirmary." She slipped out the door.

To Erin, Jim said, "I think you should be in bed."

"Going!" she agreed. "So should you."

"No rest for the wicked," Jim mock complained. "At least not yet. I've just got back and I have to give a report over the way. I'll be lucky to be back by morning."

The cottage was quiet when Anderson finally emerged from the shower. He assumed David had gone to bed, but a glance in the other bedroom showed it to be unoccupied. He walked into the room where the food was, then checked out the rest of the cottage. He was on his own, no keeper, no minder...

He heard a quiet knock on the door. If it was that woman again...

He went to the door, trying to find words to get rid of her. When he opened the door, he stared in absolute disbelief.

"God girl! If you're real, I've died and gone to heaven by mistake."

"Gerry?" Erin echoed his disbelief. "I thought you were dead. I thought..."

"I think you should come in before anyone sees you," Gerry suggested. He had to take her arm and draw her inside. He kept pulling until she was in his arms. At first she seemed stiff and then he felt her shaking.

"Hey, girl. This wasn't my idea! I mean, I'd understand if you hated me…"
He felt Erin's arms tighten around him.

"I don't! I just don't believe you are real. I don't know how you could be here."

"I thought I was going for a parole hearing. I wasn't arguing about that, even though I haven't been that good. Then that mate of yours, Haroldson, takes me on. He told me to trust him and behave myself. It was all very irregular. I still don't know what I did to deserve this. What is this place and why are you here?"

"You're here because I need you," Erin told him. "I can't tell you more than that."

"That's enough for me," Gerry said, trying to find her face, but it was still hidden on his chest. "Hey, I've already had a shower."

Gerry simply held Erin while she cried.

"You're not looking well," he said. "You're not sickening for something are you? And what happened to your hands?"

"I'm okay," Erin told him. "Better than I was."

Gerry whispered something in Erin's ear. He felt her relax.

"There are no alley's here Gerry Rand. Besides, Jim told me I should be in bed."

"There's a bed here. And I did tell you my cure for whatever ails you. We can talk later."

Erin felt like she was floating – so relaxed – so confident. She let Gerry rub his hand over the mound of her belly. He had felt the baby kick, and his look of incredulous joy mirrored her own.

Then reality hit. "What are we going to do, girl?" he asked miserably. "This is just an hallucination. I've got to go back. You have to go back. We can't have a baby. I know what it is like having an ex-con for a father. You can't bring her up in jail."

"I won't," Erin said. "I've worked it out. I asked Dad to have her."

"A man – by himself?"

"He's found a lady friend," Erin said. "She's good for him."

"Is that what you really want, girl?"

"It's what's best. I know it is."

"You are a wise woman, Erin Mason. Too good for me."

"No, I'm not."

"You must be. I'm a present for you, girl. You're not a present for me.

How long do we have?"

"I'd better be back in my carefully deserted cottage by dawn." She had realised who had arranged for Gerry and why. "Otherwise that bitch Zara Russell will start something and I will be dog meat again as far as her father is concerned."

Gerry took Erin's face in his hands. "The Zara Russell?"

"Is there more than one?"

"What did you do to make her father hate you? You know who he is, don't you?"

"Of course, chapter and verse. Other than he probably thinks I still have millions of untraced dollars somewhere, I think it is because Zara took up with some of my discards. From before you straightened me out. I was guilty by contamination."

"But still – the Secretary of State here, you here, and something hush-hush – I am definitely out of my league."

Erin leant back against Gerry, who in turn was leaning against the wall in the small meeting room. Elisabeth and Tanya were pretending to read in two chairs by the window.

"So what are we waiting here for?" Gerry asked. "Not that I'm objecting to the company."

"We might be needed," Erin told him, almost absently.

"For what?" Gerry persisted. "Whatever all the bigwigs are here for?"

"Yeah, that," Erin agreed. "Look Gerry, we are not meant to discuss it, and – I need to concentrate on something. Someone."

"What about me?" he pretended annoyance.

"You don't need help," Erin told him.

"Ah," Gerry whispered in her ear. "Like that is it girl?"

Erin nodded.

"So why am I here?"

"Because I think I am going to need you," Erin said softly.

Gerry subsided and tightened his arms around Erin.

Erin focussed back on Wanda, who was in another room further down the corridor. She knew the moment that Jenha released his hold on her memory, from the sense of her agitation. She could feel Jenha keeping her calm, and David's steadying presence.

There was nothing that Erin needed to do for her yet. The Bigwigs, as Gerry called them, hadn't started questioning her or David yet. They had called on Colonel Aldrin first, since to them, he was the only proper agent of the mission.

Erin spared a moment of thought to wonder if the Chiefs of the Armed Forces were as disbelieving of the facts of things as the Secretary of State; and if Stev Aldrin thought it best to introduce Jenha Mosellan, how he would be welcomed. She could envision those powerful men being wary of him (at best) and paranoid at worst. If her part in helping them to return was mentioned, they'd be eyeing her in the same way. More powerful enemies.

In the main conference room, Aldrin was addressing the Commanders-in-Chief. He was primed with all the information that had been discovered about the Kumatan and Atapi that had been on Earth and the descendants. Also, with information that Jenha had supplied to add to what Wanda had been told. He was ready to play the tapes of Wanda teleporting. He was the best person to try to convince them that the alien place existed. They would be less likely to think him insane.

Erin sensed when Jenha was requested to go into the room with Aldrin. For a brief moment, she felt his preference to remain anonymous, or was it that he had been ordered to draw no attention. Then he calmed his mind and Erin had a wordless sense of what it was to be a Traeger.

After two hours, Erin announced, "They have sent for Wanda and David."

Elisabeth and Tanya came over to where Erin stood and joined hands. Gerry simply hugged Erin tighter for a moment then eased his pressure, but did not let her go.

Erin sensed Wanda's apprehension, and used that to enable Elisabeth and Tanya to hear what Wanda was thinking. She simply sent a feeling of support.

From the questions directed at her, it was obvious that much of what had occurred on Korvu had been covered by Stev Aldrin and probably, Jenha.

What the Bigwigs wanted to know was how Wanda had got herself, David and Stev, between worlds.

This subject was one of the lesser things she would prefer not to talk about. Erin couldn't decide if the Bigwigs feared the ability or wanted to use it.

No one needed to tell Wanda that – for although she quite easily admitted when the ability had started, and how she could do it consciously – she stressed the personal cost in energy. She told them how she had been depleted for several days after arrival, and how she could no longer move herself.

They pounced on the fact that she had sent Stev and David back and asked how she had done it.

"Without people anchoring the arrival point, I couldn't have done it."

Erin and the others heard the words in their mind. Wanda went on, "Simply knowing the arrival place was not enough. I think some of the energy came from here – from those anchoring here."

"Could anyone be an anchor," one of the Bigwigs asked.

"No," Wanda said carefully. "I have to know them well, trust them, and they must have sufficient psychic talent to form the link."

"So, could you use your husband or Colonel Aldrin for this?" was the next question.

Wanda didn't have to read their minds to guess their thoughts. "I trust them both, implicitly, but no – neither have psychic talent."

"So who did you link to?"

"My sister and cousins," Wanda said softly. But the Bigwigs heard and Wanda knew her cousins were aware of the admission. Erin breathed easier when the next question related to how she had got home if she could not move herself. Jenha smoothly inserted, "I brought her back."

Attention went immediately to him, but he knew precisely how to phrase his answers to reduce the fears of the important men.

He referred back to what they had already been told, but had probably ignored because it was so fantastic. Wanda, he said, hadn't been called specifically, but she had the talents needed to respond. It had not been a certainty that anyone could or would respond. "We needed people who knew how to fight, but who were honourable and would only kill when necessary, not just for the love of it. Then he said it was hoped that one from Earth might be able to reach one who was herself, half human.

That had led to a discussion of how the Atapi had got to Earth, was Jenha sure they were all gone, and if any others could repeat the act. Jenha explained logically how it was very unlikely.

"Could you do that?" Jenha was asked.

"A Traeger cannot abuse the aura of Korvu that way. I could come here, with one other, only because I had been here before, and was returning one who belonged here. I am trained to do this, and the one with me, is kin to me and was linked to others who were."

From the sense of amazement, that detail had not been previously admitted to.

Wanda interrupted the overlapping questions. "I didn't know of that kinship until just before I came back. It was the only reason I was able to go there and in the end, the only reason I was able to come back. Jai Cassidy, the half human - half Atapi that I needed to find – is also related to me. She could not help me get back, except to send power with me. She, like the Atapi sorcerers, is bound to the land and can't leave."

Then came the questions that the listeners in the far room, hadn't wanted to be asked. "Who had she linked to, to get back?" The next question was "What sort of things could her sister and cousins do?"

Wanda played down their skills, to the minimum. Jenha confirmed her comments.

"Your sister is...?" someone asked.

"Elisabeth," Wanda said quickly, glancing at Jim who was sitting quietly, listening.

"Elisabeth who?"

Jim answered. "Before she was married, Wanda was Wanda Dean."

The Bigwig gave Jim a sharp look, then remembered that Jim was purportedly State Department and guessed at a need for secrecy and subsided.

Wanda continued, "I have only met Erin once and I couldn't pick anything up from her, so I don't know."

Jenha volunteered no comment – finally the Secretary of State did.

"She would have us believe that she feels emotions of other people. Do you agree with that, Professor Mosellan? Should we really call you that?"

"That title will do – it is the closest you have for that part of my normal duties. And yes, the claim is accurate. One empath can recognise another. However, this gift is little known here on Earth and she was never trained to understand and control it. An untrained empath is vulnerable to manipulation and at risk of being overwhelmed by a large volume of strong emotions. I have made a start to teach her, but I was trained for years, and I will not be here for that long."

Down the passage, Erin breathed easier when the questions turned to those about Jenha himself. Elisabeth voiced a thought, "I wonder what they would think if they realised that the three of us are eavesdropping on their meeting?"

"Paranoid," Tanya summarised. "But I can't do anything like this normally."

"Nor can I," Elisabeth agreed. "Except with Wanda."

"And only with the three of us together," Erin pointed out. "And it is only with Wanda at the other end."

"It would be smart to emphasise that," Gerry said unexpectedly.

Erin squirmed around, releasing her cousins to stare at him. "How can you know what I'm talking about?"

"Ah...from what you said," Gerry said, awkwardly.

"Were you getting like – pictures and words in your head?" Tanya demanded, eyeing Gerry thoughtfully.

He nodded, looking uncomfortable. "I wasn't going to say anything."

"Unclinch you two," Elisabeth insisted. "See if you get anything when you aren't hugging Erin."

Gerry let her go and Erin stepped forward. She re-joined hands with her cousins and once more sensed Wanda. The continuing events in the other room were clear. After a while they dropped hands again.

"Well?" Elisabeth demanded of Gerry.

"Nothing," he admitted.

"You must have been getting it from me," Erin told Gerry. "I had no idea you would."

"I don't usually, girl," Gerry told her.

Erin tried an experiment, sending a single emotion to Gerry, without touching him. She knew he succeeded when he moved forward to hug her. "Not fair, girl," he whispered in her ear, and then he whispered something that made Erin blush.

Chapter 29

The door to the room opened, Wanda, David and Stev Aldrin entered, followed by Jenha Mosellan.

Wanda looked extremely pale, and Erin wriggled free of Gerry and went to her. "What's the matter? You're shaking," Erin asked.

"Nothing," Wanda insisted. "I'm fine."

"You're not! Come and sit down," Erin insisted. She led Wanda to one of the arm chairs and gently pushed her into it.

"Go away," Wanda told Erin. She backed away, sensing the fear and revulsion from her cousin.

Wanda scanned the room, until she looked at Jenha, and then she grabbed onto David who had gone and perched on the chair arm. Elisabeth went to Wanda's other side. Jenha gave Erin a subtle signal and she went over to him.

Jenha spoke softly. "I had blocked Wanda's memories of Korvu until just before the meeting. She managed fine until asked about the blue blood aliens. Her memories over whelmed her. I have her calmed, but she cannot recall what she must. She is aware of what I have done, and it seems she thinks I am one of them."

Erin glanced at Wanda, who was hiding her head on David's chest.

"She didn't think much of me either, just then. She told me to go away," Erin admitted. "Last night, though, we talked and got on well."

"I had hoped you would," Jenha remarked. "I think perhaps she does not want to recall that time."

"Possible," Erin agreed. "So they haven't finished with her yet, so why are you here?"

"The Warriors are taking the opportunity to discuss our information while Wanda has a rest."

"How much more do you think Wanda can tell them?" Erin asked.

"The most important information is as yet unrevealed," Jenha said carefully. "Did she not say to you that she knew their weaknesses?"

Erin nodded.

"She has said nothing of that," Jenha stated. "It is important for your people to know of it, and I too need to know."

"Of course," Erin agreed, to give herself time to think. "And the information is tied to her memories of captivity?"

"Yes," Jenha agreed. "Are you ready?"

"To tease out the memories, or convince her I am not a threat?"

"The latter is the immediate priority. In that, I cannot help you."

"I can do it. How long have I got?"

"As long as you need," Jenha advised her. "Do not let the time demands of the warriors influence you."

"Then, could everyone leave – or rather I want to be in a room, just me, her and David."

"Do you not wish Gerry with you?" Jenha asked.

"Not yet – Wanda doesn't know him and I want her to feel in control. Having David there is enough. He knows I am not the enemy."

"And later?" Jenha queried.

"Yes, though when he is hugging me he can receive from me even if I am not sending to him. He can hear and see what I do."

"Indeed? Will that be a problem?"

"I don't know. I want him there, to give me strength, but I don't know how he will deal with what I will be receiving. And it is going to be bad, isn't it?"

"Yes, I believe so. I have experienced what those aliens did to some of my people and the Kimh. Wanda was with them for a long time. Bring Gerry over, I will talk to him."

Erin caught Gerry's intent look and beckoned him over.

"Go and arrange your talk with Wanda," Jenha directed.

"We need to talk," Erin told Wanda.

"Go away!"

"No, not until you tell me what I have done. Last night we talked and were friends, I thought."

"I know what you are now!" Wanda turned her head and hissed at her. There was real hatred in her tone.

"Wanda, she helped us bring you back!" Elisabeth protested.

"She helped make you better," Tanya added.

"I don't want her near me."

David and Stev Aldrin glanced at each other.

"Wanda!" Stev got her attention. "When you got back, you were quite ill. One of the things was due to something that Atapi sorcerer put on you. Erin removed the things, I saw her, but the things burnt her – that is why her hands are bandaged. She does not mean you harm."

Wanda stared at Erin. "I don't want her near me."

"I'll stand across the room," Erin offered.

"No! I heard then say you can walk across planes – you could get at me in seconds."

"What if you have me tied to a chair?" Erin suggested. "Would you let me talk to you then?"

"Why do you insist? I don't want your kind of help."

"I insist because I am not your enemy. I can help you face down your memories."

"NO!"

David stirred. "Hon, I think you should let her help you. You have to talk about things. Stradbroke told you that."

"NO!"

Aldrin decided to take control of the situation. "Let's move somewhere more private."

He took hold of Erin's arm, very gently. David helped Wanda up. Aldrin led the way to the gymnasium, and on arrival ordered two off duty marines to vacate it.

Wanda looked around. "There! That beam. Sit up there! Stev, hold her!"

"I'll need help getting up there," Erin protested mildly. She could have done it, if not for her bulging belly and bandaged hands.

Aldrin lifted her easily, and sat her gently, then held her steady.

Wanda backed off until David stopped her.

"What is this about, Wanda?" David asked.

"Ask her!" Wanda accused. "Ask her what she is!"

Aldrin whispered in Erin's ear, "I hope you know what you are doing. I don't like Wanda's mood."

"I am aware of it," Erin assured him, still having her eyes on Wanda. "Jenha has been working me up to this."

"Has he?" Aldrin mused.

"What do you think I am?" Erin challenged Wanda.

"One of them!" Wanda said with venom. Her mind was roiling with dark memories.

"Who are they?" Erin asked calmly. The level of Wanda's emotion was not enough to bother her, thanks to Jenha's training.

"You know who they are! You were there, watching, doing nothing – even when I pleaded," Wanda screamed at her.

"What about later?" Erin asked.

"You helped me – gave me false hope – then betrayed me. They always found me again." Wanda's voice was shrill. "Do you know what I did to them?"

"Yes," Erin admitted. The vision returned to her mind in graphic detail. "You killed them. One you strangled with some chain, one with a knife in the belly, and the other in the throat."

"It was in the creature's malehood! How could you possible know that if you were not there?"

David had turned pale. Wanda stepped toward Erin, reaching into her pocket for something. Belatedly, David reached for Wanda but she dived forward.

Erin felt from Wanda, something secretive, and was wary. When she dived at her, Erin couldn't dodge, but Stev Aldrin reacted with blinding speed. Before she realised he had released her, he had leapt over the beam and grabbed Wanda by the wrist, revealing that she had a scalpel in it. He made her drop it. It seemed that Jenha's calm command on her was no longer effective.

Wanda struggled like a berserker, but Stev had no trouble holding her.

"You aren't meant to be protecting her!" Wanda screamed.

"She isn't an enemy," Stev told Wanda, staring at her to reinforce his message.

Erin managed to slip off the beam without her hands hurting too much. She walked to where the scalpel had dropped and managed to pick it up with her finger tips. Wanda tried to back away, but Erin didn't come closer. Instead she deliberately scratched her arm with the scalpel. Wanda twitched and grabbed her own arm. She shoved her bleeding arm under Wanda's nose.

"I bleed red," Erin told her. "Not purple like the lizard men or blue like the aliens. RED!"

"But I can't reach your mind," Wanda said in what was almost a whisper. "I couldn't reach theirs either."

Erin dropped her arm and allowed David to do a rough bandaging job on it.

"You asked who I am," Erin said gently. "Will you listen?"

Erin gestured for Stev to release Wanda, who slumped to the floor. Erin copied her though it was far from comfortable.

"You spoke to me last night? Do you remember?" Erin asked.

"No," Wanda admitted.

Erin realised that the dark memories were trying to swamp her. She reached out to Wanda and touched her hand with the tips of her fingers, all that wasn't bandaged. Then she projected the image of the still pool, lit by sunlight.

After several minutes, Wanda let out a sob and David squatted down to hug her.

"Yes. I remember you," Wanda said. "You haunted my nightmares, but you were the only human I could reach."

"You haunted my dreams too," Erin told Wanda. "Only at the time I thought they were my nightmares. I had problems of my own back then."

"Did you try to reach my mind last night?" Erin asked.

"I didn't think to. I had just found out you were my cousin and I had had enough of the infirmary."

"Can you reach it now?"

"No – Yes." Wanda seemed confused. "What are you?"

Erin intuited what Wanda wanted to know. "I have the same freakish blood as you do. In a lot of ways I am very like you, except I don't have the telepathy stuff. I am what Jenha calls an empath. I don't get the voices and pictures unless there is also a lot of emotion with it."

She had Wanda's interest. "When you first started haunting me I was in prison with a thousand other prisoners shouting their emotions at me. It is not surprising I couldn't isolate you."

"How did you manage?" Wanda asked softly. Now that her mind was on Erin's story, her own had calmed.

"I didn't. I was in prison less than a month before they threw me into a psych facility and I was drugged up to and above my eyeballs most of the time. Mostly I was then echoing the emotional state of those around me. In the evenings, before they gave me the night drugs, sometimes I would see you or seem to be you. I would wake from those nightmares, screaming."

"You knew what they were doing to me?" Wanda asked, trembling.

"Yes. I saw it and I felt it."

"Sometimes I pleaded with you," Wanda said. "But you never reacted – but sometimes, I did begin to feel numb..."

"They'd drugged me," Erin said, still managing to maintain her own calm.

"What kind of monster are you – who can sit there now and say that you saw and felt what I went through – and still be calm?" Wanda was becoming agitated again.

"I'm not calm," Erin said, trying to handle the new agitation as well as the other emotions coming from Wanda. "Jenha has put some bracelet things on me so my emotions don't feed back onto yours."

"Slave bands?" Wanda asked. "I remember. Jenha used them on me for a bit, were you...?"

"Deranged, demented?" Erin suggested. "That depends on who you talk to. Jenha used the term 'undisciplined'."

David smothered a snort. Erin glared at him.

"That's mild compared to what a lot of the Kumatan and Kimh thought of Wanda. A woman, doing what she did. At least Jenha made no comment except to say that the women of Earth were strong."

Erin wasn't sure if Wanda knew or remembered that Jenha was related to them. So she commented, "I wonder what he thought when Jai told him you were related to his sister."

"What? Wait – I knew that, how did you know that?"

"Elisabeth and Tanya found out and told me. I told them to tell you about both the Mosellan and the Cassidy connection. It felt like it was me telling Jai that."

"How?"

Erin explained as best she could how it seemed that what Wanda had felt, she had felt. She pointed out that Wanda had twitched when she had cut her arm. "When I slept, you came to fill my dreams. It has come to be that we are closer than twins. It is still like that. At least the day voices stopped when I got here and told my other cousins to quit it."

"They reached you?"

"Yes, but I didn't know who or what they were. I was having one of my nightmares of you and I think for a brief time they sensed you too. It was during one of the periods when your mind was clear. You suddenly realised you had to get away, get out from where you were – I realised that I had to too. I did – no one knows how, but I think I did it by walking across planes."

"I tried that," Wanda said bleakly. "I couldn't. I tried to go to one of the Kumatan places I knew."

"Not place to place," Erin told her. "Across planes. And you did do it – you came here twice – touched me and went back. You couldn't stay."

"I remember – the second step was twisting darkness. But I could only do that with someone I knew or to a place I knew."

"You didn't know me then, but our blood is the same," Erin explained. She went on to describe what she had gone through – being forced west to the mountains. Only part of it was due to the cousins who had provided the direction. She omitted the parts not directly related to Wanda's need.

Finally, Erin told Wanda. "Jenha said our minds are linked at a very deep level. He says it isn't healthy for either of us – but for now, it means I can help you. You have to talk about what happened to you before it festers inside you."

"I want to forget," Wanda moaned.

Erin spoke gently, "You begged me for help to escape. You told me that you had to get away because you could tell about the weaknesses of the blue aliens. We need to know what you know."

"No," Wanda moaned.

"What if they come here?" Aldrin asked. "Anything you can tell us will help protect us, and anything you learnt might help Jenha help heal the others that were damaged."

Erin sensed that Wanda would try and sent a sense of thanks. "You won't be alone. I will be with you. There are no secrets between us. Whatever you feel, I feel too. I can halve it. Nothing that you experienced will be too bad for two of us."

It was almost as if a signal had summoned them. Jenha and Gerry, along with Magnus Goldman entered the gymnasium.

"Are you ready to start again?" Goldman asked Wanda, gently.

"We are," Erin told him. Goldman saw Wanda clinging to Erin, but said nothing. The group returned to the briefing room.

"This is a classified debriefing session," Stan Russell insisted when he saw Erin and Gerry entering.

Goldman saved Erin the need to protest.

"Mr Secretary, to obtain the information you require from Mrs Martin – you will be forcing her to relive a very traumatic time. Miss Mason is aware of much of it already and can help her. Mr Rand is willing to wear a headset to block out details, if you require it. But, both he and David Martin are required to support the women."

"Can't Professor Mosellan act in this?" Stan Russell asked.

Jenha answered that, "I mentioned, Sir, there was a bond between them that enabled Wanda's return. In this instance, I am not a suitable mentor."

The other men conferred and agreed to allow the newcomers, but did insist on Gerry using a head set.

It was a curious arrangement. Wanda was seated with Erin standing behind her, resting her hands on Wanda's shoulders. David sat beside Wanda's chair and held her nearest hand, and Gerry was hugging Erin from behind.

Wanda didn't wait for the questions, she spoke first. "This is not going to be easy for me, so I ask you to be patient. To understand what I say about them you need to understand the context of how I learnt it."

She took several deep breaths.

"I was betrayed by two of the Kumatan I was training in unarmed combat." She named the two for Jenha's benefit, although she believed both were dead. "I was transported in one of their vehicles, after being confined with chains and some kind of paralysis weapon..."

Wanda felt Erin keeping her calm and it enabled her to talk as if all had happened to someone else. Still, these earlier memories were gentle compared to later ones.

"They wanted to know why I was different from their other prisoners. They stripped me, and they all examined me, poking probes wherever they could and had some kind of machine like an x-ray thing to look inside. When they ran out of things to explore they took me back to a dark cell and chained me up – sometimes upright, sometimes inverted, sometimes in other combinations. Not only did they want to examine me – they hated me."

Wanda paused to take deep breaths. Erin spoke for her. "They took tissue samples from wherever they could – inside and out. They used different substances on her skin to see what effect they had, made cuts to see the layers inside, and crudely stitched them up. They yanked out hair samples..."

The faces of the listeners grew hard. Erin noticed that the Secretary seemed to disregard the horrific details. She directed part of what she was receiving from Wanda to him.

Wanda was pale and trembling. Her memory was returning to her the details as intensely as if she had just experienced them. Erin wasn't much better, but she was managing to numb most of the remembered pain for Wanda, but not so well for herself. In spite of the headset, she knew Gerry was feeling what she was and she felt his arms tighten in comfort.

When Wanda described the subsequent torture, done more out of hatred now, she saw the Secretary beginning to look severely ill.

Jenha touched Erin's mind. "Enough, young one, the man cannot take anymore."

Off to one side, Stev Aldrin was taking notes, for amongst the details of how the aliens had treated her, Wanda had learnt things. These were times when she had seemed apart from her body and seemed to be watching it and able to observe the aliens. These times, Wanda now knew were times when she had linked to Erin's mind for a time.

The telling sickened even the high ranking military men, both that it was done at all and done to a woman. That she had survived impressed all of her listeners, even the Secretary. That she had managed to learn so much about her captors was astounding.

The Secretary seemed to be paying more attention to Erin, as if he could not believe what she was saying when she took over speaking for Wanda, when Wanda was unable to continue. At the end of the session when all the questions had been proposed and answered, Goldman saw the pale sweating faces of the two women and the look of horror in their eyes. David and Gerry both looked sick.

As the important men left the room, Erin collapsed into Gerry's grasp. He eased her down to the floor and noticed red marks on her arms. He moved part of her clothes and saw more marks.

"What the..." he exclaimed.

Before he could finish, Wanda was beside Erin. "No! No! That's what they did to me. How could they ...it's my fault...I did this..."

"Be calm!" Jenha said firmly, touching Wanda. She subsided into racking sobs, hiding her face in her hands.

"The marks will fade. They are manifestations of what you suffered, yes, because she both felt and saw what you experienced."

"Why?" Wanda sobbed. "Why?"

Jenha gently helped Wanda up from beside Erin. "Walk with me, young one," Jenha suggested. "Erin will need rest, yes, but she is strong. I know this – when she wakes she will know the injuries are not hers."

Jenha walked out of the room, leading Wanda, but at the doorway he took Wanda – elsewhere.

Chapter 30

In the quietness of the forest glade, Jenha spoke to Wanda.

"Do not worry about Erin. She will be well and so now will you. It was necessary that you talk about what you suffered – bringing it all out into the open. Now there will be no hidden poisons festering in your mind."

"Do you mean I might have gone insane?" Wanda asked, still trying to stop crying.

"Perhaps, but you might also have weakened at a time when you needed to be strong." Jenha inserted a picture of Jim Phillips in Wanda's mind.

"And now?" Wanda asked. "Can I trust myself?"

"Yes," Jenha assured her. "You are a strong young woman. You may have felt doubt, wanted to die, anything to stop the aliens hurting you, but you were magnificent – you didn't let them win. You learnt their weaknesses and escaped them. You survived."

"I don't feel strong," Wanda gulped.

"Many Kumatan and Kimh were captured, and tortured," Jenha told Wanda. "We could not rescue them all. Many simply died of shock. The Kimh have never had to experience such things. They are in many ways, too gentle and unworldly. My people, those that chose to fight, were less innocent but it was still a dreadful shock to them to see and experience the malice of the aliens. Of those we rescued, many chose to die rather than live on after that. Those that live – thanks to you – I think I will be able to help recover. And your example has taught many of the younger Kumatan women that they too can be strong."

"I suppose, women's lib hasn't reached your world yet," Wanda wiped her eyes.

"I think they will demand a more important role in future," Jenha agreed. "And I think that is a wonder, but having met my great nieces, I cannot but see that women can be strong and intelligent and able. How though can I teach them that?"

Wanda finally looked at him. "Don't tell them that they can't do something because they are women," she said. "Women are not all suited to do what men can do, not all will want to do what men do. Some will do them as well or better."

"I must only look at my kin to see that," Jenha said. "I finally know how confined my sister must have felt. But I doubt that even she could have done what you did."

"Maybe not," Wanda agreed. "But you may not realise that Earth is not as - I won't say civilised – but perhaps as gentle a place as your world was. I would prefer to live there, but I grew up here, imbued to the fact that crime, violence, murder, wars, etc happen. So in that I was not so shocked. As for why I survived – I am too damn stubborn to let scum win. I had practice."

"Friend Jim told me much of you..."

Gerry scooped Erin up and demanded to know where the infirmary was. His face was showing his worry. David, still staring at where Wanda had gone, shook his head and offered to show the way. Several men from the briefing were still in the passage talking. Stan Russell excused himself and followed where Erin was being taken.

David found Rowan Wallace as Gerry was putting Erin onto a bed. Russell went over to Gerry. "How is she?"

Gerry had not been officially introduced to the Secretary of State, so he did not choose to be polite.

"How the hell do you think? You were there; you heard what was going on. You tell me! My girl looks like she has been tortured. I know her – she was trying to help that other poor woman – wasn't she? I felt some of it – so I know it had to be really bad – more than she could be expected to take. I don't know how either of them could be sane after this."

Russell, having felt some of it himself, could not disagree. His impression of Erin Mason had just changed – completely. He was relieved when Rowan Wallace hurried in.

"I wish her well," Russell told Gerry, before walking out. He found Goldman and told him to go with him. When they were in private he told Goldman, "You make sure that woman, Erin Mason, is put to use by us and knows what is expected of her."

Goldman agreed with a perfectly controlled face.

Erin still seemed unconscious when Jenha returned to the infirmary. Gerry was beside the bed, holding Erin's hand and barely restraining his own emotions.

"You never said it would be like this," Gerry accused him. "You should see the marks on her."

"I was afraid that this might happen," Jenha told him gently. "That is why I urged them to bring you here. What you see on Erin is a physical manifestation caused by the deep link she shares with her cousin. An example of how the mind affects the body. I suspect what she has done is retreat into a memory of the numb darkness. I think you could bring her out of it and flush the second hand memories out of her mind."

"Me?" Gerry asked hopefully.

"She means a lot to you and you to her?" Jenha asked.

"She's my life," Gerry admitted earnestly. "But I am not a psych expert."

Jenha considered his next words carefully. "Were you aware that she was sensitive to emotions?"

"I sort of knew," Gerry admitted.

"Well she told me that she found two ways to block then. One was losing herself in what she called cyberspace and the other was..."

Jenha paused, but Gerry suddenly understood. "I... know what the other was," he blurted.

"Excellent," Jenha said. "I think it will be all right if you took your 'Girl' over to her cottage. I offered young David a similar suggestion."

Goldman, Wallace, Jim and Jenha sat together later in the evening when all the important guests had departed. It had been at Jenha's request. Jim had wanted to be sure about Wanda's recovery and was relieved when Jenha said all would be well.

"I would like to spend more time with her, as I have with the other three cousins. I want to be sure she has fully integrated her talents. There was never enough time to do that when she was on my world. However, there is one point that concerns me. She tells me that she can no longer move herself, as I can. This I am sure will cause no problem in itself, but it may indicate that a minor part of the brain was affected by the aliens."

Rowan Wallace considered this. "We have the technology to look at the brain. What would we need to look for?"

Jenha held his hands out, palm upwards. "That I do not know. My people have not such means."

"I'll have her checked," Rowan promised. "What of Erin?"

"I am certain that she will recover quickly," Jenha assured them. "What is to happen with her now?"

Magnus smiled, wryly. "I have been assured that the plans we proposed to the Secretary and the President will proceed."

"Good." Jenha relaxed.

"Would someone enlighten me?" Jim asked.

Magnus explained.

Jim nodded, and turned to Jenha. "Then you would be returning home. I would be sad but you do have a family."

"Yes and much work to help survivors of the war. I too will be sad to leave behind blood kin, and friends."

"Can there be no way to maintain contact," Magnus asked.

"Even though Stev, David and Wanda did so much for us, I think it will be a long time before my people trust aliens again. I think that even the traders that we have dealt with for a generation or more will not be so readily welcomed. Still, I would wish for a way to keep in touch with friends here – but in this I will not be free to choose. I must obey those who rule Korvu."

"I have observed that four young women I know are not always obedient to rules," Rowan murmured. "And I would not be surprised if they got together to try."

Jenha smiled faintly. "I suppose it is not possible to control one's dreams?"

"How will you return?" Rowan asked.

"As I did before. I can use my connection to my kinfolk on Korvu to anchor my return. It is a skill unique to Traegers."

"What about the Atapi? Is it likely that another renegade will come here?" Magnus asked.

"They would need a relic from here – something imbued with the aura of Earth – to do it. Stak obtained such a thing from a trader who snuck into Earth some sixty of your years ago. Now, I believe, you would be able to detect such intrusions, so the traders would not risk the anger of their consortium or the feel of your weapons, to steal anything else. Furthermore, the Atapi sorcerers are bound to their tribal lands. They can't leave. Stak had lost his tribal land rights in a challenge and rather than face disgrace chose to have revenge on everyone. To come here, he drained all of his personal power relics, all life from his tribal land and nearly all the life force from his tribe. It was luck that enough survived. Now though, Jai Cassidy rules the Atapi in parallel with the Old One. Both of them and every Traeger are alert for such an event. I think your world is safe from them."

"My turn next," Erin said aloud, aware that Jim Phillips had come to stand behind her.

"Yes," he agreed. "But your escort hasn't arrived yet."

Erin sighed very softly. She hoped Gerry would behave and not have his sentence extended. He had been transferred from Washington to LA to finish his time, since one of his crimes had been committed in California.

She still heard his whispered "I'll find you, girl," as he was led off, once again handcuffed.

If anything right then, Erin was feeling emotionally numb.

"Why don't you go and be with your cousins?" Jim suggested.

"No. Wanda doesn't need me around right now. Elisabeth, Tanya and Prof Mosellan are with her. And I want to try to forget…things."

Jim nodded. He understood. "Fair enough."

They stood in comfortable silence, until Erin recalled a remark of Jim's.

"You said a few days ago about a lawyer and an appeal on my behalf. Did I hear right?"

"Yes," Jim admitted. "I asked a friend to look into things."

"And?"

"He thinks he might be able to get the rest of your sentence reduced, or altered to community service."

Erin turned to stare at Jim. "He's deluded."

"Perhaps not," Jim told her. "But following the decision about Zara Russell, and in some ways your case can be considered similar, and since you have helped solve two crimes recently…"

"What about the little matter of me getting out of that place?" Erin shuddered, both from the memory of the place and the way she might have done it.

"I think it can be proved that you were not in command of your faculties at the time and judging from the condition I found you in – it was just as well you were out of there. I think we can make a case for cruel and unusual punishment."

"So what aren't you saying?" Erin asked.

"Don't get your hopes up," Jim advised.

"I'm not. Why are you even bothering? And isn't it a bit less than legal?"

"It will be legal," Jim assured her. "As to why – I think you have learnt the necessary lessons and keeping you in prison would stifle you."

"It's meant to, isn't it?"

"It is meant to reform and rehabilitate," Jim argued gently. "I think you have reformed and such a place could only rehabilitate you for the worse."

Erin shrugged. "Well I guess I appreciate your efforts. I doubt they will change anything, but…anyway. Oh, I left the clothes I borrowed from Tracey with Elisabeth. Could you return them and say thanks?"

"Of course," Jim agreed. He only noticed then that Erin was wearing some modified fatigues. His attention was drawn to a vehicle approaching the base gates.

"I think, perhaps, this is your ride."

"Why to Government departments like black SUV's," Erin muttered to distract herself. "It's not that arrogant civilian is it?"

"No," Jim assured her. "Come on." He urged Erin towards the main door of the base.

Chapter 31

Erin recognised her escort and did not know whether to be pleased or annoyed. She ignored the policeman as she let her cousins, well two of them, give her a hug and good wishes.

Jim and Lieutenant Haroldson exchanged a brief word before Jim shooed Elisabeth and Tanya off. As they disappeared, Stan Russell and his daughter emerged from the building with their bags.

Russell greeted Haroldson and ascertained he was to escort Erin back to Washington.

"We are ready," he confirmed. "I assume, Lieutenant, that you will be following the appropriate regulations for prisoner escort." Russell glanced briefly at Erin.

Haroldson nodded, although Erin sensed a faint annoyance.

Zara Russell openly smirked as Haroldson handcuffed Erin to himself.

They were all to travel in the one car to the airport. Russell chose to sit next to the driver and Zara was told to sit next to Erin in the back.

"Next to a criminal!" she muttered. "Isn't there a law about this?" She was ignored by everyone.

At the airport, her comments continued when she realised that Erin would be travelling on the official jet with her father.

"Orders, Miss Russell," Haroldson finally told her.

She subsided after saying, "I suppose we should pack our trash back home."

"Thanks for the invitation," Erin retorted immediately, and enjoyed seeing Zara flush red. She did pause to wonder why she was travelling with them, and decided that the Secretary wanted to be sure she went back to prison.

Erin didn't answer Haroldson's attempts at conversation. For one, she didn't feel like talking, and for another, she did not want either of the Russell's to realise that Haroldson had always been an honorary Uncle to her. The only time that she spoke to him was when she needed to use the plane's little toilet. The first time she needed to, she glared at the Secretary, daring him to object when Haroldson released the handcuffs.

It was not until Haroldson was driving her from the airport in a police vehicle that she decided to speak.

"So why did they make you, the team leader of a Swat Unit, act as a jailer?

I am hardly dangerous."

"Have you considered that you might be important?" Haroldson suggested.

"No, nor do I believe it. So why you?"

"The orders came from way up. I didn't object. Do you?"

"No. It is just that I feel manipulated. Like someone knew I would not try to tarnish your reputation or I would behave for you. I know you won't let me get away with anything – you never have. At least you don't say, 'I told you so'. Maybe you should have given the same advice to ZR."

Haroldson chuckled softly. "Maybe so. I noticed she didn't like you."

"Nor does her father and I don't know why," Erin said.

"So that is why you ignored me," Haroldson mused aloud. "I thought you had decided to hate me."

"No, it's just that if someone else was taking me, I could get my mind into the right state to deal with coming back. I can't with you. I sense your concern and kindness. We are going back to WWP aren't we?"

"Yes, that was in the orders. I'm sorry."

"Don't be – I deserved what I got," Erin told him flatly.

"Not when it affected you so - you are too sensitive."

"Not any more, Uncle," Erin tried to reassure him. "I have learnt to handle things better."

"I hope so," Haroldson said. "So what have you got involved in now – beside Zara Russell's adventure?"

"If they haven't told you, Uncle, I can't discuss it." Erin wished she could discuss it with him like she used to talk to him about things.

"I had the impression," Haroldson said carefully, "that I had to ensure you stayed safe."

"From what? Or for what?"

"For that brilliant mind of yours," Haroldson suggested.

"Yeah! Goldman of OSI wants to use that, but he doesn't trust me. As for the rest, you know that sensitivity of mine - they needed me to use that in a classified matter. I can't discuss it, not that I want to. Anyone would think I was insane. It's really funny. What I can do is classified, but I would be the last person they would give a security clearance to."

"I have heard they want to question you about some computing you did to find Miss Russell," Haroldson suggested.

"Oh!" Erin was suddenly apprehensive. "I hope they accept Jim as a suitable supervisor, because I wasn't meant to be near the internet."

"I think they are more interested in how you infiltrated the computer of the two men. It led to finding some confidential papers."

"Who wants to question me?"

"CIA or FBI, I guess," Haroldson told her.

"Crap!" Erin muttered.

Haroldson decided he had said enough. Erin didn't need to know what rumours were around, about the people looking for the hacker that had revealed a spy network.

"So, how are you and your Dad? He said he had seen you."

"Fine. You have met his new friend?"

Haroldson nodded. "What do you think?"

"She's good for him," Erin admitted. She dropped her bombshell. "I have asked them to adopt this baby."

"Gerry's baby?" Haroldson asked.

"Yes..."

"It won't be easy on you," Haroldson warned her.

"It will be better for the baby, and my life isn't meant to be easy right now." She rattled the handcuffs to demonstrate her point.

Haroldson made no comment on that. Instead he said, "Don't make any more trouble once you are back inside."

"I didn't make trouble last time. It found me and I wasn't going to lie down and let it happen."

Erin felt herself grow tense as the prison loomed up in front of them. It was late afternoon and Erin recalled that it was probably the time for the exercise period. She felt resistance building up and imaged it draining into a tranquil lake. If she had been with anyone but Haroldson, she might have made an attempt to get free.

Haroldson announced himself at the outer gate. He was expected, as was Erin. They drove to where there was official parking and were met by two guards and escorted to the Warden's Office.

The warden had been told of their arrival and was waiting for them.

"You are back with us, Mason," he greeted Erin. It was a statement, not a question. "Thank you lieutenant, we can take things from here."

Haroldson didn't leave at once. Instead he pulled out an official letter from inside his tunic and gave it to the warden. "I had instructions to deliver that letter to you. It refers to the disposition of Miss Mason."

The warden accepted the letter and nodded. "Thank you, I will read over it."

When Haroldson left, Erin felt the full effect of her return, but she managed to keep her head up. She was kept standing whilst the warden read the letter. When he finished, he put it down and gave Erin a penetrating look.

"The usual treatment for prisoners who escape is a period in solitary. I see no reason to make you an exception. Tomorrow you will be brought before a judge."

Erin listened to the rest of the warden's speech with only half her attention. She had heard it before. The only difference was the bit about no special treatment because she was pregnant.

After that, the warden gestured and she was hustled off to be processed – the part Erin hated.

She had slight amusement when they could not find a standard issue dress that fit over her belly that didn't also fall off her top. Surely there had been pregnant prisoners before?

The next step was different. She was taken to the infirmary to be checked over by the doctor - a woman this time. The two guards stayed with her.

The doctor unwrapped the dressings from her hands to examine the healing burns, and decided they only needed light bandages now. She asked questions about Erin's pregnancy and examined her.

Erin had a moment of amusement when the doctor could not feel a pulse in either wrist. She could not feel the bands Jenha had put there either, but Erin was not going to mention them. Other than that, she answered the doctor's questions as honestly as possible. She still looked very thin, and she had the feeling the doctor thought she was anorexic.

Finally, she was handcuffed and taken through to the wing where the solitary cells were, but even so, she was seen by two 'trusted' prisoners and one of them she recognised and she sensed it was mutual.

The door closed with its metallic clang. Erin stood inside with clenched fists, concentrating fiercely on the image of the placid pool. The strain of keeping up appearances was exhausting her. She moved unsteadily to the unmade bed, pushed the blanket and sheet to one end and collapsed on it, facing the wall.

She was finally able to release the pent up emotion. Even when the bands on her wrists began to hum, she didn't care. In fact, this time, by comparison, they were soothing. A reminder of a better place.

After a while, because she was exhausted from the trip, the emotional reaction, and the need to concentrate on not feeling the other ambient emotions, she fell asleep.

Less than two hours later, she was woken by the arrival of the evening meal. It was bland stuff, on plastic plates with plastic cutlery. With a sigh, she ate what she could. She had barely enough time after that to use the un-private facilities when guards came to her cell and ordered her to the far wall. Both entered the cell and one watched while the other handcuffed her again. Both held her as she was marched along passages until Erin recognised the corridor with the interview rooms.

Inside the room were four men. Two were wearing FBI jackets, two were in suits. None were familiar.

Once Erin was seated, one of the FBI men got right to the point. They were indeed interested in her hacking skills. However, her sensing of the men, or their intensity, unsettled her. They were not exactly hostile, but they seemed ready to pounce on her.

"I have no objection to helping you," Erin told them. "However, there are four of you and one of me. I think I have the right to insist on some representation here."

She sensed annoyance from one of the men, as if they had hoped to avoid that.

"We are not here to charge you with anything, Miss Mason," the FBI man, who hadn't even introduced himself, hurried to assure her. "We are seeking further information about the men involved in abducting Zara Russell."

"And your anonymous friends over there?" Erin glanced at the suited men.

"We are interested in some associates of the two men mentioned," one of them advised her.

Bingo, Erin thought, sensing that they were thinking that she had to have been involved to have hacked so successfully. No harm in calling their bluff.

"Then I insist on legal rep here," she stressed. "Since I am sure you think I must be involved somehow."

They tried questions anyhow, but Erin remained mute. They were not happy when they decided to leave, issuing veiled threats about her refusal to co-operate. But she had been right. They did think her involved and were looking for evidence.

The guards must have heard the 'fail to co-operate' because they hustled her back to her cell, more roughly than was warranted.

She was taken out again, early the following morning. This time the interview room contained two men that were at first glance, both strangers.

They did not exude hostility, and one of them approached, caught her chin and studied her face. The touch was familiar and the voice a giveaway.

"How are you, Erin?"

"Jim?" Erin smiled with relief at his nod. She did not bother to ask why he was disguised.

"How did you go last night?"

"It wasn't too bad," Erin admitted. "I was able to sleep. I couldn't do that before."

"Do you think you will be alright here for a week or two?"

Erin sighed. "Yeah. It isn't the Hilton though. They have me in solitary."

"Good!" Jim said, surprising her. "I have heard the other prisoners already know you are back and a rumour of what the visitors yesterday wanted. You handled the latter very well but the former worries me. However, it was requested that you be kept away from the others until after you hearing and until the CIA and FBI finished with you."

"Yuk," Erin said. "I don't mind solitary – really – but those vultures think I have to have been mixed up in the mess."

"It will be to your advantage to co-operate," Jim warned. "That is why I have Graham here to represent you. He has been looking into your situation and will be handling your appeal."

"I am meant to be facing a judge today," Erin commented. "Will he be with me for that?"

Graham answered that. "Yes, indeed. However I have been advised that the appearance has been rescheduled to four days from now."

"I wonder why?" Erin said sarcastically. Neither Jim nor Graham needed to comment. They did not have much time to talk before the officials arrived to question Erin again.

Erin amused herself with the verbal fencing she did with her questioners. She was polite, overtly being helpful, but stubborn in her refusal to answer certain leading questions.

"What I did in that supervised session was to hack into the computer being used by Zara's so called abductors, through the website they were using as a cover. I was only interested in getting back at those two for trying to implicate me. I didn't realise that I had got through to any other site until I was told later.

"All I can say is that there must have been a link between that site and the other one that you won't talk about."

Questions. Questions. Questions.

"I have told you – I – don't – know – anything – about – that - site!"

"How did you get into the site the men were using?" the FBI man asked.

"I know how those two cretins think," Erin told him. "The rest is simply repetition."

"Run through the steps you took," the man insisted.

Erin tried, but finally told him, "I don't follow a set plan. It is more intuitive. I could show you, but I cannot really explain."

The four officials exchanged glances. Erin sat back and watched them, hiding the smirk she felt like wearing.

One of the suited types nodded slightly. "We will be back later today."

The four men left. Jim slipped out after them, leaving Graham to discuss the hearing and appeal, with Erin.

The four official questioners finally decided they had enough new information to work with, and Erin sighed with relief. Now, she could allow herself to think about the hearing, and worry.

However, the hearing was not as bad as she feared, particularly once Graham began speaking for her. She sensed the judge had softened his opinion of her. The outcome was - no further penalty for escaping, and she would remain at the women's prison, pending an appeal at a higher level.

That appeal was organised with a speed that Erin distrusted. The presentation of evidence went as smoothly as an oiled plan of Jim's. Erin had the sense of being a chess piece being moved into a certain place. Jim simply told her to trust him. She did – but with reservations.

She challenged him when the judge retired to deliberate.

"It has already been decided, hasn't it?" Erin accused. "All this is for show!"

Jim just repeated his cryptic, "Trust me."

Chapter 32

The decision, totally unexpected, made Erin speechless. It was not prison, but not freedom – not exactly.

Well, as far as she was concerned, the first part was freedom. That was being 'committed' to Professor Mosellan's care for a minimum of four months for psychiatric treatment. Then, based on his recommendations, she would receive more treatment if required. This meant until after her baby was born. Following that, the rest of her sentence would be converted to 'community service'. Try national service, Erin told herself, sensing the not so subtle mind of the Secretary of State behind that idea.

"Whose idea was it to have me hijacked into the Marine Corps?" she demanded when she was out of the court and in the private company of Jim and Graham.

"That was my suggestion," Magnus Goldman spoke from the doorway. He walked further into the room.

Erin stared at him, sensing he was quite serious.

"So you won the lottery to control my brains," she taunted him; still annoyed at the feeling she had been manipulated. "I don't know why you bothered. You don't trust me worth a damn."

"I am positive that using that intellect of yours at anything less than a national level would be wasting it," Goldman told her. He met her eyes and forced her to heed him. "As for my trust, you have to earn that. The decision means that you can prove to any other detractors that you can be trusted and will no longer be an undisciplined individual."

Erin wanted to squirm, but wasn't about to break eye contact first. Goldman seemed to sense that, for he had a faint smile on his face when he added, "At the end of your basic training and initial posting, you will be seconded to the OSI."

Well, with that carrot in front of her, Erin muttered, "Alright, damn it, you win."

She tried very hard not to show her delight with a huge grin. It was even harder when she was told that Zara Russell was to join the marines with her.

The End.

NOVELS

WANDA: FROM BAD TO WORSE

If she was going to die young, like her mother, Gwen Willard was determined to die rich and she had very few years to do it. Her first step was to leave home. She met Hooch, who taught her some exciting and illegal skills. She was the Dracos lucky mascot until she came to the attention of the police. Then her uncanny knack for predicting trouble, warned her to flee to the city and change her name.

Life wasn't easy. She was 15, had little money and no regular job, but her new skills came in handy. Then she crossed the path of an evil and unscrupulous man and she didn't want him to have his way.

WANDA: CHOOSING CRIME

Wanda was free. She was never going back to jail. But she was homeless, almost penniless and Harrison Franklin had a long and vengeful memory. Jim Phillips had a long memory too, and Wanda had saved his life. Could he save her from Franklin?

WANDA: RISKING LIFE TO LIVE

The euphoria of successful heists were what kept Wanda Dean alive. At 23, she was crime boss Harrison Franklin's top agent – well paid for absolute obedience. That's all that mattered. Until she met Mike Johnston and her boss ordered him killed. For that, the Franklins were going to pay. In Risking Life to Live, justice conflicts with loyalty and the penalty for betrayal is death.

WANDA: A NEW LIFE - HIDDEN SECRETS

Even before beginning as a covert agent for the US Government, Wanda is abducted by a foreign operative. After being rescued, there are signs that she had been subjected to hypnosis. With an important government gathering imminent, her handler must ensure she is not a security risk.

Can Wanda's psychic extra senses help her recognize and resist the implanted commands and clear her for secret work?

WANDA: A NEW LIFE - FIRST MISSION

On her first covert mission for the US Government, Wanda calls on the skills that made her a skilled thief to convince a revolutionary general that she's an ideal recruit. When her team mates' covers are blown, it is up to her to ensure that two missing scientists and confidential Government documents are not smuggled out of the US.

WANDA: FULL CIRCLE

Three generations after the alien Kumatan left Earth, their own world is suffering from alien invaders. In desperate hope, one returns to Earth seeking help - little knowing they had left one of their own behind.
Wanda, a child of the third generation, answers the call.

ERIN: THE FORCING OF WISDOM

For years, Erin has used the intricacies of cyberspace to banish unwanted emotions. Others call what she does hacking, and her manipulations criminal, but now her skill was exceptional - in, out, traceless. She was wrong. Someone betrayed her.
Travis has dangerous plans. He needs an electronics expert – one he can coerce through fear. Erin was perfect.
With the inescapable threat of prison looming, Erin accepts his offer of sanctuary. When she realises his intentions, she is in too deep. But the terrifying of innocents is unforgivable. She cannot walk away. She is an empath and shares their distress.
She has to help them, even if it means prison, and insanity…

KORVU: THE BEGINNING
The prequel to The Wild One

Jai Ansuni was the first female Atapi sorcerer for thousands of years, but she dare not reveal it. However, when tribal sorcerer, Stacion Ansuni escalates the enmity between Atapi and Kumatan to an ominous level. Jai and her womb mate, Con, try to mitigate his atrocities but can two young Atapi, not even a score of years old, win against the powerful sorcerer?

THE WILD ONE

Sixteen year old Jai Cassidy thought she was finally free of her family until she is discovered by her other relatives…the ones that aren't human. Jai uses her natural perversity and cunning to escape their control, but catapults herself into the middle of a deadly feud between two alien races.

ATAPI SORCERESS

The sequel to The Wild One
Jai Cassidy is beginning her mission of reversing the decline of the non-humanoid Atapi. As a sorceress and an Atapi-Human hybrid, she is vehemently disliked by the male Atapi sorcerers and the humanoid rulers of Korvu. Her task is complicated by the treachery of a group of alien engineers, who are inciting insurrection and harsh reprisals.

THE TYMOREAN TRUST BOOK 1 - POWER RISING

The Tymorean Trust - When peace rules Tymorea - Peace reigns in the universe.

Chosen to be the Advocates of the mystical and incorporeal Guardians of Peace, twins Tymos and Kryslie must first learn to control and use the power rising in them - or it will destroy them.

On Tymorea, only the ruling Triumvirate Governors are powerful enough to guide the strong-willed alien-bred twins until they have mastered their power.

THE TYMOREAN TRUST BOOK 2 - GREAT ONES

The peace of the Guardian Planet, Tymorea, is in deadly peril. War there will create ripples of unrest and destruction throughout the settled universe.

Tymos and Kryslie, still adolescents, have barely mastered their power and Llaimos is still less than a year old, but they are the three chosen to be Advocates of the mystical Guardians of Peace, to safeguard the Tymorean Trust.

THE TYMOREAN TRUST BOOK 3 - RETURN TO EARTH

Even before the war on Tymorea, the Elders foresaw that Great Ones Tymos and Kryslie would have an imperative mission on Earth.

But as the Tymoreans prepare to build an Earthbase to support them, they discover that specifications for two vital protective shields are missing.

Now, nearly a century later, Tymos and Kryslie must find his work and build the generator before the base is found.

THE TYMOREAN TRUST BOOK 4 - EARTH MISSION

Just before their graduation from the prestigious WSRA Washington University, Tymos and Kryslie Ward deliberately disappear.

The Great Ones have foreseen the capture and death of the new Tymorean missionaries and discovered that the leader of the Eastern Imperium plans to undermine the United World Nations.

Tymos and Kryslie must protect their kin and prevent a potentially devastating world war.

THE TYMOREAN TRUST BOOK 5 – ALIEN CONTACT

Tymos and Kryslie Ward, hide their Tymorean intelligence and abilities while working as low ranked technicians at the WSRA's lunar base. When an alien ship arrives at Lunar One, pursued by a powerful enemy who will stop at nothing to get what he wants, only the two Tymorean Great Ones have the knowledge and abilities to overcome him, but to do so they must risk their sanity, and their souls.

Great Ones Tymos and Kryslie go to rescue the crew of Earth's first deep space mission – and discover that Ciriot space pirates have discovered Earth's location. When the Ciriot invade in force, the Great Ones reveal themselves so that Earth can gain vital help. However, Kryslie becomes the victim of Ciriot, who want to control her mind and make her betray the people of Earth.

TRICKS

Tom and Jo Dwyer had a reputation for playing tricks – and getting detention. They didn't seem to care about that, so long as they made their class laugh. That was until someone began to turn their tricks against them, and it was no longer funny.

www.ingramcontent.com/pod-product-compliance
Lightning Source LLC
Chambersburg PA
CBHW032110180726
48284CB00002B/522